THE ROGUE

Volume 1
PLANETS SHAKEN

Lee W. Brainard

Soothkeep Press

This book is a work of fiction. Apart from several mere mentions of actual people, the characters are fictitious. Any resemblance to people living or dead is purely coincidental.

If perchance my conception of events—geopolitical, political, astronomical, or prophetic—proves to be uncannily close to what actually transpires, let it be known beforehand that I do not have access to inside information, nor do I have the ability and wherewithal to hack into computers storing classified information, nor am I a prophet who enjoys special communication from God. The scenario portrayed is just an educated guess based on various factors: biblical prophecy, geopolitical trends, historical precedent, ancient history, ancient cosmology, electric universe cosmology, and a fertile imagination.

Cover design: Bespoke Book Covers, Bedfordshire, UK
Formatting: Polgarus Studio

1

Ariele stared at the package perplexed. The return address was Shadowchaser, 107 Walnut Lane, Mentor, KS. The cancellation stamp said Salina, KS. Nothing rang a bell. She had no family or friends in that part of Kansas. None that she knew of anyways. And none of her friends ever used the moniker *Shadowchaser*. She double checked the address. Ariele Serrafe, 420 Hancock St., Bancroft Apts., Unit F8, Los Angeles, CA 90031. *That's definitely me*. She tweaked her mouth and raised her eyebrows. *Weird*.

She dropped the package notice into the trash receptacle stationed next to the wall of mailboxes, placed the parcel box key inside the parcel box, and shut the door. Then she turned her attention back to her mailbox, which was still sitting open, retrieved her mail, closed her box, returned her mailbox key to her purse, and headed toward her apartment, her eyes nervously scanning the area for the packs of youths that milled around aimlessly most afternoons and every evening. Her father—her dear papai—disliked her current living situation, an older, edgy neighborhood east of Chinatown. He constantly reminded her that she could afford better. True, she could afford better. But she had her life mapped out. And the first thing on her list was buying a homestead in the San Gabriels. She longed for an orchard with fruit trees, a garden, a few chickens, a hand pump, and a woodstove. Living here was part of her plan to get there. Alas, things weren't going quite as she had planned. Property values were climbing almost as fast as her savings account. She sighed.

To her relief, she saw none of the gang-looking types, who made her nervous, not even at the basketball court or the soda machine by the laundry room. She relaxed her pace and turned her attention from scanning for potential threats to surveying the monotony of her surroundings. The dreary exterior of her building near the southeast corner of the complex was indistinguishable from the other buildings. The three dozen time-worn brick buildings, one apartment deep and three stories high, were clustered around courtyards of trampled grass and aging concrete like gaunt elephants at withered waterholes. Though the scene was as familiar as the back of her hand, it was awkwardly foreign. She didn't feel at home here and likely never would.

She turned up the sidewalk to her apartment, which was in the middle of the building on the second story, bounded up the stairs to her landing, and leaned against her door, pinning the package with her belly. While holding the doorknob with one hand, she inserted the key with the other and tried to turn it. *Rats! Six calls to the manager, and I still have to fight this door knob! If I ever have a guy in my life, he's going to be a fix-it kind of guy.*

Once inside, she set the package on the kitchen table and inspected it. *Who is this Shadowchaser?* She opened her laptop and searched the White Pages for the return address. Nothing. She searched again for a Walnut Lane in Mentor, Kansas. Again nothing. She brought up a map of Mentor, Kansas, and looked for Walnut Lane. There was no such street. In fact, there almost was no town. The address appeared to be bogus.

Ariele examined the package once again, looking for tell-tale clues that she might have missed. *Aha!* There was no handwriting on the package. Both the address and the return address were printed on computer-generated mailing labels. Whoever sent the package didn't want to be traced or identified. Shadowchaser probably didn't even live in Kansas.

She removed the brown wrapping paper and uncovered a shoebox—Christian Louboutin pumps, size 7. *Probably not a guy.* She lifted the cover and peered inside. It was stuffed to overflowing with wadded pages from the Salina Journal. Under the wadding, she found a folded manila envelope with the word "ROGUE" glued on, a single "R" and "OGUE." They appeared to have been cut from the covers of women's magazines. *Probably Redbook and Vogue. That's another one for a woman.*

Her curiosity piqued, she opened the envelope with a scissor tip and dumped the contents. A single DVD and a several-page typed letter, neatly folded, spilled onto the table. Intrigued, she unfolded the letter and read the top page. It was a cryptic note.

The social was boring.
We sat on swings under the stars, swapping stories.
We laughed at conspiracy theories.
We talked about end-of-the-world scenarios.
We shared directions:
You were headed for sky time in the Golden State,
I for computer time in a cubicle out East.
We shared ambitions:
My pursuit was TNOs,
Your life focus was NEOs.
Here's an NEO you'll wish you never heard about.

A smile creased her face. The *who* part of the mystery was solved, kind of. Shadowchaser had been a classmate at California Institute of Technology, Caltech for short. They had shared numerous classes starting with Astronomy 101 during their freshman year, but they had never been close friends. Both had a passion for astronomy and were exceptionally bright—straight As from junior high through their graduate work. Both had obtained a PhD in astrophysics.

She could see her face clearly, but she was drawing a blank. *What was her name?* The name was trying to claw its way out of her subconsciousness. *Irina ... Irina Kirilenko.* The memories came flooding back. Their differences went far beyond the fact that Irina had focused on trans-Neptunian objects while she had focused on near-Earth objects. They were different, like princess and hippie chick.

Irina was religious, some kind of evangelical. Ariele wasn't religious though she was culturally Jewish and attracted to Eastern mysticism.

Irina didn't drink. Ariele did. Though she had grown out of the party scene before the end of her sophomore year, she had continued her little indulgence every Friday night with the Rat Pack as they styled themselves. The five of them studied, laughed, and sipped bitter liquors like retsina and vermouth in emulation of their favorite intellectuals and authors.

Irina was a small-town girl. She had been born and raised in Ostroh, Ukraine, where her father taught physics and mathematics at the National University Ostroh Academy. When she was fourteen, he moved their family to Yreka in Northern California, fleeing the growing specter of Russian hegemony before it was too late. He was now head of the mathematics department at the College of the Siskiyous. Ariele was a bona fide city girl having grown up in Los Angeles, where her father was a fairly well-known sound technician in the film industry.

Irina loved classical music, ballet, and ballroom dancing. Ariele's tastes were more trendy: indie, reggae, and new age. Irina was cultured and classy. Ariele was fascinated with the hippie culture, old Mother Earth News magazines, and tiny homes.

Earth to hippie chick. Ariele rolled her eyes at herself, reigned in her nostalgic reverie over her Caltech days, and returned her focus to the matter at hand. She flipped the page, walked to her favorite chair in the corner of the living room, settled in with one leg crossed under, and began reading the body of the letter.

Ariele,

You may recall my doctoral dissertation, *The Underestimated Danger Posed by Comets*, which led to an invitation to join Dr. Goldblum in his TNO program at Cornell. In this paper I pointed out that there are over one million undiscovered comets in the vast expanse beyond the Kuiper Belt. I further observed that there could be thousands of comets lurking out there which will eventually interfere with Earth whether directly or whether indirectly by altering the orbits of other bodies (like asteroids, Trojans, or Centaurs), sending them on new orbits that will eventually interfere with Earth. The solar system is a dangerous place, and the odds are against us. It is only a matter of time.

My greatest fear is low-albedo comets. As you know, they can be so dark that they reflect almost no sunlight, making them difficult to spot with optical telescopes. These dark comets, like stealthy ninjas, can move deep inside our solar system before they are noticed.

I joined Dr. Goldblum at Cornell in June 2016, excited to pursue my dream, and began setting up my program to search for TNOs and comets using image sets from nearly two dozen sources. After months of tedious preparation, I began searching in Orion in February 2017. During the next eleven weeks, I discovered four asteroid-sized TNOs and two dwarf-planet-sized TNOs, one about the size of Makemake, the other about the size of Orcus.

In late April, I turned my attention to Taurus. Several weeks later in mid-May, I discovered an occulted star above the Pleiades on a plate from April 2016. Further investigation revealed seven more occultations between March 2013 and January 2017. Initial analysis suggested, due to its apparent size and trajectory, that it was an exceptionally provocative comet, so we put it at the top of our priority list.

In September we enlisted the help of the Keck 1 at Mauna Kea, the Hooker at Mt. Wilson, and the MMT at Whipple in observing the occultation of a dim star just below the Pleiades. With their assistance, we were able to estimate the comet's diameter using the time-of-transit methodology. We were shocked to discover that its diameter was far larger than we anticipated, between 900 and 1,000 kilometers—fifteen times the diameter of Hale-Bopp, the largest known comet. The enormous size indicates that it has an extremely low albedo, maybe lower than 0.02, which is more than twice as dark as coal. Using the recent data, we were also able to confirm our prediction that the comet's orbit will take it through the asteroid belt and bring it dangerously close to Mars—within 25,000 miles.

Because the comet was extremely large and dangerous, reminiscent of an elephant gone rogue, I wanted to name it Rogue, a slight departure from the naming protocols employed by the Committee on Small Body Nomenclature.

On Monday, November 6, after six months of historical data collection and verification, we sent my report on the comet to the Minor Planet Center along with the suggestion that it be named Rogue rather than Kirilenko. Dr. Goldblum was beside himself with excitement. This was the most tantalizing space story since the Apollo 11 moon mission. A large comet was going to pass through the asteroid belt, potentially disrupting the orbits of several asteroids, and then pass terrifyingly close to Mars.

That afternoon, we received the standard formal response from the MPC acknowledging the receipt of my report. The next day, we anxiously waited for the confirmation email. We were a little surprised when the end of the day came, and we hadn't received it. Normally, the confirmation letter is sent within twenty-four hours. In the previous year, we had sent in six reports on new TNOs, and all of them had been verified within that time frame.

The next day, Wednesday, Dr. Goldblum didn't show up for work. His assistant informed us that he was attending a NASA function and would return in a few days. At the time I thought nothing of his absence.

I was on pins and needles all day, checking my email every fifteen or twenty minutes, hoping to find a confirmation letter. It never came. Instead, we received an email late in the afternoon telling us to hold off on all communication and publication about the discovery until the MPC had concluded its investigation—a very unusual request.

On Friday afternoon, Dr. Goldblum showed up in his office. When I poked my head in his door and said "good morning," he muttered "g'mornin" to me without looking up, turned his back to me, and began rummaging in a file drawer. He appeared to be ignoring me. I asked if he had seen the email. He shrugged and answered with a touch of exasperation, "Sometimes these things just take time." He obviously didn't want to talk about the discovery, so I left him alone. As I walked away, I began to wonder if the Rogue was no longer in his hands. A premonition of darkness in high places sent a shiver down my spine. Was something brewing in the cauldron, something conspiracy-theory nuts would drool over were they privy?

My mind raced. If the project had been wrenched from his hands, the deed had not been done by his colleagues or incompetent bureaucrats in the MPC or NASA. Most likely it was federal agencies with the authority and ability to control information flow. But why? There was only one possible reason. The government regarded the information we had given the MPC as dangerous. They were determined to keep it out of the hands of the public. And that implied that the Rogue posed a much greater threat to mankind than I had anticipated.

But the thought that I was embroiled in the early stages of a conspiracy of vast proportions seemed too preposterous to believe. I stepped back from my fears and determined to wait for further information.

The following week, on Wednesday, November 15, we received another standby letter from the MPC reiterating the request to refrain from communication on the matter, apologizing for the unusual delay, and explaining that the extraordinary find demanded extraordinary verification. Dr. Goldblum vented a little steam at this procrastination, but his frustration seemed hollow. I suspected then, and am convinced now, that he knew a whole lot more than he was letting on.

We finally received the confirmation email on Monday, November 27. Though I had suspected that something was brewing and had prepared myself for disappointment, the letter was still bittersweet. My discovery, it insisted, was not a string of stellar occultations caused by a comet, but a string of refractions caused by the shock wave on the nose of a growing jet from a recently formed black hole. It defended this interpretation with several dollops of ad hoc physics. Then it banned me from communicating with anyone on the phenomenon until the federal government (the MPC, NASA, JPL, the Pentagon, etc.) had finished their investigation. They regarded it as a sensitive issue. Barry Naylor himself had signed the letter.

Needless to say, this letter left me crestfallen. Instead of receiving a confirmation that I had made an exciting discovery with an apocalyptic aura, I received a notification that I had made a boring discovery, of interest only to a handful of academics. At the same time, I was dumbfounded. While I felt uneasy questioning the experts, I found myself skeptical of their interpretation that the series of stellar occultations was caused by the shock wave from a black-hole jet. Perhaps this really is a viable theory that should be considered. But why wait until now to trot it out? Why wasn't it brought up earlier with any of the dozens of comets that had been discovered earlier? Why bring this theory up for the first time with a comet candidate whose orbit would likely create havoc in the inner solar system? And why did the MPC involve the Jet Propulsion Lab if there was no potential threat to Earth?

When I questioned the interpretation that the

occultations were caused by the shock wave at the nose of a jet from a black hole, Dr. Goldblum defended it and patiently explained the theory to me. While the stars appeared to be occulted by a body passing in front of them, what was really happening was that the light waves from the star were being refracted by the shock wave, which prevented them from reaching Earth. I was a little peeved at his condescending attitude, but I bit my lip. I had a little more education under my belt than freshman physics. I wasn't questioning the legitimacy of the theory of shock-wave refraction, only its application in the present situation.

I asked him if he had any doubts at all about the black-hole interpretation. He replied that it didn't matter whether he thought the interpretation was right or wrong. It is what it is, and there is no arguing with the MPC. When I glared straight into his eyes, he glowered back with lightning in his eyes and said firmly, "I don't doubt their interpretation at all."

When I continued to protest, Dr. Goldblum told me to let the matter rest. The experts had spoken. That should be the end of the matter. It was our business to find things. It was their business to decide what those things are.

Now I was fuming mad. What in the world was going on? This was not the fiercely independent scientist I had worked with for the past year and a half. Gone was the man of sturdy common sense that always preferred less complex solutions over more complex—that lived by Occam's Razor. His response couldn't be chalked up to humility showing a little deference. It was blatant kowtowing. Men only did that for fear or for gain. So, what was he afraid of? Or did he sell his soul when a golden opportunity presented itself?

While I was stewing over the matter, he dropped a bomb on me. All research on the black hole was being turned over to a team of experts from a dozen prestigious astrophysics departments. Effective immediately, I was to terminate all my research in Taurus and return to my research in Orion. Furthermore, I was supposed to turn in all my research on the phenomenon in Taurus by the end of the day so that it could be made available to those who had been assigned to the research project.

I looked him straight in the eyes. He met my gaze with a cold stare and curtly told me that the matter was out of his control. The decision had come down from above. Hot tears welled up in my eyes, fury alone keeping me from sobs. I nodded, turned, and walked away, convinced that the powers that be were intentionally covering up the truth. They knew that a comet, the Rogue, was headed for a dangerous rendezvous with Mars. If they had really believed the shock-wave light-refraction theory, if the only danger involved was yet another academic relativity problem to give astrophysicists headaches, they would not have banned all unauthorized research on the phenomenon, much less all research in Taurus. They had done a pretty good job of hiding their hand, but the cards they played on the table made for easy card counting. As my father used to say, "Sometimes the smartest people on the planet are the dumbest people on the planet."

Two hours later, I turned over my research as requested. What I didn't tell him was that after the second standby letter from the MPC, which left me with a gut feeling that something was wrong, I made copies of every document and image in my research and gave them to Buster for safe keeping.

Ariele winced. *Buster? She knows about Buster?* Buster was a Linux-based off-shore operation that offered a suite of services including data storage with insane levels of protection. It was an arcane business loved by hackers, the underworld, and the rich and powerful. *Über-cool. There is way more to this straitlaced, churchy girl than meets the eye.*

I admit that I felt a little uncomfortable with the fact that I had kept copies of all my research, likely against the will of the federal government and not merely against the will of some highbrowed academics. But I consoled myself with the thought that my actions were more in keeping with the Old Testament story of brave Jehosheba hiding the heir to the throne from the murderous designs of Athaliah than a traitor committing treason against his own country.

I sat on this for about a year, hoping against hope that the situation might change. But nothing has. And likely nothing will. Several times, I tested the waters with Dr. Goldblum, but always got the same response, adamant insistence that I let this go and move on. But I can't do that. And I can't sit on this any longer. Something is up. I suspect that NASA and the government know full well that the Rogue is on a course that will take it dangerously close to Mars. They are afraid of the potential outcome. And they don't want this disruptive information in the hands of the public. Moreover, I fear that my time here at Cornell is soon coming to an end. I have been warned that I am on Homeland Security's list of potential threats. If I don't get this information out into the hands of others now, I may never get the chance. The truth will be buried.

The enclosed DVD includes five images of the most recent documented occultation that I have—fourteen months ago—a dim star at approximately 3h 52m 4s and 23° 47'. You will also find eight series of images that show earlier occultations. By my estimation, you should look for the next occultation in the vicinity of 3h 52m 3s and 23° 45'.

Sometimes I fear that I have blown this matter out of proportion and that I am being paranoid. I don't know for sure that it will deflect another body into an orbit that will threaten Earth. But I do know that it has made people in high places extremely nervous. Perhaps the Rogue will be the disruptor implied in Luke 21:26, "the planets of the heavens shall be shaken." Something has to shake the planets. They are not going to shake themselves. You may recall that I shared this verse with you the evening we sat on the swings and talked.

Your friend,
Shadowchaser

P.S. If nobody can reach me, it is probably because I am languishing in a FEMA camp somewhere, unarrested and uncharged, a prisoner buried deep in the shadowy Homeland Security enclaves, concealed under the veneer of the detention of white-collar criminals and soft terrorists, who pose a non-violent threat to U.S. security.

Ariele's mind was pulled in two directions. Her sober half wanted to believe that Irina was making a mountain out of a molehill, that nothing was going on that merited the kind of concern she was indulging. But her suspicious side, the side that distrusted big government, feared that Irina might really have stumbled upon a threat which was being covered up. She was, after all, one of the most sober-minded thinkers she had ever met. Not given to nonsense or exaggeration.

Moreover, the news story Ariele had heard two weeks earlier on *Down the Rabbit Hole*, the late-night talk-radio program she listened to while driving home from Mt. Wilson, meshed with Irina's account. According to Burrage Krakenhavn, the show's host, Russian hackers had obtained intel from two U.S. sources that confirmed the existence of the so-called Rogue. The same intel had also established, based on data from NEOCam and the recently refurbished WISE and Spitzer satellites, that the Rogue was vastly larger than previous estimations—larger even than Mercury! A planet-sized comet! At the time, she had laughed at the report. But Irina's letter now put that report in a whole new light.

She stared out her window dreamily, wishing she had a rural vista. *I need more information. Need to determine whether Irina's fears are well-founded or unfounded. Whether Burrage's account is based on fact or whether it's simply another late-night exaggeration fest.*

2

Ariele noticed that the late afternoon shadows were settling upon the neighborhood and remembered that she was scheduled to be on the Hooker that evening. She loved using the ancient telescope. It pleased her retro streak. She glanced at the clock. It was 4:33 p.m. Later than she thought.

She jumped up, tossed the letter back in the box on the table, grabbed her favorite sweatshirt from her closet, a tan hoodie sporting the Counter Culture Coffee logo, took a quick glance in the mirror, and sighed. *I really need to redo my hair. My roots are starting to show beneath the rose gold.* She grabbed her leather messenger bag, a treasured flea-market find which she used for her purse, tossed in two Greek yogurts and a banana, and headed for the door. Halfway there, she stopped in her tracks and doubled back to the box on the table. She placed the letter and the DVD in the envelope, hurried to her bedroom, and slipped the envelope between her mattress and box spring. Whirling around, she hustled back to the dining table, pulled her miniature shears from her messenger bag, and cut the mailing labels off the packaging. Then she deposited the pages from the Salina Journal, the grocery-bag wrapping paper, and the mailing labels in a kitchen garbage bag and tied it shut. She would drop the evidence in a convenient dumpster on the way to work. Several possibilities came to mind. *I'm probably being paranoid. What are the odds that the FBI will ever search my apartment?* Then she stowed the empty shoebox under her bed. She glanced at the clock again. It was now 4:42 p.m. *Nuts. No sunset tonight.*

The drive from her apartment to La Cañada Flintridge took thirty minutes in normal traffic, and it was another forty-five minutes from there to Mt. Wilson, weather permitting. She liked to leave about fifteen minutes early so that she had ten or fifteen minutes to prepare before her Hooker time started. That meant that she had to leave her apartment a few minutes before sunset, which was 4:45 p.m. today. If she wanted to catch the sunset view from the lower stretch of the Angeles Crest Highway as it climbed into the San Gabriels, which she tried to do once a week, she had to leave thirty-five to forty-five minutes early. That was not going to happen today.

She sighed. Several of the ridges offered a stunning view of the sunset as it dipped below the ocean horizon. She never tired of chasing sunsets. They seemed to be part of her soul. Grand. Majestic. Magnificent. Yet such descriptions fell short of doing them justice. Like the God who made them, they were beyond the tongue or pen. She stopped and tried to put the thought out of mind. She didn't like to think about God, but sunsets and sunrises often brought him to mind. And thinking about him led to thoughts about an awful day Irina had shared with her once. The day the sun was going to set on the world as we know it. She shuddered. That was not a thought she liked to entertain.

3

drive to Mount Wilson
Friday afternoon, November 30, 2018

Ariele bounced out of her apartment a few minutes before four in the afternoon, as giddy with excitement as if she were going on vacation. It was a crisp autumn evening in Southern California, and she was going to chase the sunset today. She climbed into her 1991 VW Cabriolet Special Edition—which her dad had found for her—started it, savored the distinctive chug of the diesel engine for a moment, backed out of her parking space, and headed for the Angeles Crest Highway. She loved this drive. During warmer weather, she drove through the hills with her top down, the wind blowing in her face and disheveling her hair. She relished the fragrance of the trees, especially on the draws where the evening breeze wafted the scent of eucalyptus down the slope.

As she turned onto the Angeles Crest, leaving the worst of the city traffic behind, she relaxed and allowed herself a little freedom for the rest of the drive to think and soak in the scenery. Oblivious to the fact that she was practically praying, she gave thanks once again for the fortuitous circumstances which had landed her this dream job with the Caltech NEO program. It enabled her to pursue research in NEOs and gave her telescope time two evenings a week at the Mt. Wilson Observatory on the 100-inch Hooker.

She was grateful that she had submitted to her father's counsel. In high school her heart had been set on attending MIT in Cambridge, Massachusetts. It was rated as the best in the world in her field for technical and academic excellence. But he had convinced her that Caltech was a better fit for her independent spirit and her career designs.

She was also grateful that she had decided to take her core graduate level classes with Dr. Sally Evans though her classes were less popular than the other options. Sally was a rapid-fire lecturer and a hard grader. But she was also the head of the Caltech NEO program and had strong ties with NASA. During Ariele's first year in her Master's program, they had bonded, both feeling that a strong NEO program was one of mankind's greatest needs for the future. This had led to her working on several NEO survey projects under Dr. Evans using new search protocols that she had designed herself. During these surveys, she had discovered thirty-two new NEOs, a tremendous achievement for a student. Four were exceptionally provocative. They were larger than five kilometers and likely to pass within one lunar distance of Earth in their next ten passes. Between her personality, academics, technical savvy, and pure scientific genius, she rapidly grew in esteem, being highly regarded by the faculty and enjoying near pop-star status among her fellow students.

Ariele completed the requirements for a PhD in

astrophysics in May 2016 with the defense of her thesis, *Pioneering Techniques for NEO Discovery*. Dr. Evans was her advisor. It was lauded in the astronomy community and republished in two different journals. Her savvy and success in her research programs and her thesis had led Dr. Evans to invite her to join the NEO program at Caltech, a step she took in July 2016. With the passing of the NASA Bill in November 2017, Mount Wilson Observatory came under the oversight of NASA, and the Hooker was leased to the Caltech NEO program four nights per week. That same month, Ariele had started on the Hooker. It had been twelve months now—a remarkable year.

Since then, she had not only continued to grow in her reputation as a brilliant astronomer but also in her reputation for being slightly eccentric, a reputation she enjoyed. You never knew what color her hair was going to be when she walked in the door. She regularly dyed it with organic tints in subdued hues, especially tones from rose gold to deep cherry, which she applied in ombre styling. Most of the time, her lipstick and eye shadow matched her hair. Her skirts and blouses were hippie-mod. She preferred jewelry made with polished wood, woven twine, and semi-precious stones. Sandals were her constant footwear. In cold weather she added colorful toe socks. Her associates at Caltech affectionately referred to her as Moxie.

The turnoff for Mount Wilson Road shot by on her right. She jumped on the brakes, slowed to a stop, and backed her VW up enough to make the turn. She laughed at herself. *Silly girl. Getting way too deep in reverie again.*

4

Mount Wilson
Friday evening, November 30, 2018

As Ariele prepared for another evening on the telescope, sharpening her Kitaboshi pencils and starting a pot of coffee, fresh ground organic Ethiopian Yirgacheffe, she found herself once again thinking about the mysterious letter she had received from Irina. What was this Rogue, this massive body, reputedly larger than Mercury, that was headed for a tryst with the Red Planet? Was NASA really involved in a cover-up orchestrated by the highest levels of the federal government? The whole thing seemed more like a movie on the Sci-Fi channel than reality. Whatever was going on, one thing was certain. Something was up there that made Richard Fairchild, the director of NASA, and those he answered to very nervous.

Irina was probably right that research in Taurus would not have been banned if the official position were true. NASA didn't really believe that the string of occulted stars were actually refractions of starlight by the shock wave of a growing jet from a new black hole. That was a contrived

24

explanation. They were scrambling for a cover story.

She decided to look at the area for a few minutes without logging her time. A quick glance at the clock revealed that she had twelve minutes before her assigned time began. But what would be her cover story? *Gonna need a plausible justification.*

Her resolve faced an immediate gut-check. Should she do this? She knew she was risking her job. Since the passing of the NASA Bill, Caltech's time on the telescope was limited to the NEO assignments that NASA gave them, and her time was limited to the assignment she was given by Caltech's NEO program. According to the legislation, JPL's Center for Near Earth Object Studies, or CNEOS, was charged to catalog every potential NEO threat to Earth in the next five years. This could only be accomplished if every institution involved did their assigned part. But she suspected that intensified NEO research wasn't the real reason behind the NASA Bill. The real reason posed a vastly greater threat than that posed by any of the asteroidal NEOs—the comet in Irina's letter.

While the official policy did not formally ban research in any particular sector, there was a ban on research in any sector other than one's assigned sector. Telescope time and plate research were strictly limited to one's assigned field of research. The astronomers who worked at Mt. Wilson had been warned in numerous team meetings against wasting time, energy, and hard-wrested grant money on their own free-lance projects. Freelancing on government telescopes would not be tolerated, especially if it involved any of the apocalyptic scenarios that were rife on the internet like Nibiru, Planet X, rogue planets, and brown dwarfs. Such efforts were ridiculed as foolishness that was little different than attempting to track down Spiderman. They would be answered with severe consequences.

Curiosity and her sense of right got the best of her. *Time to be decisive. If there really is a cover-up here, if there really is a massive comet on course for a potentially disastrous rendezvous with the asteroid belt and Mars, then this information ought to be in the hands of the public.* And judging by Irina's letter, she might be the only person in the world in a position to get this information into their hands. *I hope I don't regret this.*

She hit upon her cover story. She would explain that she had mistakenly assumed that spending a few minutes on the Hooker, prior to her scheduled time, investigating a rumor of a massive comet that will barely miss Mars seemed to fall within the broader scope of their NEO research. The NASA Bill had, after all, expanded the definition of an NEO to include any large object of interest that passed within 1.6 astronomical units of the sun. Moreover, a comet that size running wild in the inner solar system was too big and too dangerous to ignore. She sucked her breath in with a quiet whistle as she pondered the frightful situation. *Bigger than Mercury. Large asteroids dislodged and running amok. The ramifications for Earth are unthinkable.* It reminded her of Irina's description of the end of the Minoan empire. She had once told her that the ancient histories, based on eyewitness testimony, claimed that Minoa had been destroyed by a huge comet that had raised stupendous tsunamis, triggered massive volcanic eruptions and earthquakes, and devastated the entire region with a storm of stones and fire. In a matter of hours, the entire Mediterranean Basin had been demolished: its cities razed, its civilizations in tatters. She shuddered.

But she needed a rumor. Where was she going to get one? A Google search? Perhaps. That might fly. But both her search parameters and her source had to be kosher. They couldn't be associated with Planet X nutcases or any other dubious sources that would raise eyebrows. Tainted sources were a non-starter.

Time was running out. She decided to investigate now and worry about her cover story later. She would likely find her creative genius once she was in the heat of the fire. As her father had once said, regarding his experience in the high-pressure environment of the Hollywood film industry, "Nothing like a little pressure to bring out the best in a man."

Listening with quiet reverence to the creaks and squeaks of the lumbering giant—this was her cathedral and organ, she swung the telescope in the right general direction, then entered the coordinates that Irina had given her. *Hopefully, no one will notice that the telescope is pointed in an unauthorized direction.* The massive reflector swiveled, adjusted, and stopped. She focused and shot two images. Then she moved backward on Irina's calculated trajectory three-quarters of a camera frame and shot another two. Next, she moved forward on the trajectory to about three-quarters of a camera frame past the original location for a final set. When she was done, she swiveled the telescope back to its approximate starting point.

Mission accomplished, she saved the images in a file she named "Potential NEO near the Pleiades." Then she made two copies of the file on DVDs. She placed one disc in a folder in her file drawer which she labeled "Potential NEOs." The other she placed in a 5X7 manila envelope, which she promptly buried in her messenger bag. She glanced at her watch. *Nuts.* It was now 6:23 p.m. *Eleven minutes late.* She quickly logged in, entered the coordinates for her first assignment, poured herself a cup of coffee, and settled in for an evening of NEO verification and orbital determination, slightly on edge as she listened to the lumbering giant creak and squeak again. If anyone was paying attention, three relatively large moves inside twenty minutes was a bit unusual. She picked up her manifest and glanced at her assignment: two new asteroids, one new short-period comet, and six asteroids she had been tracking for several weeks now.

5

Los Angeles
Saturday, December 1, 2018

When she returned to her apartment that evening, shortly after midnight, Ariele was too excited to immediately go to bed as she usually did. Feverish with anticipation over what the new images might reveal, she hurried to her bedroom to retrieve Irina's DVD from under her mattress, raced back to her kitchen table, dug the Hooker DVD out of her purse, opened up her laptop, and hesitated. She winced as she pondered the trouble she could get into for having a copy of SODpro on her laptop. The Stellar Occultation Discovery Program was a proprietary program and only authorized for installation on designated Caltech computers.

Four months ago, she had noticed an installation disc sitting on the desk of one of her colleagues at the observatory and had made a copy of it, just in case. Even back then, she had sensed, based on things she had heard in team meetings—as the evasive answers given to questions on the new mission focus—that NASA was not disclosing the real cause behind the sweeping changes implemented in the

29

NASA Bill. Something big was up, but she had no idea what. So, she had appropriated a copy of the software—that sounded more legitimate than stealing it—and tossed it into her file cabinet behind the last hanging folder. It seemed like an innocuous place to store the pirated disc. By all appearances, it was either misplaced or lost. She had retrieved the disc on Tuesday evening when she was on the Hooker and had installed SODpro on her laptop the next day, figuring that she would need it to scan for occulted stars if she was going to pursue the lead that Irina had given her.

She fired up the software and waited. It took ages to load. Once it was running, she installed Irina's DVD, loaded her data, and waited. The software crept at a snail's pace. Slow CPU and too little memory. *Note to self. Buy a super-fast gaming laptop, like yesterday.* An hour and a quarter later, she confirmed the string of stellar occultations that Irina had observed. There was no way around it. A massive body was moving through the heavens somewhere in the vastness beyond Neptune.

Next, she inserted the Hooker DVD, installed and labeled the images into SODpro, and started the scanning process. Twenty minutes later, she whooped, "Bingo!" Sure enough, the zoomed-in chart of the area showed that a dim star below the Pleiades, on the trajectory Irina had predicted, was fifty-five percent occulted. It was not, however, the one she had predicted, but one slightly farther. That implied that the comet was traveling faster than she had anticipated.

Like Irina, Ariele did not buy the theory that the apparent occultations were actually light-wave diffraction from the shockwave at the nose of a still-growing jet from a black hole. That seemed like a stretch when a much simpler explanation was available. A chunk of rock traveling through our solar system was passing in front of stars, partially or entirely blocking their light. Irina was right. Dr. Goldblum, the MPC, JPL, and NASA had rejected the simple explanation of the phenomenon because they had been required to drink the Kool-Aid—embrace the official cover-up story.

She muttered in frustration. Stupidity is not ignorance. Stupidity is a moral failure—subverting reason for personal gain. One of her pet peeves in life was men who were willing to set aside common sense and embrace claptrap in order to win the favor of the movers and shakers. Such dereliction of reason was analytical suicide. What could possibly induce men like Dr. Goldblum to set aside common sense and drink the Kool-Aid? Money? Position? Reputation? Fear? Maybe there was an Orwellian juggernaut on the rise. *Enough with the muttering and the psychoanalytics. Focus.*

What next? She decided not to rush to publication. For one thing, she had no idea who she could trust to publish this sensitive information. She didn't trust the mainstream media. They fed you the news through either a left-wing or a right-wing lens. Nor did she trust the alternative media. They had their own agendas, which often led them away from common sense and integrity, especially the looney tunes that held forth on late-night radio.

For another thing, she sensed the need to investigate the comet's path. Was it going to pass as close to Mars as Irina feared? Was it going to pass on its inside or its outside? What were the odds that it could brush the Red Planet? Would it disrupt any asteroids? The latter was a troubling consideration that opened its own can of worms. Asteroidal disruptions could cause problems for centuries to come, long after the present problem had passed and was merely a chapter in the history books.

Two more occultations were needed, she figured, to have enough data to make her trajectory projections with the degree of accuracy she desired. It was now November. If she shot two sets of images per week for five months, December through April, and discovered two more occultations, which was likely as the Rogue was passing through a region densely packed with dim stars, she could have her report done in May. But settling on such a distant date seemed like an intentional delay to her impetuous spirit. The five months may as well have been five centuries. Yet, she had no other option. *That's the way it is. Deal with it.*

The big challenge was a cover story, something to mask her tracks if she were discovered doing unauthorized research. While a good story probably wouldn't keep her out of trouble, it might lighten her punishment—a verbal warning rather than termination. If it was half decent, Sally might even cover for her. But whatever story she came up with, it needed to be something plausible that she found on the internet.

She started by googling "comet + Taurus OR Pleiades." When it brought up millions of hits, she sighed. She slogged through 127 pages of results. Nothing. She found several legitimate comet articles that were completely unrelated to Irina's find. The rest were without scientific merit, a stream of mind-numbing conspiracy theories that ran the gamut from far-fetched apocalyptic scenarios like Planet X, to the reality of UFOs, to Zechariah Sitchin's comedic take on Sumerian history. She sneered. *A real conspiracy would be far more realistic and far more subtle than this stuff.*

Ariele's eyelids were heavy, and her brain was fogging out. It was now 4 a.m., and she had been at her fruitless search for over four hours. She decided to give up and go to bed. As she rose from her chair with a frustrated huff, a sudden inspiration rejuvenated her. *Think like a hacker!* If there really was a government-directed conspiracy going on, she would likely find nothing using common search terms like *comet*, *Taurus*, or the *Pleiades*. Any websites covering the Rogue story that could be found with such terms would likely have been taken down already. She was going to have to use a little more imagination. She sat down again.

Use your thinker. Mind over tired body. Surely, at least one person in the know would have had misgivings about the cover-up and leaked the information. But how would a cautious discloser hide the leak in plain sight? Alternative terminology! Of course! They would use lesser known terms. She skewed her mouth and furled her eyebrows, deep in thought. *What was the ancient term for a comet? I should know this. It was covered in Historical Astronomy.* The term was on the tip of her tongue. *Hairy stars! That's what the Greeks called them.* She turned her attention to the Pleiades. *It was seven something ... the Seven Sisters!*

She googled "hairy star + seven sisters." There were tens of thousands of hits, which elicited a dejected sigh. She spent the next two hours slogging through page after page of irrelevant results. On her sixty-second page of hits, she sat up in her chair and blurted out a loud *Kowabunga!* She had found a recent paper published by Dr. Steven Youngblood from the University of Arizona in late September, only two months earlier, entitled *Another Look at the Phenomenon Near the Seven Sisters—Is it a Hairy Star?*

The introductory paragraph stated, "A newly discovered comet of tremendous size, with an average diameter of approximately 5200 kilometers, about ten percent larger than Mercury, has been discovered on a path that will take it dangerously close to Mars—within 20,000 miles. This is close enough to the sun that it is technically classifiable as an NEO according to the expanded definition in the NASA Bill—within 1.6 astronomical units. While this body has an orbit that suggests a long-period comet, it is fifty-five times the diameter of the largest comet ever observed. Most likely, it is either a rogue planet from outside our solar system or a former planet from inside our system that somehow became dislodged from its orbit. Whatever it is, it poses a greater threat to Earth than all other known and potential NEOs put together."

She scrolled through the eighty-six pages. It looked very promising. The presentation was clear and cogent. It contained images from all eight of the occultations that Irina had discovered on historical plates, plus two that Dr. Youngblood had found, plus three observations made jointly by the Hooker at Mount Wilson, the Keck 1 at Mauna Kea, and the MMT at Whipple. It also contained recent infrared images from NEOCam, WISE, and Spitzer. On top of that, there were graphs, diagrams, and a spectrographic analysis that had been done by Spitzer, which indicated that it was essentially iron, with high amounts of nickel and platinum-group metals and significant amounts of heavy rare-earth minerals.

The mention of the NEOCam, WISE, and Spitzer space telescopes fascinated her. *I thought NEOCam was slated to be a warm mission. And the cold missions of WISE and Spitzer ended long ago. There is no way those two could obtain cold-mission data unless they were revitalized. That means NASA spent an insane amount of money to revitalize their cold-mission abilities. And that implies that this comet has NASA's undivided attention. It makes them nervous.*

On the second page, it addressed the interpretation being touted by those in the academic community who were privy to the phenomenon, the theory that the shockwave at the nose of a growing jet from a newborn black hole was causing the refraction of light waves, giving the appearance of a string of stellar occultations. The author, however, disavowed this interpretation in no uncertain terms, pleading for common sense over consensus. "If it looks like a rock, acts like a rock, and moves like a rock, it is a rock."

On page forty-two, the paper explained why the comet was currently invisible to both optical telescopes and Earth-based infrared telescopes. It was too dark for the former to see and too cold for the latter to see. It pointed out, however, that the comet would become visible to Earth-based infrared telescopes in the mid-range bands of 10, 12.2, and 14 micrometers once it neared Uranus, barring atmospheric problems caused by things like nuclear war or a Tambora-class volcanic eruption. But it would not become visible to optical telescopes until it developed a coma. While this normally occurred between Jupiter and the asteroid belt, we were entering a period of extremely low sunspot activity and decreased solar wind, which meant that the comet might not manifest a coma until it was inside the asteroid belt. When the coma did appear, however, it was going to be a show for the centuries. It would be the brightest comet in modern history by tenfold or more.

Several things stood out about the author of this paper. First of all, he was well-connected because he had access to data and tools that weren't available to Irina. Secondly, he had a tremendous grasp of the subject. Thirdly, he was savvy. His use of innovative search terms had masterfully hidden his paper from prying eyes who wanted to keep this information off the internet while making it discoverable by anyone with a little knowledge in ancient astronomy, which was true for students of catastrophism who believe that the past sheds light on the future. And fourthly, he wanted this paper to be understood by the average man because he had written it in plain English, not the typical technical jargon that only the scientist can understand. In other words, he hoped that this paper would be leaked to the public. Ariele smiled and nodded her head in agreement. She would do her part to fulfill his wish. *I sure hope I get to meet this man someday. Gotta admire his wisdom and courage.*

Ariele printed a copy for her own reading, secured it with a large clip, and placed it in a folder. Though a millennial, she still preferred paper. Then she saved a copy to a thumb drive, one to her hard drive, and another to her cloud account. With a sweet sense of relief, she closed her laptop and stood up. Finally! She could go to bed. She had her alibi in hand. With a twinge of curiosity, she glanced at her watch. It was 6:26 in the morning. *Oops! Had no idea that it was that late.* As she turned, she noticed that the faint gray of dawn was beginning to gleam in the window.

Before she had even walked two steps, she realized that she was still short one alibi. A cover story to explain how she happened to stumble upon an article on the internet about an NEO threat that is currently near the Seven Sisters. She slumped back into her chair and flipped open her laptop. Would the odyssey never end?

On a hunch, she googled "NEO + hairy star + threat," indicating that she only wanted those results that contained all three terms. She got twenty thousand hits. *Double nuts.* Frustrated, she started working her way through the pages of results, dreading the thought of another protracted search. But her fears didn't materialize. On the eleventh page, she found what she was looking for—Dr. Youngblood's article. With a sigh of relief, she closed her laptop and pushed it away. Now she had a plausible cover story. She could claim that she had stumbled on his paper while doing general research on NEO threats. No one could accuse her of finding the article while wallowing through cheesy websites that were peddling stuff like the Mayan apocalypse or Nibiru's return.

Her night was finally over, and sunlight was streaming in the window. She shook her head at her pertinacity. *I haven't stayed up all night since I was an undergrad.* After sitting in satisfied silence for a moment, she shouted "Yes!" stumbled to her bedroom, kicked her shoes off, and climbed into bed. As her tired eyes succumbed to sleep, she contemplated the situation—the letter from Irina, her own investigations, and the seriousness of the situation. Her last waking thought was the line from Irina's letter, "Here's an NEO you'll wish you never heard about."

6

Caltech
Monday, December 3, 2018

Ariele and Woody Lundstrom strolled toward Beckham Auditorium, headed for the food trucks that parked there over lunch hour except in bad weather. Woody could tell that something was on her mind. He knew her almost as well as he knew his own daughter. They had started hanging out together for lunch, more or less by default, shortly after she had arrived in the summer of 2017. The other girls in the department went to the gym during their noon break, which just wasn't Ariele. The other guys liked to get a beer with their lunch, usually at a noisy club, which wasn't Woody's preference. After sitting alone in the break room for several weeks, eating her yogurt in silence, Ariele began tagging along with Woody to the food trucks. Since then, they had become friends.

The unusual quiet unnerved Woody. He thought about prying but kept his peace. Moments later, Ariele spoke up. "Something's been bugging me all weekend. I just don't know what to do. Should I go forward with a course of

LEE W. BRAINARD

action that I'm contemplating? Or should I just walk away?"

"Depends. What's on your mind?"

"Let's say you were working for a big corporation that claimed they were only interested in human welfare, but you became privy to information that proved they were covering something up that was detrimental to man's well-being. What would you do? Would you abide by your confidentiality agreement? Or would you disseminate the information by some means like Whistleblowers or WikiLeaks or The New York Times or what have you?"

Woody weighed his response, then replied, "That would really come down to the seriousness of the infraction. If it involved a threat to health or privacy or freedom, definitely *yes*. You would have a moral obligation to disseminate the information. You couldn't just walk away."

"How about hiding information, information that would enable people to protect themselves from harm that is lurking in their neighborhood?"

"You mean like not releasing information on dangerous pollutants that a local corporation has allowed to leach into the water system, leaving communities unwarned?"

"Yeah. Something like that."

"That kind of information needs to be in the hands of the public, without exception. If the government chooses to either ignore the warnings or conceal the information, then folks need to skirt the government and take matters into their own hands."

"What if you risk your job or your freedom by sharing the information?"

"The amount of risk we face doesn't affect the principle we are trying to uphold. It only changes the cost we might have to pay."

Ariele chewed on Woody's advice for a moment, then smiled and nodded her head. He smiled back. He knew the look. She had made up her mind to go forward, whatever it was that was on her mind. She grinned—back to her perky self—and exclaimed, "I'm feeling adventurous. Let's go to the Hoagie Magician and try the hot sandwich we haven't tried, Calabrese salami with asiago and pepperoncini."

7

Irina fidgeted nervously. For months she had looked forward to defending her thesis *The Underestimated Danger Posed by Comets*. Now the day was here, and she was filled with dread. Her confidence had vanished. She faced six seasoned scientists, and one of them, Dr. James Gardner, was a well-known skeptic of NEO danger. He loved to berate the NEO-apocalypse theory, insisting that astronomers hyped and exaggerated the danger so they could procure funding to buy cool equipment.

He argued that the solar system had been in existence for billions of years and that if anyone intelligently considered the ramifications of this fact, they would realize that Earth had long ago swept its orbit clear of every major threat. There was zero danger of a catastrophic event much less an extinction event, not from an asteroid, not from a comet. In his estimation, the only extinction threat we faced was the death of the sun, and that was millions of years in the future.

We had millions of years to prepare. Millions of years to move civilization to a younger star elsewhere in the galaxy. Irina could practically recite his mini-lecture denying NEO threat. She had taken two required courses from him and had heard it twenty times.

Fearing that Dr. Gardner would mercilessly pick her thesis apart, Irina had asked her advisor several times to exclude him from her examination committee. But Dr. Shannon Benson had refused. "Life is tough," she said. "The corporate and academic world can be vicious. It won't hurt you to start your career with a stiff dose of professional opposition. Besides, the truth has never been hurt by the crucible."

Dr. Benson opened the session. "Your thesis statement opines, 'The threat posed to Earth by comets is vastly underestimated.' Expand on this. What is the crucial point that you believe scientists have overlooked?"

Irina drew in a deep breath and began. "The threat posed by long-period comets is significantly heightened if the theory be true, as a growing community of scientists insists, that comets are stony bodies with the same composition and origin as the asteroids."

"Pffff!" Dr. Gardner snorted. Irina felt her heart skip a beat. She was more intimidated by him than all the others put together. Not only was he virulently opposed to the NEO-apocalypse theory, he was also a champion of the dirty-snowball theory against the fledgling theory that comets were rocky bodies. He had written several academic articles against this upstart view, directing all his savvy and his extensive pejorative vocabulary in scathing attacks upon the theory and its advocates. The rocky-comet groupies as he styled them, whether from mainstream circles or the electric universe camp, were guilty of the same pseudoscience as those who believed in a flat Earth.

She looked over in his direction. Dr. Gardner scowled back with eyebrows furrowed and foot tapping a million miles an hour. He did that when he was angry. Irina grimaced. *Way to go! Offend the Hedgehog on the first question.* This could be the longest two hours of her life. She had hoped to avoid his prickliness, but somehow she had managed to rub his fur the wrong way in the first few minutes.

Several long seconds of silence hung in the air like a frozen slice of eternity. Then he barked, "A stoner! Is this your coming-out statement?"

Ouch. *Stoner.* Her eyes stung and welled with tears. A lump rose in her throat. Her lower lip quivered. He had used his favorite derogatory term for those who believed that comets were essentially the same as asteroids except for their orbits. She felt panic-stricken and wished she could crawl under a rock or suffer a heart attack. She took a deep breath. She was stalling. She tried to slow her racing pulse.

"How dare you trot out such nonsense on my watch! This is a thesis committee, not a testimony meeting. Do we get your conversion story too? Since when do science and fairy tales belong in the same room?"

She felt the hot magma of indignation start to rise. *What a pompous mule! What arrogance!* Trying to hold her tongue was hard, like trying to wrestle a crocodile. She sensed the white-hot. She turned and stared defiantly into his eyes. Her body shook with volcanic paroxysms. She couldn't hold it in any longer. She was going to unsheathe her sword and flay the old coot.

"Mercy crowns the protector." All eyes stared at Dr. Jonathan Goldblum. The visiting professor had sat in silence until now. Normally, he chaired the Astrophysics Department at Cornell, but he was at Caltech this semester in a faculty exchange with Dr. Erica Melrose. They were teaching each other's courses and filling in for each other on dissertation committees.

"Go easy on the young lady, Jim. The guardians of the faith need to show some mercy to the acolytes. Besides, you know as well as I do that many in the scientific community, even in the highest echelons, have begun to consider the stony-comet theory. You can't continue to bury your head in the sand. You need to seriously consider the evidence of the past decade that has scientists scratching their heads. The once fine line between asteroids and comets has become blurred. What if the stony-comet proponents are right?"

"They aren't right," the flustered professor groused, staring off into the distance. He refused to meet the gaze of the man who dared to challenge him, an unusual response for the cantankerous old man. Was he intimidated? Unable to answer? Bristling with indignation, he turned his attention back to the shaking candidate and said, cold as ice water, "Continue."

Emboldened by the courage of the knight that had risen

to her defense, she blurted out with enough boldness to startle herself, "I do believe that comets have the same origin and composition as asteroids and that they differ only in their orbital habits. I have taken this position on the basis of five observations that men ought to consider.

"First of all, jets, plumes, and comas have been detected on asteroids, bodies which everyone agrees are composed of stone. The dirty-snowball theory and the sublimation of ice can't explain the existence of these phenomena on these stone bodies. Perhaps they don't explain their existence on comets either.

"Secondly, the comets we have visited with probes have differed widely from the snowball model. They all looked like stone and were as hard as stone. A troublesome fact that gave the experts fits and forced them to resort to the ad hoc explanation that they were stone-covered snowballs.

"Thirdly, the theory that comets are dirty snowballs is based on the theory that comets were formed by large-scale adhesion effected through low-velocity collision. This is an unproven theory that has never been observed in nature or reproduced in any laboratory.

"Fourthly, most of the comets which we have visited exhibit minerals which suggest an extremely hot origin, 1400 Kelvin or hotter, rather than an extremely cold origin in the distant reaches of the Oort Cloud. Forsterite and pyroxene are two examples.

"Fifthly, the electrolysis of hydrocarbons better explains the coma than the sublimation of water ice does. No one has ever demonstrated the sublimation of water ice in a vacuum at temperatures from minus -125° Celsius to -200° Celsius when subjected to remote sources of light or heat. The electric model of the coma, on the other hand, can be easily replicated in the laboratory using well-known principles of electrochemistry which are comprehensible by any electrical engineering student.

"As a comet approaches the sun, a charge imbalance develops, which produces cathode sparks. These sparks strip atoms of oxygen away from the mineral surface and ionize them. These ions are then accelerated away from the comet in electric jets and mingled with hydrogen ions from the sun's solar wind to form the coma, a cloud of ionized atoms. Some of the oxygen ions combine with hydrogen ions to form hydroxyls like hydrogen peroxide that are evident in the coma.

"In the light of such observations, I am convinced that comets are rocky bodies, not icy bodies, and that the coma is the result of electrically induced ionization, not the sublimation of ice. The bright coma we see on a comet, in other words, should be compared to the bright glow of the northern lights, not to the dull cloud made by dry ice in the kitchen sink." *That felt good. Way better than erupting.*

The examiners sat in stunned silence, surprised by this unexpected display of spunkiness. Several melted into broad smiles. She hoped they were pleasant-surprise smiles and not nervous-reaction smiles. But perhaps it didn't matter.

Dr. Naismith enquired, "What do you mean when you say that comets and asteroids share a common origin?"

Irina hesitated, nervous that she was under attack again.

"I mean that when you examine the similarities between comets and asteroids, you are drawn to the conclusion that they share a common origin."

"What do you think this common origin was?" He glared coldly at her, waiting for her to step into his trap. "You do have an opinion, don't you? A cherished model on the origin of your rocky comets? Why be evasive? Why not simply acknowledge that your rocky-comet theory is dependent on the assumption of the exploded-planet theory? The theory that there used to be a planet orbiting between Mars and Jupiter and that this planet was hit by a larger planet and exploded."

He cocked his head haughtily and continued, "You are aware, aren't you, that the exploded-planet theory has been debunked? ... that the asteroids only tally about five percent of the necessary mass for a planet the size of Mars ... that even if you throw in all the comets and all the meteorites that have impacted Earth, you are still lacking ninety percent of the required mass." When he finished his attack, he sat back in his chair, folded his arms, and smugly stared her down, obviously proud of the prowess he had just displayed in destroying her position.

Irina groaned inside. *This is getting started on the wrong foot right out of the gate.* "First of all, observational science does not depend on explanatory theory to be valid. Secondly, I do believe that a planet once orbited between Mars and Jupiter ... that somewhere in the distant past it tangled with a larger planet and lost the altercation ... that it was shattered and scattered ... that those fragments which stayed in the same orbital plane became the asteroid belt ... that those which took on long-period orbits became comets ... that others became Centaurs and Hilda asteroids ... and that others yet were captured by planets becoming Trojans and moons. Thirdly, my own investigations and calculations suggest that there is no missing-mass problem."

But Dr. Naismith was not going to let the matter rest. "So, when did this event occur?"

"Whether this event occurred in recent history or whether it occurred tens of millions of years ago is irrelevant to the question of gauging the threat that the fragments pose to our planet."

"You didn't answer my question. In your opinion, when did this event occur?"

Irina took two deep breaths, trying to relax. She racked her brain searching for some repartee to extricate herself from this baited question without looking small. She cleared her throat and hesitatingly began, "Well ... I um ..."

"I myself am inclined toward Miss Kirilenko's theory," Dr. Goldblum interjected, addressing the whole group, "that the asteroids and the stony comets both trace their origin to a former planet that exploded in the past, though I would date that seminal event at tens of millions, if not hundreds of millions of years ago. And I agree with her that the time of that event is somewhat academic while the threat which the remnants of that event pose for Earth is of paramount importance. So, for the sake of focusing on the real issue, let's accept her thesis of planetary origin as a legitimate working model, turn our attention away from theories on *when* this planet exploded, and focus on the threat that we face from comets if her model is true in its primary points."

Irina breathed a sigh of relief. Her knight had ridden to her rescue once again.

Dr. Evans, herself attracted to Irina's theory, took the questioning in a different direction. "Assuming that comets are fragments of a former planet rather than conglomerations of ice and dust formed in the Oort Cloud, then how many comets do you suppose there are?"

Relieved to field a question from an ally, Irina calmly replied, "I estimate that the number of comets of significant size is approximately 1.25 million."

Dr. Gardner snarled, "Define significant size." He was obviously still feeling ornery.

"By significant size, I mean significant enough to cause significant damage on Earth." She winced. *That was lame. Using significant to define significant.*

"How about giving an objective size for a definition," he retorted, "rather than an amateur display of subjective terminology? Significant is not quantifiable."

Irina calmed herself and replied, "I utilized the commonly employed threshold of one kilometer or larger in diameter."

Dr. Naismith interjected, "Why do you stick to the bottom of the estimate range for the number of comets in our solar system rather than employing at least the median or the average of the estimate range? Either one would still give the appearance of a conservative estimate. It seems strange to use such a diminutive estimate when your aim is to impress the academic world with an argument that Earth faces a serious threat from comets."

Irina was fuming inside. Dr. Gardner's little sycophant was testing her patience. "Because I am constrained by the parameters of my own theory. I believe that comets have the same origin as asteroids, therefore I am not at liberty to bolster my case with the vast estimates—hundreds of millions or billions—that are based on the theory that comets originate in the Oort Cloud. And if comets have the same origin as the asteroids, then the number of comets is correlated with the number of asteroids. The estimates for the number of asteroids larger than one kilometer in diameter range from 800,000 to 1.25 million. I settled on 1 million for my estimate, which is approximately in the middle."

Dr. Goldblum raised his eyebrows and asked, "If you have 1.25 million comets and 1 million asteroids, you have a ratio of 1.25 to 1. How did you arrive at this correlation?"

"Based on my crude estimates of the mass, size, angle, and speed of the destroyed body and the destroying body— the former being about the size of Mars and orbiting in the center of the current asteroid belt, the latter being Venus and approaching it in approximately the same direction at a forty-degree angle—I calculated that the escaped fragments would exceed the retained fragments by a ratio of 2.5 to 1. Half of the escaped fragments, 1.25 million, became comets, and the other half became Trojans, Centaurs, TNOs, Hilda asteroids, and moons.

"Crude estimations?" Dr. Naismith sneered.

"Many an advance in science started with a crude idea, crude theory, or crude estimate," Irina retorted a little testily. The little wiener was really starting to get under her skin.

Dr. Goldblum's face slowly crept into a restrained grin. With a twinkle in his eye, he shook his head in disbelief, or was it amazement?

I think he likes what he is hearing. Hard to tell, though, whether or not he agrees with what I'm saying. Maybe he just likes independent thinkers.

He broke his silence. "I am intrigued by your opinion that there is no missing mass problem. What insight have the rest of us missed?"

"The missing factor is the size distribution of the fragments that would be expected if a Mars-sized planet was shattered by a Venus-sized planet that trespassed its Roche limit at an angle of forty degrees. Dr. Gregory Jenkins of Jet Propulsion Laboratory, a well-known pioneer in the rocky-comet field, calculated the probable size distribution of the fragments in such a scenario. He discovered that the greater the diameter, the higher the percentage of the fragments that would be ejected. When plotted for size, the ratios of ejected fragments to retained fragments make a parabolic curve.

"He made similar calculations for the distribution of the ejected fragments. The greater the diameter, the higher the percentage of the fragments that would resist capture and maintain a cometary orbit. Captured fragments became Hilda asteroids, Centaurs, Trojans, moons, and TNOs. When plotted across the range of sizes, the ratios of comet fragments to captured fragments make a parabolic curve.

"Based on his calculations, I was able to make two estimations. First of all, four percent of the mass would have stayed in the original orbital plane and become the asteroid belt, eight percent of the mass would have been ejected and captured as Hilda asteroids, Trojans, Centaurs, moons, and TNOs, and eighty-eight percent of the mass would have been ejected and taken up cometary orbits.

"Secondly, there are approximately one million comets that are one to fifty kilometers in diameter, about the same as the asteroid belt ... four hundred that are fifty to two hundred kilometers in diameter, which is twice as many as the asteroid belt ... seventy that are two hundred to five hundred kilometers in diameter, which is five times more than the asteroid belt ... plus fifteen fragments that are greater than five hundred kilometers, which is fifteen times more than the asteroid belt, plus one or more moons. I also—"

Dr. Goldblum arched his eyebrows in wonder. "Moons?"

The corners of Irina's mouth turned up in an impish grin. "Yes, moons. As many have pointed out, the largest asteroid, Ceres, does not exhibit the shattered-piece look exhibited by the asteroids but instead exhibits a planet-like look. I believe it was one of the moons of the former planet. I suspect that there is at least one more, if not two or three more, orbiting the sun as comets."

"That idea is unique and intriguing. I don't recall reading anywhere in the literature that some of the comets might be former moons. But I interrupted you. You were going to say something more on size distribution."

"Yes. I was going to bring up the iron core. On top of the large fragments and possible former moons in cometary orbit, I suspect that there is also an extremely large iron core lurking out there that is approximately the size of Mercury, assuming that the core remained intact when the crust and mantle were broken up."

Dr. Goldblum looked away and stared blankly out the window, muttering to himself, "a planetary core the size of Mercury ... the fragments are the mantle and the crust ... comets include the bulk of the mid-size fragments and almost all of the large fragments ... add in the mass of the asteroids ... add in the mass of the Trojans, Centaurs, and Hilda asteroids ... add in the moons and TNOs." He nodded and uttered to no one in particular, "Fascinating. I think that really could add up to the mass of a Mars-sized planet."

He turned back to Irina and addressed her theory, without indicating whether he liked or disliked it. "Well, that would certainly resolve the missing-mass dilemma that has long haunted those who embrace the planet-explosion theory as the explanation for the origin of the asteroids and comets."

Irina felt like wielding her wit but bit her tongue. *Of course it resolves the dilemma. It has elegant solution and Occam's razor written all over it.* "I agree. There is no missing-mass dilemma. The mass is scattered all over the solar system, the preponderance of it in the comets.

"And our comet-strewn solar system is a dangerous

neighborhood. There are at least a million chunks of rock larger than one kilometer in diameter hurtling around the sun on long-period orbits. Thousands of them will eventually visit Earth. These fateful encounters are programmed into the calendar of our solar system. They are only matters of time. While the next one could be hundreds of years away, it could also be just around the corner. We cannot avoid these impending disasters. Nor can we avert them, certainly not with any current technology. We can only hope that we observe trouble coming far enough in advance that we can prepare for it. Maybe we can minimize the death and destruction that would result from the fateful rendezvous. But whether prepared or unprepared when the awful day arrives, we will watch an apocalyptic scenario unfold before our eyes, and it won't be CGI on a movie screen."

Dr. Gardner barked, "Are you lecturing us, young lady?"

"No sir," Irina replied, cowering, "just emphasizing the fact that we face a very real danger." Inwardly she groaned, *Why did I have to add that CGI comment? It sounded more like a prophecy preacher than a scientist.* She reminded herself to follow her father's advice—"Don't try too hard. An extra olive does not make a better martini."

While she mulled her gaffe, Dr. Gardner stood up with a vigorous movement that pushed his chair backward hard, tipping it over with a clatter on the tile floor. Without saying a word, he wheeled around and stormed out, pulling the door shut with enough vigor to let everyone know that his ego had been affronted.

Six pairs of eyes followed him out of the room. After his unceremonious exit, the committee members stared at Irina, unsure what to say. Dr. Benson smiled at the shaken female, attempting to encourage her.

Dr. Goldblum broke the silence. "Let that be an object lesson, Miss Kirilenko. Are you prepared to pay the price professionally for defending a position which the majority of scientists believe is indefensible? To maintain the stony-comet position comes with a hefty price tag. Your academic capital will take a hit, you will be unpublishable, your papers will be rejected by peer-reviewed journals, your options are going to be greatly limited, and you may never find a position in the field of astronomy. You could very well end up being an outcast—an unemployable pariah."

He's testing me. I think he's considering me for his TNO program. "I understand. But if I am going to be a scientist worthy of the name, I have to follow the facts to their logical conclusion even if that conclusion challenges the status quo. I am convinced that comets are stony bodies. I may not be as bold in the defense of this position as I should be, or as adept with the arguments as I could be, but I am committed to it. I can't be intimidated into surrendering the point. I would rather wait on tables all my life in a truck-stop diner than sacrifice my beliefs just to curry favor or land a position." *I can't believe I said that. Hope it didn't come out sounding too over the top.*

"Men are going to challenge you."

"I know. But if anyone wants to take me to task, let them at least have the decency to bring real evidence to the table, observations that support the dirty-snowball theory. Men forsake the scientific method when the only things they bring to the table are their sacred theory and crafty explanations to neutralize the evidence that challenges their sacred theory. That's not science. That's cultish religion." *I really went out on a limb now. Hope I don't end up regretting this. I really don't want to work in a diner.*

Dr. Goldblum replied, with a hint of a smile, "Speaking of posing challenges to a theory, what do you do with the low densities that comets manifest, densities which suggest that their structure is more like ice cream than solid rock? Don't those densities challenge your rocky-comet theory?"

Looks like the whole cat is coming out of the bag and not just his whiskers. "This is really a matter of observational science versus theoretical science. If we observe that a comet is composed of solid rock, yet our calculations of its density suggest that it has the density of ice cream, then something is wrong with the method we use for calculating density. In my estimation, our theory of gravity is the weak link.

"The fact is, using the supposed gravitational constant to calculate the mass of a comet will always result in masses and densities which imply that comets are composed of rock-flavored ice cream.

"I suggest that gravity is not a constant, but a variable, the electrostatic polarization of a body's subatomic particles. Under this electric universe view, we expect to see changes in calculated mass with changes in the electrical environment if we calculate mass using an unchanging value for gravity. For instance, the calculated mass of a cubic kilometer of rock orbiting the sun as a comet would be notably lower than the calculated mass of a cubic kilometer of identical rock on the surface of Earth.

"On the other hand, if we directly calculated the actual gravitational values, then used these gravitational values to calculate the masses, the calculated masses for the identical cubes of rock would be identical.

"So, how can we definitively determine whether gravity is a constant or a variable? How can we prove whether comets have a density that is like ice cream or a density that is like rock?

"Two simple physical tests would answer these questions once and for all if the standard-model advocates are willing to man up and face the challenge. A two-foot-long carbide-tip drill bit probing the surface on several comets would tell us whether their surfaces were solid rock or the accreted granules and dust of the dirty-snowball theory. And ground-penetrating radar employed on several comets would tell us whether their interiors were solid rock or mysterious foam or hollow or methane snow. And if comets prove to be solid rock, then our theory of gravity is wrong."

Irina looked around. The committee members, except for Dr. Goldblum, seemed shocked as if they were having a hard time digesting what they had heard. No one spoke. Once again, a grin crept across his face, only this time he didn't restrain it. Irina was nervous. Was he graciously shunting her gravity explanation aside as hilariously bad, or was he subtly acknowledging it as worthy of consideration? She watched him for some facial or verbal clarification of his position. Nothing. *That rascal. Just like a guy. He persuades you to tell him your secrets but won't reveal his.*

Dr. Evans broke the quiet that had settled on the group. "Your theory makes the solar system look more menacing."

Irina's face wrinkled in a wry smile, and her eyes sparkled as she responded, "No doubt about it. If comets are actually solid rock, then they would be far more dangerous than dirty-snowball comets. I see four factors that heighten the danger they pose.

"The first is, obviously, the increased density. Assuming equal diameters, a rocky comet would release significantly more energy than a snowball comet in both impact and bolide events. The greater the mass, the more energy there is to be released.

"The second is greater size. If comets and asteroids originated together in a planetary explosion, then the size distribution of comets would be similar to that evidenced in the asteroids. This implies that the largest comets are more in keeping with the range of the largest asteroids (150 to 900 kilometers in diameter) than the range generally assumed for the largest comets (25 to 150 kilometers in diameter).

"The third is shorter orbits. If comets originated in the immediate solar system from the disintegration of a planet, then their orbits would be vastly shorter than if they had their origin in the Oort Cloud. Consequently, they would cross paths with the bodies of the inner solar system on a much shorter timescale than currently assumed. Perhaps three or four times more often, if not ten times.

"The fourth is the swarm effect. If comets are actually the fragments of a planet that once orbited between Mars and

Jupiter, and these fragments were all sent into orbit with the same explosion, then the bulk of the comets will likely return together in an apparent swarm that could bombard the inner solar system and Earth for decades if not centuries. We will be forewarned of the approach of this swarm for in the decade or two prior to its arrival, there will be an exponential increase in the number and size of comet events: shooting stars, debris showers, bolides, impacts, and other cometary phenomena.

"But the coming swarm of long-period comets will be the second swarm of fragments. The first swarm was comprised of short-period comets and asteroids whose orbits intersected Earth. I believe that this is the true explanation for the waves of comets and stone showers we read about in ancient history that terrified the inhabitants of Earth during the Bronze Age and the Iron Age."

Another silence fell upon the committee as they absorbed this information. The swarm aspect, in particular, caught them by surprise, an electrifying addition to their first significant exposure to the rocky-comet theory.

Dr. Benson probed the subject further. "If the stony-comet theory is true, wouldn't that also overthrow the assumption that asteroids pose a greater threat to Earth than comets?"

Irina smiled. She had hoped this question would come. "It would shatter that viewpoint for three significant reasons.

"First of all, asteroids tend to strike Earth with glancing blows from the side or from behind. This reduces their effective speed, which reduces the force of their impact.

Comets, on the other hand, often impact Earth on more direct angles, even head-on. This increases their effective speed, which increases the force of their impact.

"Secondly, comets are typically traveling three times as fast as asteroids. This has terrifying ramifications because the impact energy of a body increases with the square of its velocity. If a comet and an asteroid of the same size were both coming in at the same angle, the comet impact would have nine times the force of the asteroid impact."

"Thirdly, Earth has already swept its path clear of the vast majority of the asteroids and short-period comets that intersect it. That happened during the comet barrage of the Bronze Age and Iron Age. But long-period comets have barely started testing Earth's path. When the future barrage of comets arrives, it will be thicker and more devastating than the first wave."

"I'm not as interested," Dr. Goldblum challenged, "in the theoretical threat that we face from comets in the distant future as I am the actual threat we presently face from them. Quantify the threat that we face right now on a recurring basis."

Irina's heart skipped a beat. She had feared that this question might come up. With a little reticence, she replied, "During the past six hundred years, we have averaged three major comet events per century, some destroying entire towns or large portions of major cities."

He raised his eyebrows, cocked his head slightly, and looked inquisitively at Irina.

My dog used to do that when he wasn't sure what I was doing or saying.

"Three major impacts per century? The only destructive comet event I am aware of that occurred in the past couple of centuries is the well-known bolide event over Tunguska in the Siberian taiga, and that was an airburst."

Irina felt awkward and hesitated for a moment as she framed her answer. *How do you correct a man you are trying to impress?* She shrugged internally and determined to say what needed to be said even if it seemed a little gauche. "I need to clarify a point. I did not say *impacts* but *events*. Our planet has averaged three major comet events per century.

"We need to discard our artificial focus on impact events and embrace a perspective that incorporates the whole gamut of comet events. Because of this focus, many comet events have gone unrecognized as such. Men have often been puzzled over the centuries by mysterious events that caused immense destruction: showers of stones, showers of fire and sulfur, balls of plasma fire, toxicity, radioactivity, mysterious fires accompanied with electrical phenomena, and destructive red rain. They did not make any connection between the comet that passed overhead and the destruction that followed it except for the old superstition that comets are omens of evil."

Dr. Goldblum was skeptical. "Give me a few examples of unrecognized comet events from the past two centuries that caused widespread death and destruction."

Irina was raw nerves. Excitement and nervousness were tangled up inside. "Three mysterious events occurred in the nineteenth century which cannot be explained by any known physical or meteorological phenomena, but can be readily explained if comets are electrically charged bodies."

"The first is the New Madrid earthquake, a two-month series of quakes and shocks with the three largest occurring on December 16, 1811; January 23, 1812; and February 7, 1812. The first occurred while the great comet of 1811 was yet visible in the skies. When the first quake hit, the ground rolled like the waves of the sea. Shortly after it hit, a cloud of charcoal-like substance descended, darkening the skies till it was darker than night and filling the air with a sulfur-like odor, which made men nauseous. The dust was so thick that it left men with shortness of breath and prevented their lamps from being lit. Earthquake lights and explosion-like flashes appeared everywhere. Lightning and sparks ran along the ground. Metal objects attached themselves to stone walls as if magnetism was involved. And survivors recalled feeling a tingling sensation in their bodies. I suspect that all of these phenomena are to be traced to Earth passing through the dust and electrical fields of the tail of the comet.

"The second is the Great Moscow Fire, which began on September 15, 1812, as Napoleon's advance troops entered the city. Witnesses were awakened by a bright ball of light descending from heaven which illuminated the entire city. Stone buildings, including the palace, were almost instantly turned into piles of ash and rubble. The ball of fire expanded outward in every direction, destroying many buildings and filling ditches with stone rubble. Some of the ditches were over ten meters deep and thirty meters across. Many of the French soldiers died instantly. Many others died from an unknown ailment over the following week with symptoms that suggest radiation poisoning: bloody diarrhea, extreme weakness in the limbs, hair falling out, nails falling off, dizziness, nausea, vomiting, and ulcers. Their horses died too, covered with ulcers and sores. To this day the radiation levels in Moscow are very high. The destruction and death appear to have been caused by a meteorite that was both flammable and radioactive, likely a fragment of the Pons-Brook Comet which came down burning and exploded upon impact.

"The third is the Midwest fires, which started on October 8, 1871, most notably the Peshtigo fire and the Chicago fire. The Peshtigo fire started with a blinding aerial flash and thunderous detonation followed by balls of fire falling from the sky, which ignited hundreds of fires at the same time. But buildings also burst into flames when no fire was nearby. The flames were so hot that stone buildings were turned into piles of calcinated ash within minutes. A rain of choking red dust and sand followed the fireballs. Over two thousand people died within a few minutes, many of them exhibiting no indication of burning but only evidence of suffocation from lack of oxygen. Some of the victims were found with metal objects on their bodies or in their pockets that were melted, though they themselves were unburned.

"The standard explanation is that the wind turned a few small fires into a blazing inferno, but this explanation does not explain all the facts. First of all, while the day was breezy, the event occurred in the evening after the wind had died. Secondly, some of the phenomena cannot be explained by a typical forest fire: the red dust, buildings catching fire when no fire was nearby, the calcination of stone buildings, and the fusing of metal on unburned victims.

"Likewise, the Chicago fire began with balls of fire falling from heaven. These fiery missiles were accompanied with odd phenomena including colorful flames running along the cornices of the buildings, glowing discharges from the sharp edges of the roofs, a rain of red dust, and spontaneous combustion where no fireballs had fallen. The fires burned extremely hot—many of the flames were blue. Iron ingots melted and flowed like a stream into Lake Michigan. Iron, glass, and granite were melted together into grotesque lumps. Six-story-high stone buildings caught fire and turned into piles of ash in five minutes. Even fire-proof materials were fused together.

"The standard explanation claims that this was a wind-driven wood-structure fire, but this contradicts the facts. First of all, the fire rapidly expanded in the face of a forty-mile-per-hour gale. Secondly, the fires burned far hotter than any wood-structure fire is capable of burning."

Dr. Goldblum sat silently for a few moments, processing this information, then replied in a noncommittal way, "Hmm. Fascinating."

That's it? Just fascinating? Was that an "interested" fascinating or a "skeptical" fascinating? Am I being lumped with Edwin Hubble or with sasquatch researchers?

The professor continued, "The concept that the Peshtigo, Chicago, and Moscow fires involved some sort of fire from heaven is plausible. And the idea that Earth could pass through the tail of a comet is plausible. But the notion that some of the phenomena evidenced in the Moscow fire, the Midwest fires, and the New Madrid earthquake were electrical, well—to put it bluntly—you're stretching me. I'm just not prepared to embrace the theory that comets are electrically charged bodies and their comas are clouds of charged particles."

Irina felt her heart deflating. *I guess that classes me with the sasquatch researchers.* But she resisted the impulse to sink into defeat. With a little sass she replied, "If we look at the facts of what transpired in these types of events, we are forced to conclude that there are dynamics involved which require much more research to understand and explain. But we are far better off if we own the facts of what occurred even if we don't understand them than if we sweep those facts under the rug and pretend that they didn't happen. It's not science when we sweep inconvenient facts under the rug and continue our allegiance to theories that are challenged by the facts under the rug."

Dr. Goldblum stroked his chin reflectively, appreciating her sass. "Okay. You gave me three examples that merit further investigation. But does the historical record really indicate that we can expect three events of this magnitude per century?"

"It certainly does. But the point demands clarification. There are no official records of comet events that are publicly archived in government publications such as we find with volcanoes, hurricanes, and earthquakes. We can't just go to the library and ask for the comet publication. The accounts of unrecognized comet events must be ferreted out from tens of thousands of sources. And while a handful of academics and amateurs have taken it upon themselves to publish the results of their investigations in this field, both online and in books, these collections are far from complete. They only scratch the surface."

Dr. Goldblum nodded. He understood the complexity of the situation.

"What was the rationale behind your classification system?" Dr. Evans asked, nudging the exam in a different direction.

"My system is based on the pragmatic observation that it is vastly more practical to classify comet events by the damage they cause rather than their estimated size."

"And you divided comet events into six classes, correct?"

"Yes. My system divides comet events, regardless of the manifested phenomena, into six classes.

"Class F events result in minor damage like a small meteorite punching a hole in a roof, or making a tiny crater in someone's backyard, or destroying a small shed.

"Class E events result in localized destruction that ranges from a house to a city block in extent.

"Class D events result in more extensive devastation that ranges from a city block to a small village in extent.

"Class C events result in widespread damage that ranges from a town to a city in extent. The Peshtigo fire, the Chicago fire, and the Moscow fire are recent examples. In urban areas, this class can result in dozens or even hundreds of fatalities along with the devastation.

"Class B events result in vast destruction that can engulf

dozens of square kilometers. Tunguska in 1908, Rio Curucu in 1930, and West Marudi Mountain in 1935 are three recent examples. Thankfully, all of them landed in forested regions. A Tunguska-size blast would level New York City.

"Class A events, also known as Minoa class, result in regional devastation comparable to the cataclysm which devastated the Minoan, Mycenaean, and Hittite empires, and brought the Bronze Age to a close. The world, of course, hasn't witnessed a Class A event since that awful day some 3500 years ago."

Dr. Evans sought a little clarification. "When you say three major events per century, do you meant three events that are class C or larger?"

"Correct. But I would add two caveats. First of all, the past two centuries saw four class C or higher events. And the last century saw three class B events. This uptick could be the harbinger of the coming swarm. Secondly, class A events must be regarded as black swans. We do not have a large enough sample of occurrences to make predictions on their frequency."

The group took a ten-minute recess. Irina was glad for the break. It gave her a chance to relax and refocus. While she was satisfied with how the first half of the exam went, she was nervous about the upcoming hour when she would present her methodology for searching for comets and TNOs. While she wanted her exam to be well-received by the committee as a whole, she was especially concerned about making a positive impression on Dr. Goldblum. When she first heard that he was going to teach a semester at Caltech in an exchange program, she was ecstatic. Not only did he lead one of the most prestigious TNO programs in the world at Cornell University, he also had a reputation for being a maverick. He wasn't intimidated by the high priests of relativity who maintained domination through a peer-review system that required everyone to utter the sacred shibboleths if they wanted to be published. He was friendly toward the electric universe theory though he had not endorsed it, at least not publicly. Perhaps this was her golden opportunity to land a position in TNO research, despite her heresy.

Dr. Goldblum opened the second hour. "Expound a little on your ninja terminology."

"Ninjas were a class of Japanese warriors," Irina replied, "renowned for their stealthiness. Likewise, ninja comets are known for their exceptional ability to avoid detection. While all comets are stealthy, being cooled in deep space to such low temperatures that Earth-based infrared telescopes can't detect them until they warm up—usually inside Neptune—ninjas have enhanced stealthiness that stems from four traits: two innate and two external.

"The first innate stealth factor is low albedo. A comet with an albedo under 0.03 would be twice as dark as coal, making it difficult to see. A comet the size of Makemake with an albedo of 0.0145, the lowest recorded value for a single face, would be so dark that it could sneak inside Jupiter without being detected by optical telescopes until it formed a coma.

"The second innate factor is low angle of approach. If a

comet was approaching Earth at or near the ecliptic, it would be difficult to detect with standard image-scanning software. These programs are designed to exclude objects moving less than 1.5 arcseconds per hour in an effort to eliminate false positives. This is problematic for comets approaching our planet at low angles because they are generally moving less than 1.5 arcseconds per hour.

"The first external stealth factor is low sunspot activity. Normally, comets develop a coma between Jupiter and the asteroid belt. During low sunspot cycles, the solar wind decreases significantly, allowing comets to draw closer to the sun before they form a coma. During an extended period of low sunspot activity with an unusual doldrum of solar-wind activity, a comet might not develop a coma until somewhere between the asteroid belt and Mars. That would leave us with very little warning.

"The second external stealth factor is poor atmospheric conditions on Earth. If the upper atmosphere was clouded by ash from a Tambora-class volcanic eruption in the equatorial region, the ability of Earth-based telescopes to detect comets would be significantly degraded for several years."

Dr. Goldblum raised a challenge. "Your sunspot activity point is contingent on the electric-universe assumption that the coma is formed by ionization, not sublimation."

"Yes. But I do not regard ionization as an assumption. When you examine the correlation between solar-wind speed and the distance a comet penetrates the solar system before it develops a coma, you realize that the coma isn't caused by sublimation. If it were caused by sublimation, then the coma would always appear at the same distance from the sun, within a relatively tight range."

He ignored her response and moved on. "So, what is your suggestion for an early-warning system?"

"We need to have several satellites devoted to the search for incoming comets, medium-band infrared eyes in the sky. This will significantly increase our forewarning time. The plates should be analyzed immediately by a dedicated team utilizing software that doesn't automatically exclude motion less than 1.5 arcseconds per hour as a false positive. And the satellites should have the ability to broadcast data back to Earth even if our atmosphere is blanketed with volcanic ash.

"The way things stand right now, we often face a huge information lag. Sometimes months, if not years, pass before bodies are discovered on the plates by researchers. While this isn't a big deal when dealing with asteroids and TNOs, it can be a tragic loss of preparation time when dealing with comets."

Dr. Goldblum nodded slightly—was that a twinkle in his eye?—and then continued as if nothing noteworthy had been said.

He turned to Irina's methodology. "How do you propose to conduct an Earth-based early-warning search program for long-period comets that threaten Earth?"

Irina suppressed a grin. "My methodology employs an indirect detection strategy rather than direct. It searches for the occultation of stars on optical and infrared plates using software that I designed myself. The program runs several scans, including two that search for very low arcsecond changes, lower than any existing software, enabling the detection of comets approaching Earth at or near the ecliptic."

"If you intend to scan for low-arcsecond changes," Dr. Goldblum replied, "how are you going to prevent your program from overwhelming you with false positives?"

"My program eliminates most false positives because it only flags positives based on two or more consecutive plate changes. The number is adjustable. The program can also skip plates if desired. For instance, if a team is examining two years of plates taken one week apart, they can set the program to skip every other plate so they are examining movement over a two-week window instead of a one-week window. They can set the program to give them odd plates or even plates or alternated plates—like one and three, two and four, three and five, et cetera—or customized sequences."

Dr. Goldblum nodded agreeably. "I like your ideas. We are on the same page in this regard. Stellar occultation is the methodology of choice. And your idea to mix a multi-plate-identification function with a plate-skipping function is the best way to eliminate false positives. You may be interested to know that we happen to be working on a similar search program at Cornell."

Irina perked up again. *Was that a hint that I might be a good fit at Cornell? That I might get to take in a concert at Tannery Pond this fall?*

The remainder of the examination was a blur of technical questions: delving into the inner workings of her software, seeking technical clarification on how her search program differed from those currently in use, and inquiring how her program manages the differences between searching for TNOs and searching for comets. Irina answered the questions satisfactorily, but the endless barrage wore her down.

She had just started to pray that her trial might soon pass when Dr. Benson brought the examination to a close. "Well, that wraps it up for the technical questions. But I have one further question, a personal question, I would like to ask before turning it over to Dr. Goldblum for closing remarks." She turned to Irina. "What do you hope to accomplish in the field of astronomy?"

The candidate responded, "I would love to discover several TNOs and at least one long-period comet. But more importantly, I want to change the NEO landscape. People aren't worried about them. As long as no asteroid lands in their backyard, they don't care. They have a hard time imagining how a one-kilometer asteroid landing in some other country thousands of miles away would affect them apart from dominating the evening news or interrupting the ball game. The way they see things, they will still be able to buy a cheeseburger and fries the next day.

"I want them to understand that the worst-case scenario is not a one-kilometer asteroid landing in a distant corner of Earth. It is a much larger comet devastating their own neighborhood with a Tunguska-size cataclysm or larger. And I want them to understand that such devastation is not an IF question but a WHEN question. The odds are against us. It is only a matter of time. Will we be prepared?" *Hope that wasn't too melodramatic. Seemed pretty tame compared to some of my earlier remarks.*

Dr. Benson turned and nodded to Dr. Goldblum, whom she had invited to close the examination with a few remarks.

He nodded back, looked at Irina, and began. "I appreciate your theory that comets are rocky bodies with the same origin and composition as asteroids. My own views are similar, though I blend the rocky-comet theory and the dirty-snowball theory. Personally, I believe that the planetary explosion occurred in prehistory millions of years ago.

"Despite a few minor quirks, your thesis makes a valuable contribution to comet work, both in regards to risk analysis and in regards to cost-effective search methods that can help us discern threatening comets years before they arrive in the inner solar system."

The room was quiet. Dr. Benson smiled at her, and so did Dr. Evans. Dr. Naismith rose from his chair, and the rest of the committee members followed suit. It was over. It was really over. Irina slumped in her chair. She felt like laughing, crying, and hibernating all at the same time.

The committee members filed out into the hallway, shut the door behind them, and talked animatedly for several minutes. Then they filed back in. Dr. Benson took the warrant out of her folder, set it on the table near the coffee urn, and signed it herself. One by one, with Dr. Naismith last in line, they signed it.

Dr. Benson shook Irina's hand, congratulated her, picked up the warrant, and went on a mission to track down Dr. Gardner. She later related the story to Irina, and the two of them shared a good laugh over it. The old curmudgeon took some convincing, but he did finally and grudgingly sign it, muttering, "How can such a bright girl be a stoner?"

Irina shook hands with each of the committee members, Dr. Goldblum holding back for the end of the line. When his turn came, she said "Thank you" with more warmth than she had intended. He gripped her hand with a firm masculine handshake, pumped her hand vigorously, then withdrew his hand, reached into his suit-coat pocket, pulled out one of his business cards, quickly scribbled a note on the back, and handed it to her. "Give me a call next week at my office, anytime after Monday." As he walked away, he thought to himself. *On the negative side, she's a little bit of a religious fanatic. On the positive side, she's an exceptionally brilliant, independent thinker. Not to mention, she's classy and sassy.*

She turned the card over. It said, *"Consider Cornell."* There was nothing to consider. If he wanted her to join his research program at Cornell, it was a done deal.

As she walked back to her car, she felt like an emotional train wreck, both worn out and excited. It was time for a bowl of her favorite ice cream. She could almost taste the cherries, the walnut and pecan slivers, the fudge and caramel globs, and the dark-chocolate-covered coffee beans thickly scattered in a coffee-toffee swirl. *Train Wreck here I come.*

8

**Washington, D.C.
Wednesday, May 18, 2016**

Jack Lundstrom, Woody's cousin, sat in his usual booth at Madigan's, slowly picking away at his steak and fries and watching the news on the big-screen television. He ate most of his evening meals here. Apart from occasionally grilling on weekends, he simply didn't like to cook. He had settled on this place two years ago, shortly after his wife Emily had passed away. He liked the food. More importantly, he liked the atmosphere. It was quieter than the restaurants haunted by college students and boisterous millennials on the first rung or two of their career path. The clientele were older professionals and government officials—few were under forty. No loud tables ordered round after round of beer. The television was always tuned to CVN, the Conservative Viewpoint Network.

He shook his head and sighed as he absorbed another dose of bad news. *Definitely not the world I grew up in.* Another bombing in Europe, this time in Paris, France. More extremist activity in Iraq and Afghanistan. *Are we actually fighting the extremists or just playing an aggressive game of bloody knuckles?* The proxy war going on in Syria. More boots headed to Iraq. Another police brutality case— was the cop an unfit goon in blue or an innocent man being framed for political gain? More riots in Baltimore and Boston. More slimy dealings on Wall Street. More mudslinging in the primaries. The crap was six feet high and rising.

Head propped in hand, he stared at the screen, listening as the commentators provided the latest news on Iran's efforts to build a ballistic-missile arsenal, the growing frustration among the Palestinians, the simmering ambition of many of Israel's neighbors to get revenge for their past defeats, Iran's threat—echoed by other nations—to drive Israel into the sea, and Israel's vow that the next war will be the last war. *Lots of pressure building up in the Middle East. Reminds me of the quasi-Shakespearean quote, "An ill wind doth blow." Seems like the stage is being set for the last days to begin and the Middle East to explode. Woody and I definitely won't lack for things to talk about this summer in Montana.*

9

Sierra Coffee Company, Glendale, CA
Friday, March 24, 2017

It was an unusually cool spring day. Wet snowflakes had been falling that morning when Woody first looked out the window and had continued to fall during his drive from Glendale to Caltech. Now, during his drive home, the San Gabriels were white with a fresh blanket of snow, more than eight inches at Mt. Wilson. The temperature had never risen above forty-four degrees, and it had been blustery and rainy the entire day, the kind of day that made you think of hot chocolate and a cozy fire. Such nippy days always reminded him of the winter he spent in the mountains of Bosnia with the Special Forces. *Has it really been twenty-one years since I was making hot chocolate in my canteen cup over an old dual-fuel stove? How the time flies.* His thoughts wandered in a different direction. *I wonder how my body would hold out today if I had to hike a miserably long hump at a blistering pace over terrain that rugged carrying a pack? Not sure I want to find out.*

He was getting close to the corner for Sierra Coffee

Company, and—tightwad that he was—he was still wrestling with whether or not he should stop. He loved stopping there and did so several times a week after work to unwind, chat with the regulars, and drink a mocha. (He enjoyed his coffee black in the morning but preferred mocha later in the day.) His hesitation was based on straightforward math. He had already stopped three times this week, his normal maximum. But the urge to indulge got the best of his miserly disposition. *It just feels like a Cinnamon Griz' day.* He pulled into the right-turn lane just in time to make the corner and immediately turned right again into the parking lot. The tightwad laughed at himself. *What a scrooge.* He rarely spent all of his budgeted fun money, not even on his annual Montana trip. Shoot. He still had his original glass piggy bank—chock full of pennies, nickels, and dimes—that his grandfather gave him when he was six.

When he entered, none of the regulars nodded or waved. They were all distracted, leaning over the shoulders of a man he didn't recognize, eyes fixed on a tablet propped up on the table. He faintly made out the garbled drone of a news broadcast. Intrigued, he sauntered over and took a gander.

A knot began to tighten in his stomach. What absorbed them was not a piece of twisted humor on YouTube but a nerve-racking development in the Middle East, the kind that leaves men wondering if World War Three is just around the corner. As he peeked over a shoulder, the local afternoon news program was just signing off. "That concludes our coverage of the new ground offensive in Basra. Stay tuned for the *World Report* for accurate and unbiased news, both national and international." Woody grit his teeth. He hated commercials. Now he had to endure two or three before he could satisfy the curiosity that had been awakened. But no commercial followed. The program immediately started. That was highly unusual. *Must be big*, Wood mused.

"Good evening from New York City. This is the *World Report*, broadcast live seven nights a week at 8 p.m. Eastern time, and I'm Tom Overbright. Thank you for joining us tonight. We apologize to our sponsors for skipping their advertisements and cutting straight to our program, but we felt an obligation to present without delay the latest updates on the gut-wrenching situation in the Middle East, a situation that has the entire world on edge.

"There are two breaking stories tonight. The first is that a large force of U.S. and allied ground troops began a massive offensive two hours ago, at 2 a.m. Iraqi time, to crush the Shia militants in the southeastern Iraqi town of Basra. The militants, aided and incited by more than two thousand members of Iran's Revolutionary Guard, have been a tremendous hindrance to both the peace process and a stable government in Iraq. Iran, not surprisingly, has vilified the American government over this in two official releases, one from Ayatollah Ali Khamenei and one from President Rouhani. This new-found resolve on the part of the United States threatens to deal Iran a serious blow to her influence in Iraqi politics. Iran has threatened military response, but defense experts in the West are skeptical that Iran will do little more than posture. So far, the Russian response has been muted.

"The assault force is comprised of twenty-five thousand American troops—led by the First Marine Expeditionary Brigade and a brigade each from the 101st Airborne Division and the 82nd Airborne Division, two brigades of mechanized infantry, two battalions of Rangers, and two hundred SEAL and Delta Force operators—along with five thousand troops from Australia, the UK, and Iraq. The assault force is being supported by four brigades of armor and cavalry, who have surrounded the city to prevent any militants from escaping.

"Reporters on the ground tell us that the night air is heavy with the acrid smell of smoke and exploded ordinance, the din of small-arms fire, and the incessant reverberations of explosions from bombs, missiles, mortar fire, and artillery rounds. It appears that President Weston's promise to put an end to all extremist and militant groups in Iraq—Sunni or Shia—beginning with the Shiite militias in the South, was no mere threat. His policy, enunciated in his recent speech and endorsed two weeks ago by the Iraqi government, is that no groups in Iraq except the Armed Forces, the Iraqi Police, and the semi-autonomous Kurdish Peshmerga, will be allowed to possess weapons or military hardware. Any other persons or groups found in possession of these things will be regarded as enemies of Iraq."

Woody was startled out of his absorption by someone tapping him on the shoulder. He turned and faced Joby, who was holding out his mocha. Woody nodded, took his drink, and watched Joby walk away, shaking his head at men who could be so fascinated with war. Joby was a peacenik, deeply influenced by pacifist thought. *Not enough painful experience in life yet. Someday, harsh reality will overturn his idealistic boat as it drifts down the river of life, forcing him to swim in its cold waters, forcing him to come to his senses.* That was usually all it took for men to realize that pacifism, which refuses to meet and defeat aggression, is an extreme that is just as stupid and immoral as aggression itself. Pacifism in a world filled with criminals, terrorists, and belligerent nations doesn't bring peace. It encourages the bad guys to grow bolder.

He turned back to the broadcast. "The second breaking story this hour is that last night at 2 a.m. Riyadh time—concurrent with the U.S. effort in Basra—joint forces from Saudi Arabia, Egypt, Jordan, Qatar, and the UAE launched a formidable invasion of Yemen at the behest of President Hadi. According to an official news bulletin released by the coalition headquarters to Al Jazeera, the invasion is intended to accomplish two ends. The first is to eradicate the Houthi rebels in Yemen, which have brought the country into civil war, and deport their Iranian advisors. The second is to crush every al-Qaeda cell in the region.

"Initial reports, which we have obtained from an Al-Jazeera correspondent embedded with Saudi troops on the front lines, indicate that this attack has been merciless—even ruthless. Every known Houthi stronghold is being shelled and bombed into oblivion without regard for collateral damage among civilians. When asked about this, the reporter merely shrugged his shoulders and observed that the Arab conscience isn't saddled with the same scruples that hinder American operations. The coalition also appears to be unconcerned about the death toll among the Iranian advisors, who are widely rumored to number in the thousands.

"Iran is incensed over this invasion. She insists that her armed forces in Yemen are only engaged in peacekeeping and humanitarian missions. This claim, however, is rejected by Saudi intelligence, which insists that at least five hundred members of the Iranian special forces, known as Quds Force, are engaged in direct combat against the coalition forces, many of them leading Houthi units in combat operations. Iran is threatening to go to war with the coalition over this aggression and has directed two pointed warnings against Saudi Arabia and Egypt. But regional experts doubt that Iran has either the resolve or the resources necessary to engage the coalition, much less defeat them."

Woody swirled the last of his mocha, lofting the dregs, and drained the remaining swallows. Then he bid his friends goodbye and headed back to his Jeep, brooding. The new developments in the Middle East made him very uneasy. *Things are going to get worse before they get better, a whole lot worse. Looking forward to Jack's take on this stuff.*

10

Cornell University
Monday, May 22, 2017

Irina locked the BMW that her father had given her for a
doctoral present—a 2006, low-mileage 5 Series, bought for
a song from a fellow professor who was retiring to
Bermuda—and strolled across the asphalt, still amazed at the
way that things had worked out for her. She had been at
Cornell for ten months now, and she was living the dream.

Her theory of comet origin and threat had impressed Dr.
Goldblum, and he had extended a formal invitation in June
2016 to join his TNO-research program at Cornell, which
she accepted. The next week, she had packed her possessions
into her car, except for her baby grand piano, and started on
a leisurely eight-day drive to New York. On her way she had
visited the Grand Canyon, Taos and the Sangre de Christo
range, the Colorado Rockies, and the Appalachians. She
loved the mountains, not so much to hike in them as to soak
in their majesty.

She had arrived in Ithaca the third week of June, found
an apartment within two days, and started hunting for a

church. After visiting several, she chose New Life Church. It had an awesome worship team and exuded an aura of excitement and success, the same things that had drawn her to Resurrection Fellowship when she lived in California. She also appreciated the fact that Pastor Colin Jellineck was both highly educated, with an earned doctorate in Theology, and a dynamic speaker.

Her new position had begun the second week of July. The first week had been spent in orientation: getting to know the layout of the buildings and meeting her program directors, department faculty, and colleagues. The following week, she had begun setting up her algorithmic program which looked for occultations of fixed stars on optical and infra-red plates. Once the software and hardware were ready, she had assembled a collection of images much larger than she had anticipated, with sets from the CFHT Legacy Survey, OSSOS, WISE, 2MASS, NOAO Science Archive, Hubble, Spitzer, Pan-STARRS, New Horizons, IRAS, and twenty other sources.

Best of all, her Orion research had succeeded far beyond both her own and Dr. Goldblum's expectations. Between February and April, she had discovered six TNOs, an unparalleled stretch of TNO serendipity. Two of them were large enough to classify as dwarf planets: one the size of Makemake, the other slightly smaller. No earthly joy had ever been half as satisfying as the joy of sending her dwarf-planet discoveries to the MPC.

But she was facing one small bump in the road: what to name the dwarf planets. While she was indifferent to the naming of the smaller TNOs, she did care about the names that the dwarves would bear. Her dilemma was that TNOs were traditionally named after mythological creation deities. She laughed. Typical bureaucratic short-sightedness. What are they going to do for names when they run out of creation deities? She really wanted to name them Methuselah and Melchizedek, names associated with pivotal moments in man's history, but she suspected that this nod to the Bible would be unacceptable to the Committee on Small Body Nomenclature. She shook her head. Mythical deities are okay, but major figures from the Bible are banned. What an upside down world.

Finding herself at the doors of the Cornell Center for Astrophysics and Planetary Science, she left memory lane behind, bounded into the building with a song in her heart—*I love my job*—practically skipped down the hall, then waltzed into her office. She began the day with her usual Monday ritual: pouring a cup of coffee, putting on Beethoven's *Fifth Symphony*, sitting back in her chair, clutching her cup with both hands, and mentally preparing for the week.

She was now three weeks into her Taurus project, and things were going well. She had found two TNO candidates that were early in the verification process and had made a few tweaks to the program which tightened the parameters for detecting bodies close to the ecliptic. She savored the feeling of accomplishment—finally enjoying her dream job after years of hard work and preparation. She reached for another piece of her favorite dark chocolate, Sage and

Juniper from Evocative Nuances. It evoked magical hints of cowboys and the rugged West. She started to wistfully drift into romantic thoughts of being swept off her feet by a cowboy.

Chirp, chirp, chirp. The alarm for a potential TNO interrupted her evening ride down a pine-covered ridge on a palomino behind a blonde cowboy, her arms wrapped around his waist. *This had better be the apocalypse on the way.*

Irina swiveled to her computer, brought up the hits that had registered since she logged out on Friday, and sent them to the printer. She could have pulled up the readout on her monitor but, like her father, she preferred the feel of real books and real paper in her hands. The printer quickly spit the page out. She retrieved it and scanned the results. There were twenty-eight that had registered less than five percent occultation, almost certainly false positives. Four others had registered five to ten percent occultation, most likely false positives too. But one of the hits leaped off the page. Some unknown body had entirely occulted a star next to the Pleiades in late April 2016.

She identified the star, a string of numbers and letters which would seem nondescript to an outsider, then entered its name and location into her verification program and set up a perimeter search centered on the star. A half hour later, her computer spit out the answer. Four occultations of dim stars lined up in a row with the original occultation: one in January 2017, one in November 2015, one in March 2015, and another in August 2014, all slightly above the Pleiades and close together. She entered the coordinates for a search on the general trajectory that might take it back another couple years. Three more hits on dim stars were returned: one in February 2014, one in July 2013, and one in March 2013.

Hands shaking, she punched the coordinates for the eight occultations into NASA's trajectory-calculation program. After several minutes, a map of the solar system popped up on her monitor with a green line indicating the known historical path of the unknown body and a broken green line forecasting its future path. It had the trajectory of a long-period comet and would pass within 25,000 miles of Mars. She didn't bother to check it against the database of known TNOs. Instead, she checked it against the database of long-period comets. There were no matches. It appeared that she had discovered a new comet.

Irina started to tremble. Chills ran down her spine. She reached for her coffee. It was cold, too cold. She walked numbly to the break room, emptied her cold coffee into the sink, and poured a fresh cup. *Why am I so nervous? I discovered a comet with a long-period orbit. Astronomers discover them every year.* But something was out of place. *The corona!* Of course. There was no corona, not even the faintest hint, around the occluded star. The truth dawned on her. It wasn't a run-of-the-mill comet that had occulted the star It was a large comet—a very large comet. Her mind began to run wild. *Extraordinary comet! Nice to have on the resume! Collect yourself girl. Stay objective.*

Instead of returning to her desk, she merely dropped off her coffee, then continued down the hall to Dr. Goldblum's office, where he usually ensconced himself on Monday mornings. His door was open, so she knocked and entered almost in one motion. He looked up from the astronomy journal he was reading with an empty stare that suggested she was intruding.

The excited female blurted out, "I found something highly unusual!"

He looked quizzically at her. "A new dwarf planet or perhaps Planet X?"

Is he serious, or is he pulling my leg? "Definitely more extraordinary than finding another dwarf planet. More like finding Planet X."

"So, what have you found that belongs in the same category as the discovery of Planet X?"

"I'm pretty sure that I have discovered a large comet, an extremely large comet, on a trajectory that will take it close to Mars." As the words tumbled out of her mouth, she started to feel a little sheepish. *That was pretty lame.* A new comet was an exciting discovery, but it didn't belong in the same category as Planet X. And most long-period comets journey inside Jupiter, with many of them passing close to Mars. But as he pierced her with his eyes, she recovered her courage and reminded herself that it was unique—it was unusually large. "I'm pretty sure that it is unusually large for a comet, Hale-Bopp size or even bigger."

He nodded. "Pretty sure isn't science."

She winced. Now that the knight in shining armor had hooked her and reeled her in, he wasn't quite as sweet as he had been when he was wooing her. It wasn't that he was mean. But when he was focused on a project, he tended to be curt and callous, even cold.

Dr. Goldblum continued in a sterile staccato as if he were repeating his instructions from memory, "Do the standard follow-up and verification. Contact Sally Evans at Mt. Wilson, George Wilkins at Whipple, and Gloria Kamealoha at Mauna Kea. Give them all the data you currently have, the next star in its path, and an approximate date for the next occultation. We need current observations. Dig a little deeper for earlier occultations. Verify and reverify the orbit. We not only want proof, we want a clear presentation of the proof. We don't want to send a mistake-laden or poorly-prepared case to the MPC. The last thing you want is for Barry's crew to toss your letter into the wastebasket." He looked at her intently, like someone watching their dog to see if it was going to obey.

Irina nodded, said "Will do," turned about, and trudged back to her desk, a little sullen. She was sorely tempted to indulge some self-pity, but advice from her father blocked the way—"Just because a carpenter doesn't stop pounding nails when you ask him a question doesn't mean that he doesn't appreciate you. It means he's busy." She squelched a laugh, dropped into her chair, retrieved her cup, and clutched her coffee, still quite warm, with both hands. *Time for that chocolate.*

11

Three weeks after Irina had presented Dr. Goldblum with a folder of observations and calculations suggesting that her discovery was more than just another run-of-the-mill comet—to her chagrin, he had appeared to ignore it—he showed up at her cubicle and apologized for treating her and the comet with such aloofness. He explained that he had been so focused on meeting a looming deadline for his prospectus on institutional cooperation with NASA in the search for NEOs that he didn't have time to think about anything else. Sheepishly he confessed that he hadn't even glanced at her folder. But now the monkey was off his back, and he was free to give his undivided attention to her discovery.

She accepted his apology but looked at him as if waiting for further clarification. He noticed her concern and added, "Yesterday afternoon, after eight weeks of brain-numbing effort, I shipped my prospectus to Richard Fairchild at NASA via overnight air. I hope I never have to get so entangled in government bureaucracy again. But I was way too exhausted and numb to immediately take up your comet. I went home, collapsed in my recliner for the evening with a glass of scotch in my hand, and watched Humphrey Bogart until I fell asleep. But here I am today, ready and raring to give your discovery the attention that it deserves." He waved her folder as he spoke.

She smiled. "Better late than never."

When he saw her smile, he knew things were going to be okay. He smiled back and walked away.

Several hours later, Dr. Goldblum, after checking and rechecking Irina's observations and calculations, and running a few calculations of his own, sat at his desk trembling with mingled apprehension and exuberance. That moment, a career-defining epiphany was enshrined in his ego. Irina's comet, as she had tried to tell him, wasn't just another typical long-period comet. It was stupendously enormous. It was paradigm shattering. It was like discovering concrete evidence that Sasquatch really did exist after all. When he ran simulated occultations of Irina's occulted star with a Hale-Bopp-size comet, the star manifested a corona. When he ran simulations with a comet twice the diameter of Hale-Bopp, the occluded star still manifested a faint corona. There was no doubt about it, a comet significantly larger than Hale-Bopp was going to smash its way through the asteroid belt and pass very close, dangerously close, to Mars. He stared off into space, overcome with the magnitude of the discovery that had fallen into his lap.

From that moment, he was a changed man, electrified, driven with a passion that made his former self look like a slacker. He gave the comet priority attention and took charge of the entire project, directing and organizing every aspect: research, analysis, calculations, and projections. He kept in continual contact with Sally at Mt. Wilson, George at Whipple, and Gloria at Mauna Kea, whom he had enlisted for help with the project. And he helped Irina prepare a journal article so they would be ready to publish when that day came.

At first, Irina was glad for his generous help, but over the next few weeks, it slowly dawned on her that he wasn't assisting. He was domineering. His involvement was more than a boss micro-managing his team or overly involving himself in their projects. His involvement was egotistical, self-promoting, and coldly calculated. Here was a man with a big ego making sure that one of the biggest astronomical feathers of the past century, if not the biggest, was stuck in his hat. Lady Luck had given him a golden opportunity to upgrade his status in the astronomical world from rising star to superstar, and he was making every effort to capitalize on it. Irina felt vulnerable, like he was trying to take ownership of her baby, but there was nothing she could do about it. She steeled her inner woman and pressed forward, committing the painful situation into the hands of God.

12

Cornell University
September 2017

Dr. Goldblum delayed sending the report for Irina's discovery to the MPC. This wasn't a matter of uncertainty regarding the identification, size, and direction of the comet. It was a matter of political investment. His future—his destiny—was linked to this comet. If he was going report a planet-sized comet on a dangerous trajectory, he was going to do so with a presentation ready at hand for the big shots, a presentation that was bulletproof, that left no stone unturned, that was forward-looking, that would impress the movers and shakers in the astronomy world, and the White House, and whatever other hallowed enclaves mattered.

Inflamed by this spirit, he pressed his team, pushing them to put together a sheaf of research that went far beyond the already stringent criteria that he had set for Cornell's TNO program. The climate became so intense that some of the team members joked that they had been baptized into a cult. Even Sally at Mt. Wilson had started to feel like his requests for data were really demands. While she didn't sour on him, she did feel hurt, similar to the way she felt when in a relationship where she was giving but not receiving back.

***

After reviewing the latest round of data he had ordered from Mt. Wilson, Whipple, and Mauna Kea on the transit time for the occultation, Dr. Goldblum was shell-shocked. The diameter of the comet was vastly larger than they had anticipated. The new calculations pegged it at 900-1000 kilometers in diameter, about fifteen times the size of Hale-Bopp comet. It was an outlier of gigantic proportions.

The new data also confirmed earlier calculations that the comet's path would directly intersect the orbitary path of Mars and would come within 25,000 miles of the planet. This made for an extremely unsettling situation. Theoretically, it could collide with Mars.

Another unnerving observation was the extremely low albedo that the comet exhibited. Although it was 900-1000 kilometers in diameter and only a little ways past Pluto, yet it was still invisible to optical telescopes, even Keck's 394-inch at Mauna Kea. By way of contrast, Eris, which is twice the size but three times more distant, was discovered with the 48-inch telescope at Mt. Palomar. It seemed to have been a stroke of luck—or the providence of God—that Irina had discovered this comet. If it hadn't been for her almost quixotic desire to look for occultations in Taurus starting in the region of the Pleiades—traced to her fascination with the prominence that *the Bull* and *the Seven Sisters* enjoyed in ancient mythology—the comet could have passed deep into the solar system before anyone noticed its presence.

When Irina looked over the new data and calculations, she felt a cold chill from head to toe. It upped the scare factor to apocalyptic proportions unknown to modern man except in Hollywood productions. She shuddered to think what would happen if this wandering giant knocked two or three large asteroids into eccentric orbits. That could spell disaster for Earth, maybe not in the immediate future, but looming on the horizon. Worse. What if it was deflected by Mars into an orbit that would eventually intersect Earth?

The situation filled her with inner turmoil. She didn't—couldn't—feel the same elation that she had felt over the discovery of the two dwarf planets and the other TNOs. Her usual sense of scientific satisfaction was muted by a nagging uneasiness. She knew exactly why. TNOs weren't a threat. They were benign. But this comet was ominous. It posed a tangible threat to Earth. She smiled at her naiveté. She wasn't handling this as well as she had imagined she would. It was one thing to grapple with a dangerous comet as a theoretical concept in a thesis. It was another thing to discover one that was headed for your neighborhood.

Her usual enthusiasm for prophecy was also somewhat subdued. While it was exciting to think that this comet might have something to do with Bible prophecy—maybe it was the impetus that causes the terror of Luke 21:26, "the planets of the heavens shall be loosed from their orbits"—yet the apocalypse spelled sorrow for the inhabitants of the world.

Dr. Goldblum, on the other hand, wasn't experiencing

emotional struggles like Irina. Though he could articulate the potential threats which the comet posed to Earth, he was emotionally removed from that aspect of the subject. His eyes were fixed on what the comet could do for him: name recognition, promotion, NASA, maybe even a book deal. Increasingly he exuded haughty self-importance, a trait that tarnished him in Irina's eyes. While an inflated ego might be desirable in some circles, to her it was an unsightly blemish.

13

Cornell University
early October 2017

Dr. Goldblum contacted Hugh Beckinsall, a high-level systems analyst at NASA, and asked him for a threat analysis for a hypothetical situation in which a 1000-kilometer comet passed through the asteroid belt and threatened one of the inner planets like Mars or Venus. Hugh laughed at the request and jokingly replied that that was like asking for a threat analysis on the damage we could expect were Godzilla to show up on the shores of Japan near Tokyo. When Dr. Goldblum said he was serious and pressed him for help, Hugh said that he would look into the matter but doubted that he would find anything.

To his surprise, Dr. Goldblum received a 106-page study in the mail three days later with the provocative title *Rogue Apocalypse*. It wasn't exactly what he was looking for as the hypothetical scenario involved a comet which was a mere hundred kilometers in diameter, but it did contain a wealth of research, dozens of graphs and charts, and a bibliography. It was more than ample to kickstart his own threat analysis.

He breezed through the introduction. The study had been published three years earlier by a JPL analyst who was known for thinking outside the box, the under-appreciated Mitchell Grand. He had run a thousand simulations of the scenario and then derived probabilities from them for such a rogue knocking a large asteroid out of its orbit and for the displaced asteroid impacting Earth.

When he turned to the conclusion, he had the wind taken from his sails. The author had concluded that there was only a twenty percent probability that such a rogue would displace a large asteroid and a less than one percent probability that the displaced asteroid would impact Earth within a thousand years. Such low probabilities weren't sufficient to impress the folks he wanted to impress. He needed numbers with a little more wow factor.

He pulled out his legal pad and scribbled some rough estimations and calculations. His comet—he liked the ring of that—was in a class of its own, about ten times the diameter of the comet that was hypothesized in the study. So it wasn't unreasonable to figure that it was a virtual certainty—nearly one hundred percent probability—that his comet would displace a few asteroids that were one kilometer or larger in diameter. And there was a good chance—say a ten percent probability—that one of these dislodged asteroids would impact Earth in the next century.

The numbers pleased him. The ten percent probability of impact seemed like an ideal working figure. High enough to garner attention. Low enough to avoid panic. He hoped that further investigation and calculations would validate this hunch. He needed to make a big splash with his colleagues and with the heavyweights. The hunger to be a power player at NASA gnawed away. He had to make the best of this opportunity. While Irina had actually discovered the comet, he shared in the credit because the discovery had occurred under his supervision. But close association only opened the door. It wouldn't usher him in. His golden ticket was going to have to be expertise. He smirked to himself. It was within his reach to be regarded as the foremost expert in the world on this comet in threat estimation and threat preparation if he greased the proper wheels and did his homework.

14

Cornell University
mid-October, 2017

"Run a few more simulations," Dr. Goldblum insisted, "using slightly larger numbers. I have a hunch that we're underestimating the size of the comet." He started to walk away, then wheeled back around. "Oh, before I forget. Meet me for lunch today. There are a few things I would like to discuss with you regarding our discovery."

"Sure," Irina replied, shaking her head to herself, trying to frame what she had just heard in good light, fighting a sense of indignation that was straining against the leash. *"Our" discovery? How does that not sound presumptuous in your ears?*

"Let's rendezvous for lunch, say about twenty minutes after one. Will that work for you? I know it's late. I wish I could make it earlier. But I have two important phone conferences over our usual lunch break, one with Mitchell Grand at JPL and one with Gloria Kamealoha at Mauna Kea."

"No problem." She turned and started to walk away.

He pressed her. "Is everything okay, Irina? You seem a little distant lately."

She stopped in the doorway, cast a nonchalant glance in his general direction, and replied, "I'm fine. Just focused on my work." But the hint of an edge in her voice and her unusually laconic interaction suggested otherwise. She was perturbed at the knight in crusty armor. *I'm not fine! And if you can't figure out what's bugging me, you don't deserve to have a woman in your life!* She cringed. *Probably a little harsh.*

***

They settled into a booth at Dr. Goldblum's favorite sushi restaurant. Irina didn't like eating here. She wasn't wild about sushi and loathed the atmosphere. It was just another raucous bar, except that you got good sushi with your beer instead of a mediocre hamburger. But this is where he brought her when he took her out for lunch. It was a status-symbol thing for him. She agonized over the menu—she wasn't much of a Japanese food fan—and finally settled on the swordfish. To humor him, she ordered a sushi appetizer and ate most of it. The squid stayed on the plate. She couldn't stomach the taste and texture, and she couldn't fathom how could anyone enjoy cooked rubber.

After they had finished their meal and made Caltech small talk for a few minutes, Dr. Goldblum reached into his satchel, pulled out a copy of the research paper he had gotten from his contact at NASA, and slapped it ceremoniously and rather noisily on the counter in front of her. "You gotta check this out, girl!"

Irina stared at the paper for a moment, taken aback by his clownish antic. "A man is but a beer away from a buffoon," her mom used to say. Then she rotated the paper so the cover faced her. *Rogue Apocalypse*. She liked that. It was a captivating title. *Apocalypse* was a term that had often been on her mind since she had discovered the invisible leviathan. And *Rogue* had a ring to it, hinting of unpredictability and danger. It was the right name for her comet. She could picture it wreaking havoc in the inner solar system, like a jumbo elephant gone rogue and trampling a village. But she was skeptical that the CSBN, the Committee for Small Body Nomenclature, would bite on the idea. The time-honored convention would name the comet after her, the discoverer, assuming that she was the first to report it. And they, like most institutions, tended to be married to their conventions. But maybe if she convinced Dr. Goldblum, he might add a little weight to her case.

"I think the comet should be called the Rogue," she proposed. "I know that cuts across the grain of naming protocol, but it doesn't seem right to name something this big and dangerous after …" She trailed off.

"After a classy female," Dr. Goldblum said, finishing her sentence.

She smiled sheepishly. "I was going to say *a woman*. But I changed my mind. Kind of a sexist statement when you consider that women can be as mean and nasty as men."

"You have a valid point," he responded, putting on a more professional air. "Naming it after any human being, regardless of sex, seems out of place. But try convincing the traditionalists at CSBN."

Irina laughed. "On the other hand, it could be argued that Rogue is my nickname. My babushka used to call me шахрай (shock-ray) because I preferred hot dogs to borscht and classical music to Ukrainian folk music."

But Dr. Goldblum was no longer paying attention. He was drifting. The wheels were turning. He wasn't sure if the CSBN would agree to name the comet Rogue, but he was sure that he would use the handle, at least informally. It was apropos and had a stickiness to it. It would definitely catch on. He imagined himself dropping the name in a room full of big shots—NASA, bureaucrats, and military—and watching a sea of heads nod in approval.

15

Irina read, for the third time, the report she was going to send to the MPC on the discovery of her comet. She fumed a bit as she read, still peeved with Dr. Goldblum and his foot-dragging. Normally, they would have invested two months maximum in preparing a report, but he seemed to have his own agenda in the matter. While she had spent six months analyzing plates and data and adjusting her calculations on the comet's orbit and diameter, he had been working on his own project, which was obviously associated with the comet, but which he was tenaciously secretive about.

She thought the report was ready, but still she hesitated. Her own perfectionist streak was satisfied, but she wasn't sure what Dr. Goldblum would make of it. She walked to his office and poked her head in the door. "Here's the report, ready to send to the MPC."

He glanced up from the project on his desk—several books and papers on comet impact, a legal pad filled with notations, and his timeworn Texas Instruments calculator—

and gestured to a spot on his desk that was only half-cluttered. She sighed to herself and placed the manila folder holding her MPC report on a chaotic pile of astronomy periodicals, photocopied articles, and letters, wondering how he could possibly find anything in this mess.

"I'll get to that within the hour," he said. "Then, if everything is in order, we can send our report to the MPC."

She shook her head—*there's that "our" again*—and stared at him for a moment with that nice-ice look that some women are capable of, a thin veil of pleasantry covering an iceberg of displeasure or scorn. She turned and started back to her cubicle, then spun the other way and made her way to the break room. Her nerves were frazzled. *Coffee break is coming early this morning.*

Three hours later, right before lunch, Dr. Goldblum summoned Irina back to his office. "Everything looks good on the MPC report," he exclaimed. "Shall we?"

Irina nodded. He placed the pages in the hopper on his fax machine and hit the *send* button. She braced herself. The sounds that fax machines made were extremely obnoxious, like fingernails on a chalkboard. *You would think, with all the techno-wizardry at our fingertips, that manufacturers could program them to make sounds that didn't sound like chintzy, B-grade, sci-fi sound effects.* But this time she hardly noticed the sounds. Her eyes were glued to the panel, watching the lights as they flashed: sending, sending, sending, received. She relaxed. Her long odyssey was over.

"Done!" he said triumphantly. "Now we wait."

At 4:49 p.m. as they were winding things up for the day,

Irina heard the fax machine chirp and whine. When she stepped into Dr. Goldblum's office, he smiled and handed her the page. As she suspected, it was her acknowledgment of receipt from the MPC. She looked at him and grinned, then glided out of his office and down the hall.

16

Irina arrived at work early, about 7:45 a.m., buoyant with anticipation. Today, she would receive her confirmation letter from the MPC. She stuck her head in Dr. Goldblum's office. It was empty. She looked around dumbfounded. His chair was still pushed in. His coffee cup was cold and empty. That was strange. He was always at his desk by 7:30 a.m. unless he had a conference or a meeting somewhere. And when he was going to be gone, he let everyone know at least a few days in advance. *Maybe he gave me a heads-up, and I wasn't paying attention.*

She headed to Valentina's office. Mrs. Constantia, Val to her friends, would know where Dr. Goldblum was. She always knew where he was. She had been his assistant for eleven years and knew his schedule and appointments better than he did.

"Is Dr. Goldblum coming in late today?" she enquired. "Did he have a meeting this morning at the country club?"

"No dear," she replied, in her rich, Hispanic tones. "He

left a message last night on my office phone that he would be at a NASA function for the next two or three days. Said he might be back on Friday. Otherwise, we shouldn't expect to see him until Monday."

"That's strange. He didn't say anything to me about a NASA function, and I don't recall seeing anything on his calendar."

Val replied, "I didn't hear anything about it myself until this morning. And you're right. It is unusual—very unusual. He always gives me a heads-up well in advance when he is going to be gone, sometimes months ahead. But I suspect that it has something to do with the NASA Bill. I feel sorry for him. That project has already consumed a year of his life and will certainly consume even more. My guess is that he received a phone call for an urgent face-to-face conference to discuss last-minute changes to the bill, which is scheduled to be debated in Congress this coming week."

Irina shrugged her shoulders, muttered, "Okay, thanks," and walked to her cubicle. *Could this have something to do with the Rogue? Nah! Probably nothing. Silly girl. You have watched way too many conspiracy movies.*

She was antsy the entire day. Once or twice per hour, she jumped up and walked to Dr. Goldblum's office to check the fax machine, just in case her confirmation letter had come in, and she hadn't heard the characteristic chirps and screeches. It would have been far more convenient for her if they had sent the report in with her email account instead of his fax machine. She wondered why Dr. Goldblum had such a love affair with the noisy dinosaur. It was old tech and headed for extinction, yet he insisted on using it whenever he had the option. She suspected it was pride. It made him feel important when the relic raised a ruckus. It telegraphed to the entire department that he was sending and receiving important messages.

At 4:36 p.m. the fax machine came to life, its grating whine echoing down the hall. Irina's heart began to race. She rose out of her chair and strode quickly down the hall to Dr. Goldblum's office. The page was starting to roll out. She grabbed it anxiously, barely able to wait for it to finish printing. When it finally spit out, she snatched it up and was crestfallen. It was from the MPC. But it was not a confirmation letter. It was a standby letter.

Dear Miss Kirilenko:

Thank you for your recent communication on a possible comet in Taurus. We here at the MPC, along with teams at NASA, JPL, and PDCO are still in the process of investigating the anomaly that you have discovered. We must require you, under the guidance and authority of NASA and other federal agencies, to refrain from all communication or publication on this discovery, both public and private, until we have concluded our investigation of this phenomenon.

We also request that you forward to us the names and associations of every party with whom you have communicated on this phenomenon.

We need to get a handle on this unique situation
posthaste.

Respectfully,

Barry Naylor, Director, MPC

The letter seemed odd—obscure. Why did Barry himself
send the letter? Usually, the underlings take care of the day-to-
day transactions of the MPC. Anomaly? Phenomenon? That
was pretty bizarre language to describe what appeared to be,
except for its size, a straightforward case for a long-period
comet. Why involve the Jet Propulsion Lab and the Planetary
Defense Coordination Office? They aren't normally involved
in a discovery unless there is a significant threat of impact. A
ban on communication? That was unprecedented. The names
of every individual with whom she had spoken regarding the
comet? That was inconceivable. It sounded more like the FBI
than the MPC or NASA.

She wrestled with the possibilities. What was going on
here? Was NASA exercising caution lest anyone come to
unwarranted conclusions? Or were they exercising caution
lest anyone come to warranted conclusions? Was this the
subtle tip of a cover-up? Were the authorities trying to keep
the knowledge of the comet from the public? Or was she in
danger of sliding into a misguided conspiracy mentality? She
was at an impasse. She didn't know for sure what was going
on. She could do nothing but wait.

17

Cornell University
Friday, November 10, 2017

As she pulled into the parking lot, she noticed Dr. Goldblum's Mercedes sitting in its usual spot. *Hallelujah! Now we can talk about the strange letter from the MPC.* She went straight to his office and stood in his doorway.

"Good morning, boss," she exclaimed cheerfully.

Without looking up, he muttered "g'mornin," turned his back to her, and started rifling through the top drawer on his right file cabinet, looking for something.

Irina watched and waited for a moment. She wasn't sure, but he seemed to be ignoring her.

"So, how did your meeting go?" she asked.

He shook his head and groused, "Same old bureaucratic horse apples, just a bigger wagon load."

"Did you read the fax yet?"

"Fax? What fax?" he muttered.

Really? No idea what I'm talking about? "The fax from the MPC."

Dr. Goldblum shrugged his shoulders and, with his back

yet turned toward her, retorted with a touch of exasperation, "Sometimes these things just take time."

Irina was a little stunned. He obviously didn't want to talk about the comet, and she didn't feel like pursuing the matter further. Dejected, she slunk away. She could hear him continue to paw in his file drawer almost frantically, like a hungry bear tearing apart a rotten log hunting for grubs.

As she walked down the hallway, a premonition sent a shiver down her spine. What if the Rogue was no longer in his hands or hers? What if there really was a conspiracy brewing in the cauldron, something that would make the conspiracy mavens drool if they found out about it?

But if the project had been wrenched from his hands, the perpetrators were not his colleagues in astronomical circles. Nor were they incompetent bureaucrats in the upper echelons of the aerospace agencies. Dr. Goldblum would probably have bulldozed his way with such men or at least wrestled some significant concessions out of them. This could only be the work of agencies that were over the MPC and NASA, agencies determined and able to squelch information flow. But why? She suspected why, but she hardly dared to admit that it might be true. The federal government regarded the comet—its existence, diameter, and trajectory—as sensitive information. They were determined to keep this information out of the hands of the public as long as possible. If true, the Rogue posed a greater threat to Earth than she had imagined.

Irina realized that she had been standing at her desk, holding her coffee cup with both hands, staring into space, deep in thought. She recovered herself—*back to the here-*

and-now—and tried to disengage herself from her fears and concerns about a potential cover-up. *Get a hold of yourself girl.* Sure it was possible that there was a conspiracy here, a cover-up in the making. But the concept was a pretty big leap emotionally and intellectually. It seemed preposterous. Before she could allow herself to go down that path, she needed more information. She didn't want to be guilty of the shortcoming Pastor Vargas disdained in men inflamed with the conspiracy mindset, "strong on fear, weak on facts."

18

Shortly after morning coffee break, Irina was standing near the fax machine talking to Dr. Goldblum when it began to chirp. She nearly jumped out of her skin. Anxiously she watched as the first page rolled out. She recognized the MPC letterhead. Her heart skipped a beat. *Finally!* But once again, her expectations were dashed. It was another standby letter, apologizing for the unusual delay and reiterating the ban on all communication regarding the phenomenon. This course was defended with the hackneyed observation, "Extraordinary finds demand extraordinary verification." She groaned to herself. *Clichés and agency-speak can't hide the lack of transparency.*

She handed the letter to Dr. Goldblum. Despite the coolness and aloofness he had shown since he came back from his recent NASA trip, he put on a pretty decent act. He almost seemed genuinely frustrated. "A whole week without an answer?" he snorted. "This is beyond unusual. In twenty-some years of dealing with the MPC, I have never heard of such a thing. What's going on down there? Are they taking their cues from Congress on how to get things done? Are they all on vacation? Maybe our report clued them in that the world is coming to an end, and they are busy moving their operation to the Cheyenne Mountain Complex."

While Irina wanted to believe that Dr. Goldblum was sincere in his little tirade, it seemed hollow and over-the-top. Looking back, she wondered whether the last statement was a Freudian slip or a crude attempt at humor. At any rate, she had a nagging suspicion that he was privy to the content of this letter before it arrived and that he already knew the content of the next one too. She felt like Christmas had been canceled. The day would still come, but there would be no presents and no tree.

19

Cornell University
Tuesday, November 21, 2017

Dr. Goldblum failed to show up for work again. Val knew nothing beyond a brief note in her voicemail—sent at 8:15 the prior evening—informing her that he had another meeting at NASA come up at the last minute. He might be back on Friday. If not, then Monday.

"Sorry dear," she said to Irina. "I have no other details. Wished I knew more myself. The Jonathan of the past few weeks ..." She trailed off, sighed glumly, and shrugged her shoulders. "I feel like I'm dealing with a different man." She looked at Irina, started to say something, hesitated, looked down at her desk for a moment, then back to Irina.

The frazzled woman poured her heart out. "I don't know if I should tell you this or not, but I got a strange phone call last night from my friend Margie, who happens to live across the street and two doors down from Jonathan. She plays bridge with us on Wednesday nights. Anyways, she said that she saw a black SUV pull up to his house last night at about 8:30. There were two men wearing suits and ties in the front seat and another in the back seat. The one in the back seat got out, walked up to the door, and rang the doorbell. Jonathan emerged from his house carrying a suitcase and a suit bag, followed the man to the SUV, and climbed in the back seat. I have to admit, that does sound strange. Margie is afraid that he has gotten himself tied up with organized crime. Maybe selling cocaine or one of the new designer drugs. I assured her that he would never do something like that. But how can I know for sure? The whole thing … I don't even want to think about it." Her lower lip started to quiver.

Irina watched with compassion as the distraught woman fought back the tears and tried to compose herself. *Poor thing.*

Val wiped her eyes with a tissue, composed herself, and spoke with a force and finality that caught Irina off guard. "Well, I need to get back to work." She was done talking.

"I need to get to work too," Irina replied, then graciously retreated. Her mind started racing. *Dr. Goldblum was picked up by men wearing suits and driving a black SUV. That's not NASA. That's not a cab. Plus, he would have driven himself to the airport if he was going to a NASA meeting. Something is definitely fishy here.*

20

Around 2 a.m. Irina woke up from a vivid dream that seemed to warn her that her fears were right, that there was a cover-up brewing, and that if she didn't do something soon, the window of opportunity was going to close. In the dream she handed her research to Dr. Goldblum. He flipped through it, nodding approvingly a few times. Then his face changed into a sinister demeanor, and he tossed her research into a garbage can with a cavalier wave of his hand. When she protested, he warned her not to retrieve it. He turned to a chalkboard, wrote the word *comet*, then crossed it out and wrote *anomaly*. He then proceeded to fill the chalkboard with physics gibberish trying to prove that what appeared to be a comet wasn't actually a comet. While she protested against the nonsensical arguments, agents wearing suits and ties entered the room and placed her in handcuffs. At this juncture, furious at Dr. Goldblum and the government, she woke up.

Irina didn't believe that the dream was a direct revelation from God. But she did suspect that he had providentially prodded her subconscious mind to warn her that a cover-up was in play and that time was short if she was going to do something about it.

Her mind was racing. She slowed it down and tried to focus. The first thing she needed to do was safeguard her research. But how? She needed to download it onto her thumb drive and upload it to Buster. She trembled as she mulled this idea. She had always been a good girl. This seemed like it was crossing the line. On the other hand, if her hunch was right, if there really was a cover-up going on, then protecting the material wouldn't be wrong. It would be like protecting the Jews during World War Two. It was the Nazis and their evil designs that had crossed the line. On the other hand, if her suspicions were wrong, then such a course of action would run afoul of school policy and could result in her dismissal.

She was conflicted and wished she could call her father and ask his advice. But that was out of the question. If there really was a cover-up being overseen by the highest levels of government as she feared, then talking to him about the situation would endanger her entire family: father, mother, and three siblings yet at home. The price was simply too high. She would have to walk the dark road alone.

After turning the issue over in her mind several times, she decided that safeguarding her comet research was the right choice. It had to be available to the public if time proved that she was right. Too much was at stake. *Just need to buy a 50 GB thumb drive tomorrow during lunch break.*

That brought up the next step, a plan to disseminate her

research. Several ideas came to mind, but as she tried to compare and consider them, drowsiness weighed upon her weary eyes, and she decided not to fight it. The first step was figured out. The next step could be dealt with later. She rolled onto her side and drifted off to sleep.

***

Irina stayed late at work that day, trying to appear busy at her desk. At 5:11 p.m., ten minutes after the last person besides herself had left for the day, she reached into her bag for her thumb drive, then wavered. Should she? Shouldn't she? She had been certain last night, now she was embattled with doubts. Gripped with anxiety and uncertainty, she found strength in her grandfather's sage advice. "Things don't look as clear in the heat of battle as they do on the drawing board." She laughed to herself and decided to execute the plan she had formulated in the comfort of her own bed. *Here goes. The start of my new career as a spy and conspiracy vigilante.*

She placed the thumb drive in her workstation, opened up the file transfer window, and started the download of all her files on the Rogue. Then she settled into her chair, knowing it would take a few minutes, cradled her coffee mug with both hands—*silly me, the coffee's not even hot anymore*—and watched the green bars that marked the progress. A subdued smile crept across her face. Despite her frazzled nerves over the sneaky operation, she felt a sense of satisfaction for answering the call of duty in the face of risk.

When the transfer finished, she placed the thumb drive

in her purse and purged the log for the activity. *Glad dad made me read that book on security and privacy.* Then she opened her *Loose Notes* file and quickly entered a page and a half of thoughts and observations from her legal pad. Information entry would be her cover story, if one was needed, for logging out late. After she finished, she logged out, slumped back in her chair, and breathed out a deep, slow sigh. She was done. If her fears were founded in reality, she would be ready.

***

When Irina returned to her apartment that evening, she skipped her customary practice of immediately putting on a pot of coffee. Instead, she pulled out her laptop and logged into her local network. She wanted to put this spy stuff behind her as fast as possible.

Mentally she walked through the steps her dad had taught her about using the internet securely and getting a Buster account. *I got this, I think.* She started by downloading the TOR browser bundle for Firefox. Then, utilizing TOR and its onion routing, she navigated to Buster to set up an account. As her father had described, it was simple and anonymous. No names. No addresses. No Social Security numbers. Just a twelve-digit username and a twenty-digit password that used small caps, large caps, numbers, and symbols. When it came to the payment step, she waffled a bit. It was $199 per year, quite a bit steeper than she had anticipated, and they only accepted payment with Bitcoin or with an anonymous or alias debit card. She had neither one.

She rolled her eyes at herself. Now she remembered. Dad had said something about needing an anonymous debit card and that they could be purchased at major drug store chains. She got up from her barely started project, grabbed her purse and coat, and headed out the door. Soon she was pawing through the rack of gift cards and debit cards at Rite Aid, looking for a name that sounded familiar. *Vanilla Visa. That rings a bell. Think that's the one dad likes.* She picked up two of the hundred-dollar cards and walked to the register.

Once back home, she navigated to the card activation site, entered an alias name and address—Wheremy Cowboy, 123 Cactus Lane, Branding Station, TX 56789—and activated her card. *That felt a little weird, too much like lying. Yet such a spoof that it's hard to regard it as lying.* Then she logged back into Buster, finished the payment process, activated her account, and set up her preferences.

Next, she created a new folder, named it *Rogue*, and queued up all of her files on the mother of all comets. Once the upload started, she raced to the kitchen and brewed herself a pot of coffee. Then she paced the floor, eyeing the dripping brew like a child eyeing the cotton candy at the local fair. *Coffee always brews slower when you need it fast.* When she finally lifted a cup of the elixir to her lips, she noticed that her hand was shaking. *Guess I'm not cut out to be a spy. Just a little bit out of my league.*

An hour and fifteen minutes later, the upload was done. She logged out of Buster and reformatted her thumb drive. Then she breathed a sigh of relief. Now she could relax. But she couldn't. She found herself haunted by a vague sense that her job wasn't done yet. *I uploaded all of my research. What else is there to be concerned about?* She was just about to put her concerns out of mind when the oversight dawned on her. *Of course, the research paper from Dr. Goldblum's NASA acquaintance!*

She hurried to her closet and rifled through the top layer of the box she jokingly referred to as her *someday box*. It was overflowing with periodicals, excerpted articles, and technical papers she intended to read someday. Underneath several recent additions—paper-clipped journal articles— she found the research paper Dr. Goldblum had given her several weeks earlier titled *Rogue Apocalypse*. When she had come home that day, she had nonchalantly tossed it into the box, more likely to be forgotten than read. She retrieved the paper, scurried back to her printer, and scanned the entire work into her computer, including Dr. Goldblum's notes in the back. Then she logged back into Buster, created a new subfolder called *Other Materials*, uploaded the paper, and logged back out.

Finally, she really could relax, glad the day was over. She hoped that her involvement with intrigue and conspiracy would begin and end with this little caper. Hopefully, there was no cover-up. Hopefully, all the excitement was in her hyperactive imagination. Playing spy was not her cup of tea. She put on Satie's *Gymnopédie No. 1*, kicked off her shoes, stretched herself out on the couch, closed her eyes, and lost herself in rhapsody. A few minutes later, she was sound asleep, a victim of emotional exhaustion.

21

Shortly after 2 p.m., Irina heard the fax machine whine and chatter. Several minutes later, Dr. Goldblum sauntered up to her cubicle and said, putting on an air of swagger, "You're going to want to see this, Miss Kirilenko," then handed her a confirmation letter from the MPC. "If you can keep your nose clean, you are going to be a rock star in the astronomy world. Magazines and talk shows will seek interviews with you. What you have discovered in Taurus is far more rare and far more interesting than a comet."

Irina looked at him dumbfounded, then it dawned on her what was coming. *The government has decided to officially deny that the Rogue is a comet. They are trying to buy my compliance. They want me to sell my soul.* She said nothing and took the letter from his hands with a heavy heart.

> Dear Miss Kirilenko:
> Congratulations! The anomaly that you have discovered is associated with a black hole—a near-

neighborhood black hole, a tremendous first for the field of astronomy. The experts investigating the phenomenon are in almost unanimous agreement that the apparent occultations which you traced are not actually occultations by an approaching comet (a reasonable assumption on your part) but the refraction of light waves by the emission lobe—the shock horizon or bow shock—of the growing jet of a recently formed black hole.

By a tremendous stroke of luck, we have the privilege from our observation point on Earth to look almost straight down the barrel, so to speak, of the jet. This explains why we don't see the jet, but only infer its existence from the stellar occultations caused by its shock horizon as it extends across our galactic neighborhood. The jet has not shown up in the infrared, ultraviolet, and x-ray photographs of the region because this class of black holes emits only radio waves and low-frequency microwaves.

The most likely explanation for the shock horizon causing stellar occultations is that refractive lensing is occurring where the shock horizon impacts the interstellar medium, bending the Earth-bound visible-light waves emitted from the star and directing them on a tangent that makes them invisible to viewers here on Earth.

The apparent path of the phenomenon in the direction of our solar system is due to the fact that the jet is still growing, which means that the shock wave at its nose is continually extending further outward. This apparent travel in the direction of our solar system will cease when the jet reaches maximum sustainable extension. At that point the jet will begin to pulsate, alternating between minor retreats and re-extensions.

The curved path of the occultations, which bears a remarkable similarity to the orbit of a long-period comet, is caused by axial precession. The spinning black hole makes tiny changes in its spin. And these tiny movements cause the nose of the jet to move in a large circle. If we had the luxury of watching this phenomenon for several thousand years, we would observe the occultations trace a full circle.

Our estimations of the distance of this black hole and its jet, based on the work of many experts in the astronomical community, suggest that neither one poses a threat to our solar system.

Despite the fact that we are confident of this interpretation of the phenomenon, we request that you say nothing about it to anyone. This is not public information. The decision-making parties involved in this research—the MPC, NASA, JPL, the Pentagon, and other federal institutions—have decided not to go public with the story until the research teams have finished their investigation. We anticipate releasing their findings in perhaps eighteen months. We trust that you will honor this request to neither publish nor communicate anything about your research in Taurus, especially this phenomenon. The federal government regards this phenomenon as a sensitive issue and is currently overseeing its investigation.

Thank you for your important contribution to astronomy and astrophysics.

Sincerely,

Barry Naylor, Director, MPC

Irina mused. *A sensitive issue though it poses no threat to the solar system? JPL? Hmm! They don't get involved unless a body poses a credible threat to Earth. Why the Pentagon? Why other federal agencies? This is no mere scientific investigation. People in high places are worried.*

A half hour later, Dr. Goldblum called her into his office and asked her to sit down, something he had never done before. *This must be big*, she thought to herself.

"I don't know how to break this to you easily, so I will just be blunt and give you the cold, hard facts. NASA has been obligated by the federal government to implement the expanded CNEOS and PDCO programs, despite the fact that she is already juggling two massive projects—the Mars mission and the moon base—while struggling with an under-funded budget. Under the NASA Bill, all federal and state-funded observatories and all large private observatories are being brought under the NASA umbrella. We are no longer partners." He hesitated for effect. "We are now subordinates. We answer directly to them."

Irina looked at him, slightly bewildered, wondering what was coming next.

He continued, "NASA's first cost-cutting measure is eliminating unnecessary research overlap so vital research goals can be pursued in the most efficient and cost-effective manner."

She swallowed hard. She didn't like where this seemed to be going.

"This affects astronomical institutions in several ways. The most important is that research programs must now be authorized by NASA and will on occasion be assigned by them. For most astronomers, this will only be a minor inconvenience, another layer of bureaucracy and some extra paperwork. It won't affect either their current research projects or their future research preferences. But on rare occasions, projects will be canceled, denied, or modified. Further, researchers may be reassigned according to NASA's directives and priorities. Sadly, you are one of the rare occasions." He paused and stared intently at her.

She met his gaze with the embers of defiance glowing hot in her heart.

"Research on the anomaly in Taurus has been assigned to select teams at a dozen elite institutions, and general research in Taurus is in the process of being reallocated to them. You may continue your research in Orion, but you have been formally requested by NASA to cease all research in Taurus. You are further requested to forward all of your research that pertains to the anomaly to NASA, via me, so it can be forwarded to the proper institutions."

She looked at him in shock. *Select institutions? Other institutions? Proper institutions?* It was hard to stifle the tears. Even harder to repress the anger rising inside. She was furious and crushed, like a mother whose baby was being taken from her. For a moment, she felt like clawing his eyes out, but she managed to gather herself and maintain her composure.

"Furthermore," Dr. Goldblum added, "we have been given a strict advisory notice from NASA, valid until formally notified otherwise, that they do not want any unauthorized persons writing or talking about the phenomenon in Taurus. There is to be no discussion, not even a mention. Not with family, friends, co-workers, priests, counselors, or nosy government officials. Every breach of this notice will result in immediate termination. No exceptions. This is the most important research project in the world. It has immense ramifications for national defense and astrophysical research. It must not be compromised."

He stopped his harangue for a moment and looked Irina straight in the eyes, drilling deep into her psyche. "Do you understand?"

She met his glare with her own and responded crisply, "Of course I understand. You were speaking English, and I do have a PhD. Do you think I need a little mansplaining to help me understand the big words?"

He stifled an explosive outburst at her impertinence. "Will you comply?" he demanded.

"Do I have a choice?" she countered.

"No. You don't have a choice. But I want an answer, not

a rhetorical question from a hot-shot rookie astronomer. Will you comply?"

Irina nodded, but inside she was not nodding. She was seething mad. They didn't want anyone to know about the looming menace she had nicknamed the Rogue.

"I don't want a mere nod. I want a straight answer. Will you comply?"

"Yes," she snarled. *I will outwardly comply for as long as necessary until I have a good opportunity to unleash my inner noncompliance.* She felt a twinge of conscience. *Was that lying? Did I just lie?* She determined not to worry about it too much. Her situation reminded her of the account in the Old Testament where Hushai used deception to defeat the counsel of Ahithophel, thus saving King David's life. Whatever God had in mind when he banned lying, he sure seemed to approve of Hushai's effort at misinformation. That was her take on the matter anyway.

An awkward silence hung in the air for a few moments. Then Irina's patience burst. She couldn't hold her exasperation in any longer and exploded with a flurry of questions.

"Do you really believe this black-hole-jet theory? Pretty lame interpretation, don't you think?"

"Of course, I believe it. The brightest minds in the entire astronomical world have concluded, unanimously, that it is the very best explanation for the phenomenon."

"Why are they trotting out the black-hole-jet theory now? How come astronomers never brought this theory up in the past when they observed a series of occulted stars?"

"Because no series of occulted stars observed in the past produced phenomena that met the criteria for consideration as a black-hole-jet situation."

"And what phenomena are they referring to? What phenomena indicates that we are observing refraction from the shock horizon of a black-hole jet and not the common occultation of a star by a planetary or cometary body?"

"Are you challenging the world's greatest astronomers? Listen. The brightest minds in the astronomical world have concluded, unanimously, that the black-hole-jet theory is the best explanation for the phenomenon."

Pity and disgust wrestled in her breast. The fact that he countered by repeating the same argument reminded her of something her dad used to say. "When men sound like a stuck record, they are speaking off a script." *Somebody is telling him what to believe and what to say.*

She continued her protest, "Why do they still refer to it as the anomaly or the phenomenon if they really believe it is the shock wave of a black-hole jet?" Before he could answer, she posed another puzzler, "If it really is a black-hole jet, and it really poses no threat to Earth, then why the secrecy?"

Dr. Goldblum was taken aback, knowing full well that she had him cornered. But surrendering the point was not an option. So he took a different tack. He relaxed a little bit and looked upon her as if he pitied her. "Irina," he began, shaking his head slowly as if he couldn't comprehend her dullness, "Try to see this from a practical perspective. You are way too idealistic."

"Practical?"

"Yes, practical! Listen! Things don't always go the way we would like them to go in life. Life is a rough-and-tumble sandbox. And it is even rougher if a person is idealistic or dogmatic or always trying to make things go their way."

Irina knew she tended toward idealism but didn't think her idealism had any bearing on the question of whether the occulted stars had been obscured by a comet or a black-hole jet. "What do you mean by that?" she demanded. "What are you implying?"

"I am implying that if you don't watch yourself, your idealism will get out of hand, and you will step on toes you don't want to step on, or ask questions that are extremely unwise to ask, or appear to be a threat to people who have the power to crush you."

"Can you be a little more straightforward? That sounds like a cryptic threat made in a movie by henchmen from the Mafia. How is my inquisitiveness going to negatively affect me? What particular consequences are you talking about?"

"If you refuse to comply with NASA's advisory notice or challenge the official position of NASA in this matter, you will be stripped of access to any telescope or plate collection under NASA's jurisdiction, and you will be treated like a leper by every astronomy department and observatory in America and Europe. You will be undesirable in the job market and unpublishable in peer-reviewed periodicals. Your career in astronomy will be over. You will be squashed like a bug."

"That's not fair or right. What happened to academic freedom? What happened to the long-standing tradition of independent thought and independent research?"

"Welcome to the real world, sweetheart. The world where grownups work. Where you don't have as much freedom as you think you have. Where you must deal with politics, egos, and deceit if you want to climb the food chain. And unless you make it to the top, you are part of the food chain. You don't dictate. You are dictated to. You don't make the rules. You play by the rules. That is the harsh reality. Either deal with it or get on the porch and quit running with the big dogs."

She couldn't pretend that the possibility of being blacklisted in the astronomy world didn't make her uneasy. She had dreamed of being an astronomer since she was eight years old. But she had her priorities: integrity first, career ambitions second. Nonetheless, though she was willing to choose integrity over her career ambitions, she didn't care to precipitate or hasten the loss of her career by a careless tongue. *The tongue is a fire, a world of iniquity.* She calmed her outward fluster and asked, "So, what do you suggest that I do?" But she was only putting on a face. Inwardly she was still fuming. She knew that she could neither comply nor take his advice. *That's not in the rule book that I play by.*

He continued his onslaught, "Comply. Sticking up for your beliefs doesn't put food on the table or pay the bills. Rocking the boat doesn't earn promotions. You are going to have to figure out, sooner or later, that there are times when being right is wrong. On top of that, you don't realize the gravity of the situation. You don't grasp how dangerous wrong decisions in this matter really are."

She looked quizzically at him. *Dangerous? Was he upping the ante a little?*

He glared back. "We are allowed to play in the sandbox, but only if we comply with the rules. Most of the time noncompliance merely results in the loss of some of our sandbox privileges. There are times, however ..." He paused, unsure how to make his point in a discreet manner. "Let me just say this. If you cross the agencies who have given us the rules for playing in the sandbox, it will get real ugly—uglier than you care to know." He let the last phrase drop like a brick on her head.

The revelation left Irina trembling. *Very telling. There is a big difference between a warning with academic consequences and a warning with ominous consequences.* He had divulged far more than he had intended. She was now certain that offending the astronomical community was the least of her worries. She needed to worry about offending Big Brother. This also cleared things up about the changes she had seen in Dr. Goldblum. Someone with a lot of clout had stepped on him.

Dr. Goldblum was a fighter. He would have stuck to his guns. He was so tenacious in controversy that his friends referred to him as the Iberian Tiger, alluding to his courage and Spanish lineage. His family had moved from Bavaria to Andalusia in the eighteenth century. But the tiger had been tamed. It had to be someone high up in the government, likely in one of the federal agencies. Someone who could crush him or buy him. As Pastor Vargas had once said in a sermon, "If the watchdog stops barking, someone threw him a bone." She was wondering what kind of bone could have enticed him when she was startled by the sound of a chair being shoved backward. Embarrassed, she realized that she had wandered off deep in thought. She looked up and saw Dr. Goldblum standing up. *Perhaps the storm is over,* she hoped.

But the confrontation wasn't over. The worst was yet to come. Dr. Goldblum came around to the front of his desk, sat on the edge, crossed his arms, and looked down on Irina. "We have some unfinished business to take care of. As I mentioned at the start of this conversation, your research project in Taurus has been shuttered. All research on the anomaly has been transferred to hand-picked teams at elite institutions. Consequently," he paused for dramatic effect, "you have two hours to turn in all your research on the phenomenon in Taurus—everything in your possession whether paper files, electronic files, thumb drives, legal pads and notebooks, graphs and charts. Everything."

Irina nodded, tears welling up in her eyes. She turned and fled, fighting the sobs, and ran to her car. She needed a few minutes alone.

After she had composed herself, she walked back into the building to find a box to put her research in. She felt dejected, like she was shopping for a coffin for her own funeral. Nobody in her department had a box. An associate suggested she contact the custodial staff, but the custodial room was locked, and nobody was around. She fretted. She didn't have time to drive to her apartment and back. She wasn't going to walk to the university store and purchase a box for three dollars. What should she do? *Think, girl! Where am I most likely to find boxes?* In her mind she could see a delivery truck unloading lots of boxes. *Where was that? I saw it last week while driving to work … the liquor store!*

A few minutes later, she pulled into the parking lot of the liquor store, which was about ten blocks from the campus. When she entered, she was a little tense as she had never been in a liquor store before. She nervously asked the man at the counter for a box. He smiled broadly and asked, "What size?" She held up her hands about sixteen inches apart and replied, "About this big." He hustled into the back room and returned with several boxes for her to choose from. One stood out and made her chuckle, perfect in its size and its message. It was a Bad Daddy Tequila box with a macho logo that included the phrase, "Grow a set!" She eagerly took the box from his hands with a flamboyant "Thank you" and hurried back to her car. In a moment the painful task had been given a measure of twisted pleasure.

A half hour later, she marched into Dr. Goldblum's office with a stiff upper lip, the box in her arms, and a growing sense of equilibrium in her new identification, a covert operator in a cloak-and-dagger operation. A voice in the wilderness warning the world about the existential threat that the government was covering up, warning them before it was too late. But for now, she must exercise caution, patiently biding her time until the right opportunity presented itself.

She halted in front of his desk, made eye contact, and held it. She was not going to be intimidated.

"Is this everything?" he demanded.

"Yes." *You have everything that I have.*

"Do you have copies of any of this material in your possession?"

"No, I do not." *Not saying I don't have access to copies.*

He nodded toward his desk, indicating that he wanted her to set the box down on its cluttered surface.

She placed the box on his desk, turned it so he could see the Bad Daddy logo with its "Grow a Set" quip, swiftly turned around, and marched out of his office.

He did see it. His lip quivered in anger. He hated it with a passion when he was upstaged or outsmarted.

22

Irina was not one who could easily let things rest when something bugged her, especially if it seemed wrong. The present situation was no exception. The letters from the MPC and Dr. Goldblum's antics had convinced her that NASA was engaged in covering up the comet she had discovered in Taurus. And though she wasn't absolutely certain, she was inclined to believe that this cover-up extended to the highest levels of government. She was hopping mad and wanted to do something about the situation. But what?

Her first inclination was to send her files ASAP to some organization like WikiLeaks. But she nixed the idea. She just wasn't that convinced yet. Maybe she should have been, but she wasn't. She was still a little nervous about the fiasco it would turn into if there really wasn't a Hollywood-worthy conspiracy in the making. What if she was reading more into the letters from the MPC than the facts warranted?

Maybe the cover-up was merely an ordinary cloak of secrecy as was often seen in such fields as technology and weapons development. But why would the heavyweights in technology or the military-industrial complex cover up the comet? Maybe it was a gold mine of minerals containing helium-3 or some other extremely valuable commodities. *Nah! Not a viable mining opportunity no matter how valuable the mineral or rich the concentration. Bottom line, hard to imagine any plausible scenario for covering up a comet with a run-of-the-mill cloak of secrecy.*

She choked on her next thought. Maybe it really was a black-hole jet, and she was just too married to her belief that it was a gargantuan comet to see the truth. At first glance, the black-hole theory did seem to fit better with the cloak of secrecy view. Maybe the government saw the potential for some amazing technological advance which they believed would give them a huge military or aerospace advantage.

But there were holes in this interpretation. For one thing, it seemed like a chapter from science fiction to capitalize on the potential of a black hole. Right in there with wormholes and time travel. For another thing, even if there really was some technological potential, it was light years away— impossibly distant. No, the black-hole theory was too far-fetched. It was a story without a story behind it. It was just a cover story. And she couldn't hide from the fact that the evidence was the exact same evidence that had always been accepted as a comet.

Irina was back to where she started—a real comet and a real conspiracy. But she hesitated and flip-flopped, leaning toward conspiracy, then leaning toward aerospace-military secrecy, then back again.

After a couple weeks of wrestling with the question, she decided to be proactive rather than simply waiting for the answer to materialize. She would test the waters. Determine beyond all shadow of doubt whether there really was a federal cover-up or whether it was just another instance of commonplace aerospace-military secrecy. And if there was a cover-up, determine how serious NASA was about their ban on communication. How much muscle was behind it. With this decision made, she felt much more relaxed about the situation. Her fears that a conspiracy was being fostered upon America would either be confirmed or allayed. If they were allayed, she would let the matter rest. If they were confirmed, well, that meant more danger and adventure than she cared to experience.

But what could she do to test the waters? The most obvious way would be to try and get her research published anonymously, then watch and see what happened. But what publisher? If the ban was as strict as they had implied it was, she likely wouldn't get any scientific publication to bite. She needed to find a publication that wasn't a big blip on the radar. The prepper and survivalist magazines? Maybe. But likely not. Judging by the intense scrutiny they were now facing—preppers and patriots were specifically mentioned in the Homeland Security Act—she suspected that they were already infiltrated by feds and informers and that she would have a hard time getting her story past the editor and into print. It was probably a non-starter.

She decided to try science fiction. After a quick internet search using TOR to hide her trail, she found her candidate,

Sci-Fi Today. They were a new entry in the field—only two years old—but enjoyed stellar reviews and a growing readership. Plus, they were based in Texas, the state that was the most resistant to the Security Act's uncomfortably broad treatment of homegrown security threats. While their flagship offering was science fiction, they also featured a column on cutting-edge technology that held out promise for space exploration and colonization, as well as occasional pieces on apocalyptic scenarios that involved heaven-sent phenomena like asteroids and EMPs. *Perfect.*

With coffee at hand, she logged into Buster, opened Open Office, and began writing, careful not to divulge any information that might enable investigators to determine her identity. The article opened with a startling statement. "What would you do if you were made privy to research which indicated that Earth faced a potentially apocalyptic scenario, but were forbidden to divulge the information because the government had determined that covering up the truth was in America's best interest? Would you abide by the ban? Or would you alert the public? Would you still choose to alert the American public if divulging the information meant that you might have to answer to the FBI?"

The introduction to the author followed. "No doubt you are wondering who the anonymous author is. I am an educated professional who was in the right place at the right time for this information to fall into my lap."

Without further ado, the article launched into an outline of the salient facts. It gave a brief description of the process for finding TNOs and comets with stellar occultation when they are still a long way away from Earth, too far away to detect with optical and too cold to detect with infrared. For examples of the process, it used two recent discoveries of TNOs by graduate students at Caltech and Harvard, material which had recently been published in *Astronomy*. For each example, it included photos which exhibited the waxing and the waning of the occultation. Having laid the foundation for the science, it then produced the evidence for the comet, nine series of photos which exhibited the occultation of nine stars in Taurus over a period of four and a half years. This was followed by an illustration which demonstrated that if you drew a line through the occulted stars and extended it, the line passed through a thick patch of the asteroid belt and directly intersected the path of Mars, coming within 25,000 miles of the Red Planet sometime in 2024—a terrifying scenario.

This threat was approaching Earth like a ninja, stealthy and unobserved. Its albedo was so low that it would be deep in the solar system, possibly as far as the asteroid belt, before it became visible to Earth-based optical telescopes. The earliest Earth-based observations of the comet would likely occur in 2020 when it was somewhere between Neptune and Uranus and had warmed up enough that infrared in the 10- to 15-micrometer range would begin picking up its signature.

A brief outline of the cover-up followed, including the official explanation that the phenomenon was the refraction of starlight by the shock wave of a growing jet on a new black hole.

The article closed with a plea for honest men to

investigate and weigh the facts. What is the most probable explanation for the occultation of the stars? The new theory on the refraction of stellar light by the shock wave of a jet on a black hole? Or the commonplace occultation of stellar light when a body passes in front of it?

At 2:30 in the morning, after eight hours of intense labor, Irina finished. *Hallelujah!* Though she really wanted to go to bed—her eyes ached—she knew she wouldn't be able to sleep until the article had been sent. She opened Buster's email program, GASmail (Guaranteed Anonymous Sender), composed a brief cover letter, attached her article, filled in the email address for the editor at *Sci-Fi Today*, and hit the *send* button. With a sigh of relief, she relaxed in her chair and cradled her coffee cup though it was long cold and nearly empty. A jumble of emotions jostled for attention. Relief because the article was done and sent. Apprehension that she might be opening a can of worms. Sadness that her career appeared to be on the shoals. Pride because she had done right in the matter. *Might have been a little easier on the emotions if I had pursued a career in music instead.*

23

Irina stared, dumbfounded and dazed, at the headline story in the evening CVN newsfeed. There was a picture of dozens of federal agents raiding the office of *Sci-Fi Today* crowned with the headline "Terrorist Front in Fort Worth Raided."

She blazed through the story. At 8:30 Central Time that morning, a large force of FBI and Homeland Security agents had conducted the raid, accompanied by SWAT officers in full combat gear and six armored cars. The CVN reporter estimated that there were about 150 agents and officers on the scene. *A little overkill, ya think.* Twenty-four people had been led away in handcuffs.

The last person to be led out of the building had been in the restroom when the federal agents barged in. He had been able to send a few short texts on the development before he was apprehended. His last text was, "They are battering the bathroom door down." The FBI had confiscated every phone and computer in the building and loaded them into two vans. After the suspects had been taken away, and the

145

armored vehicles and SWAT crews had departed, a semi-truck pulled up. Federal agents then loaded the trailer with dozens of boxes taken from the building, six 55-gallon drums, and several pieces of equipment that looked like they could be the computerized control modules for the printing press.

An accompanying video concluded with a snippet of the local police chief's appearance on television, reading a brief statement which declared that the operation had been a front for a terrorist organization and that all of the employees were now in custody, being held on unspecified Homeland Security violations. When asked where the suspects had been taken, he replied that they were currently being transferred to a classified location for questioning and holding.

Irina was racked with grief. Not only did the raid on the *Sci-Fi Today* office bring her publication plan to naught, but she feared that she might be responsible for their misfortune. She hoped she wasn't. Perhaps this was just a coincidence. Perhaps they were already under suspicion or investigation. But *perhaps* didn't do much to salve her conscience. It seemed like wishful thinking.

She continued reading below the video. In an operation widely believed to be associated with the *Sci-Fi Today* raid, the WikiLeaks website and three similar websites had been shut down by the FBI and the NSA that morning. There had been no official statement from the government yet, but an insider, speaking on condition of anonymity, claimed that both the *Sci-Fi Today* raid and the WikiLeaks closure were tactical responses to a huge national security leak, perhaps the most damaging ever.

In association with the website closures, some six dozen persons affiliated with the websites had been arrested and charged with complicity in the leak. Two dozen others had been arrested and accused of being the hackers who, in the dark belly of Anonymous, had originally obtained and leaked the classified information. Human rights advocates, however, disputed the validity of these arrests. They insisted that none of the reputed hackers had ever been associated with Anonymous. Some weren't even legitimate hackers at all. A soundbite was circulating on the internet where a young man said, brushing away the tears from his eyes, "I know Cody like nobody knows Cody. We been gamin' together almost every day since we wuz in junior high. He ain't no big-time hacker. Fact is, my bro' couldn't even hack his way into his sister's email."

Irina searched for more information on the story. On the right-wing website *Torchbearer*, she stumbled upon a recent post which caught her attention, "Unusual Arrests in Fort Worth Incident." A local SWAT officer, who had been on the scene and had asked to not be identified, had called the *Torchbearer* and informed them that none of the arrested had been recited their Miranda rights. The reporter who answered the call suspected that this denial of rights was related to the recently passed Homeland Security Act. He called the Fort Worth Police Department and asked for clarification on the arrest procedures at the *Sci-Fi Today* incident. They told him to contact the FBI. He asked them for a copy of the police report. Again he was told to contact the FBI. When he called the Dallas Field Office, he was informed that they had no information that could be released to the public. He turned to several contacts in prominent law firms and discovered that none of the arrested had been allowed to call an attorney or family members. Moreover, the firms themselves had struck out trying to obtain a copy of the police report and ascertain what charges had been filed against the detained.

Her mind reeled. This was disturbing. No Miranda rights. No police report. No formal charges. And no access to a lawyer. *Seriously? That brand of law enforcement wasn't unusual in Russia. But America?*

She continued to read. The author compared the Fort Worth incident to eight similar Security Act incidents across America in the past two weeks. Then he opined, based on several inside tips, that those arrested in these incidents were being detained at a secret FEMA camp that housed only Security Act arrests. *Really? FEMA Camps?* That sounded far-fetched to Irina as FEMA camps, which had only been operating for two weeks, were the cornerstone of a brand new federal program known as Fresh Start that was being touted as America's best hope to get the homeless off the streets and give them a new start in life. Besides, the idea that the government was using FEMA camps as secret prisons was an old urban legend that had been in circulation for at least a decade. It was still a favorite soundbite for the firebrands in the prepper and patriot camps.

While she was parsing the nuance of an insinuating statement three paragraphs later, the article vanished. The page was replaced by a "404 Page Not Found" error message. She tried to navigate to the homepage and discovered that the entire website was down. Confounded and spooked, she stared at the screen. Was this related to the WikiLeaks closure? Or was it a mere coincidence? *Lot of strange coincidences for one day.*

24

Dr. Goldblum stormed into Irina's cubicle and slapped a magazine on her desk. It was the February edition of *Sci-Fi Today*. Her eyes practically jumped out of their sockets when she saw the splashy cover, a picture of an enormous comet headed for Earth, and the provocative headline "Cover-up or Ludicrous Conspiracy Theory?" *Wow. They really were going to run my story.*

"Follow me to my office," he said quietly, but firmly. Then he picked up the magazine and wheeled about. She got up and followed him. He closed his door behind them with agitated force and motioned for her to sit in the chair across from his desk. She obliged.

He stood directly in front of her, perched his backside on the edge of his desk with his feet still solidly on the floor, tossed the magazine into her lap, crossed his arms, scowled at her for a moment, then growled, "What do you know about this article?"

She looked up at him. He was livid, and he seemed a bit

worried too. "Not much. I haven't read it. In fact, I've never even read the magazine before."

Dr. Goldblum clenched his jaw. "Are you positive?"

She met his glare and said, a little coolly, "As positive as positive can be." *I am positive that I have never read the magazine before, and I am positive that I haven't read the editor's version of that article, and I am positive that "not much" is a good subjective answer when telling the truth seems to be a worse crime than a deceptive answer.*

"Somebody leaked highly classified information which ended up in the hands of this pseudo-science rag, and now I have federal agents in my office asking a thousand questions. We are going to get to the bottom of this, and the responsible party is going to pay—pay dearly."

Thanks for the juicy niblet. It confirms my fears. We are definitely dealing with a government cover-up and not merely corporate secrecy. But what's this "we" stuff? Has the FBI made you a junior investigator?

He continued, "We don't know who leaked the sensitive information, whether an insider or a hacker. But if it was an inside job, it won't take us long to figure out who the culprit is because there are fewer than seventy people who are privy to the information that was leaked."

Good thing I didn't know that. If I had known how few people were in the know, I might not have mustered up the courage to send the article.

"Are you listening, Miss Kirilenko? We have a situation on our hands, a security breach that threatens the stability of the entire nation and has the entire security infrastructure engaged. People in high places are demanding answers."

She nodded. *Bet he's unaware how much he just divulged. This goes all the way to the top. The president and his cabinet are calling the shots here.*

"Thankfully, we got lucky and the breach was nipped in the bud before the information was leaked to the public. An assistant editor had gotten a little nervous about the story and called Homeland Security the day before their scheduled press run to ask about its legality. It turns out that he had been on vacation when the story arrived by an anonymous email, so he was unaware of its existence. On the evening that he returned from vacation, his boss called him at home to inform him that he would be attending a one-day seminar on HSA 2017 the next morning in Dallas. The legislation required all media outlets and publications to train their employees on the ramifications of this bill for their industry. Every company was required to send an individual to a training session and appoint them to be their security representative, who would then be responsible for training the rest of the company.

"The day after the seminar, his first day back to work, the story was placed on his desk by an associate, not for editing but to bring him up to speed on the upcoming issue. The story piqued his interest, but it also raised a few alarms based on the information he had learned the previous day. He now knew that apocalyptic fear mongering, a long-standing and deeply-revered tradition among the religious right, was now regarded as a federal offense. During his lunch break, he called the 800 number he had been given, a hotline for concerns about efforts to create panic with supposed impending apocalyptic scenarios. He called because he wanted to know whether the story would pass muster with Homeland Security. The counselor on the other end of the line—the lines were manned by FBI and Homeland Security agents—told him that he would gladly look into it for him, gave him a fax number, and advised him to fax the story ASAP, but not from his office. He suggested that he drive to the FedEx Print & Ship eight blocks south of him.

"The next morning, FBI and Homeland Security agents arrived just as *Sci-Fi Today* was firing up the presses. They stopped the presses, took the employees into custody, and confiscated everything pertinent to the security breach. Less than a hundred copies were printed, and all of them are in our possession. We dodged a bullet this time."

"We" dodged a bullet? In "our" possession? What is he hinting at? Is he a big player in this game? Or is he suffering from delusions of grandeur?

"Loose tongues may have talked to spouses or friends, but steps have been taken to ensure that those exposed to this classified material will never compromise the sensitive information that was divulged to them."

Steps? That sounds pretty cold-blooded. What kind of steps? Sequestering them in a gulag like they did in the old Soviet Union?

Dr. Goldblum fixed a cold stare on her for about a half a minute. Irina found it unnerving and fought a sudden wave of uneasiness that bordered on panic. *Does he know more than he is letting on?*

Then he sprang an unexpected angle on her. "The sender was probably an amateur. He left a trail of crumbs that the NSA thinks it will be able to trace in the next forty-eight hours." He cocked his head and looked at her knowingly as if he expected her to fess up and get it over with.

She cringed and hoped that he hadn't noticed. "Well, I hope the wrongdoers in this matter get the justice that they deserve."

"Oh, they will," he replied matter-of-factly. His cold, soulless glare continued. She hoped this conversation would end soon. It was hard to listen to his agitated voice. It reminded her of the rasping drone of an air conditioner on its last legs. Moreover, she was tired of the mind games that he was trying to play with her. *Good thing he's an amateur at psychological manipulation.*

"One more thing. NASA has decided to remove you from the Orion project and make you a department assistant. You will aid the other researchers: entering data, typing reports, running errands, whatever they need you to do—"

"What?" she interrupted as a stab of pain shot through her breast, making her wince. She hadn't seen this coming. Her voice rose. "First, you removed me from my research in Taurus. Now you're removing me from Orion and demoting me." She wiped the hot tears that glistened on her cheeks. "Why?" she demanded, her tone lowered, but still obviously aggravated.

"Because you can't be trusted. It was a stretch in the first place to bring you on board because of your association with the religious right. Since then, you have shown yourself to be insubordinate, independent, and unbalanced. You challenge authority, refuse to be a team player, make your own rules, and squabble with accepted science."

He paused for a moment. "On top of that, we took into consideration the fact that you were enough of a security risk to be on the FBI's list of insiders who were the most likely suspects for the *Sci-Fi Today* incident. The fact is, if the FBI hadn't received credible claims from several Anonymous hackers insisting that their organization was behind the leak—they had hacked into a secure network at a NASA-linked university, downloaded hundreds of files, and passed them on to *Sci-Fi Today*—and if the FBI hadn't found these files on several computers confiscated from the *Sci-Fi Today* office, you wouldn't be sitting here with me today. You would be sitting in a dismal interrogation room wired up to Casper—an acronym for Cerebral Stimulation Pattern Recognition, the newest hi-tech lie detector—answering a stream of questions posed by FBI interrogators."

Praise the Lord! Someone at Sci-Fi Today contacted Anonymous hoping to verify my story. Anonymous verified the story and forwarded the proof to Sci-Fi Today. The FBI found this information on their computers. Thank you, Lord, for delivering me from the mouths of the lions.

"Are you listening to what I'm saying? You need to take this seriously. Don't think that you are out of hot water. You may be in the clear as far as the *Sci-Fi Today* incident is concerned. But you are still on the FBI's list of problematic insiders, people *in the know* on the Taurus phenomenon whom they regard as potential troublemakers. You need to be on your best behavior. If you give them any further reason for concern, you will not only find yourself no longer employed by Cornell University, you won't be employed anywhere ever again." He spoke the last line with a dark tone designed to intimidate her. Irina cowered and stared blankly at him, unsure what he meant, but certain it wasn't good. He continued, "Let's just say that the authorities will put you in a situation where you and your unhealthy ways will be kept at bay permanently. No contact with the outside world. No legal recourse. No escape."

Irina's heart sank. *Maybe the rumors about Homeland Security arrestees being held in secret FEMA camps are true after all?* She sat in silence, occasionally touching a Kleenex to her moist eyes, wishing she could retreat to her apartment and have a good cry. She was hurting. She was battered into compliance for the time being. But she was unbroken and far from submission. Her tears merely salted her resolve.

Dr. Goldblum softened a little on seeing the change in her demeanor, not certain she was in the process of changing her ways, but hopeful. "If you keep your nose clean for the next six months and stay out of trouble, we might be able to pitch another research proposal for you. If you do your part, I will see what I can do about it. Okay?"

"Okay," she replied meekly. When he didn't continue with his onslaught but cracked a faint, slightly forced smile, Irina assumed that her ordeal was over and stood up to leave.

He motioned to her to remain sitting. "I might be done talking to you, but there are others who are waiting for their turn."

She nodded glumly and sat there trembling, not so much from fear, but from weariness and frustration.

Dr. Goldblum strode out, briskly walked down the hall to the unused room, and summoned two agents who had been patiently waiting. Without speaking a word, they rose and followed him back to his office.

Irina wasn't too surprised when two young men wearing suits and ties walked in. She looked down and noted their freshly polished black wingtips. *Feds. The government must be dead serious about the ban on communication.*

They were polite but curt. The taller one began, "We would like to ask you some questions."

Irina fixed her gaze on the one that had spoken. "What is the purpose of this visit? Why am I being interrogated?"

With a hint of a Boston accent, he replied, "Ma'am. We are not here to answer your questions. We are here to ask you questions."

She shot back, "That's miss, not ma'am."

"My apologies, miss." Their eyes locked for a moment, then he continued, "Do you have or have you ever had any association with Anonymous?"

"No."

"Do you know anything about the leak of classified information to *Sci-Fi Today*?"

"Only that somebody leaked classified information to *Sci-Fi Today*."

The questioning continued in this vein for a little over an hour. Abruptly they changed the tenor of the conversation from interrogation to pressure. "Are you willing to set aside your personal beliefs and work as a team player with your fellow team members?"

She looked intently at them, processing the question and her answer. *I have to comply. Otherwise, I may never have an opportunity to disseminate the truth about the Rogue.* "Yes. I can do that."

"Will you do that?"

"Yes. I will do that."

The grilling continued for another thirty minutes. They probed her commitment to her understanding of the anomaly in Taurus, her willingness to sacrifice her own opinions for corporate good, and her view on the apocalyptic teachings of the Bible. They enquired whether she thought it was possible that she might be reading her views on Bible prophecy into current events, imagining fulfillment where none exists. The questions were nerve-racking, but she figured she must have answered them satisfactorily because nothing came of her answers.

The taller agent brought the session to a close without warning. "That will be all. Thank you for your cooperation, Miss Kirilenko. There will be no further questioning at this time." With that, the two stood up and prepared to exit.

Irina blurted out, "Out of curiosity. What would happen to someone if they didn't comply? Let's say, for instance, that someone thought this situation called for Copernicus to challenge the 'accepted' paradigm? What if they believed that political expediency was trampling on science?"

"Then they would be taken into custody."

"On what basis would they be arrested?"

"I didn't say *arrested*. I said *taken into custody*."

"Then what does take into custody mean?"

The taller agent hesitated and looked to his partner. The shorter agent calmly answered, "It means to be treated like a prisoner of war: without rights, legal representation, or recourse. Criminals, who mistreat their fellow human beings, are arrested. Terrorists and security threats, who threaten the well-being of the entire nation, are taken into custody." He peered deep into her eyes. "You aren't rethinking your compliance are you?"

"No, sir." Irina was compliant on the outside. Her inner tiger, however, wanted to run amok and fix the stupidity that seemed to reign whenever politics got the upper hand over science. But she kept a firm grip on the tiger's chain, her grandfather's counsel echoing in her ear. "Outbursts of anger never fix anything. They break things. You need intelligent, controlled anger if you want to fix things."

After that day, the agents stopped by two or three times a week. They snooped around. They observed. And they made everyone feel nervous. Not even Dr. Goldblum seemed to appreciate their presence. But it was their detached and aloof demeanor that made folks the most nervous. They rarely talked. And they never smiled or laughed. Eventually, they became an inside joke at the Cahill Center. They were really experimental cyborgs developed in Area 51.

25

**Washington, D.C.
Thursday, June 28, 2018**

Jack slumped into his familiar booth at Madigan's—it had been a tough day at work—and made eye contact with the waitress. He and his entire department had been busting their butts with an extensive security upgrade for the past six months, working sixty to seventy hours per week. Now they were approaching their deadline, and things had gotten even more intense. As soon as dinner was over, he would be headed back to his office for another four or five hours of work. He was a little peeved. His bed tonight would be a cot, and his breakfast would be fast-food breakfast sandwiches, which always gave him indigestion. A shower wasn't going to happen, nor a shave. If he didn't put in north of a hundred hours this week, it would be a miracle.

He propped his right elbow on the table, leaned his head on his hand, and ruffled his hair, an odd little habit that he indulged when he was either frustrated or exhausted. He understood the push, the urgency. The president's security program was absolutely necessary to meet the threats and contingencies America faced in the increasingly complex world. We needed a massive technological gap between ourselves and the rest of the world so we could hack them, but they couldn't hack us. We needed this advantage in the face of the arms race with Russia and China, the ramping up of the war against terrorism and insurgency, and the war against the illicit drug trade and the illegal arms trade. But why did NASA need the same security and intelligence measures as the CIA and the NSA? Was something going on in high places that he wasn't privy to? Were the space race and the arms race now inseparably entangled? He wished he knew.

Jack was startled from his reflections when he noticed that Darleen was at his side with the coffee pot. "Let me guess," she said with a smile and her delightful Southern drawl, "the 12-ounce bourbon-soaked sirloin, medium rare, with western fries, and salad with ranch dressing."

"You get an *A* for the day, Darleen. I wish my new hires fresh out of college had a memory like that. My job would be twice as easy. They have political correctness coming out of their ears, and they can master video games like they were as easy as learning to eat pizza, but they struggle with applying the math and programming skills they supposedly learned, and they can't even remember basic office protocol. My name isn't *Dude*, it's *Jack*."

She smiled and departed with a little bounce in her step. He was pretty sure she was interested in him. But he wasn't ready for another relationship. Besides, he had his eye on a different woman, a highly unusual blonde. He hoped their paths crossed again some day. He caught himself indulging fond memories of her laughter and her adventuresome spirit. *Let it go, Jack. It probably isn't meant to be.*

While he ate his steak and fries, he turned his attention to the evening news with Geoff Seaworthy. "The Middle East is not, however, the only hot spot in the world. Europe is experiencing its own share of tensions. The tensest place this week is certainly Ukraine, where pro-Russia riots and violent insurgency are dominating the headlines again. Over the past three weeks, the violence in Kharkiv, Luhansk, and Donetsk has spiraled into full-blown war. The cease-fire is in tatters. The past week alone has seen many hundreds of Ukrainians killed, thousands more wounded, and the Ukrainian army in retreat. Officials in Kiev insist that the insurgency in Kharkiv and the Donbass has been transformed from ragtag units that were merely Russian armed to full-fledged battalions that are strengthened with Russian troops, including veteran NCOs, and commanded by Russian officers. They claim that more than twenty thousand Russian soldiers are operating in these two oblasts alone. This has drastically changed the dynamics on the battlefield, and the Ukrainian Armed Forces have proved no match for the Russian military. Again this morning, Kiev issued yet another plea to NATO, begging for intervention from the West before it is too late, before Ukraine is absorbed into the Russian Federation. To this point, NATO has done little more than posture, send a few token companies to the Baltic states, and bolster the Marine Corps presence at the U.S. embassy.

"But the violence in Ukraine is no longer limited to the East. The once relatively peaceful pro-Russia demonstrations in Zaporizhia, Dnipropetrovsk, Kherson, Mykolaiv, and Odessa have intensified into widespread violence and armed insurgency. In all five of these oblasts, well-armed separatist groups—the so-called local defense forces—have engaged in fierce gun battles with Ukrainian police and soldiers who were attempting to break up demonstrations that had gotten out of hand, with the demonstrators overturning cars, breaking windows, and setting fire to buildings and piles of tires. Ukraine intelligence believes there are ten thousand Russian soldiers in these oblasts masquerading as local separatists, stirring up discontent, and gathering Ukrainian membership. But, they warn us, this is just the beginning of the nightmare. There are another hundred thousand Russian soldiers at Rostov, Russia, near the border being trained in insurgency tactics and guerilla warfare, plus more than twenty thousand Ukrainians, who shall soon join their pro-Russia comrades in the local defense forces in the inflamed oblasts. If the West doesn't respond adequately, in a few short months these oblasts will be under full-blown Russian siege like the Donbass and Kharkiv are today.

"We sought interviews with the pro-Russia protesters and members of the local defense forces, but few would talk to us. A regional defense-force commander in Odessa, who was probably a Russian army officer, did agree to answer a few questions regarding the purpose of the protests and the local defense forces, but only if we came with no cameras or recorders. His answers were short and blunt. The primary purpose of the protests is the call for a referendum to secede from Ukraine and join the Russian Federation. The purpose of the local defense forces is to protect the protesters' right to protest and defend them from the illegal aggressions of the Ukrainian police force and the Ukrainian army. When we asked why they wanted to secede, he was equally blunt. He insisted that the Ukrainian people have far more in common with Russia than they do Europe and America and that they are far more likely to find peace and prosperity under the watchful eye of Mother Russia than the empty promises of Europe and America.

"We asked Ukrainian officials what branches of the Russian military they believed were behind the upheaval in eastern and Crimean Ukraine. They insisted that not only are SVR agents and Spetsnaz behind the recent upheaval in the troubled oblasts, but Russian volunteers from infantry and airborne units comprise over fifty percent of the members of the separatist groups. Moreover, they believe that the number of genuine pro-Russia volunteers is greatly inflated. In their estimation, the majority of the Ukrainian volunteers are troublemakers that have been lured by free cigarettes, vodka, and the prestige of carrying a Kalashnikov.

"We spoke with representatives of the Kremlin and asked them for their view of the situation and their response to the Ukrainian charges. They staunchly objected to the claim that Russia is behind the recent violence and vehemently denied that there are Russian troops in Ukraine other than a few peacekeepers in the Donbass. The Kremlin lays the blame for the situation solely on incompetent leadership in Kiev."

I wonder what Woody thinks about this turn of events in Ukraine? Jack mused. *He's been skeptical of my warnings about the return of the Russian Bear. It would be hard to stay skeptical in the face of news like this. Sure looking forward to our time together this summer. Gonna have lots to talk about around the campfires at night. Wanna hear Jordy's take on this matter too.*

The broadcast continued with its stream of bad news: the drought in Africa, Islamic radicals in Sudan beheading Christians, Greenland's melting glaciers and global warming, Russian involvement in Libya, five more states legalizing marijuana, another meteorite. Jack had just stood up to go pay for his dinner—he had heard enough unsettling news for a day—but when he heard the word *meteorite*, his ears perked up, and he sat back down. Meteorites and comets always caught his attention.

"Last night, the northern hemisphere experienced yet another large meteorite. Shortly after midnight Central time, a meteorite similar in size to the one that rattled Chelyabinsk made impact in the Canadian wilderness about seventy-five kilometers west of Churchill, Manitoba and ten kilometers south of the Seal River. Scientists are rushing to the area to search for the impact site in the hope that they can recover fragments for study. This impact, which they are calling the Churchill impact, was accompanied with many reports of exceptionally brilliant meteors along the sixtieth parallel—in eastern Canada, Greenland, Scotland, Scandinavia, the Baltic states, and western Russia—including an exceptionally large, bright-green bolide over Scotland."

Jack had an ominous feeling about the sharply increasing

numbers of meteors and meteorites. He was more nervous than ever that they were edging into the last days mentioned in Bible prophecy. *It seems surreal. It's starting to look like I might actually be around to see the end of the world.* As he contemplated the situation, he sensed a familiar jumble of emotions, the intertwined excitement and fear that enervate the soldier facing combat. *Let it come.*

26

Irina lay awake, fretting about the situation unfolding in America. The pieces were starting to fit together. The cover-up was massive. The government was taking enormous steps to keep the public ignorant of the Rogue. They had inaugurated their deception with three pieces of legislation in November 2017 that were blatant pretexts. Their duplicity was working like a charm. The populace was oblivious to the subtle cover-up being foisted upon them.

The NASA Bill had vastly expanded NASA's authority, giving them control over all of the nation's observatories, even privately owned facilities. This included the prerogative to assign and deny research projects. The stated purpose of this intrusive management was eliminating research overlap so NASA could expedite the CNEOS's objective to find and catalog NEOs. But the real purpose was to ensure that no astronomer stumbled upon the Rogue. Only a tiny handful of elite astronomers, vetted with Top Secret clearance, were made privy to the comet and allowed to conduct research in

Taurus. All other requests to conduct research in Taurus were turned down, and the applicant was given their second or third choice.

The Homeland Security Act had given federal law enforcement agencies the legal muscle they needed to stop Rogue leaks dead in their tracks. It outlined broad definitions of domestic terrorism and espionage. It expanded the concept of sensitive information that posed a threat to the security of the United States. And it authorized the detention of anyone suspected of the unauthorized possession or dissemination of sensitive information. Moreover, those detained under the Security Act were treated like prisoners of war: no Miranda warning, no formal arrest, no formal charge, no due process, and no access to an attorney.

While arrests under the Act covered a broad spectrum of security issues, internet rumor suggested that more than sixty percent involved the threat which had precipitated the Act in the first place—the Rogue. To mask the true reason behind Rogue arrests, the government leaked reports to the media which alleged that the arrested parties belonged to terrorist front organizations in cahoots with rogue nations like Russia, China, and Iran. Even CVN, the most conservative of all the major news agencies, had bought into this official version.

The Homeland Security Act had also made it a federal offense to disseminate reports which claimed or implied that the world faced an impending apocalyptic threat from the heavens. Such reports, per official communiqués explaining the Security Act, were regarded as a threat to America, liable to promote unrest and destabilize the nation. The media, at the behest of the government, further blackened the reports, portraying them as the subtle efforts of Russian agents, both SVR and GRU, to destabilize the country. This explanation seemed to satisfy the public.

The FEMA Bill was two-pronged. The first prong had enlarged FEMA and given it a directive to ensure that every state and local government was prepared for extreme-disaster eventualities like massive earthquakes, volcanoes, EMPs from the sun, terrorism (chemical, biological, or nuclear), and nuclear war. They were required to take whatever steps were necessary to protect their infrastructure, services, and citizens in the event of such calamities. But they were on their own for funding. No federal subsidies were available. And penalties would be imposed for noncompliance.

This bill had kicked off a flurry of construction efforts nationwide. State and local governments worked around-the-clock on underground shelters, government offices, supply depots, emergency infrastructure, water sources, and power supplies. Banks and technology companies moved their data centers and critical components underground. Here again, the media—serving up endless stories that fomented concern over Russian and Chinese aggression, nuclear terrorism, and EMPs from the sun—helped the government conceal the real reason for the construction, which was the Rogue.

The second prong had introduced FEMA camps as a convenient and inexpensive way to provide for the needs of the homeless. By the time the gates officially opened on the first dozen camps, however, the concept had been expanded to include the removal of the chronically unemployed from the government dole and the eradication of a broad range of undesirables infesting the cities: like drug runners, addicts, and prostitutes. Six weeks later, FEMA opened its first white-collar camp to house non-violent criminals like tax evaders, embezzlers, gambling cheats, and Ponzi schemers. Shortly thereafter, it was revealed that FEMA was also using them to hold soft terrorists, who were guilty of the unlawful possession and dissemination of sensitive information or the promotion of civil unrest with apocalyptic stories.

But the original and underlying purpose for the FEMA camps, as internet rumors had long insisted, was segregating individuals with knowledge of the Rogue from the rest of society. The other camp programs, derelict and white-collar, had originally been designed as a cover for this effort. They had worked so well, however, that they had gained a life of their own and were accepted by both sides of the political aisle as a brilliant solution to several long-standing problems.

Irina sighed. While there had been significant minority opposition to recent legislation on hate laws, homeschooling, alternative medicine, and gun rights, there was little uproar over the Homeland Security Act and the FEMA Bill. She could understand why most Americans wouldn't be upset if they saw the homeless and criminals being removed from the streets and placed in FEMA camps. But didn't it bother anyone that Bible-believing pastors, radio personalities, and internet-media moguls were disappearing into the abyss of the FEMA camps? How could this be happening in the land of the free? How did this sit right with the average Joe? Was the public entirely in the dark on what was really going on? Would her family and friends believe the Russian-agent nonsense when she was eventually taken into custody?

She shuddered and longed for the America that she had enjoyed when a teenager, where nobody disappeared over vague security infractions. Freedom was slowly going down the drain on the pretense of making America more secure, and men didn't seem to notice or care.

Weary of the cover-up and tired of thinking about it, she tried to put it out of mind. But she couldn't escape its ugly tentacles. Though trying to picture herself in a cabin in the Rockies with a fireplace, a grand piano, and a ballet barre, she found herself fretting about tomorrow morning when she had to sit through yet another two-hour training session on domestic terrorism, espionage, and security—a quarterly requirement for all employees of the Cahill Center since the Security Act. But exhaustion overwhelmed her worries, her eyelids grew heavy, and consciousness fled her.

***

Irina woke up again in the wee hours of the morning, still thinking about the cover-up and impatient with herself. It had been eight months since she had confirmed her fear that the government was covering up the approach of the Rogue, and she was still waiting for the right opportunity to get the information into good hands. Part of the problem was that she didn't have a workable plan. Who should she send the information to? When should she send it? How should she send it? And how could she access the information? The last hurdle was her biggest. Her usual means of access—work computer, laptop, and cellphone—were being monitored, so she couldn't access her documents without exposing their existence. Nor could she easily use an alternative means of access like a public computer or one belonging to a friend because she was being trailed.

But thinking about her need to come up with a plan touched the nerve of another problem she faced, the question of whether it was right for a Christian to engage in the kind of illegal activity that she was contemplating. She had been grappling with this moral dilemma off and on for months, and every time she had come to the same conclusion. Civil disobedience, active disobedience, and evasiveness were all commendable when dealing with governments that were severely corrupted. Then it was a right, even a duty, to do so.

There was no question that the French Underground was right to do so under the Nazi puppets of Vichy France. And she was convinced that activities like smuggling Bibles into countries that banned them or preaching the gospel in nations that ban evangelism were praiseworthy in God's eyes. But the efforts of the present administration to cover up the evidence that a comet threatened Earth with an apocalypse of biblical magnitude didn't seem to be quite the same. It did seem wrong. But was it wrong enough? The agents and the education officials certainly had a way of making her feel wrong—guilty—for her concealed desire to buck the ban and let the world know. Sometimes, she wished she could just forget about the comet and go on with life.

But she couldn't. Surrendering to convenience or taking a path that reeked of quisling-esque principles was not in her blood.

Her father's advice challenged her. "It never feels right to do right when everyone thinks that right is wrong. You can't trust your feelings in a firestorm. Right isn't a feeling. Right isn't comfortable. Right is a path, a path often difficult and reproached." Irked at herself, she resolved that she was done worrying about the matter. It was time for action, time to seize the day. *Just suck it up and own it, girl.* She just needed to start going forward and, God helping her, do whatever needed to be done. There was too much at stake, including innocent lives. She prayed that God would open doors and coordinate things. That part was out of her league. If he opened doors, she would take them. If he coordinated, she would capitalize. Immediately, she felt bathed in peace, the calm that comes with resolve, and soon drifted off to sleep once again.

***

Two days later, Dr. Goldblum called her into his office and informed her that she was going to be allowed to take a Thanksgiving vacation after all. As of that morning—he waved a letterhead in front of her—she was officially removed from Homeland Security's Orange One list. That meant that she was free from her domestic travel restriction.

She nodded and silently thanked God. She had acted unwisely in the matter of the congratulation letter from the MPC, and that indiscretion had led to her demotion at the time of the *Sci-Fi Today* raid. Since that time, she had gone to great lengths to improve her image and be a model employee. The efforts had paid off. Now she might actually get an opportunity to repay their duplicity with her own.

He snapped his finger and caught her attention. "Are you still with me, Miss Kirilenko?" He held her gaze for a moment. "I am glad that you have been removed from Orange One. However, you are still on Orange Two. You are still regarded by the FBI as a threat. Please exercise caution. Don't abuse your freedom. One misstep, and you'll be back on Orange One permanently. One big slip-up, and you'll be living with the lowlifes in a FEMA camp, eating horsemeat and outdated hotdogs."

27

It was a gorgeous fall day, and Irina was enjoying an evening stroll in the park, marveling at the myriad hues of the autumn foliage. But her primary reason for the walk wasn't indulging the beauty of nature. It was figuring out a solution for her situation. Walking cleared her mind and helped her grapple with perplexing questions. Time was running out. She needed to get the evidence for the Rogue into capable hands, hands that wouldn't ignore or bury the unsettling information for the sake of convenience or gain. She knew several people she could trust, but the recipient needed more than trustworthiness. They needed access to suitable astronomical software and the expertise to operate it. Moreover, they needed to be fearless and cunning, ensuring that the information would get disseminated regardless of the obstacles. She only had one shot. In her brother Illya's military lingo, it was a go/no-go operation.

Her contemplations were distracted by a group of young ladies—they appeared to be Renaissance buffs—wearing period dresses, sporting flowers in their hair, and carrying pitchers and woven baskets. They were having their pictures taken in poses, alone and in groups, by a photographer. The scene reminded her of Ariele Serrafe, a quirky acquaintance from her Caltech days. She was unique—a hippie chick with a stunning IQ, like Rainbow Family meets Einstein. Irina smiled as memories danced through her head. She liked her, but they had never hit it off as friends. They were just too different, like night and day. *Wait a minute. Ariele is precisely the person I need.* She was trustworthy. She was an exceptionally intelligent astronomer. She had access to the necessary software. Her moral compass was exactly what the situation called for. She was death on corruption and duplicity, and she was relentless and fearless for causes that she believed were right. She could be trusted to do the right thing with the information.

Having settled on her contact, the rest of her plan in its rough details came together easily. She decided to mail the information to Ariele during Thanksgiving break. The five days she would have off would give her plenty of time to access her Buster account, load the documents and images onto a DVD, package it anonymously, drive to a distant location, mail the package, and drive back. She just had to work through the details, including how to shake the agents that would almost certainly be tailing her.

With the load off her shoulders and a sense of serenity returning, she turned her focus back on the wonders of God's creation. In the distance the hoot of an owl echoed through the trees. Overhead, a flock of geese was noisily preparing to land on a nearby lake. A squirrel scampered up a white pine and scolded her. And the sinking sun was bathing the clouds in majestic reds and oranges. *God is still in charge, and things are going to work out. They may not work out the way that I would like them to. But they will definitely work out.*

28

Irina entered the CCAPS building and found it strangely quiet. When she walked into her department, it was empty. No one was at their workstations. The offices were empty. The silence—like the still of a graveyard—was unnerving. *This is really odd.* She glanced at her watch in case she had shown up an hour early. After all, she did occasionally have her blonde moments. Her grandpa used to tease her about dying her hair brunette. It was 7:48 a.m. That was a few minutes early, but not early enough for her to be the first one to arrive. Now she was thoroughly confused.

She fished her cell phone out of her purse and checked the day. It was definitely Monday as she had thought. *What is going on?* Had there been an emergency or an emergency drill? Did she forget about a scheduled meeting? Where was her cubicle mate? Sandy's chair was pushed back from her workstation and turned as if she had just stepped away. She walked up for a closer investigation and noticed that she was logged in and her program was open. *Strange.* She reached out and touched Sandy's coffee cup. It was still quite warm. *Really strange.*

Her thoughts were interrupted by muffled human voices. She walked around the corner to investigate and heard what sounded like the droning of a television in the distance. As she approached the break room at the end of the hallway, a cacophony of exclamations erupted which drowned out the programming: "Wow!," "Whoa!," "Insane!," along with a bevy of coarse expressions. She hurried down the hall and peeked into the room to see what the commotion was about.

A female newscaster was pointing on a map of Asia to a red circle near the center of Mongolia and talking a mile a minute. "Early Monday morning, around 2 a.m. Ulaanbaatar time, an extremely large meteor streaked across the East China Sea in a north-westerly direction, then across eastern China, and ultimately impacted in the mountainous region of Övörkhangai, southwest of Ulaanbaatar. There were only a handful of witnesses, all in Mongolia. Apparently, the meteor came in at a fairly low angle, traveled unseen across the open spaces of the Pacific Ocean, passed between Taiwan and the Okinawa Islands while both were socked in by heavy clouds from Typhoon Usagi, then passed over an overcast eastern China and Gobi Desert before dropping beneath the clouds deep in Mongolia.

"The witnesses, we have been told, were a few nomadic families who were grazing their livestock in the area and an Englishman on assignment with National Geographic. This area will be very difficult for the authorities and researchers to reach. The Englishman, who was staying with one of the families, informed us that they were camped about two days horse ride from the nearest road and that the impact site is another seven or eight hours further away. Apparently, there are three families missing and feared dead. As of this time, the Mongolian government has said pointedly that they cannot comment on the matter until their investigation is completed. It is believed that they have people at the site at this time, assisted by a team from China. China is not saying anything. The Russian news outlets are silent. Both countries have banned all air traffic over their territory adjacent to Mongolia until further notice, effectively hindering access by any outside observers to the site.

"The impact was so forceful that originally the suspicion among U.S. intelligence was that a nuclear device had been detonated, most likely an illegal test by North Korea, China, or Russia. But when triangulation traced the event to Mongolia, authorities were nonplussed. For the next sixteen hours, the government officials and agencies involved were stumped. Various theories and conjectures were floated, but none gained any traction except the meteorite-impact theory. Nobody was certain though, and the agencies involved were in a holding pattern, waiting for more information.

"Less than an hour ago, however, we received a phone call from the BBC that one of their contacts in Mongolia, the Englishman mentioned a moment ago, had breaking news. The seismic event appears to have been a meteor that made impact early Monday morning, Ulaanbaatar time.

"Joining us live from Övörkhangai aimag—province—in Mongolia via satellite feed, approximately forty kilometers from the impact site, is Harry Wetherington. Good evening, Harry."

"Good morning to you, Heather."

"I understand, Harry, that you are currently returning from a visit to the impact site."

"That is correct. We are around forty kilometers from the impact site and about sixteen kilometers from our ger, often called a yurt in the outside world. It has been a long, grueling day on horseback, traversing extremely rugged territory."

"What time is it there now?"

"Heather, it is 7:55 p.m. The sky is blanketed with stars, and we are enjoying a magnificent view of the Milky Way, the kind you can only experience in the remotest regions of Earth."

"Wish I could see that for myself. Not much of a night sky here in the Big Apple. But back to our story. It is my understanding, Harry, that you are the sole source of intel coming out of Mongolia at this time."

"That's what I have been told, Heather. And it wouldn't surprise me if that were true. There is no cell-phone service for over a hundred kilometers. Nobody in the region except myself has a satellite phone. None of the locals would have had time yet to ride out to civilization because we are two long, hard days on horseback—with blankets, mind you, not saddles—from the nearest road. And that barely qualifies as a road. It is four-wheel drive only. You need a Land Rover, a Russian UAZ, or something similar to negotiate it."

"Are there any officials or investigators at the site?"

"Yes, there are, Heather. At around 3 p.m. local time, we

observed two large helicopters flying over the site with Chinese markings, accompanied by a smaller helicopter that belonged to the Mongolian Air Force. A half hour later, two more helicopters arrived. They landed approximately two kilometers from our observation point and disembarked soldiers which appeared to be both Chinese and Mongolian. It was hard to determine with certainty. At that distance, my binoculars were unable to resolve the uniform details."

"Were they setting up a perimeter?"

"No. They spread out in small teams and appeared to be searching the area. Several were using what appeared to be Geiger counters, and others were gathering soil and air samples."

"Does there appear to be any danger from radiation or poison?"

"I have no information at this time except that I don't see any panic or haste among the soldiers. But if my hair falls out, I'll give you a call." *Where do they come up with these questions? I carry a lot of cool tools in my duffel, but I don't carry a Geiger counter or a chemistry set.*

"How long do you think it will be before the Mongolian officials give us an official news release on this event?"

Gee, let me turn on my ESP for a few minutes and tap into their brains, and I'll get back to you shortly. "Well, Heather, the Mongolian officials and their Chinese partners have only been at the site for approximately seven hours. Their investigation is still in its early stages. I'm guessing that we might have to wait another forty-eight hours before they release an initial statement." *If it were only the Mongolians, we would likely have heard something already. But with the Chinese involved, we may be forced to wait a week or two. They love to annoy the West with such tactics.*

"Tell us your story."

"Certainly, Heather. I have been in the area since May, living with a nomadic family in their summer ger, working on a project for National Geographic. Last night we stayed up late around a campfire, drinking airag—fermented horse milk—with four hunting guides who were passing through. The men swapped tales of run-ins with wolves, bandits, poachers, opium smugglers, and Chinese soldiers. We had let the fire die down and were getting ready for bed around 2 a.m. local time when a large glow in the low-hanging clouds streaked across the north-eastern horizon, followed by a large flash behind the mountains to our north, followed shortly after by a loud explosion. My heart raced. I thought to myself, 'that was either one blooming huge bomb or one blooming huge meteorite.' I watched the horizon for several minutes, a tad nervous, but the flash was not followed by a mushroom cloud, so I figured I would probably still be alive in the morning. Relieved, I went to bed.

"Early the next morning, my host, his brother, his cousin, the four guides, and I crawled out of bed, quickly downed our breakfast—a bowl of milk tea with millet and lamb jerky—saddled our horses, and headed north from the ger about 7 a.m., shortly before sunrise. We wanted to investigate the situation. It took us seven hours to reach the ridge that overlooked the area of the explosion. It was in a shambles. The trees had been blown over into a tangled mess, making access very difficult. On the far side of the valley, about two kilometers away, we observed a crater around three hundred meters in diameter. Everything in the immediate area was burned or blackened. The trees were knocked down for more than two kilometers from the destruction zone, both up and down the valley. The pungent odor of sulfur hung heavy in the air.

"Heather, the devastation from this meteor was simply enormous. If it had landed on or near a small town, it would have been decimated.

"About a half hour after we arrived on the ridge, we were joined by a weeping woman, with her husband and children, who explained that her parents and two brothers, with their wives and families, had pitched their gers in this valley a few weeks earlier and that she feared that the flying death worm had killed them. She and her husband had seen the death worm fly over their heads, burning with red, yellow, and blue flames.

"About 2:40 p.m., while we were observing the site, two jets flew in from the north about five kilometers west of us, circled back around, then flew directly over the area low and slow, giving us the opportunity to positively identify them as Russian. When they finished their flyover, they accelerated on their northward flight, presumably returning to Belaya Air Base in Irkutsk.

"Twenty minutes later, around 3 p.m., the first of the Chinese and Mongolian helicopters arrived on site and made several runs over the impact area in a fairly tight formation. As I mentioned earlier, they were later joined by two further helicopters which landed in the valley bottom, about half a kilometer from the impact crater and unloaded soldiers, civilians, and equipment. We continued to observe the site and the operation until shortly before 4 p.m. when two smaller Chinese helicopters arrived and began flying patrol around the perimeter of the area. On their first pass over the ridge we were on, they noticed us. They circled back around twice and buzzed us. Both times, we held our ground. The third time, the door gunner opened fire about two hundred meters before our position and continued firing until they were about thirty meters from us. We got the message. We picked up our gear, scrambled our way back over the fallen timber to our horses—a little spooked from the gunfire—untethered them, mounted up, and headed back toward our peaceful ger."

"You mentioned that the meteor had colored flames. Do you have any idea what significance the colored flames might hold?"

"Heather, I have no idea why the flames were multi-colored. *For crying out loud, I studied photography and cultural anthropology, not chemistry.* I can only tell you that the locals saw what appeared to them to be a flying death worm with red, yellow, and blue flames. And it scared them half to death."

The interview ended, and the commentator turned to her next guest in the studio, an expert on meteors and meteorites at the Smithsonian Institute. "Dr. Franconi, what do you think the significance of the colored flames is?"

"I am going to guess that the yellow indicates sodium,

the blue sulfur, and the red probably strontium."

"Is there any chance that this death worm might actually have deadly qualities like radioactivity?"

"Great question, Heather. I am curious about that myself. The red flames are provocative, for they suggest strontium. And some isotopes, like strontium-89 and strontium-90, are radioactive. While these isotopes do not occur naturally here on Earth, that doesn't mean that they don't occur in other parts of the solar system."

"Are there any other potentially deadly traits that can be associated with meteors?"

"Yes. Some comets have evidenced cyanogen gas in their tails. If such a comet made impact in a populated area, that could be problematic."

"And what kind of physical evidence can the parties on the ground expect to find apart from the crater, the ash, and the devastation?"

"Fragments of the meteor, which are technically referred to as meteorites, along with impact diamonds, fullerenes, and minerals that are indicative of extraterrestrial origin."

After several more minutes of discussion on the minerals, poisons, and radioactivity that could be associated with an impact event, the interview grew less interesting, and the crew began to disperse.

Dr. Goldblum sauntered up to Irina and crowed, "Maybe this death worm is the beginning of a parabolic increase in comet activity as your theory suggests? Wouldn't that be exciting if your theory was vindicated?" He studied her face, looking for affirmation. She managed a feeble smile. He continued fishing for praise, "I sent an email to The Meteoritical Society and suggested that they name the Mongolian event Deathworm. Has a dark ring to it, don't you think?" She nodded morosely. She wasn't in the mood for conversation, much less stroking his ego. The narcissist flashed an uneasy smile and retreated to his office.

Irina felt a heaviness in her breast as she watched her boss walk away. If she was right, this impact belonged to the early contractions before the actual labor pains. Things were going to get a whole lot worse. Her heaviness contrasted with Dr. Goldblum's creepy glee. All he was thinking about was the opportunity for fame and glory that might accrue for hotshot astronomers if her apocalyptic scenario proved true. As for the name Deathworm, it was certainly appropriate. But she still didn't like it. It sounded too much like Wormwood.

29

Two weeks before she received the life-altering package from Irina, Ariele was enjoying a late-night drive through the San Gabriels on her way back from Mt. Wilson. She noticed that the clock on the radio dial said 11:01, so she switched from her fave indie/reggae station to YMMR so she could catch the *Down the Rabbit Hole* program with Burrage "Butch" Krakenhavn. It came on the air seven days a week at 11 p.m. A golden, husky voice resonated, "We cover the world's biggest stories without the usual dollop of media bias, report the news that the news doesn't report, investigate conspiracy stories—real and imagined, and dive into that mysterious realm where it is sometimes difficult to tell the truth from fiction."

She enjoyed listening to Butch. He had a wonderful radio voice, once voted the best voice on California radio. More importantly, she appreciated his commentary on news and politics. He was his own man—a bit of a maverick—who followed no political or religious party line. On some issues he was right-leaning and others left-leaning, but on most he was an even-keeled independent. If he had a downside, it was his penchant for conspiracy theories and X Files type stuff. He also had a man-crush fascination with a prophecy in the Bible in the book of Ezekiel about Russia.

While the quirky stuff held little attraction for her, it did serve a useful purpose. It kept his program on the air. Most of his audience, judging by his callers, ate that stuff up. She snirkled—her whimsical and fleeting snorty-laugh—as she contemplated the gullibility of such folks. They were loose on the hinges and lived in their own little world, a conspiracy-infested world, where it was easier to catch a conspiracy than a cold.

Overall, she enjoyed his program. Whether she was nodding in agreement, or amused at his lunacy, or angered at one of his positions, he was always interesting enough to keep her awake and on the road while driving home at night.

He was on his Russia hobbyhorse again. "Tonight, we bring you more developments in our continuing coverage of the rise of the Gog and Magog juggernaut. If you are new to our program, Gog and Magog, along with Rosh and Tubal, are ancient peoples mentioned in the prophecy in Ezekiel 38 and 39, who inhabited the region from the Black Sea to the Baltic Sea. Over the twenty-six centuries since this prophecy was given, these peoples melded together, digested an inflow of Scandinavian peoples, and became the modern nation of Russia.

"As you already know, Russia annexed the eastern third of Ukraine five months ago. Now they are stretching their tentacles further. Over the past few weeks, the riots that roiled the East prior to its annexation have introduced turmoil to many towns in the West. The cry of the rioters is 'No divided Ukraine,' and this seems to resonate with the man on the street. There is a growing consensus among Ukrainians that it would be better to be united under Russian hegemony than divided. They regard the loss of freedom under Russian domination as more bearable than trying to exist under a West Ukraine and East Ukraine dichotomy.

"But Ukraine is not the only place in Europe where pro-Russia fomentation is upsetting the population. Over the past month, as we have reported on several occasions, pro-Russia riots have turned violent in major cities in Belarus and the Baltic states: Minsk, Vilnius, and Riga to name a few.

"This does not surprise me. We have been following the rise of both Belarusian and Baltic pro-Russia separatist groups for the past eight months. Whether the sleepwalkers in the West believe it or not, this hankering for a return to the glory of the Soviet Union, which I have dubbed *Motherland Spring*, is rapidly spreading in the former Soviet satellites. Before it finishes running its course, every former satellite that is not completely integrated with the West will be given an ultimatum: either get crushed in a bloodbath or return to the Motherland.

"In the past seventy-two hours, we have received reports that the violence has turned up a notch in Belarus, Lithuania, and Latvia, with gunfights between regular army troops and the separatists. Our contact in Belarus, a former colonel in the Soviet army, claims that Russian Spetsnaz and SVR agents are working with the separatist groups, providing leadership, training, and weapons.

"This raises a frightening question. Will Belarus and the Baltic states fall to Russia as Crimea, the Donbass, and eastern Ukraine have fallen, and western Ukraine appears poised to fall? In my estimation, the answer is an emphatic *yes*. Not only do we see Russian-aided insurgency groups destabilizing Belarus and the Baltic states, but the Russian government is expanding and upgrading the supposedly decommissioned Smolensk North air base and amassing enormous amounts of troops and equipment there, including two armored divisions, two airborne divisions, and more than two hundred aircraft. And we see large numbers of troops and equipment being massed at another dozen locations along the Belarussian and Latvian borders.

"It does not take three decades of experience in the CIA with the Office of Russian and European Analysis to see that the Russian government is determined to link the landlocked archipelago of Kaliningrad with Mother Russia and gain access to the port at Riga. Whether they accomplish this with a mere show of force that intimidates Belarus and the Baltic states into capitulation, or whether they find it necessary to invade, rest assured, they will occupy these unfortunate states and make them vassals of the Russian Federation. Folks, this is going to happen. It's only a matter of time. Come out of your stupor. Quit drinking that Neville Chamberlain Kool-Aid. Wake up. Russia is no more to be trusted than Nazi Germany.

"There are two other Russian stories in the news today. The first is that both Iran and Libya signed a mutual defense pact with Russia this week and an associated agreement that permits her to build naval and air bases in their sovereign territories. This offers mutual benefits. On Russia's side, it vastly expands her regional and strategic capabilities, giving her, among other things, valuable warm water ports in the Indian Ocean and the Mediterranean Sea. On the Iranian and Libyan side, it buffers these nations from their enemies. We can only imagine how nervous this must make the brass in the hallowed halls of the Pentagon. It certainly changes the balance of power in the Mediterranean and the Persian Gulf.

"The second is that Russia has begun the construction of facilities at twelve military bases in the western and southern regions of Iran and at fourteen of Iran's most vital nuclear sites. All of these facilities are being built by Russian personnel in immediate proximity to existing Iranian missile and nuclear sites. Furthermore, these facilities will fly the Russian flag and will be manned and operated by Russian personnel. This puts Israel in an impossibly difficult position. She now risks killing Russian civilians and military personnel were she to attempt to destroy any of Iran's most significant missile or nuclear sites. On top of this, were she to invade Iranian airspace, she would find herself facing Russian jets as well as Iranian. No matter how you slice it, Israel now has no viable options to defend herself from the Iranian threat. Humanly speaking, it looks as if Iran now holds all the trump cards.

"In related Gog and Magog juggernaut news, Germany distanced herself even further this week from her EU and NATO partners. Against their advice, she signed an economic cooperation package with Russia which includes importing natural gas and oil at a discount and exporting German goods and technology on favorable terms. This is in keeping with a slow but steady Rusward trend we have been watching for a while. Over the past few years, Germany has often expressed her desire to enjoy closer ties with Russia and her frustration at NATO's unwillingness to cooperate with Russia in the Middle East.

"This became a major point of contention last September at the NATO summit in Istanbul when Germany criticized the West, in particular the U.S., for seeming to delight in antagonizing and ostracizing Russia. Things came to a head in October when Germany stormed out of the EU summit in Luxembourg, angered by policies she claimed were designed to punish strong economies and reward weak ones. She vowed she would no longer carry the European economy on her back. Her trade agreement two weeks ago with Russia seems to prove that this was no empty threat.

"What can we expect next? There are rumors afloat that Germany has been engaged in secret talks with Russia on the possibility of military cooperation and alliance. If this is true, the writing is on the wall. Such talks are nothing less than a harbinger of Germany's eventual departure from both NATO and the EU and her realignment with her Slavic cousins in Russia, a change we have long anticipated and predicted based on the ancient prophecy found in Ezekiel 38 and 39."

Ariele found herself strangely allured by this report and the Ezekiel prophecy. It seemed like God was drawing her to something much bigger than herself, like she had a date with destiny. This was an unusual feeling for her as she had shunned religion for years. She hadn't felt strong religious inclinations since she was ten years old. But the seed had been planted. She vaguely recalled her grandfather on her mother's side, a devout Orthodox Jew of Sephardic lineage, talking about this prophecy when she was a little girl, insisting that God was going to deliver Israel from her enemies in the last days by a fiery vengeance from heaven. They weren't going to deliver themselves. America wasn't going to deliver them. God himself was going to deliver them. For the first time since her childhood, she felt a desire to tap into whatever it is that Jewish people were supposed to tap into. *GOD, help me to find whatever I'm supposed to find and do whatever I'm supposed to do.*

She was interrupted by a riff from the theme music of *The Da Vinci Code* which opened the conspiracy segment of the program. "Our big conspiracy story this evening is the arrest yesterday of a dozen prominent webcasters, owners of some of the biggest conspiracy websites, men who have long tried to bring the American people the truth on topics like reptilians, Big Brother government, Planet X, and the end of the world. The official report coming from the major media outlets claims that the arrests were pursuant to the Homeland Security Act and that the arrested were members of a terrorist network whose purpose is promoting anarchy in America. Yada, yada, yada.

"While we have no confirmation, these reporters were probably taken to FEMA camps, where they will be given an opportunity to mend their ways and become productive citizens. In other words, they will be taught to think and say only what they are permitted to think and say.

"As for the arrests, while the official account is certainly plausible for there are real terrorists in America, I and my associates suspect that something deeper is going on here.

"First of all, as many of you already know, Security Act arrests are dubious. Many have been charged with the possession of sensitive information merely for being privy to the Rogue. Others have been charged with promoting civil disorder merely for preaching that the asteroid impacts in the book of Revelation are real and will happen soon. The fact is, arrests under the Security Act have nothing to do with genuine terrorism. Real terrorists are always charged under older terrorism legislation.

"Secondly, the arrested have one thing in common. Last week, they broke an intriguing story about a potential Planet X scenario based on material leaked by Anonymous. That story, like the *Sci-Fi Today* story a year ago, exploded on the internet. Supposedly, a massive comet has been discovered that is currently about five hundred million miles beyond Neptune. This invader, nicknamed the Rogue, will smash its way through the asteroid belt and pass within 20,000 miles of Mars, directly intersecting the Red Planet's orbital path.

"Thirdly, a rumor has been spreading through the internet grapevine claiming that the websites of the arrested were shut down, that their employees and volunteer help were also arrested, and that the contents of their homes were confiscated and loaded into semi-trucks. We are currently trying to verify these reports. At this time, the only thing we can verify is that all twelve websites are now showing '404 Not Found' error messages.

"By the way, as is usual with Security Act arrests in the past six months, most of these recent arrests were made by plainclothes agents who declined to identify which agency they worked for. When asked, they merely replied, 'That is classified.' Folks, are you wondering like I am, who in the habanero these mysterious plainclothesmen are? We intend to get to the bottom of this question in a future episode. So, don't miss a single hour of this program. You never know when we are going to *out* the truth you need to hear.

"But let's move on to the Planet X story itself. Folks, this massive comet is MASSIVE. According to the leaked information, based on data from the NEOCam, Spitzer, and WISE space telescopes, the comet is shaped like a rutabaga, measuring 5800 kilometers tip to top and 4900 kilometers across the top. It has approximately the same mass as a spherical body with a diameter of 5200 kilometers. The irregular shape is why the original measurement was so far off. During the occultation in September 2017, only the tip of the comet transited the star, leaving astronomers with the impression that it had a diameter of 900 to 1000 kilometers.

"Furthermore, not only is the comet extremely large, it is extremely dense. A spectrographic survey conducted by the Spitzer space telescope indicates that it is essentially iron, with large amounts of nickel, platinum-group metals, and heavy rare-earth minerals.

"Let me put the size and density in perspective. This comet is eighty percent of the diameter of Mars. That is unbelievably gargantuan. And it is so dense that its mass is approximately the same as that of the Red Planet.

"If there is any truth at all to this story, we are facing a terrifying scenario, one that exposes the hollowness of most of our apocalyptic talk. This comet could easily knock a few asteroids into elliptical orbits when it passes through the asteroid belt, posing an eventual threat to Earth. We don't even want to think about what might happen were it to collide with Mars.

"By the way, the simple fact that the NEOCam, WISE, and Spitzer space telescopes are involved in this story is an intelligence gold mine. Bear in mind that the NEOCam was originally slated to be a warm mission. She was supposed to be fitted with sensors that are sensitive to relatively warm temperatures, an outfitting ideal for the search for asteroids in the asteroid belt. But her warm-mission sensors would have been unable to observe a comet in the frigid regions beyond Uranus. This implies that NASA must have retooled the NEOCam before launch, replacing at least one of its slated sensors with one able to detect colder temperatures.

"The WISE and the Spitzer telescopes would have also required retooling before employment in a cold mission. The former had long ago used up its liquid hydrogen coolant and the latter its liquid helium coolant. Until recently, both were used only for warm missions, primarily asteroid research in the asteroid belt. So, NASA must have revitalized them: replenishing their coolant, reprogramming them with new mission instructions, and replacing the original sensors in the WISE. Otherwise, they would not have been able to take images and surveys of the comet while it was yet far beyond Neptune.

"The bottom line is, the government implemented a huge change in mission when they had NASA retool the NEOCam telescope prior to launch, and they threw a ton of money at NASA to revitalize the WISE and Spitzer space telescopes. The Anonymous leak claims NASA spent over seven billion dollars to refurbish Space Shuttle Atlantis, fast track the mission to revitalize the two space telescopes, and actually execute the mission. The retooling, the vast expenditure, and the fast-track priority imply that the White House and NASA are worried about this comet—very worried."

Burrage trotted out his Paul Harvey impersonation. "And now you know the real reason why NASA brought Space Shuttle Atlantis out of retirement in January of 2018 and had her ready for launch by August 2018." She snickered at his miserable attempt as he continued in his normal voice, "I hope my listeners remember that I went out on a limb at the time and claimed that the official story—deployment of two sensitive satellites, solar-wind experiments, and a graviton-deflection experiment—were a crock of malarkey.

"So, what is my analysis of this story? How high does it score on the world-famous Krakenhavn Meter? Let me preface my score with two observations.

"First of all, those who listen to this show regularly know that I believe that most of the internet doomsday and X Files type stuff is written by whack jobs who prefer sensationalism over journalism, confuse superstition with facts, and pretend that their tabloid drivel is investigative reporting. I don't exempt Planet X stories from this judgment. It has been my position for years that the vast majority of Planet X stories belong in the same category as bigfoot, the Loch Ness monster, and green men from Mars.

"Secondly, even if this is just another bogus Planet X story, what is the harm? Where is the harm for society if Planet X is just an apocalyptic tall tale? So what if a handful of unstable, gullible folks think that an extinction event that happens once every thirty thousand years is likely to happen in their lifetime? So what if these folks store up food and bottled water in their basement? Who are they hurting? What unrest are they spreading in society? They only thing they are spreading is a few laughs. And their panic buying is good for the economy.

"But having said this, well, I am going to give it the highest score I have ever given a space-threat story. I am going to rate it a very high eighty-five percent probability that the core of the story is true even if the details need to be revisited. And let me tell you why.

"The feds are not going around shutting down websites and arresting webmasters for propagating bigfoot stories, or spinning yarns of an ancient civilization on Mars, or claiming contact with UFOs. But they have been shutting down websites and arresting webmasters over Planet X stories—not the mere theory, but real-life candidates for a Planet X scenario. Most of these arrests have involved the mysterious, unseen comet known as the Rogue. This raises a big question mark in my mind. Is it possible that the doomsdayers have actually uncovered something that the government doesn't want to be uncovered? What if amidst all the nonsense, paranoia, and sensationalism there was a kernel of truth that the government was bent on covering up until it could no longer be covered up? Think about it." The closing music started to play.

"If you enjoyed our coverage today on Planet X intrigue, then don't miss the rest of the story. Over the next few weeks, we will bring you more information on the rogue comet that many believe is headed for a rendezvous with Mars. The information we have received is truly startling. Not mere theories cranked out by crackpots, but purported facts from apparently reputable sources.

"Well, our time is up. Tune in tomorrow evening. I will be covering the legendary Paulding Light. Is it supernatural or natural? This is Burrage Krakenhavn signing off. Don't believe anything you hear on late-night radio unless you hear it here."

Ariele laughed. Sometimes, they make this stuff sound so realistic that you almost feel compelled to believe it. This comet story certainly belonged in that category. It was one of Butch's best yet. A comet that was eighty percent the size of Mars knocking asteroids around like pool balls on a pool table, sending them on orbits which could pose a threat to Earth? That would make a decent summer blockbuster.

30

As it turned out, Irina's Thanksgiving vacation didn't land on Thanksgiving weekend. New guidelines had been issued in October for every institution and agency involved in the Minoa Project. One of the new stipulations was a requirement to maintain a minimum of fifty percent of staff on duty at all times. This meant that federal holidays would be observed in split shifts. Irina was assigned to team B, who were informed that they would be taking their vacation a week early. She didn't mind. She was just thankful that she was given vacation time, providing her the opportunity she needed to do her spy thing. Thankfully, the change didn't affect the cover story she had planned, a ski trip with friends in the Adirondacks. In mid-November two early snowstorms had arrived back-to-back, blanketing upstate New York with four feet of snow.

Her plan was to join three friends from her church for a girls' outing to Lake Placid, where they would stay at the Courtyard, a hotel in the Marriott family. Her friends were going to spend their days tackling the slopes at Whiteface

Mountain while she was going to spend hers, supposedly, holed up in her room, soaking in the hot tub and catching up on her reading—Tolstoy's *War and Peace*, cover to cover, in the original Russian. In the evenings they would rendezvous for dinner and shopping.

The group arrived at the hotel in Olivia's green Outback shortly after ten. They checked in, carried their luggage to their rooms, and ordered pizza. While they were waiting for their dinner, Irina pulled Olivia aside. "Olivia, can I borrow your car? I need to go somewhere." Olivia's Subaru was ideal because it was all-wheel drive and didn't have GPS.

"Sure. Where?"

"I can't … I don't … I'll tell you later."

"How long are you going to be gone? A couple hours?"

Irina grimaced, embarrassed. "Until Sunday afternoon."

"What?!" Olivia snapped. "That's the whole weekend! I thought we were doing a girl thing together. That was the point of this whole trip, wasn't it? You were the one that suggested it, planned it, and talked us all into it."

Irina tried to soothe the situation. "I understand your disappointment. I am truly sorry. But I just have to do this."

"This? What is *this*? And where will you be doing *this*? What is so important that you need three days to do it, and you can't even talk about it to one of your friends?"

"I'd rather not talk about it. Not yet anyway. I promise that I will tell you everything after things have run their course whether for good or for bad."

Olivia brightened a bit. "Wait a minute. Is there a guy in your life? Is this why you keep turning Cameron Braddick down? What have you been hiding from me, girl? This guy must be quite the catch. You had us all wondering if you didn't have a guy on the string somewhere. Otherwise, we couldn't understand why you would turn down the hottest, hunkiest, most eligible bachelor at New Life Church."

Guy angle. Hmmm. Maybe I can work this. "Yeah. There is a big fella involved. He's a rogue in the eyes of many, but ever since I discovered him, I've found myself strangely attracted to him. I believe the whole situation is a matter of divine destiny."

"But why now? Why this weekend? Why do you have to bail on your girlfriends at the last minute? Couldn't you take care of this at some other time?"

"Things came together pretty quickly. And the way they came together didn't leave me any other options. With the direction he is going, and the way things are going in my life, this weekend was my best, maybe my only, shot. I might not get another chance. The folks that are trying to keep us apart have been pretty successful up to this point."

"This rogue fella isn't a married man is he?"

Irina laughed. "No. Absolutely not. I would never even consider such a relationship."

"Okay. Just be careful Irina. I don't want you to get into trouble."

"I promise, I won't get myself into trouble." *Make that moral trouble. Can't promise that I won't get into trouble.*

Olivia relented and handed over her keys, still a little reluctant. "Here you go. We won't need the car because we are planning to take the shuttle to the ski slopes." She looked

Irina in the eyes. "Girl. I'm trusting you. Please don't make me regret this."

Irina hugged her. "Thanks. You won't regret this once you understand." When she stepped back, she added, "I promise I'll be back by early afternoon on Sunday."

Olivia, disappointed, shrugged her shoulders and walked back into her room to join the other girls, who were getting ready to watch the classic chick flick *You've Got Mail*.

Irina stood there for a moment, feeling like a witch because she was not only deceiving her friends but potentially dragging them into trouble with the authorities. She pushed the unpleasant thought out of mind. She was only doing what she had to do. She had no choice. With her resolve intact, she returned to her own room and began her preparations for her escapade. *Here goes my own inept version of Mission Impossible. With a little help from above, I can pull this off.*

She plugged her cell phone in and placed it on the desk. She was leaving it behind. That should buy her some time. Those tracking her would think that she was still in her room. After all, everyone knew that she never went anywhere without her phone. Then she plugged her thumb drive into her phone, installed a busy-signal app, which gave every call a busy signal, and activated it. If her boss attempted to call her, perhaps under the prompting of the feds, it would appear that she was talking to someone.

Just in case agents got suspicious about her phone ploy and decided to search her room, she left misleading signs that might buy her a few more hours. She filled the hot tub and turned the heater on, tossed a bag in the corner with one and a half days of dirty clothes, crumpled the bed, moved the TV guide to the bed stand, set her tablet on top of it, tucked a bookmark into page two hundred sixty-four of *War and Peace*, poured several cans of Coca-Cola down the drain and tossed the empty cans in the wastebasket, hung the "Do Not Clean" sign on the doorknob, left a half-eaten bag of Salt-N-Vinegar chips on the table, spread her hygiene and cosmetic items on the bathroom counter, left her suitcase unzipped on the floor, and left her main purse on the desk, taking only her clutch purse. That should do it. *Looks like I'm actually living here and just went out for a while.*

Next up was her disguise. She pulled on a pair of jeans and a plaid shirt, a combination she never wore. She didn't mind dressing country-classy but felt a little hick in plaid. *Maybe on a real camping trip.* Then she retrieved a blonde wig from her tennis duffel, which she had stowed away in her suitcase, donned it, and primped in front of the mirror. *Definitely think I look better brunette.* Finally, she donned a powder-blue Eddie Bauer ski jacket purchased just for this trip.

She did a last-minute double-check of her preparations, then left the room with nothing but her clutch purse and her tennis duffel, the latter holding the things needed for her mission: a shoebox, a plain brown grocery bag, a manila envelope, tape, a DVD, a small laser printer with USB cable, a dozen sheets of 60-bond paper, several sheets of mailing labels, three five-dollar stamps, a pouch of quarters and dimes for the toll roads, a change of underclothes, and some baby wipes. She had added the last two because she couldn't bear the thought of going two days without washing up at least once. She briskly walked down the hall, bounded down the stairs, and headed for the internet room just around the corner from the lobby. *Slow down girl, you're a little too antsy.*

Thankfully, no one else was in the room. She had it to herself. She opened the browser, navigated to Startpage, and then to Buster. She logged in, opened Open Office, and began writing to Ariele. Preferably, the letter would have already been written, but she hadn't dared to access Buster or Startpage or to use TOR after she had come under suspicion, figuring that such actions would be regarded as subversive by those who were tracking her every move on the internet. Twenty-three minutes later, she finished, connected the USB cable for the printer, and printed the letter. *Step one done.*

Now the uncertain part. Would she find a mailing-label template on Buster that matched one of the three sizes she had brought with her? She hoped so. Her backup plan was filling out the labels with her left hand. It would look like chicken scratching, but it would be legible. Thankfully, she did find a template for the smallest labels. She placed the correct sheet into the printer, entered the sender and receiver, and printed the labels. Then she disconnected the cable and put the printer back into her bag. *Step two done.*

On to the last step. Irina put her double-density DVD into the drive, selected the files, images, and documents she wanted in the download queue, and started the download. She wished she had a cup of coffee. This was going to take a while. After twenty-six minutes that seemed like days, the download was completed. She retrieved her DVD, logged out of Buster, closed the browser, and cleared the computer's browsing history and temp files. It had taken her sixty-eight minutes to do her computer stuff, twice as long as she had anticipated. *Off to a great start, Miss Super Spy.* At least she was done.

She gathered up her spook-trade items, placed them in her duffel bag, and zipped up her jacket. It was 12:47 a.m., early Friday morning, and she was ready to go at last. As she walked out the front door, she fretted. *Hopefully, this disguise works and throws off the fed boys who are almost certainly tailing me.*

Whether the disguise worked or whether nobody was tailing her, she never found out, but there were no headlights behind her when she pulled out of the hotel parking lot, nor when she turned north on Sentinel Road. While she did see headlights behind her a few times on Main Street and Sara Placid Road, nobody stayed behind her. By the time she was heading west out of town on State 86 with no headlights behind her, she was starting to relax, and her pulse was returning to normal. *Salina, Kansas, here I come.*

31

After a grueling drive without stopping, except for fuel and caffeine, she arrived in Salina at 2:36 a.m. Saturday, her eyes heavy and sore. She was exhausted to a degree she had never experienced before. The last four hours, she had driven with her window down and the radio going full tilt on an obnoxious heavy-metal station. She desperately wanted to lay down and sleep for a while. But sleep was out of the question until she had done what she had come to do.

Her first stop was the Pilot Travel Center where she filled the tank and purchased a copy of the Salina Journal. While paying, she asked the attendant if he knew where she could find a drop box for mail nearby. He replied, "At the Petro Salina on the other side of the interstate. The truckers drop their mail and small packages there."

She drove to a quiet corner of the truck stop and parked. It was time to place her *baby* in a box—kind of like Moses—and trust the providence of God that the precious cargo would be protected. She laid the manila envelope containing her letter and DVD on the bottom of the shoebox, stuffed the box with crumpled newspaper pages, placed the cover on the shoebox, and taped it shut. Then she wrapped the shoebox with a plain brown grocery bag and attached her labels and stamps. *Okay, I'm ready. Let's do this.*

She drove to the Petro Salina, found the collection box right away, and with a bit of a squeeze got her package in. A huge weight fell off her chest. It was done. It was finally done.

But she still had to get rid of the trash. She returned to the Pilot Travel Center, pulled up to a dumpster, and threw away the remaining pages of the Salinas Journal, all her receipts, her food and beverage containers, the printer, the extra labels and paper, anything that might suggest that she had been in Kansas or why she had been in Kansas.

Now, finally, she could sleep. She found an empty spot on the far edge of the automobile section, parked, crawled into the back seat, donned her coat and hat, wrapped her legs with Olivia's car blanket, laid herself down with a sigh of relief, uttered a brief prayer of thanks, closed her eyes, and she was out.

***

Irina woke with a start, nervous, not remembering where she was or why, dead tired and desperately wanting to go back to sleep, but sensing she needed to wake up and get going. Fighting the weariness and grogginess, she forced herself to sit up, rubbed her aching eyes, and tried to piece things together. The fog started lifting. With a jolt she remembered her mission, spun her head around quickly, and surveyed her surroundings. The sun was higher on the horizon than it should have been. She checked her watch. *Oh, my!* It was 9:35 a.m. *I overslept!* She had to get going if she was going to be back in Lake Placid by the time she had promised.

She started the car, put the defroster on high, ran inside, used the ladies' room, purchased eight Doubleshots and six Krispy Kreme donuts, ran back to the car, wiped the fog off the inside of the windows, and headed out. Once she got on the interstate, she set the cruise at four miles per hour over the speed limit. Then she focused on her growling stomach, wolfing down two of the donuts and slamming two of the heavenly-rich coffee beverages, a combination that was definitely not her normal breakfast. *My ballet teacher would have a cow. But just in case today is the end of freedom for me, I want my last meal in freedom to be the splurge of a lifetime.* While she hoped she would make it back before her absence was noted by the agents assigned to her, she knew the odds were against her.

The determined gal pushed hard through the morning and afternoon, keeping herself awake with caffeine-laced energy drinks and cracking black-pepper sunflower seeds, a trick learned from her brother Vasyl, who was a traveling software salesman. Normally, she refused to chew sunflower seeds, especially in cars, because they were so messy. But protocol goes out the window in desperate situations, and she desperately needed to stay awake.

She hated to admit it, but chewing sunflower seeds was actually kind of fun, though it was disgusting that the floor and seat were littered with cracked shells that had missed the thirty-two-ounce plastic coke cup. *Maybe around a campfire. Just spit 'em into the flames.* Her female mind quickly made the jump from sunflower seeds and a campfire to cowboys, then her cowboy wherever and whoever he was. She lost herself in reverie.

Early in the evening, bone-tired and unable to fight the sandman any longer, Irina realized that she needed to sleep for a couple hours. She took the 465 loop under Indianapolis and headed for the Pilot truck stop where she had stopped on the way to Kansas. There, she figured, she could rest her weary frame. But she never got her nap. Unbeknownst to her, the FBI had recently broadened their search, and that step had enabled them to get a location on her.

The original APB for Irina had been sent out at 8:56 p.m. Friday night—covering the New England states, the northern Appalachian states, the seaboard states, and Ohio—after the FBI had determined, upon questioning her friends, that she had fled to parts unknown. When she left under mysterious circumstances, the girls had assumed that she had snuck off to meet a guy, like a secret boyfriend or an online contact, a dubious venture that seemed out of step with her reputation. They were horrified to learn that the sweet young lady whose company they enjoyed was sought by the FBI and Homeland Security as a serious threat to the security of the United States. Olivia's distress, however, far surpassed the discomfort that her friends felt. The FBI confiscated her Outback without recompense.

At 6 p.m. on Saturday, the FBI expanded the APB to

include all states east of the Mississippi River. This quickly brought Irina's escapade to an end. At 7:25 p.m. an overpass camera on the west side of Indianapolis reported the license plate of the Outback. Five minutes later, just as she signaled for the exit that would take her to the Pilot truck stop, Irina noticed a patrolman on her tail with lights flashing. She negotiated the exit and slowed to a stop on the ramp. *It's over*, she thought to herself. *Glad I splurged on the Krispy Kremes.* He waited until a backup arrived about three minutes later. Then the two patrolmen approached her with pistols drawn. The first one ordered her to step out of her car. After she complied, he barked, "Hands on the vehicle. Walk your feet backward. Spread your feet."

She remained in that uncomfortable position—made even worse by the inconvenient fact that she desperately needed to empty her bladder—for several minutes. "How long do I have to wait like this!" she blurted out. Nobody answered.

Several minutes later, she heard cars pull up, doors open, and footsteps walk up to her. But there was no conversation between the agents and the patrolmen, not even muffled whispers. *Strange.* She sensed motion on both sides of her, then cringed as both of her arms were wrenched behind her back. Cold metal touched her wrists, and handcuffs clicked shut, a click that symbolized a new era of her life.

"Why are you arresting me?" she demanded.

"You are not being arrested. You are being taken into custody for questioning," one of the agents answered, almost mechanically.

"Then what?"

The question went unanswered. They spun her around, marched her to the second SUV, and pushed her toward the open back door. She clambered in, awkwardly banging her head on the opening and munching her fingers on the seat. *Nothing like climbing into an SUV after dark on uneven ground with your hands handcuffed behind your back when you have to use the ladies' room.* They took her to the Indianapolis Field Office, where she was questioned, often intensely, by the Counterterrorism Division and Homeland Security agents assigned to a regional Joint Terrorism Task Force team.

Irina didn't remember much about the next four days— a blur of interrogation sessions, paper cups of bad coffee, and transfers to other facilities. She was polygraphed three times and harnessed to Casper. She talked freely, even blithely, but gave them no information that could jeopardize her effort to warn the world about the Rogue. Though they threatened to use whatever means necessary to make her talk, her fears that she might face the waterboard or some other formidable tool of the trade never materialized. *Maybe they only use that stuff on real terrorists.*

32

Irina woke when the nondescript transfer van halted at the gate of a bleak-looking, fenced facility. *Wonder where I am?* Nothing offered the least hint. There were no signs. The two vehicles she could see both had federal plates. *What time is it?* She checked her watch. It was gone. *Oh yeah. Forgot. They confiscated it when they took me into custody.* She felt a tinge of melancholy. The Baume and Mercier had been a graduation gift from her grandfather for earning her PhD. *I'll have to improvise.* She glanced around, observed a hint of the sun behind the clouds about halfway up the horizon, and estimated that it was midmorning.

A guard trotted out of the guardhouse, an Army-castoff M16 draped over his shoulder, looked over the driver's identification and paperwork, had the driver sign a log sheet on a clipboard, then looked over the transfer manifest for the three persons in the van: Irina, a long-haired hippie-looking guy that appeared to be in his early sixties, and a petite blonde in her late thirties or early forties. They had been seated apart and ordered to maintain silence, so Irina hadn't had an opportunity to learn their names.

Everything must have been in order. The guard motioned to his partner in the guard shack. With a lurch, the chain-link gate began creeping sideways. When it stopped moving, the guard nodded to the driver, and he slowly drove through the narrow opening into the facility. Irina craned her head to look back. The gate was slowly closing, locking her into an unchosen and undesired fate, a fitting metaphor for her life. But she wasn't giving up. *The gates of hell shall not prevail.*

The driver cautiously guided the van across the pot-hole-filled blacktop to a gaunt brick structure that looked like it could be a hundred years old. He stopped at one of the side entrances, opened the sliding door for the passenger compartment, and told the detainees to follow him. He led them into a dimly lit entryway with three small offices on either side, poked his head into the middle doorway on the left, and said, "Got three more for you, Bob."

A voice answered, "Seat them in the chairs, Bart. I'll be with them in a minute."

The driver pointed to a cluster of worn vinyl chairs facing Bob's door, muttered "Bob is the facility director," and hustled for the exit. The place gave him the creeps.

Irina took stock of her new surroundings. She noted that the interior of the building was even more neglected than the exterior. The paint was faded and peeling. The ceiling tiles were yellowed with age and stained. Her eyes lingered on the office doors in front of her. The hammered glass panes in two of them were cracked. The center one, Bob's door, was held open by a torn stuff chair. Apparently, the doors didn't stay open by themselves. The building had probably settled. She was comforted by the faint sound of laughter and banter echoing down the hallway. *That's a good sign. They seem to enjoy a little freedom here.*

Her thoughts were interrupted by a voice barking out of the office, "Burrage Krakenhavn. You're first." The long-haired fellow stood up, looking careworn and exhausted, and shuffled into the office. The name rang a bell. *Krakenhavn. I know that name from somewhere.* She tried to recollect where but drew a blank.

Twenty minutes later, Irina received her summons into the dingy office. While he was not impolite, Bob engaged in no pleasantries. He asked her to verify her name and Social Security number. He rattled off the rules and regulations that she was expected to abide by. Then he warned her that those who were detained here were regarded as serious security threats by the government. He emphasized the word *serious*. Heads would roll if any of the detainees were allowed to escape and circulate in society. To prevent escape, the camp was surrounded by a fifteen-foot tall chain-link fence topped with concertina wire, the gate was manned by armed guards, and the perimeter was monitored by cameras. Moreover, he was authorized to use deadly force in any escape attempt, and he would not hesitate to do so. While he was a church-going man who took no pleasure in violence, he had mouths to feed at home and college educations to pay, so if push came to shove, he was not going to lose any sleep if his guards were forced to fatally shoot a detainee whom the government regarded as a threat to the country.

He stared coolly into her eyes as if he were trying to gauge her reaction. "Do you understand the things I have just gone over, and do you agree to abide by them?" She nodded. He handed her an acknowledgment form which stated that he had explained the rules and policies and that she understood them and agreed to abide by them. She signed her name and handed it back.

Bob lightened up a little bit. "Now for the mundane stuff. First up, your work assignment. Would you prefer to work in housekeeping, in maintenance, in the laundry, or in the kitchen?"

Hate cleaning toilets. Don't have a clue how to fix toilets. Laundry sounds boring. "I'll take the kitchen."

He nodded. "Report at 5 a.m. to the kitchen for the morning shift. Francis Ferguson will be your supervisor."

"Secondly, practical directions and pointers. The kitchen is down the hall to the right. Breakfast is served from 7 to 7:45 a.m., lunch from noon to 12:45 p.m., and dinner from 5 to 5:45 p.m. The supply room and the commissary are also down the hall to your right. Both are open from 8 a.m. to noon and from 1 to 5 p.m. Monday through Friday. The ladies' sleeping quarters are on the second floor, and the men's are on the third. The stairs that lead to the sleeping quarters are down the hall to the left. The women are housed twelve per section. Sections A, B, and C are filled. You may take any available bed in section D. Just let brunette Joyce know the bed number. Each bed comes with a dresser and a closet rod. If you need anything beyond that, you are on your own. There are two bathrooms on the second floor with ample sinks and toilets. No showers are provided, but the boys in maintenance have rigged up some crude showers in the warehouse. They have also set up a makeshift laundry room back there.

"When you leave here, stop at Room 7, also known as the supply room. There you will be issued some necessary personal items and allowed to choose necessary clothing from the racks and bins. You will also be given your first five-dollar allotment for purchases at the commissary. The allotment is distributed every Friday."

He remained silent for a moment, rubbed his chin as if mentally running through his checklist, then said, "That will be all. You are dismissed. Oh, one more thing. I don't want to see your face in here unless the sky is falling."

Irina nodded but remained standing, her eyes fixed on him pensively as if waiting for permission to speak.

"Yes?"

"Where am I? And what is this place called?"

Irina sensed that he was trying not to smirk. "Classified and classified," he replied dryly. Then he pointed toward the door. "Bye."

She gladly retreated from his office and made her way to Room 7. An attractive older woman behind the counter greeted her with a friendly smile. "Hi, newbie. My name is Cassie, Cassie Morrison." Handing Irina a set of sheets she said, "Sorry that we're all out of 800 count," and grinned broadly. Then she set a selection of blankets on the counter. "We got wool, acrylic, bedspreads, and quilts."

Irina selected a pastel-pink acrylic blanket and a boys' bedspread with four vignettes of John Wayne riding his favorite film horses: Duke, Banner, Beau, and Dollar.

"That's quite the combination," Cassie said, muffling a giggle.

Irina, seeing the irony herself, sheepishly replied, "I've liked cowboys since I was a little girl."

"Have you roped one yet?" Cassie enquired.

"No, I haven't," she replied, blushing.

"Well, God bless you, darling. I hope you find a man who comes with integrity, honor, and courage. Most of them today come with a big ego, a wussy button, a lazy streak, and a wagon full of games and toys." Irina laughed. Cassie handed her a small box with the rest of her stuff: a tan pillowcase that would match her bedspread, a toothbrush and container, a tube of toothpaste, a soap dish and bar of soap, a small pouch to hold her hygiene articles, two washcloths, two towels, a laundry bag, a hairbrush, and a worn five-dollar bill.

Irina glanced at the clock. It was getting close to noon. She picked up her box and said, "Thanks, Cassie. I'll come back after lunch for some clothes," bolted out the door, and raced down the hall to the commissary.

Bursting into the next room, she asked about shampoo and a watch before she even got to the counter. "No time for small talk, hon'?" replied the blonde behind the counter, who appeared to be in her forties. "Is the town hall on fire?"

Irina laughed, enjoying the humor and the fact that both the supply room and the commissary were manned by Southern girls. *Lots of Southern drawl around here. I can get used to that.*

The sassy gal continued, "My name is Joyce, Joyce Meribeth Lee, but I'm usually referred to as blonde Joyce to distinguish me from brunette Joyce."

Irina smiled awkwardly, a little embarrassed that she hadn't introduced herself, and apologized, "Sorry. My name is Irina Kirilenko."

Joyce grabbed her three-ring binder, wrote *Kirilenko, Irina* at the top left of a clean page, and placed the page in its proper place alphabetically. "I'll have to start an account for you. The only watches I have cost more than the five bucks in your pocket." She reached into her case and pulled out several samples. "We carry a mediocre selection of Timex offerings and Fossil knock-offs." Irina picked the sturdiest looking women's Timex and handed Joyce her five-dollar bill. Joyce gave her four dollars in change and wrote *Timex— twelve dollars* on the first line. Underneath the entry, she wrote *one dollar paid* and recorded the date. "Trust me. You'll be glad you have the four dollars in your pocket."

Anxious to select her bed, put her things away, and wash up before lunch, Irina said goodbye, scurried out the door, and hastened down the hallway, looking for the stairwell. Finding it at the end of the hall on the right, she bounded up the stairs and burst into the second-floor hallway. *This will be easier than I thought.* The doors on the right-hand side had letters painted on them, A to F.

She walked into D. *Interesting.* The room was set up in an open-bay fashion with twelve single beds. The dressers were a haphazard assortment of styles from hotels and second-hand stores. Most of the closet rods were salvaged from retail stores, but some were merely pieces of black pipe fastened to a 2X4 frame with a diagonal support for stability. She noticed that three of the claimed beds had desks: one a small wooden desk, the second a cheap computer desk, and the third a piece of plywood set on milk crates. The scene was almost quaint. She appreciated the ingenuity she saw here. It brought one of Pastor Vargas' quips to mind. "Those who adapt, survive. Those who adapt well, thrive."

She chose bed number eleven because it came with a large dresser and a real clothes rack, tossed her belongings onto it, grabbed the things she needed to wash up, and raced down the hall to find the ladies' room. *For a bad situation, this isn't too bad. Just wish I wasn't still wearing the same jeans that I wore for my disguise.*

33

Standing in the lunch line, Irina heard two middle-aged guys in front of her say in unison, "It's Wednesday. We always have chicken nuggets on Wednesday." Then they chortled. *Must be a line from a movie before my time.* A woman jested, "Hey. We get three different kinds today." A husky voice bantered back, "Outdated fast food, outdated school lunch, and outdated supermarket." Several snickers followed. The scene reminded her of high school. But there was something deeper there, more evidence of adapting. It brought to mind something her grandfather had observed as an airborne commander in Afghanistan during the Russian occupation. "A sense of humor in harsh conditions indicates resilience. The men haven't lost heart."

When she arrived at the serving counter, she said *yes* to the chicken nuggets and french fries, chose cucumber slices and carrot sticks, selected a yogurt and a can of sparkling lemon water, and filled one of the divisions in her tray with Miracle Whip. Dipping fries in catsup was okay, but she preferred mayonnaise or Miracle Whip. With her tray full, she turned to look for Cassie or blonde Joyce but didn't see either, so she sat down at a table by herself. An attractive brunette quickly joined her and identified herself as Joyce Howatt. Irina grinned. *Must be brunette Joyce.* It was. Not waiting for Irina to introduce herself, she continued, "If you haven't already figured it out, I'm brunette Joyce."

"Glad to meet you. I'm Irina Kirilenko." She paused for a moment then added, "Before I forget, I'm supposed to give you my bed number. I chose eleven."

"Already figured that out, dear. Cassie told me that you had taken the John Wayne blanket. I saw the blanket on bed eleven. Simple math."

Irina looked a little unsettled as if she regarded this as nosiness.

Joyce explained, "Don't worry hon'. It's not like we're a bunch of talebearers with nothing better to do than gossip. It's just a small world in here. There's very little privacy and even fewer secrets."

Irina noticed that Joyce was trying to stifle a smile. She cocked her head and asked, "What gives?"

"Nothing really. Just laughing about the John Wayne blanket. That blanket was here when Cassie arrived and took over the supply room. She passed out more than eighty blankets since that day and nobody wanted it. She started a joke a while back that the blanket was waiting for the chosen one to come. Whoever picked the blanket would be the one that would foil the evil empire's cover-up of the Rogue. They would also be the first one to escape." She continued while stifling a giggle, "We never imagined that a woman would pick the blanket, much less a classy girl who looks and acts more like a model than a cowgirl."

Irina pointed to her shirt.

"Hon', your jeans and plaid shirt don't fool anyone."

Irina, blushing in spades, said nothing.

Joyce noticed that her new acquaintance was uneasy, so she changed the subject. "So, Irina, why are you here?" Without waiting for a reply, she continued, "Let me guess. Either you were made privy to information on the Rogue which you were not authorized to know, or you were part of a Minoa team and disseminated information about the Rogue to people who were not authorized to know."

Irina raised her eyebrows. "How did you guess?"

"It wasn't a guess." Smiling knowingly, she explained, "Welcome to FEMA 286, generally referred to in internet media and government circles as simply 286. This is where the federal government sends folks who pose a threat to their Rogue cover-up. Everyone here, except for Francis the cook and Dr. Andy Gordon our physician, was sent here for the illegal possession or dissemination of sensitive information on the Rogue. Some were part of a Minoa team whether research, government, or enforcement. Some stumbled upon this information. Some were party to the Anonymous effort to steal and leak the information. Some were members of the media who published the information that Anonymous stole. The government keeps us all together in several camps, isolated from the other classes of detainees and prisoners, so we can't make converts to our conspiracy theory." She made

quote marks with her fingers as she said *conspiracy.* "So, were you a leaker, a hacker, a webbie, or just an unlucky duck?"

"A leaker. Actually, I am the one who discovered the Rogue. I discovered it in May of last year while working under Dr. Goldblum at Cornell."

"So you're the whiz kid?" Joyce remarked, not really asking a question but expressing a eureka moment.

But Irina was more interested in learning about 286 than talking about what she did to get here. That could come later. "So where are we?" she asked.

"Frenchie says we're in an old industrial park on the outskirts of Syracuse, New York, that has been empty since he was a teenager nearly twenty years ago. He claims he and his friends used to sneak in here and party. From some of the windows on the third floor, you can see several businesses just outside the park that he recognizes, like Jiffy LTL Delivery and Sonny's Salvage and Recycling."

"Tell me about the FEMA camps."

"There are three classes of FEMA camps. The 100 series, which were the original camps, are used for getting the unwanted off the streets and out of society: the homeless, drug users, non-violent dealers and criminals, unlicensed prostitutes, and the chronically unemployed. The 200 series are designated for white-collar criminals, troublemaking religionists, and the so-called soft terrorists, who pose zero threat of violence. The Rogue camps are a special class in the 200 series. The 300 series are for security risks who are potentially violent, like patriots who have threatened to fight for freedom and deucers who have vowed to defend their second-amendment rights.

"A bipartisan think tank first came up with the idea, and time has proved them correct that it would be far cheaper to keep derelicts and non-violent criminals in FEMA camps than in other government programs or jails. Although some have expressed concern that the camps are run like 'nice' POW camps, the public as a whole has a favorable opinion of them. The bottom line is, the camps work. They keep the homeless and other unwanteds off the streets. They have lowered welfare, unemployment, and law enforcement costs. They have freed up law enforcement so they can focus on bigger issues. And they cost very little to run.

"The fact is, many of the camps are actually run at a profit. They are all housed in government-owned properties like closed military bases or abandoned industrial parks. They are all engaged in a business, as light manufacturing, recycling precious metals and specialty alloys, and repairing electronics and appliances for the second-hand market. The detainees do their own cleaning, cooking, and maintenance. If a sink leaks or a toilet breaks, they fix it with salvaged materials as far as possible. If a washing machine or a refrigerator breaks, they fix it or replace it with another second-hand model.

"The camps are given an annual headcount-based budget, and the directors are given a bonus of twenty-five percent of the savings which they accomplish under budget, which can be a significant sum. Some of them double their government salary. And they are given tremendous freedom to attain savings. They are permitted to buy used items, government surplus, and outdated goods from the USDA's *Safe Outdated Goods* list. They are allowed to turn the thermostat down to 64 degrees during the day and 56 degrees at night. They are permitted to turn the hot-water heaters down to 125 degrees, except in the kitchen. They are not required to provide hot water to any laundry facilities. They are permitted to obtain clothing from second-hand stores and warehouse clearance sales. And they can require detainees to purchase clothing and personal items from a commissary.

"Detainees are paid five dollars per week regardless of what kind of work they do in the camp whether in the camp trade, or in the kitchen, or in maintenance. These funds are derived from the camp's assets and business income."

Irina was stunned. "Camp assets?"

"That's right. The camps are flush with cash. They are lucrative even without a profitable camp business. When someone is detained, the government seizes their assets. Half goes to the general treasury for FEMA camps and half to the camp that the detainee is assigned to."

"The nerve!" Irina interrupted. "Selling my possessions to pay my room and board! Where's the decency? Shouldn't my possessions go to my family if I'm going to be locked up for the rest of my life? I'll bet my watch and car alone cover my expenses in this dump for four or five years."

Joyce nodded in agreement. "I hear ya, dear. I had nearly two hundred thousand in an IRA, over two hundred thousand in my 401K, some valuable heirloom jewelry, a Jaguar, and a three-story brownstone overlooking Central

Park that was nearly paid for. I like to think that it's my money that buys us all outdated supermarket pizzas for dinner twice a week." She paused for a moment. "I suspect that part of their reason for the confiscation of our property is that it enhances their deceptive claim that we are security threats to this country, a charge that implies terrorism in the minds of the mindless masses."

Irina frowned. "I hope my parents don't think that I've become a terrorist. They were worried about me when I left the Orthodox church and joined an Evangelical church. They thought I was headed down an extreme path. I wonder what they'll think now?"

"Don't think about it," Joyce counseled. "That will lead to worrying about it, which will lead to a disengaged mind, or maybe even mental breakdown. Find something to focus on here that will keep your mind off unprofitable worries. Be an asset to the team, not a weight."

"Is there any hope for discharge from a FEMA camp?"

"Folks can get discharged from the derelict camps if they show evidence that they will be productive citizens upon discharge. And people will be discharged from 200-series camps if they were imprisoned for white-collar crimes and have finished their term. It's a little more sketchy for those in 300-series camps and those detained in 200-series camps for civil disorder charges. Supposedly, they can be discharged if they finish the reeducation program, pass a Casper exam, which includes promising not to stir up trouble any longer, and meet several other stringent conditions.

"But no one is discharged from the Minoa camps, where

the Rogue problems are detained. These camps are like black holes. People enter. People never leave. Being sent to a Minoa camp, like 286 here, is essentially a life sentence. The worst part about it is …" she paused for a moment, "nobody knows that we are here."

"What!?" Irina exclaimed. "Nobody knows we're here?"

"That's right hon'. Nobody knows. The government does not notify the detainee's family when they detain them. They wait a few weeks, then send them a letter that states that their child or spouse or parent or whatever has been detained by Homeland Security at an unspecified location on unspecified security charges. They leave them with the awful suspicion that their loved one was a closet terrorist. No opportunity for contact is offered. All requests for contact are turned down."

"How do you know so much about the FEMA camps?"

"I was an investigative reporter for the New York Times and was doing a story on the FEMA camps. As I dug deeper, I realized that FEMA camps were being used for more than getting derelicts and petty criminals off the streets, slackers off the government dole, and white-collar criminals off the prison roles. They were being used to silence voices who, right or wrong, saw themselves as John the Baptist types crying in the wilderness. My boss told me that I was getting in over my head and that I was going to end up in a FEMA camp. I thought he was joking. He wasn't. So here I am." She shook her head and laughed. "I'm over it now. It is what it is. But if I ever get the chance, I would still like to get my story published. Maybe one of the Russian news sites that are operating beyond the reach of the American government or maybe one of the underground news outlets."

"What does 286 do for its trade?"

"We repair appliances and furniture for the Salvation Army store in Syracuse. Some they sell on location, and some they transfer to other stores. Once a week, we unload a box truck of appliances that need repair, then reload it with repaired units. The trucks are driven by FEMA drivers, who supervise the unloading and reloading. Every two weeks, we receive a load of damaged furniture, then reload the truck with pieces that have been mended or renovated. And every six weeks, we receive a load of crates filled with kitchen and household appliances that need attention—blenders, toasters, vacuums, coffee pots, microwaves, and the like— then reload the truck with crates of refurbished items. Many of the repairs are made by cannibalizing parts, so we end up with quite a bit of waste. Some of the waste gets recycled. Some we find innovative uses for. Some ends up in the landfill.

"We have also received, on several occasions, shipments of crates and boxes filled with appliance parts in the original packages, most likely overstock from warehouses or salvage from repair shops that went out of business.

"One of the perks of this business is that we have first dibs on the items that come in, so we have nice appliances in our kitchen, good washers and dryers in the laundry room, and fairly decent furniture. We also have three big screen televisions, which have been placed in different rec rooms. So no one is forced to watch sports."

Irina snickered, then asked, "Where do the appliances and furniture come from?"

"Mostly donations from second-hand stores and retailers glutted with trade-ins. On occasion we receive seconds from manufacturers."

"Bob mentioned showers."

"Yeah, we got showers. The maintenance department put together two makeshift shower rooms in the back, one for the guys and one for the gals. There is plenty of hot water from mid-fall to mid-spring. They jimmy-rigged a system to siphon heat off the boiler. The rest of the time, the water is only warm."

"Is there internet access?"

"Yes, there is. We have quite a few computers, mostly older models, set up in the computer room and convenient locations like the kitchen, the supply room, the commissary, the maintenance shop, the infirmary, and the repair business. But unfortunately, we can't upload or send anything except prescriptions and orders which are sent through Bob Drake. We have no communication with the outside."

"If I want a desk, who do I see?"

"See Arnie in maintenance."

"Arnie. Interesting name. Is he Norwegian?"

"No. He's Italian. His real name is Stephan Gallo. We call him Arnie because he lifts weights in his spare time and has really bulked up since he got here. He was a webcaster focused on threats from heaven like comets and NEOs. His website was called *Impact Today*, and he was well-known for having far more science and far less over-the-top speculation than most of his peers. He published some information on the Rogue given to him by Anonymous, and within forty-eight hours his website was shut down, and he was in custody. Within a week he was working in maintenance." Joyce glanced at the clock. "Hey, we only have fifteen minutes left on our lunch break. We better eat fast."

34

Irina sat on the edge of her bed, frustrated because of the limitations she faced in clothing and cosmetics. She wiped a tear from the corner of her eye. This was a big step down. In the past she wouldn't have gone to a church picnic wearing the outfit she would be wearing today. With a sigh, she determined to make the best of it. *It is what it is.*

Her mind turned to the chapel service. Would she enjoy it? The two Joyces loved it. But she had low expectations. She had gotten spoiled under the rousing messages of Pastor Jellineck at New Life Church and the expository Bible teaching of Pastor Vargas at Resurrection Fellowship in Glendale. And the bar had been set pretty high for music too as both churches had employed highly skilled worship teams.

She set her feelings aside and left for the meeting early so she could enjoy some quiet time. As she walked in the door, the chapel wooed her, as it had Wednesday night at the prayer meeting, with its quaint charm. There was grandeur

233

in its simplicity. Set up in an unused section of the warehouse, it was separated from the open floor by makeshift walls of pallets and wooden crates stacked eight feet high. A plywood platform stood in the front, adorned with a simple podium. Behind the podium was a large screen and an old-fashioned overhead projector for song lyrics. In front of the platform stood a card table draped with a white sheet. On top of the table sat a small loaf on a small kitchen plate, a pitcher of grape juice, and two serving trays loaded with a variety of shot glasses.

The seating was an assortment of plastic chairs and folding chairs with several wooden chairs. Along the far wall was a set of shelves that held a modest selection of Bibles and books. Along the near wall was a folding table which offered a coffee pot, an odd assortment of coffee cups, an urn for hot water, a selection of tea bags, and several packages of outdated cookies. It wasn't much. But it was more than enough.

The only lack that they felt was a piano—their furniture supplier was on the lookout for an inexpensive console. But they were content to continue with their guitars.

People started trickling in, milling around, chatting, and drinking coffee. At 9:30 a.m. the two song leaders took the platform, repaired guitars in hand, and placed the first song on the overhead. Irina was encouraged to see how well attended the meeting was—she estimated mid-thirties—considering that there were only 114 detainees at the camp.

After a half hour of singing, Jeremy Hendricks took the podium with his Bible and a sheaf of notes. He was one of the two who did most of the Bible teaching. He was also the one who had organized the chapel when he arrived at 286 in January. His message was based on the text, "Though the outer man perishes, the inner man is renewed day by day." During the second hour, the Sunday School class, he walked the congregation through a number of passages on spiritual essentials and priorities, things necessary for the growth of the inner man. He exhorted them to not let themselves get distracted by superficial things that have no real spiritual or eternal value.

That afternoon, reflecting on the meeting, she realized that she appreciated it far more than she had expected. While Jeremy wouldn't win any awards for his oratory skills, his message was insightful and heartfelt. And the singing, while far from polished, exuded a sense of heart-reality that made a profound impression on her. She found herself strangely drawn to the spartan chapel. Its attraction brought to mind the Messiah's draw for the believer. "There is no beauty in him that we should desire him."

The little chapel at 286, which invited comparison with the underground churches during the Soviet socialist regime, had everything that really mattered for a vibrant testimony: God, the Bible, and earnest believers. She felt a twinge of shame as the truth dawned on her. *I've put too much emphasis on superficial things, not enough on spiritual basics. Too much focus on the outer woman, not enough on the inner woman. Too bad it took a few days in 286 to see that I didn't have my priorities right.*

35

After taking her first unauthorized images of the Rogue a
week after she had received the package from Irina, Ariele
began taking two sets of images per week, one on Tuesday
evening and another on Friday. She directed the images to a
temporary folder in SODpro and then transferred them,
after the shoot was finished, onto a two-TB flash drive she
had purchased just for this illicit project. It was a pricey
gizmo. The expense was grudged a bit because the money
had come out of her homestead nest egg. But it could hold
a dozen stellar images at high resolution. When she returned
to her apartment later in the night, she downloaded the
images into her copy of SODpro—her pirated copy.

Throughout January and February, Ariele spent all of her
free time searching the archives, optical and infrared, which
Dr. Youngblood had posted with his research paper *Another
Look at the Phenomenon Near the Seven Sisters*. It was an
exhausting endeavor, leaving her—a tireless astronomy buff
since she was nine years old—weary of stars, charts, and

images by the time Valentine's Day came around. She moped and sulked the entire day. *Some Cupid Day this is. Chasing a hunk of rock instead of being chased by a hunk. Where is my valentine? Where is my box of chocolates?*

Despite feeling burned out, she pushed herself hard. On the last evening of February, she finished scanning the last of the 126 archives that Dr. Youngblood had attached to his post, supposedly every known Taurian archive from May 2008 to August 2018, drawn from thirty-six collections. Her searches uncovered the same thirteen occultations that he had included in his online paper: the eight that Irina had discovered, the three joint observations made by the Keck, the Hooker, and the MMT, and the two prediscoveries that Irina had missed. One was a twenty percent occultation that was first observed on Sunday, November 10, 2013. The other was the earliest known record of the intruder, the complete occultation of a dim star above the Pleiades on December 21, 2012.

The last date sounded familiar. *Why does that ring a bell?* She furled her eyebrows and thought for a moment. *No way! The Mayan apocalypse.* She shook her head and chuckled to herself. *It's probably just a coincidence. But then again who knows? Maybe the Mayan-calendar nuts were right after all?* The more sober-minded Mayan experts, after all, had suggested that the December date was not the end of the world per se but the threshold of a new era, which would bring the world into a time of testing, purging, and renewal similar to the last days of Christian prophecy.

***

On Friday, April 12, Ariele snapped the final images of the occultation of a dim binary pair, giving her the second of the two occultations that she needed to have a large enough sample of occulted stars to calculate the Rogue's orbit with the accuracy that she desired. The first had been discovered and documented in January. As she was loading the images onto her flash drive, she breathed a sigh of relief. She was finally done with her furtive—and risky—research, a project which had kept her on edge like a cat in a dog kennel.

During her drive home that night, all she could think about was the Rogue data. With her finds, there were now sixteen occulted stars—four faint and twelve very faint—that made a dim trail of footprints in the heavens, starting a little above the Pleiades in December 2012 and ending a little below the Pleiades in April 2019. Even to her trained mind, it seemed strange that such a feeble display in the heavens would have any significance for man. Nonetheless, it was undeniable that a comet was headed for our neighborhood.

But what would the data reveal? Was the Rogue really as dangerous as Irina had feared, Burrage had reported, and Dr. Youngblood had estimated? Was it really going to give Mars a close shave? She didn't want to doubt her friend, much less experts like Dr. Youngblood, but a comet as massive as Mars playing bumper cars with the Red Planet seemed over-the-top. It was surreal. Her mind ran a hundred miles per hour as she grappled with the scenario and its complexities. When she turned off Orange Grove Avenue and onto Highway 110, her home stretch, she realized that she wasn't going to bed anytime soon tonight. She was way too wired.

Not knowing what to expect, she placed her key in the lock, and to her surprise—*holy guacamole*—it turned easily. The WD-40 trick she had tried that afternoon had actually worked. She stumbled into her apartment, physically tired and emotionally drained, but laser-focused. *Time to rumble.*

She flung her purse on the table, raced to her bedroom, reached under bed, retrieved her gaming laptop and external hard drive, darted back to the kitchen, set the high-powered unit on the table, turned it on, plugged it in, and fired up her orbital calculation software, Caltech's GUI version of OrbFit. Shaking with excitement, she carefully entered the dates and stellar nomenclature for all sixteen occultations, started moving her cursor toward the *calculate* button, then hesitated. The gravity of the moment weighed heavily on her.

With a nervous puff of her bangs, she moved the cursor to the *calculate* button, tapped her touchpad, trembling as if it were the *launch* button for a nuclear missile, and waited in suspense. The laptop chugged along, maxing out the CPU and the memory. She jumped up, paced the floor anxiously, broke out a few dance moves to relieve her frustration, and returned to her chair at the table. Even with her gaming laptop, the calculation was processing at a snail's pace compared to her workstation at Caltech.

After seven long minutes, the results panel popped up, giving her three options for viewing. She selected *Slow Animation Mode.* The dotted green line worked its way through the asteroid belt, entered the inner sanctum of the solar system, and—she quit chewing her gum, stared in wide-eyed amazement, and whispered *holy mackerel.* The green dotted line directly intersected Mars in August 2024. The red box in the lower right corner, which warned her that the calculations could be up to 25,000 miles off, did nothing to relieve her fear. A comet of this size passing that close to Mars would perturb the orbits of both bodies whether or not the electric universe theory was true. She sat in stunned silence. The concerns enunciated in Irina's letter, Dr. Youngblood's paper, and Burrage's report on the *Down the Rabbit Hole* program were not exaggerated. They were entirely vindicated.

This changed the dynamics of the situation. She could no longer indulge the hope that perhaps those sounding the alarm were overstating the case, that maybe the only real threat posed by the Rogue was dislodging a few asteroids when it passed through the main belt, sending them into orbits which could threaten Earth. Now the situation looked dire. Either the comet would brush Mars, perturbing the orbits of both, or the comet would directly impact Mars. Either scenario raised the specter of an existential threat that far surpassed anything that Hollywood had ever conceived.

She felt vulnerable. The comet wasn't merely a point on a trajectory on a computer screen that held no interest for Earth beyond academic consideration. It was a projectile in space that threatened Earth. And whatever this projectile was—whether an undiscovered planet with an elliptical orbit of prodigious periodicity as some Nibiru fanatics supposed, or a rogue planet from outside the solar system as Dr.

Youngblood had suggested, or the iron core of a former planet as Irina had theorized—it was stupendously massive. What would happen if a body far larger than Mercury with a mass equal to Mars slammed into Mars while traveling at 100,000 to 300,000 miles per hour? How big would the pieces be? Where would the pieces go? The thought made her shudder.

She also felt conflicted. While her scientific side enjoyed a sense of satisfaction for the part she had played in the most profound astronomical discovery in modern times, her moral side felt guilty for finding enjoyment in a discovery that posed a serious threat to the inhabitants of this planet. She rolled her eyes at herself. *Deal with it, chick. There's no shame in science. Just get the message out. Redeem the research.*

Ariele did what she always did when overwhelmed with cares. She started a deep bath with a chamomile ball, added a little Epsom salt, and lit a sandalwood-beeswax candle. Then she walked into the kitchen and made herself a large mug of organic hot cocoa with half-and-half. It was time to relax, rejuvenate, and refocus. She couldn't make the trouble go away. But she could face it with a revitalized spirit.

36

Ariele was rounding a curve halfway down the Angeles Crest when the analogy struck her. Her life over the past six months had been very much like this highway, winding and dangerous, yet invigorating. All because she was chasing the Rogue. Chasing it was like chasing Moby Dick—pursuing something so big and so elusive that most who heard about it regarded it as mythical. But some dark day, the Rogue was going to rear its ugly head close to our little boat, and then all the make-believe talk would go overboard.

Silly girl. Got to get my mind off this Rogue issue. To help get her mind off the subject, she moved the dial off her favorite indie station and started scrolling, hoping she might find a late-night talk show. She didn't care what they talked about: far-left politics, far-right politics, the supernatural, or UFOs. She just wanted something that could distract her. It didn't matter whether it made her laugh or made her angry. Anything but worry. *Too bad the "Down the Rabbit Hole" program went off the air.* The official story was that the FCC

242

had taken it off the air after FBI agents determined that it was a front for an anti-American group working to promote instability and anarchy here in America. She suspected that the real reason was that the program's owner and host, Mr. Krakenhavn, had divulged knowledge about the Rogue that people in high places did not want to be divulged.

As she rolled through the channels, she thought she heard the word *Rogue* among the garbled squawks and words. She turned the dial back and tuned in the channel. *Bummer.* It was the *Smackdown* show—Lou Hendrickson's obnoxious voice gave it away—probably her least favorite of the night-time radio programs. While she often agreed with him, she was annoyed by his constant vitriolic diatribe against "imbecilic conspiracy theories" as he labeled them.

He mocked those who claimed that GMOs weren't safe and the FDA wasn't neutral. He reviled the notion that groups like the Illuminati, the CFR, the Trilateral Commission, and the Federal Reserve were conspiratorially aligned in an effort to manipulate the world's economic system, American foreign policy, and international affairs. And he derided those who claimed that the global warming message was really a globalist agenda aimed at weakening the industrial and economic strength of the West. Maybe she was naive, but it seemed to her that his program would be improved if he majored in facts and minored in pejorative insults.

Lou's raspy voice roused her from her drifting thoughts. "Reports have been circulating on late-night talk radio, on conspiracy websites, and on a few nutjob YouTube channels claiming that the *Down the Rabbit Hole* program has been resurrected from the dead. There are even several recently uploaded podcasts and YouTube videos that claim to have been produced by Krakenhavn and his team. But why the computer-generated voice? Wouldn't you use your real voice if you were doing a comeback? Wouldn't that be key to proving to your listeners that it really is you? I think the odds that Krakenhavn's show has come back from the dead and produced these podcasts and videos are zero. Zilch. Nada. Those whack jobs were a Russian front that posed a serious security threat to America, and now they have met their fate in a God-forsaken FEMA camp. I feel no pity for them, and neither should you. I hope they choke to death on maggot-infested, horse-meat stew. Sadly, there are droves of people out there gullible enough to believe this rubbish.

"By the way, I forced myself to watch several of the purported *Down the Rabbit Hole* videos earlier today, all three of which were riding the latest iteration of the Planet X hobby horse, the outrageous claim that there is a comet far larger than Mercury that is going to smash its way through the asteroid belt, sending a wave of asteroids on orbits which could threaten Earth, then pass terrifyingly close to Mars. The latest report from these wackos claims that the Rogue is now inside Neptune.

"Folks, there is no such comet. This story has been debunked by NASA, JPL, the ESA, the American Astronomical Society, the Pentagon, and the White House. Besides, if there really were a planet-sized body in Neptune's neighborhood, we would be able to see it from our own backyards with any large backyard telescope. But not a single telescope in the world, not even the largest on the planet, has observed this body. That means there is no comet. Folks, don't let the fearmongers get you into a panic with their end-of-the-world apocalypse scenarios. The next extinction event is not mere years away. It is tens of millions of years away."

Ariele muttered to herself, *Thus saith the gods from their thrones in the pantheon of science.*

Lou continued, "As a footnote, we received a bulletin this morning that the feds have rounded up another dozen conspiracy-theory fruitcakes who were foolish enough to post videos or blogs on the non-existent comet which they claim is lurking in the shadows of Neptune and threatens to bring the end of the world as we know it. My hat is off to the FBI and Homeland Security for looking out for the interests of the American public. These scoundrels ought to be removed from the internet and talk radio."

The reminder that Krakenhavn was likely being detained in a FEMA camp somewhere rekindled her mental battle on whether or not she should give her research on the Rogue to her boss. If she did give it to Sally, she was risking arrest and worse, disappearing in a FEMA camp. She shuddered at the thought. On the other hand, if she didn't give it to Sally, then to whom could she give it? She had no other options.

She was torn. Common sense told her she shouldn't trust Sally because she was one of the heavyweights in the astronomical world. She might even be privy to the cover-up. Gut instinct said she could trust Sally, though doing so seemed like leaning a ladder against a cloud. But what did she expect from Sally? Did she expect her to right the ship? Possibly. She was influential, one of the leading scientists in NEO research and the CNEOS project. If anyone could right the ship, she could. Unless, of course, the ship couldn't be righted. Did she think that Sally would run off and join the Rogue Underground if such a group actually existed? Maybe.

Despite her waffling, which had persisted for weeks, she sensed, instinctively, that she ought to give her research to Sally and press her on the threat that the Rogue posed to the world. Though it was a risky move, it was her only viable option. She would just have to leave the results in God's hands, kind of like Esther in the Tanakh.

In case things went south with this venture, she archived a copy of her research in Buster and GASmailed copies of the files to her ProtonMail account, giving her backups in two secure locations. When she finished, she was glowing with satisfaction. Knowing how to use cool security tools gave her the same sense of reward that she got when roasting and grinding her own coffee beans. While she was by no means a hack—she was clueless on how to breach security— she did have some savvy when it came to protecting herself on the internet and avoiding prying eyes whether voyeurs, crooks, or Big Brother.

37

Sierra Coffee Company, Glendale, CA
Monday, June 3, 2019

Woody swung into his favorite pitstop, the Sierra Coffee Company. Several times a week, he stopped here to unwind after work, enjoy a mocha, and chat with the regulars. As he passed through the door to the familiar sound of bear bells jangling, Joby looked up and grinned. Woody acknowledged his friend with a nod, a good western chin jut and two seconds of eye contact. They had met here five years ago and had slowly developed a relationship. Joby had helped Woody with a few furniture projects, and Woody had visited him several times at his homestead in the San Gabriels when two sets of hands were needed.

Joby was a good-looking young man in his twenty-seventh year, sporting a medium build, an infectious smile, a light Latin complexion, piercing blue eyes, and sandy-blonde hair that was naturally curly. But it was his sentiments that Woody found fascinating. He was a back-to-the-land, do-it-yourself type, with a counter-culture streak. While still in his teens, he had attended a few Rainbow Family gatherings, but hadn't been impressed with the movement—too much pot, too little hard work—and had decided that their worldview and lifestyle wasn't compatible with his own. Since then, he had carved his own path of self-reliance, though he still shared in their abhorrence of the big controllers. He distrusted big government, big agribusiness, big pharma, big banks, and major media. In his mind, they made a living by forcing crap on men that was bad for them.

Six years ago, he had purchased a ten-acre parcel in the San Gabriels from a relative on his mother's side who needed quick cash to pay an unexpectedly large tax bill. It was a gem, an old mining plot surrounded by national forest, with a year-round spring. He had torn down the old homestead his first two summers on the property. Only the foundation and stone cellar remained. The projects he had finished showed a creative flair that impressed Woody: a quaint micro house with a sleeping loft, a garden shed, a chicken coop, and a workshop with an attached lean-to.

Every week, he worked three twelve-hour shifts at the Sierra Coffee Company as a barista. While the hourly pay wasn't that great, he enjoyed the work. He was a people person and loved organic origin coffees. More importantly, he enjoyed having four days a week off.

He supplemented his income by selling chairs, tables, and other pieces of furniture that he repaired and refinished. In the evening on his way home from work, he swung by his favorite haunts, looking for repairables and resellables, and placed his finds in the back of his 1972 Toyota Hilux. In the morning on his way to work, he dropped his refurbished projects off at the Junken Treasure. It never ceased to amaze him what a guy could find in dumpsters and on the curbside. He didn't talk much about this part of his life though. People, especially the educated women that he found himself attracted to, didn't tend to be impressed by a man who made a career out of dumpster diving and curb shopping. But it was too lucrative and too utilitarian to give up, yet.

Joby's real name was Joseph Rosenthal. His mother was a Chilean Jewess of Italian descent, and his father was from an old German family with Scandinavian infusion. They had met at a grape and wine conference three decades earlier. Her family owned a vineyard in Napa Valley, and he worked as a wine taster.

Joseph picked up his nickname Joby during the summer after his junior year in high school. After his third misdemeanor, the local sheriff, a family friend, got him assigned to a trail crew in the Klamath Mountains—eleven weeks without access to alcohol or marijuana. The summer changed him. He hadn't been in trouble with the law since. He enjoyed the hard work, the mountains, and the freedom from the gang mentality. Early in the summer, his crewmates tagged him with the moniker Joe Bandana because his usual headgear was a bandana. Eventually, this was shortened to Joby. The name stuck. Even his family used it.

When it was Woody's turn to order, Joby smiled and rattled off the order from memory, "Cinnamon Griz': double mocha with extra cream, lots of cinnamon, a dash of nutmeg, and two heaping tablespoons of malt powder." Then he leaned in close and said quietly, "I have a message for you. Western Style says that it's time to float the Sundown River. He also says you should bring a real fly rod along."

For a moment Woody stared vacantly at Joby, then nodded as if he understood and blurted out, "Sounds like a good idea to me." But even as the words were leaving his mouth, the significance of the message hammered its way into his conscious mind. The Sundown River. He hadn't heard that phrase for years or thought about it. He had scoffed that he would live to see this day. Now it was here. A cold chill spawned goosebumps throughout his body.

As Joby prepared his mocha, Woody mused upon the note's author. *That's so Jack. His sense of humor stays intact in the worst circumstances. Sends me a message to warn me that the world is coming to an end and can't pass up the opportunity to remind me that he's a traditionalist who isn't impressed with tenkara. Don't understand why he won't even try Japanese fly fishing.*

When Woody turned around with his Cinnamon Griz' in hand, the man in line behind him—a short, pudgy fellow wearing a freshly pressed Bahama shirt, a brand-new Orvis hat, and unscratched Oakley sunglasses dangling around his neck—said quizzically, "I know all of the floatable trout streams in California and Oregon and most of them west of the Continental Divide. But I've never heard of the Sundown River. Where is it located? The Cascades? Colorado?"

Woody just smiled and said, "Sorry bud. That's a trade secret." As he surveyed the pudgy fisherman's face, warning bells began to go off in his gut. Something didn't add up.

He felt the same uneasiness that he had sensed on several occasions during the First Gulf War when locals pretended to be friendly but later proved to have malicious intentions. His battle instincts came online. This fisherman shouldn't be trusted … if he actually was a fisherman. *I doubt that he even knows a nymph from a scud.* Woody decided to change his normal pattern. Instead of enjoying his mocha at a window table with a view of the foothills, he nodded to the fisherman and headed straight for the exit. As he passed through the door, he felt eyes honing in on his back like a laser target designator.

Woody climbed into his Jeep and decided to dawdle a bit, hoping to get some indication of who the awkward dude in the Orvis hat was and what his intentions were. He pulled out a map of Angeles National Forest and pretended to be looking for backcountry roads to explore. As he waited for the dubious angler, his mind was racing in high gear. Float the Sundown River. What had precipitated this message? Whatever the cause, he knew it had to be serious. His cousin, Jack Lundstrom, wouldn't have sent this message unless the planet faced an existential threat.

When he figured he had waited long enough for Pudgy to get his coffees, he folded his map carefully and put it back in the glove box, started his Jeep, pulled out of his parking spot, and stopped at the street entrance, waiting for the light to change at the intersection. When the light turned yellow, he pulled out into the street. That bought him a couple minutes. Scanning his rearview mirror every few seconds, he noticed Mr. Orvis walking across the parking lot, carrying a tray with three coffees. He walked up to a black SUV, fumbled with the door, climbed into the back seat, and handed coffees to the two men in the front who were wearing suits—*likely agents.*

He smiled to himself. *Looks like Big Brother has me on their radar. Most likely because they have Jack on their radar. And Jack is on their radar because he is privy to sensitive information on a potentially apocalyptic scenario that Big Brother doesn't want anyone to know about. Guess it's time to make my way to Montana. Wonder if Jack knows that they are on to him?*

The light turned green, and he proceeded up the street, distracted, trying to come up with a plan, frustrated with himself. He had written off the possibility of an apocalyptic-size threat. To him, the probability seemed astronomically small. He had never even given the matter a serious thought. Now apocalyptic trouble was knocking on his door, and he didn't have a plan. *Way to go Woody. Right in character. A day late and a dollar short.*

His mind drifted back to the phrase "Sundown River" and the first time he had heard it. He and Jack were at Camp Eagle II during the First Gulf War, he with Delta Force and Jack with the Seals. While eating lunch on the tailgate of a deuce-and-a-half on a rare cloudy day, Jack laid out his head-for-the-hills plan should Earth ever face an apocalyptic threat from the heavens. Whoever learned of the threat first would send the other the warning message "Time to float the Sundown River." Then each would make their way to Montana, where they would rendezvous at their favorite campsite on the Musselshell River. Woody grunted and said, "Okay." He doubted they would ever need the phrase and filed it away in the back of his mind with things he regarded as useless trivia.

The plan had been modified twice over the years. In 2006 Jack had changed the rendezvous site to Bob Reddington's lodge at the base of the Crazy Mountains. In 2011 he had changed their communication method.

At the time Woody had regarded the latter change as a pain in the butt. Two years prior to the Snowden affair, Jack informed him that the NSA's massive invasion of privacy necessitated a change in procedure. Calls, text messages, and emails were too easy to intercept or block. The new plan was to relay the message through trustworthy acquaintances. If Jack got the scoop on a heaven-sent apocalyptic scenario, he would give the message to his acquaintance, who would anonymously email it to Woody's acquaintance, who would pass it on to Woody. If Woody was the first to learn of an inbound disaster from above, the process would be reversed.

This plan was definitely more NSA-proof, but it had one vulnerability. Their acquaintances would have no idea that they were part of a secret message system until they found themselves playing messenger. That meant that they had to be men of exceptional character and discretion. Jack also specified four other conditions. They couldn't be friends because they would be questioned by the authorities. They must be leery of Big Brother government. They must be familiar with anonymous email. And they must be deeply rooted, that is, unlikely to move.

After thinking through this—grudgingly—for several days, Woody chose Joby, his barista acquaintance at the Sierra Coffee Company. Jack picked Thomas "Buzz" Mason, a semi-retired SWAT officer who belonged to the motorcycle club that he rode with from time to time.

Woody's train of thought jumped back to the present, bringing a fresh jolt of frustration. The warning he figured he would never hear had just been delivered. The words danced around in his head like ball lightning—"Time to float the Sundown River." He shook his head at his blunder. Once again, his cousin had been right. He was always right. The unthinkable was on its way. Perhaps the biblical apocalypse would prove to be literal after all, and the events in Revelation would shake out in his lifetime. Regardless of what was coming, however, he wasn't ready. But he would get ready. After dinner, he would sit in his chair with his legal pad and a hot toddy and start making plans.

38

Burrage Krakenhavn had been caught by surprise when federal agents showed up at his studio and detained him for Homeland Security Act violations. At first, he thought he was being pranked by one of his competitors. He laughed at the agents and told them to go tell whoever sent them that they should find better actors next time. When they handcuffed him and ushered him outside to load him in a van, he started panicking and demanded to know who they were and where they were taking him. But they ignored all of his questions. He didn't find out why he was in custody until his first interrogation session at the FBI field station in Los Angeles.

He was incredulous when they started asking questions about the Rogue. He tried to tell them that he didn't believe anything that he said on air, that he did the show because it was a lot of fun and paid well, and that he had a hard time believing that anyone took the stuff seriously. When the intel came in about the Rogue, he thought it was another bogus story that would be fun to tell. He was wrong—very wrong.

His first month at 286, he nearly went insane. He had lost everything: his upscale house, his baby-blue corvette, his Irish Setters, his art collection, and his brandy cellar. And he had no hope of ever getting any of it back. He despaired of ever having a life of any kind again. But with encouragement and positive redirection from Jeremy Hendricks, a flicker of hope started to glow in his inner man. He saw that he wasn't alone in his pain. Everyone in 286 had lost everything: possessions, positions, spouses, and family. But they were all there in God's purpose, a tangible purpose, a purpose they could discover and capitalize on. Jeremy challenged him to find his purpose and make the best of his opportunity.

Burrage started attending chapel services, and slowly the light came on. God was after a relationship, not religion. The proof of this was the son of God himself becoming a man. With a warmed heart, he began reading the Bible to discover the plans that the Creator had for man and for the world. By Christmas Eve, he was smiling again and joined the others in the festivities. He even helped the Norwegian Legion in the kitchen with lefse, julekake, and rosettes.

With a new-found appetite for the Bible, the rejuvenated man, long a voracious reader, spent many hours every day perusing its pages. What he found was the greatest untold story on Earth. No conspiracy was more villainous than the blindness which kept these exhilarating themes and prophecies hidden from the minds and hearts of mankind. He burned to master this material and make it known.

***

In early February, Burrage sat down with Jeremy and shared a vision that was growing on him. He wanted to revive the *Down the Rabbit Hole* show, but this time around he only wanted to cover issues that were both factual and significant in the big picture. His primary focus would be prophecies on the last days like the Gog and Magog invasion of Israel in Ezekiel. He would also give a significant amount of time to the Rogue because the massive comet could well prove to be the event that precipitates the loosing of the planets mentioned in the Gospel of Luke, "the powers of the heavens shall be shaken."

Jeremy was excited about the project, but he did have a few questions. "How do you intend to broadcast your messages from the confines of Camp 286?"

"I don't intend to broadcast from here. My plan is to get my messages out to a loyal friend who would turn my notes into podcasts and my slideshows into YouTube videos. To re-establish and re-identify the brand, he would use the *Down the Rabbit Hole* logo and theme music."

"But if he was recognized as one of your friends, then the messages could be traced back to you and 286."

"Yeah. I thought about that. He would have to use voice-masking software to conceal his identity."

"But how do you intend to get this information out? We have no ability to upload to the internet, call on the phone, or send email. It's like a black hole here. Stuff comes in, but nothing goes out."

"I have been working on an idea," Burrage continued, "that the boys in the shop might be able to help us with.

How about setting up our own long-range Wi-Fi system that operates independently of the facility's communications systems? If we could locate an 18-Db, high-gain panel antenna, some low-loss cable, and a high-power wireless adapter, we would be able to pick up a strong Wi-Fi signal up to a mile away. Frenchie thinks we might be able to tap into the network at Sonny's Salvage and Recycling. Apparently, they have a pretty powerful network that gives them clear communication between the main office, the shop, and their many barns and sheds."

"But wouldn't people be able to see the antenna? And what about the cameras that focus on the building 24/7?"

"We need to set up a system in the men's dorm that is hidden in plain sight. My idea is to build a raised captain's bed with a cozy office underneath, where I will appear to be busy with a weekly newspaper for 286. In reality, I will spend much of my time preparing material for the *Down the Rabbit Hole* podcasts and videos.

"On the window end of the bunk, a bookshelf will conceal a shallow compartment, where the Wi-Fi stuff will be kept. When we want to send or receive, we swing out the bookshelf, which hangs on concealed hinges, fold down the table, set up the laptop, connect the cables and power, swing out the antenna arm and extend it toward the window, turn the system on, catch the signal, and—VOILA—we can send and receive. I estimate it would take less than two minutes to set up. If we put curtains on the windows, the setup would be hidden from the cameras, and there would be no significant loss of signal strength.

"However, we would have to limit the system to official business. We can't afford to communicate with family and friends lest we get discovered, and our Wi-Fi system gets shut down."

A broad grin spread across Jeremy's face, and he nodded with approval. He was on board. "That's a smashing idea. I think it could actually work. Let's go down and talk to the maintenance boys and get things rolling. I'll bet Bryce and his crew can pull this off." He turned and started walking briskly to the shop.

Burrage laughed and got up to follow him. *Life is good again.*

Using their make-shift ordering system, Bryce ordered the needed Wi-Fi parts from their contact at the Salvation Army store in Syracuse. They didn't know who their supply-angel was, but they were grateful. The system had started months earlier when they began finding stuff hidden inside items like couches, ovens, and dressers, and they realized that they had a friend on the outside. A note had been attached to one of the first gifts which said, "If you have any requests, hide it inside the thirteenth item on your shipping manifest. I won't make any promises, but I will do what I can." On a whim, they requested a bag of Liquorice Allsorts, which they received the next week to their amazement. Things developed from there. Over the next six months, they procured books, tools, medical supplies, and more candy.

As usual, they concealed their order inside the thirteenth item on the manifest of repaired items headed to the store for resale, this time inside the motor housing of a blender. Due to the exceptional expense this order entailed, they enclosed two hundred dollars in cash with it, which they collected by asking the camp residents for small donations.

While waiting for their order, they began preparing the men's dorm for their secret Wi-Fi station. They covered the windows with green curtains, which they made from dyed sheets. Using salvaged dunnage, and lumber from crates and pallets, they made twelve captain's beds with bookshelves on one end which they spread out among B, D, and E sections.

As planned, Burrage's bed concealed a compartment behind the bookshelf, where they installed a fold-down table, a rack for the laptop, a rack for the external hard drive and the Wi-Fi adapter, a mount for the power strip, a swing arm for the antenna, and a loop for the extension cord. Across the top they painted the *Down the Rabbit Hole* logo and the quote "Fortune favors the bold."

On Friday, March 1, the maintenance shop received a load of furniture for repair and found their Wi-Fi treasures hidden inside several couches. The project team began work immediately, and late Tuesday afternoon they had the system ready. Burrage spent the next two afternoons trying to hack into the network at Sonny's Salvage and Recycling before he discovered that the password was *platinum.*

Burrage and his advisors decided to use the Wi-Fi in the afternoon for two reasons. The first was that Bob Drake almost never poked around during the day while the night director, David St. Germain, walked the floor almost every night. The second was their fear that middle-of-the-night logins at Sonny's would stand out like a sore thumb in their network log.

On Friday afternoon, Krake, as his friends affectionately called him, began operation. He logged into Irina's Buster account, set up an email account for himself, logged into his Bitcoin account—thankfully his Casper interrogators hadn't asked him if he had more than one Bitcoin account—and paid for five years of premium service in her Buster account. Then he sent a GASmail to Nicholas Flieger's secure email account—Nick was a long-time friend—asking him if he would be willing to help with his new *Down the Rabbit Hole* ministry. The focus would be Bible prophecy—with a focus on biblical catastrophism and the geopolitical stage in the last days, particularly as it involved the reunified Roman Empire and the Russian juggernaut. If Nick was interested, his part would be to turn raw material into podcasts and YouTube slide shows.

Nicholas was a good choice for this project. He was a retired professor who had taught Russian at Columbia University and had worked as a language consultant for the State Department. His fluency in Russian was exceptional and his expertise in Russian history and foreign affairs was unsurpassed. He was also a Southern Baptist who loved the Bible and had assiduously studied prophecy and apologetics. Many times in the past, Burrage had turned to him for help on thorny Bible issues. Now he was turning to him again.

The next day, they heard back from Dr. Flieger. "Glad to hear that the *Down the Rabbit Hole* program is coming back online, this time with a focus on the apocalypse. Count me in. I definitely want to be part of this." Burrage was thrilled. He immediately threw himself into the work, devoting most of his time to research, writing messages, and making slides. Once or twice a week, he sent files to Nicholas.

His first message covered the prophecy in Luke 21:26, which states that the powers of the heavens shall be shaken in the last days. He pointed out that much of the prophetic terminology of the New Testament is derived from the Greek translation of the Old Testament (the Septuagint), that the word in this verse translated *powers* is *dunamai*, the plural of *dunamis*, that this word was often used in the Septuagint to refer to the planets in association with the sun, the moon, and the stars, and that the ancients feared and worshipped the host of heaven—the planets—as well as the sun and moon.

His second and third messages covered the evidence for planetary catastrophism in the accounts of the Babylonians, Greeks, Norse, Mayans, and other ancient civilizations. He produced passages that indicated that some of the planets once had very different orbits than those they have today. In particular, he demonstrated that Mars and Venus had highly elliptical orbits that intersected with each other and Earth. Their intersections with each other were the source of the ancient tales of trysts and spats between the god and the goddess. Their devastating intersections with Earth led to the ancient tales of the god of war (Mars) trampling Earth and the goddess (Venus) being a two-faced witch, who could be as deadly as she was beautiful. These visitations were the reason that men feared and worshiped these two planets. They were not terrified by the morning star and the tiny red twinkle that we are familiar with.

His fourth and fifth messages worked through the Old Testament passages which support the claim of many ancient historians that the planets once had highly elliptical orbits that occasionally passed very close to Earth. He covered men fearing and worshipping the planets, awful storms of stones and fire falling from heaven, mountains melting, mountains skipping, the heavens bowing down, the morning turning to night (Earth spinning or rolling on its axis), and Jehovah riding a cherub in the heavens, bringing judgment with him.

A sixth message addressed the near pass of a cometized planet which brought the Bronze Age to a close when it rained fire upon Earth from northern Europe to Ethiopia, devastating hundreds of cities and destroying the Mycenaean and Minoan empires. The fire that fell at this time was hot enough to turn stone blocks into ash as evidenced in the so-called burn layer. This visitation was the means God used to bring fire and pestilence on Egypt at the time of Israel's Exodus. And it introduced forty years of clouded skies over the entire globe, a dark and desolate time remembered by many ancient cultures around the world.

A seventh message addressed the planetary visitation that brought the Silver Age to an end when it rained fire across Europe and the Mediterranean region. This near pass also tipped Earth, causing a polar shift that sent Scandinavia and Siberia north to their present location, ending their temperate climate in one fell swoop. This same polar shift, likewise, sent Antarctica south to its present location, where the entire continent was soon buried under many hundreds of layers of ice, ice that is now two to three miles thick.

***

Burrage's sixtieth birthday rolled around on the first of May, and his friends threw him a party with ice cream and German Sweet Chocolate cake from a box. After blowing out his candles, the cry went up, "Speech!" Tearfully he shared his testimony … that he had thought his life was over … that he had found purpose and joy in his new work … that it had taken a harsh trial to open his eyes to the real meaning of life … that fulfillment is more a matter of purpose than circumstances. He closed with a line of wisdom Irina had shared with him, which she had gleaned from Pastor Vargas. "The end of the line isn't the end of the line if you are still breathing."

39

First thing Monday morning, Ariele walked into Sally's office and cheerfully greeted her, "Good morning."

"It's definitely morning, but the good part is debatable," her boss replied sardonically as she scurried about her office. "Would be a lot nicer if CNEOS wasn't constantly on my back over NEO stuff: NEO discovery, NEO cataloging, NEO preparation, NEO meetings, NEO this, NEO that. I'm supposed to be going to Washington again later this month for another NEO meeting. That's six times since the first of the year."

An uneasy tension hung in the air. Sally turned to Ariele. "Sorry for the outburst. I shouldn't take it out on you. I'm just tired of this whole NEO thing. I want my life back. I don't like being at the beck and call of bureaucrats in Washington or their lackeys in NASA. I don't like sitting in stuffy meetings and listening to windbags telling me what to think, how to think, and when to think."

Ariele's estimation of Sally's frustration went down a

different track. *Maybe tired of the whole Rogue thing would be more accurate?* She met Sally's eyes. "Sorry to hear that you're struggling with pressure from the thrones in D.C. I can identify. I don't like being told what and how to think either. It's even worse when men pressure you to swallow a camel on the plea that it's best for everyone involved."

The young astronomer girded herself. It was time to lay all her cards on the table. "I have something I would like you to read." Sally took her chair and looked over with eyebrows raised, her curiosity piqued by the unusual request. Ariele, her confidence quickly vanishing, handed Sally a thin binder which held her research on the comet along with a copy of Dr. Youngblood's paper. *Hope I'm doing the right thing.*

Sally opened the binder and bit her lip nervously when she saw the title *Comet or Shock Wave From Black-Hole Jet* and the subtitle *Another Look at the Phenomenon in Taurus.* She rose from her desk with a muffled sigh of dismay and walked to the south window, visibly shaken, where she stood with her back turned. Ariele heard the ruffling of pages. Abruptly Sally swiveled back to her protégé. "I will look at this material and get back in touch with you."

Looking on expectantly, her head cocked slightly, Ariele sought a little clarification on this open-ended promise.

"I meant sometime today, Moxie," Sally said, forcing a smile through her pain, "not sometime in the next decade."

Ariele smiled back, said "Thanks," and scurried out, fear and hope sloshing together in her heart.

An hour later, Sally summoned Ariele back to her office and motioned for her to close the door. "Ariele," she began with a heavy heart, "how did you find out that some people dispute the accepted explanation of the anomaly in Taurus?"

Anomaly? People trot that word out when they don't like an observation that inconveniently stands in their way. "The information just landed in my lap. I stumbled upon the paper by Dr. Youngblood while doing internet research on NEOs. On a whim I googled "NEO + hairy star + threat," and his paper appeared on the eleventh page of the results."

"Do you think his paper is valid?"

"I do. His interpretation of the data is vastly preferable to the accepted interpretation."

"Ariele," she reasoned, "You do understand that you are opposing the entire astronomical community, don't you? The experts are all agreed on the best explanation of this phenomenon. The apparent occultation of the stars is actually refraction of the stellar-light waves by the shock wave from the expanding jet of a recently formed black hole. Do you really believe that you alone have the correct interpretation of the apparent stellar occultations and that the entire body of experts has erred?" She watched Ariele, hoping to see some indication that her young colleague might be willing to back down.

Seeing none, Sally continued to press her point, "The experts are agreed that a fairly large star in the local universe went nova in recent cosmological history, collapsed into a black hole, then rebounded and started to expand. In its expansion, it extended jets out of its polar regions as black holes often do. From our point of observation here on Earth, we are looking straight down the barrel of one of the jets, so to speak. As the shock wave at the nose of the jet moves outward, it bends the light of the stars in its path through diffraction, giving the impression that a body is moving through space and obscuring the stars. While this is based on debated aspects of relativity, with only scant references in black-hole literature, this explanation has been unanimously agreed upon as the best explanation."

Ariele fumed. *You don't feel tension between the official interpretation and its status as Top Secret? If this really is merely the harmless effect of a nearby black hole, why the cover-up? Why the strict secrecy?*

Sally pulled the ace out of her sleeve, "You also need to know that the paper you based your research on is a forgery. The supposed author, Dr. Steven Youngblood, could not possibly have written this paper. He died three years ago, well before this Taurian controversy erupted. I know that for a fact. He was a colleague of mine. I attended his funeral."

This information stunned Ariele, but she processed it on the fly. *Why did she say controversy? She knows more than she is admitting Not Dr. Youngblood? Hmm!? Whoever wrote the paper has a technical knowledge of the subject, is an exceptional communicator, and is an insider. Somebody inside is trying to warn the world!* Ariele pressed her own perspective. "If the shock-horizon theory is true, then why do we only see one star at one point of the shock horizon being occulted? Why not many stars in a larger area?"

"The experts suspect," Sally replied, "that we only see diffraction at one point because the tip of the shock horizon is bullet shaped. We are observing the phenomenon from the perfect angle, looking directly at the tip, the odds of which are probably one in a hundred trillion. If we could observe the tip from a side angle, we would see refracted stars in a larger bullet-shaped area, and their refractions would be different, likely moved instead of occulted. As objects can be viewed through a sheet of glass without diffraction, yet when viewed through the cut edge they appear moved through diffraction, so stars can be observed through the body of the jet without diffraction, yet when they are observed through the shock horizon, the stars are displaced through diffraction. In our case, they are so far diffracted that they appear occulted."

Ariele wasn't buying the explanation. She objected and tried to argue her point further. But Sally cut her off. "Ariele, such anomalies are for the experts to debate, not workhorses like you and me. We do our job. They do theirs."

The recalcitrant astronomer stared forcefully into Sally's eyes. Sally returned the intensity. But Ariele was not going to budge. When she believed she was right, she could be as stubborn as a mule. And Sally's last statement—on experts and workhorses—had thrown down the gauntlet in challenge to her moral code. *There's that word "anomaly" again, a tacit admission that something doesn't fit your theory. Do you really believe that men should unplug their brains and listen to the experts just because things are debated? Not thinking is a problem in my book. How do you not see that as a problem?*

When Sally observed that Ariele was determined to stand her ground, she changed tactics. If reason was ineffective at convincing her to back down and let it go, maybe a threat would work better. "Ariele, you need to realize that you are in possession of highly confidential information that is far above your security clearance. The mere possession of this information is regarded as a serious security threat by the government. If you won't back down, if you won't let this matter go, I *will* have to report you. This is much deeper than you think. Please don't force me to turn you in." Sally winced. *That was an unfortunate choice of words.*

The phrase "turn you in" grabbed Ariele's attention. *She's privy to the whole shebang. She knows what's going on, but she's trying to protect me. Why?* "Turn me in? To who? NASA? The FBI?"

Sally edgily replied, "We don't want to go there," and held Ariele's eyes. She was not going to back down. She had to turn this straying sheep before she hurt herself.

Ariele waffled. She hated to surrender when she knew, or was at least reasonably certain, that she was right. On the other hand, she had to do something to defuse the situation. Maybe she should just play along. Playing along wasn't surrendering even if it looked like surrendering. It was just waiting for a more opportune time. She nodded as if she was conceding. "Okay, Sally, I'll let it go."

"You have to promise me that you won't publish this, or distribute it, or open your mouth to anyone about it for any reason. One infraction and the boom will fall."

"Okay, I promise." *But I don't promise that I won't let someone else publish it, or distribute it, or open their mouth. I might be a hippie chick, but I have read Sun Tzu's "The Art of*

War," and I have no qualms about responding to deception with deception.

Sally informed Ariele that she was going to keep the report, warned her to delete or destroy any copies in her possession, and dismissed her. *God, don't let that headstrong young lady hurt herself.*

About thirty seconds after Ariele's departure, Sterling Fitzgerald, Sally's associate department head and the only other person at Caltech that was privy to Minoa, walked into her office, leaned against her file cabinets, crossed his arms, and said as their eyes met, "You have to report her." He watched her reaction for a moment, then continued, "Those are the rules. You have zero discretion in the matter—nada. All unauthorized research in Taurus must be immediately reported. All knowledge or apparent knowledge of RN13 must be reported immediately when it is discovered. We do the tattling. They do the deciding."

Sally glared at him. She hoped she was making him feel small, but she doubted it. His ego was big enough to sink an aircraft carrier. "I know my duties and I will fulfill them."

"Fine. So do your job. If you don't make the phone call right here and now, I will. And if I make the call, you will go from a woman with a resume to a woman with a dossier."

Fuming mad on the inside—*What an egotistical, rooster-strutting, piece of road-kill trash*—Sally reluctantly picked up the phone and dialed the FBI hotline. When a receptionist answered, she said "Minoa Hotline," and was transferred to the Minoa Enforcement department. After a ten minute wait, an agent came on the line. With a heavy heart, she informed him of the situation, leaving out no salient details. She had no choice. The arrogant dirtbag was watching her like a hawk.

When she hung up, her heart felt like death warmed over. She was mad at herself. She was mad at Sterling. She was mad at the government. But there was nothing she could do.

Sterling stood smiling triumphantly, like he had saved the day and deserved a medal.

She wanted to shred him with some cutting remark, but refrained. You can't cut a heart of stone. Besides, it would be interpreted by him as a sign of weakness.

A couple hours later, two FBI agents showed up, took a deposition from Sally, which they had her sign, and took custody of the binder. As they were departing, they received a phone call. They stood in the hallway for a few minutes while one of them discussed the situation with a superior. The muffled chatter stopped, and the two agents walked back into Sally's office.

The older one addressed Sally. "The SAC, sorry, our boss, the Special Agent in Charge, has concluded, given the circumstances, that interviewing Ariele is not a pressing matter and that it could be handled at a later date, likely tomorrow afternoon. Her file indicates that she has already been approved by the FBI for Minoa clearance and that she is in the final stage of approval by the Minoa Project leadership at NASA for addition to your Minoa team here at Caltech. In a few weeks, she will likely be cleared to handle the material that was confiscated today. On this basis he has determined that Ariele's research doesn't constitute a threat to American security but merely an indiscretion, howbeit an indiscretion that merits a warning on straying from assigned duty." When the agent had finished conveying the message, he said, "Good day," nodded slightly, turned briskly, and headed back out her door with his partner at his heels.

Sally thought the agents appeared to be in a hurry, as if some situation far more pressing demanded their attention. *Probably the Antelope Valley terrorist organization. Been in the news the past forty-eight hours for possessing subversive literature that threatens the security of the United States.*

After they had filed out of her office, she closed the door behind them, leaned against the wall, and covered her face with her hands. She was overwhelmed with an avalanche of emotions. After staggering to her desk, she slumped in her chair and wept at her desk with stifled sobs, relieved, yet confused and scared. She wanted to believe that she and Ariele were out of danger. But the dark cloud wouldn't go away. She knew why—Sterling. She didn't trust that self-seeking sycophant. Things could still go south in a hurry.

When she regained her composure, she summoned Ariele to her office once again. With eyes still moist and lips still quivering, she quietly said, "Meet me here in my office after work, say 3:45 p.m. We need to talk some more." There was a little uneasiness in the air. Neither wanted to look in the other's eyes. Neither was sure they could trust the other.

Ariele bit her lip nervously. "Okay."

Sally forced a smile. "See you at 3:45 p.m."

40

Ariele walked into Sally's office a few minutes early. Sally wasn't there, but she had left a note on her whiteboard. "Moxie. Meeting until 4:30 p.m. Wait. Help self to walnut-date bars and Kenya AA coffee from Trader Joe's. ☺"

A sly thought stole into her mind. This was a golden opportunity to hack into Sally's computer. She drew a deep breath, then checked herself. *Should I do this? If I do, the bridge is burned. There is no turning back. On the other hand, my career is already damaged, maybe derailed. I can probably play the game for a little while longer, but I can't play forever.* She hesitated. *I have to find out more about this cover-up. What do they know about the Rogue and its threat that they are trying to hide? Besides, Sally knew she had this meeting and still asked me to come early. Why? Is she testing me or giving me a chance to snoop?*

Before she could stop herself, she logged in with Sally's username and password, which she had stealthily skimmed over the past three years, one keystroke at a time. When she had started skimming them, the operation had merely been a challenging game. She had no idea that she would ever need or use them. But after she received the package from Irina, and had begun to suspect that Sally's trips to Washington D.C. involved the Rogue and the cover-up, she had pursued her skimming game in dead earnest.

After she was in, she went straight for Sally's email, looking for folders that had something to do with the Rogue. No folder bore that name. She searched for *Rogue*. That pulled up eight emails from a folder entitled Minoa. She opened the first. It concerned the efforts to keep the comet's existence under wraps. *Minoa? Interesting. Why associate the approaching comet with Minoa? Minoa was destroyed by the eruption of Mt. Santorini. Maybe the use of Minoa is a hint that the government fears that the Rogue will cause vast devastation on Earth.*

She opened the Minoa folder. *Bingo!* There were hundreds of emails on the Rogue, though they referred to it as RN13. She inserted her thumb drive, downloaded the last fifty, the first fifty, and another forty or so with interesting headers. It took her eleven minutes. She was starting to feel extremely nervous. Sally's meetings often ended early. She retrieved her thumb drive, deposited it in her purse, and logged out of the network.

To help calm her rattled nerves, she fetched herself a cup of coffee from Sally's vacuum carafe and two walnut-date bars. *Gotta admit, Sally has good taste in food and clothes. Not sure about men though. Don't know why she isn't taking a good look at Woody.*

When Sally walked in, she found Ariele sitting in her chair, eating a walnut-date bar, and flipping through the May edition of *Astronomy*. She motioned for her to take one of the other chairs and sank heavily into her own. Neither felt like talking. Fidgeting with her hands, Sally forced herself to speak up and glumly filled Ariele in on the situation. "Ariele … I … I turned you in. I didn't want to do it. It killed me to do it. But I had no choice in the matter. It would have cost me my job if I hadn't called the proper authorities when you stepped out of bounds."

Ariele's mind started racing with questions. *Turn me in? Proper authorities? That doesn't sound promising.* But she didn't defend herself. She knew that she had been out of line. She nodded, resigned to her fate. "I understand. No worries. I should have used more discretion."

"Two agents came by this morning and picked up your report. They are going to question you, probably tomorrow afternoon."

"Agents?" Ariele asked. "What kind of agents?" She was playing dumb. She knew they were federal investigators.

Sally hesitated and averted her gaze. She didn't want to answer. But Ariele repeated her question. When Sally turned her gaze back to Ariele, Ariele bored her deep with her eyes. Sally relented. "It's the FBI."

"The FBI?" Ariele replied, startled, though she had expected the answer.

"Nothing to worry about. You aren't in serious trouble." Ariele looked at her, perplexed. "I sent an email to the Special Agent in Charge after I called the Minoa hotline and went to bat for you. I argued that you were doing reasonable research in a reasonable direction and unwisely wandered outside the confines of your assignment. I painted your effort as misdirected zeal for the mission rather than a threat to it. I also pointed out that you have been vetted by the FBI for Minoa clearance and that you are in the final stage of approval by the Minoa Project leadership at NASA for permanent assignment to my Minoa team here at Caltech."

Ariele was pleasantly surprised to hear the semi-positive news, but it didn't avert her sinking feeling that things were going to get worse, no matter how hard Sally massaged the situation. "Thanks, Sally. I appreciate your honesty and your help." She started to get up, assuming that the conversation was over. It was. Sally waved her out of the room with a friendly wave and a glimmer of a smile. It was good to see Sally smile again. As she walked to her car, she realized that her feelings of trust for Sally had somehow emerged intact from the ugly situation. On the other hand, could she trust her feelings?

41

Ariele left for work early and sat in the parking lot waiting for Woody. She was very uneasy about the situation despite Sally's assurances and wanted his advice. When he pulled into his parking place, she jumped out of her car and exposed her burdened heart before he had finished climbing out of his Jeep. "I need to talk to you at lunch."

Woody looked at her slightly perplexed. *We talk almost every day at lunch.* "Sure. We can do that. What do you need to talk about?" He turned and started walking towards the Cahill Center, the agitated female at his side.

"I'm kind of in a jam, and I need some advice on what I should do. I would tell you now, but we don't have enough time this morning." She felt relieved already. She trusted Woody and liked him. He was a true gentleman and always treated her like a daughter, which had earned her respect and gratitude.

When noon rolled around, they met as usual at the north doors and began walking to Beckham Auditorium, where

the food trucks parked. Ariele began her tale: Irina's letter …
a planet-sized comet beyond Neptune that was headed for a
close shave with Mars … her unauthorized search in Taurus
near the Pleiades … her observation of a stellar occultation
at the location Irina had predicted … and her six months of
observations that confirmed Irina's discovery.

She noticed that they were close to the food trucks.
Wanting to finish her story without interruption, she leaned
against a jacaranda tree and continued her account: giving
Sally her report on the comet … Sally's emotional response
to the report … Sally's muted defense of the official position
that the occultations were caused by the shock wave of an
expanding jet from a black hole … Sally's phone call to the
FBI's Minoa hotline … Sally's encouragement not to worry
because she had things under control … her desire to trust
Sally … and her hunch that the situation was spiraling out
of control.

When she finished, she looked at Woody expectantly, a
little puzzled that the man of few words had been unusually
silent while she unfolded her story. Apart from an occasional
nod, he hadn't responded at all but had listened attentively,
trying to absorb the salient facts. He met her gaze with a
distant look. She knew that look. She had seen it many times
before. He was weighing his response. But it was more than
that. He was correlating her report of a gigantic comet
headed for Mars with the Sundown River message that he
had received from Jack yesterday. He no longer wondered
what Jack's warning was about. Now he knew, and it made
him nervous.

But he was more worried about the threat they faced from the government than he was the threat they faced from the comet itself. If the authorities wanted this matter covered up, then it could be costly for anyone lucky enough, or unlucky enough, to possess information on it. And the two threats together, the comet and the government, spelled a heap of trouble. Life as they knew it, for all practical purposes, was now derailed.

Woody broke his silence. "I'm not going to deny the evidence that Earth is facing a potential extinction-level event, that the government knows it, that the government is trying to suppress this information, and that we could be in deep doo-doo merely for possessing this information, even incarceration in a FEMA camp on Security Act charges. But panic is counterproductive. We have plenty of time to make plans. In the meantime, you have to play the game. Don't make any waves. Go along with Sally's directions and suggestions. Pretend that you really believe that you only strayed a little bit, that you trust her assurance that your infraction will be treated as minor, and that you are weighing the official explanation, fully willing to be convinced. I know how hard pretending will be for you. But this is your best chance for survival."

She nodded. "Okay. I can do that. I'll feel like a phony car salesman, but I can do that."

"One more thing. This is bigger than you think. Keep me posted if anything changes or you learn something new. I will do the same. If things go south faster than we anticipate, then we'll have to change our plans accordingly."

Bigger than I think? Does he know more about this than he is letting on? "What if things go south before we come up with a good plan?"

Woody smiled. "Then we'll have to make plans on the fly. Come on. Let's go get lunch."

They ordered sandwiches and coffee from Henry's Gyros, their favorite food truck, then sat on a ledge under an olive tree and continued to talk. Ariele gave him more details from Irina's letter and from her own research. She told him about the online article *Another Look at the Phenomenon Near the Seven Sisters* that had been posted under the name of Dr. Youngblood last August. He asked her a few questions about her friend Irina and about Sally, particularly her perceived changes over the past year. He too had thought the frequency of her visits to Washington, D.C. was a little strange, certainly not necessary for generic NEO research.

As Ariele devoured the last bite of her sandwich, Woody checked his watch. He was old school and still wore one, an older model Breitling that Bob Reddington had given him years ago. "Hey, we need to head back. We're already a few minutes late."

On the walk back, Woody encouraged his young friend. "Life is like the zany Martians screensaver. You have to pound the problems down as they pop up, or they will overwhelm you. But don't make the mistake of thinking that the goal is to reduce your problems to extinction because no matter how many problems you pound into the ground, there will always be a steady stream of problems popping up."

Ariele smiled. Everyone at Caltech knew about the silly screensaver that Woody referred to. In 2016 some Caltech students had hacked a Windows 95 era screensaver, the one with goofy-looking Martians that pop up randomly from big holes, and you have to hammer them back down with a big mallet. They rewrote the code so that it worked on Windows, macOS, Unix, and Linux, and they added one significant detail—the Martians were all wearing MIT sweatshirts or waving MIT pennants. Most of the Caltech students and faculty now had the Martian screensaver on their computers. She played it once in a while to relieve stress. She laughed when she pictured her problems as funny-looking Martians and pictured herself pounding them back into the cold ground from whence they came. By the time they got back to the building, they were both laughing.

42

At 1:30 p.m. sharp, two agents rapped on Sally's door and walked into her office. "Good afternoon, Ms. Evans. We need you to summon Miss Serrafe to your office so we can visit with her."

"What's going to happen to her?"

"That isn't for us to decide. We are merely field agents. Our responsibility is to gather the necessary information so the proper authorities can determine the best course of action to take with Miss Serrafe."

"So, what are the possible courses of action?"

The older agent rattled off an answer that sounded like it was memorized. "If it is determined that she doesn't pose a security risk, she will be retained here as a member of your Minoa team with limited Minoa clearance as per your recent application. If it is decided that she poses a security risk, she will be detained and placed in an environment that will neutralize the risk she poses."

"A FEMA camp?"

"We are not authorized to say."

"How long will this process take?"

"They will make their decision before midnight tonight."

Sally sighed a hopeless sigh and felt herself descending into the abyss of forlorn heaviness. *Ariele, you are walking on thin ice. Please be on your best behavior.*

A few minutes later, Sally escorted Ariele into her office. One of the agents motioned for Ariele to take a seat at the table. She obliged. Then they motioned for Sally to leave the room. Sally exited, a little alarmed. *This may be much more serious than I anticipated.* The agents took their seats across from Ariele and stared at her with emotionless faces. She thought to herself, *I hope their cold facades are just an act, otherwise, these poor guys are doomed to bachelorhood.* She tried to disarm them with her most winsome smile, but they seemed impervious to warmth. They just sat there and stared at her. She might as well have tried to charm a tombstone.

The younger agent began the session, constantly glancing at his notes. "The agencies concerned express their gratitude for your willingness to go above and beyond the call of duty in the prosecution of your assigned mission. Nonetheless, there is always a danger when going above and beyond the call of duty that you may overstep reasonable bounds." He paused for emphasis, then added, "The government believes that you have overstepped reasonable bounds in this matter. Do you concur?"

"Yes. I definitely overstepped what they have determined to be reasonable bounds." *Not saying whether I think their bounds actually are reasonable.*

"Do you understand why the government is enforcing a ban on apocalyptic fearmongering?"

She nodded affirmatively. But to herself she thought, *to prevent the man on the street from learning the truth about an impending disaster.*

"The ban is part of a larger effort by the government to quell a groundswell of unhealthy interest in apocalyptic theories among the American public. This mania has resulted in hundreds of wild reports circulating on the internet and talk radio about existential threats lurking in our solar system that are headed in the direction of Earth. Despite the fact that these reports are fostered by fringe groups like conspiracy theorists, preppers, and Bible-thumping fundamentalists, their unhealthy influence has managed to reach deep into the psyche of mainstream America. Because this interest has swelled into a nationwide delusion that leaves the average man unable to discern the difference between fabrication and truth, the government has stepped into the chaos and banned all fearmongering with apocalyptic theories.

"America doesn't need this apocalyptic drama. It is the position of the government that we have too much instability in our nation already: political tensions, religious tensions, racial tensions, and the uproar over climate change. They don't want end-of-the-world fearmongering adding yet more volatility to an already explosive situation.

"If these reports of apocalyptic doom were permitted to circulate among the general population, which is predisposed to end-times gullibility, the results would be devastating.

Panic would destabilize the nation. There would be rioting and looting, runs on banks, and bare shelves in stores. People would walk away from homes and jobs. America would go up in the flames of anarchy. Thankfully, the government has determined to deal summarily with the apocalyptic nonsense and the sick minds who propagate it. Both will be rooted out and removed from society."

The agents were making Ariele nervous. The way they talked, many of her family and friends were enemies of the state. She might disagree with her conservative family and friends ideologically and her Christian friends theologically, and she might think that her far-left friends were drinking bad tequila, but America was supposed to be a completely free marketplace of ideas, not a fixed marketplace, where a domineering viewpoint bans every idea that challenges it. Any ban on free speech was a dangerous precedent. Let the ideas fight it out in the marketplace.

The younger agent continued, "Do you understand why there is a ban on Taurus that covers research, publication, and communication?"

Ariele replied, "I wasn't informed by anyone that our research efforts were limited by a ban on Taurus. I was told that we were implementing CNEOS protocols, that we were being assigned research sectors. We were led to believe that this constraint was budget driven, eliminating overlap so CNEOS could maximize their limited man-hours and dollars, allowing them to catalog the entire body of significant-size NEOs at the earliest possible date. My effort on my own time cost the federal government nothing."

"The government is definitely concerned," he observed, "to catalog every NEO larger than 140 meters and calculate the threat they pose. But they are more concerned about the security issues that are caused by loose lips than they are the security issues that are spawned by NEOs with impact orbits. They regard the public's chaotic reaction to threats, real or perceived, as a greater problem than the damage that would result from the impact of any known NEO.

"Therefore, when it became apparent that the conspiracy kooks, the apocalyptic wackos, and the sensationalists on the internet were drawn to the anomaly in Taurus like bugs to a light bulb and that the anomaly had become the primary focus of everyone who was engaged in apocalyptic fearmongering, the government decided that the ban on apocalyptic fearmongering absolutely had to be expanded to include a ban on all research, publication, and reporting on Taurus. It was not enough to ban the fire. They also had to remove the source of fuel that fed the fire."

Ariele's brain was starting to fire on all cylinders. *Loose lips. Lying tongues. Most are groundless speculation. Some have a grain of truth. A special ban on the anomaly in Taurus because it is too attractive as an apocalyptic story.* She decided to gamble. "So, am I right or wrong that a threat is approaching the inner solar system from Taurus that poses a catastrophic threat to the world?"

The older agent shook his head in frustration. "We have no idea what the heavens have in store for us, and we don't care. We are FBI field agents, not astronomers. But we are required to remind you that the astronomical experts are universally agreed that the phenomenon is caused by a harmless, near-neighborhood black hole. This view is satisfactory to the sober-minded majority. Moreover, even if there were an apocalyptic threat headed for Earth, and we were privy to the fact, we wouldn't be able to either deny or affirm your question. Such information would be beyond your present security clearance."

She seethed at their willingness to walk around in a fog. *The truth is right under your noses. Can't you think for yourselves for five honest minutes?* "Where do truth and facts fit into the equation?"

"The government does not care," he replied, "whether you are right or wrong. They care about the stability of the United States and her infrastructure. They take every threat to this great country seriously."

Ariele hazarded another question. "Does the government regard me as a threat?"

The younger agent responded. "In their estimation, any story about an apocalyptic threat in the heavens that is currently circulating, whether true or false, threatens the stability and infrastructure of the United States. And anyone who spreads such stories is regarded as a threat to our national interest and security."

"Well, I am guilty of neither."

"No matter, because the government regards the possession of classified information on apocalyptic threats in the heavens without the proper clearance as a threat to the stability and infrastructure of the United States. And you, Miss Serrafe, are in illegal possession of classified information."

Ariele looked down, brooding. *It's not looking good right now.*

"Were you aware," the agent probed, "that the research paper you cited was a bogus research paper?"

"I wasn't aware until yesterday when Dr. Evans informed me that Dr. Youngblood wasn't the actual author of the paper." *Regardless of who the real author is, the paper is definitely not bogus.*

"Professor Youngblood was actually deceased for several years before the publication date of the paper posted under his name. An unidentified person had the audacity to hack the University of Arizona network using his stolen identity, set up a hidden folder that was invisible on the local network yet could be accessed from the internet, and publish a paper that not only bypassed the protocols for academic publishing, but diverged so widely from mainstream science in its stated position that it would never have passed peer review.

"That paper was a cunning effort to get around the ban on research and publication on Taurus, particularly the debated phenomenon in Taurus. Whoever the culprit was, and it is widely suspected that the culprit is a Minoa insider, when they are caught, the government will not deal lightly with their treasonous act. They will spend the rest of their life in a secure facility.

"May we remind you, Miss Serrafe, that there is a ban on research in Taurus. Only authorized persons are allowed to conduct research in that sector. Unauthorized research—by telescope, plates, or online—is forbidden. And those who are authorized to pursue research are not permitted to talk to anyone about the subject. Not colleagues. Not friends. Not family. Every breach in this matter is regarded as a threat to the security of the United States. And every violation will be prosecuted by the authorities pursuant to the applicable laws under the Homeland Security Act."

The agent paused and locked eyes with Ariele. "Will you comply with the ban?"

"Yes. From now on my actions at both Caltech and Mt. Wilson will be fully compliant with the ban."

"Are you prepared to reconsider your interpretation of the phenomenon in Taurus?"

"Certainly. I am prepared to go wherever the facts lead me." *But I will stand in mud up to my armpits with Jeremiah the prophet before I give up my candor. And in my world assertion is not confused with argument, and theory is not confused with fact.*

"Do you agree that withholding classified information from the public is in the best interest of the American public and is necessary for the sake of preserving the security of this nation?"

"I understand the government's logic and resolve in this matter. If that is what the government has determined must be done to preserve America, then every law-abiding citizen must comply with it."

"Will you keep the information you have to yourself and only speak of it with those who the government deems have a need to know?

"I will." *Until I decide I won't.*

"That's all for now, Miss Serrafe. You will have a visit with the Casper team later on this evening. Your case will be decided by midnight tonight. If we have any more questions, we will summon you. You are dismissed."

She got up to leave, shaken but determined not to show it. *Casper? I might be able to beat a polygraph. Nobody beats Casper. To be decided by midnight? Unless GOD parts the Red Sea, I am pretty much screwed … GOD, I don't talk to you much, but I need help.*

43

Woody was leaving the break room with a cup of coffee when he noticed that the two federal agents had returned. They knocked on Sally's door and barged in without waiting for an invitation. That was a bad omen. She knew they were coming. She was in cahoots with them. Something ugly was brewing. Almost immediately, Sally walked out of her office and headed toward the cubicle area where he and Ariele worked. She was walking slowly, however, not with her usual sense of purpose. That was contrary evidence. It implied she wasn't in cahoots with them.

He paused by the break room door, pretending he was reading the material posted on the bulletin board. Hopefully, he didn't look too conspicuous. Did anyone actually read this stuff? He wasn't surprised when moments later Ariele shuffled to the office behind Sally. He kept his eyes glued to the board, steeling himself to not look up. Out of the corner of his eye, he noticed Sally eyeing him as they passed. *Interest? Likely not. Suspicion? Hopefully not.*

Woody knew that Ariele had breached operation policy when she had searched in the neighborhood of the Pleiades. But federal agents were a bit of an overkill if her only crime was merely looking in an unassigned sector. Her suspicions were probably correct. There really was a gigantic comet, and the government knew or feared that it posed an existential threat to mankind. They were treating it as a matter of national security, trying to cover up its existence, trying to avoid nationwide panic.

An hour later, a visibly shaken Ariele returned to her cubicle. She glanced feebly at Woody. He smiled back. *Poor girl.* He smelled trouble. He knew he had to come up with a plan fast and communicate it to her. But he couldn't risk contacting her via cellphone, text message, or email. Nor could he just walk up and talk to her. People would overhear. He needed to use a discreet form of communication.

Another cup of coffee seemed to be in order. Maybe the walk and the caffeine would stimulate some cerebral activity. As he turned up the hallway, he noticed Sterling at Sally's office door talking to the two agents, then the three of them walked into her office and closed the door. *Not good.* Woody neither trusted nor liked the man. He was an arrogant heinie-smoocher who coveted Sally's job. *If he gets her job, I'm officially in the job market. I'll recycle aluminum cans before I'll work for that preening opportunist.*

His curiosity, or perhaps special-ops instinct, got the best of him. He again pretended to be reading the bulletin board, feeling even more self-conscious than previously. *I've read this stupid board more today than I have since I started.* He heard Sterling's booming voice through the door. "You can't trust Ariele or Sally." He winced. Though he couldn't make out everything that was said, he overheard enough over the next five minutes to figure out that Sterling's report on Ariele was as negative as Sally's was positive. He portrayed Ariele as a serious threat who couldn't be trusted, who was concealing her real beliefs for convenience sake, who was convinced that the comet interpretation was the only valid interpretation, who believed that the public should be told the truth about the comet. He also painted Sally as a weak leader who wanted to cover Ariele's transgression instead of turning her in and would have done so if he hadn't forced her hand.

Woody groaned. This made a bad situation worse. He had to contact Ariele and warn her. Things were going to happen fast. Her case would likely be upgraded very shortly. They would start tailing her within the next hour or two. He felt awful. *She doesn't deserve this. She is such a sweetheart. Wait a minute. Sweethearts. Of course!.* He remembered that he had several bags of Valentine's Day hearts left in his desk drawer. *A little overboard on the candy this year.*

Back at his desk, he opened his stash drawer, counted out four Styrofoam bowls, which he kept in his desk drawer for hot soup on cold winter days, grabbed the top bag of candy hearts, opened it, and poured out a pile into each of the bowls. *Hopefully, this will work.* He began pawing through the bowls, searching for words or syllables that he could use. As he found suitable hearts, he scratched off the words and letters he didn't need. When he had found what he needed, he flipped the top layer in Ariele's bowl so all the writing was facing down, then arranged his doctored hearts with the letters facing up so they spelled out his message: "danger … meet me … ros-as … at six … take two whee-ls … back way … back door … care-ful." It only took him sixteen hearts. He had lucked out with the phrase *meet me* and ten whole words. He smiled with confidence. Ariele was a bright girl. She would understand the message, eat the evidence, and stir the bowl. *Eat your heart out NSA.* He stacked the other bowls on top of Ariele's and sauntered off to distribute his treats to the girls in their cubicles.

Ariele quickly figured out the message. She knew Rosa's well. It was a Mexican and Western restaurant conveniently located for Woody, near Caltech and on his usual route to and from work. He enjoyed the cooking, the waitresses, and the atmosphere. Several times a week, he ate his breakfast and dinner there. On occasion Ariele joined him for dinner when she was in the mood for dining out.

Within seconds after she had figured out the message, all sixteen hearts were in her mouth, almost too much and too tart to chew and swallow. *Not doing that again.*

How could she respond, she wondered, without anyone knowing it was a response except Woody. Nothing came to mind. She drew a blank. While she was pretty savvy with math and science, she didn't have his creativity. He could write poetry, paint, carve, and come up with ingenious solutions on the fly, even in difficult situations. *A valentine-heart message. That's so Woody. Brilliant, original, and funny. Wait a minute! Funny … humor … of course!*

She scrolled through her personal email, found the corny joke that her brother had forwarded to her a couple days earlier, claiming that there was a culture of prejudice against brunettes because no one told "dumb brunette jokes," added "Yes!" to the comment line, and forwarded it to Woody and several other friends. She had a strong suspicion that he would both understand the communication and appreciate the joke.

44

Ariele walked to her car with a heavy heart after work. After she climbed inside, she slumped on her steering wheel and tried to zen away the feeling of being crushed. It didn't work. With a sigh, she started her VW and headed for home. As she pulled onto East California Boulevard, she noticed a black SUV in her rearview mirror. *Am I being followed?* After a few blocks, it vanished. *Must have been a false alarm.* But a few blocks later, the black vehicle, or another one just like it, reappeared not far behind her. *Rats.* Then it was gone again. Then it appeared again. *Maybe I really am being tailed.* This happened several times during her drive home. She hoped that the SUV appearances were a coincidence and that she was just being paranoid. But she wouldn't bet on it.

When she entered her apartment, she tossed her purse on the table and headed straight for the kitchen. *Time for some comfort food.* She reached into the antique cookie jar on her counter for a handful of chocolate-covered coffee beans, her favorite snack, placed them in a small bowl, and popped one in her mouth. Next, she made a fruit smoothie: blueberries, raspberries, strawberries, a banana, and yogurt for thickener. Then she poured a bowl of habanero salsa and a bowl of Red Hot Blues. Finally, she grabbed two Cajun chicken wings from the box she had purchased at Whole Foods.

She felt slightly guilty for eating a full meal now though she was meeting Woody at six at Rosa's. *Oh well. I'll just have a piece of peanut butter pie and a cup of coffee.* With her table spread, she sat down, picked up a chip, reached for the salsa, hesitated, and for the first time in years said her prayers: on this occasion HeEtz, HaAdama, and SheHakol. It felt awkward but comfortable, like returning home after a long absence. She had been running from her Jewishness for years. Lately, for some profound reason, she found herself drawn to it.

As she ate, she thought about her meeting with Woody. He was obviously nervous about the situation. *Danger* was the first word in his message. *If Woody thinks that I'm in danger, that speaks volumes. That means my fears are not groundless. But if I'm in danger, what can I do? How do I get out? Not gonna worry about it. Woody will know what to do. He's been in many sticky situations over the years. He knows how to get out of a jam.*

But if Woody got her out of her predicament, would he be able to extricate himself? She was tormented with anguish for dragging him into this mess. This could spell the end of his career, not that he had much of one. It had fizzled out six years ago because of his unacceptable views.

Her mind wandered into contemplations on the courage

and character of her gray-haired friend. She admired the independent-thinking maverick who stuck to his guns, no matter what the cost. He had paid a steep price for holding "obscurantist" views that challenged the "accepted" theories of modern physics. He had been demoted from his position as department head at the Cahill Center and marginalized— banned from the major telescopes, blacklisted by the peer-review journals, shunned by the industry publishers. He now labored in grunt work, with occasional time on the Hooker, though he was fully qualified, apart from his publishing record, to head most astronomy departments in the country.

She didn't think his "obscurantist" views were opposed to knowledge and scientific advance, much less dangerous. They actually sounded plausible. The universe is infinite and static (non-expanding) … all galactic motion is orbital and the galaxies orbit in radial equilibrium … redshift is not proof of an expanding universe … redshift is not a function of speed at a steady acceleration rate and therefore cannot be used to calculate distance … redshift is a composite of plain-vanilla factors including galactic composition, density of galactic and intergalactic plasma fields, and Doppler effect from orbital motion relative to Earth.

Who was right, she wasn't sure. But his view did seem to explain how quasars that are connected to the same galaxy by filaments can have widely different redshifts.

His protest against gravity as the preeminent force in the universe was her favorite. He loved to point out that gravity is a comparatively weak force … that electromagnetic energy is a billion billion billion billion times stronger than gravity … that a fridge magnet can lift a washer off a table, overcoming the gravitational attraction of the entire planet … that electromagnetic energy is the force that holds the universe together and maintains its orbital relationships … that once you own the preeminence of electromagnetic energy, there is no need for theoretical contrivances like black holes, dark matter, and dark energy to find enough gravity to hold the universe together.

Woody had also offended the movers and shakers with his belief that the complexity of the universe pointed to intelligent design. The universe can no more self-exist or self-assemble than a Rolex watch. For him, this was merely a matter of scientific and philosophic honesty. He wasn't a practicing Christian. *Enough with the wandering, girl. Eat! Gotta get ready and go.*

After putting her dishes in the sink, she changed into an outfit that would be more comfortable for her bike ride to Rosa's: a pair of coffee-brown gauchos, an eggshell peasant top with colorful embroidery, and brown trail shoes.

She was almost ready to go when she noticed, out the front window, a black SUV parked outside. The two men sitting in the front seat were dressed in suits and ties like the FBI agents that had talked to her earlier that day. *That pretty much proves that I'm not being paranoid. I'll bet Woody expected that this might happen. That's probably why he told me to take the back route.*

Her survival instincts kicked in. She felt the same rush of adrenalin that had energized her body on several occasions when she had been accosted by gangbangers in the park. On one of those instances, she had maced three mouthy punks and left them cursing and crying. The other two times, she had simply outrun the scuzzballs who threatened to rape her. This time she made hasty preparations for a stealthy escape.

She grabbed her Counter Culture Coffee sweatshirt out of her closet and stuffed it in her daypack. Then she added two changes of socks and underclothes, a pair of jeans, two blouses, and her sandals. From the bathroom, she retrieved her personal hygiene kit and a package of baby wipes. In the kitchen, she snagged a dozen Clif Bars, four bottles of water, two sports drinks, and her vitamin C tabs.

A wave of doubts washed over her and left her second-guessing herself. *Maybe I'm overreacting. Maybe they're just insurance salesmen or Mormon missionaries.* She walked by the window and glanced out of the corner of her eye. The SUV was still there and so were the goons in ties. They weren't getting out of the vehicle. They weren't retrieving literature from large leather bags. The one in the passenger seat was working on a laptop. And the vehicle sported federal plates. *Better finish packing.*

She opened her desk drawer and grabbed her stash of cash, two gift cards, a write-anywhere pen, a waterproof notebook, a swiss knife, and a no-battery flashlight—stuffing them all in her purse. Then she shoved her purse into her daypack, along with the emergency kit which her father had given her for Hanukkah two years ago. Almost as an afterthought, she added her Kindle reader and a solar charger. *Think that should do it. No, wait! My laptop.* She fetched it and stuffed it into her pack. *Glad I didn't forget that.* Not only was it a pricey unit, it contained her scanning software and all of her files on the comet. She suspected it would come in handy in the future, wherever that might take her. Not to mention, she definitely didn't want to leave it lying around for the FBI to find. After one last mental checklist, she cinched up her pack and clasped the flap.

With the kind of shock you feel when you almost screw up in a big way, she remembered her phone. *Thank you, GOD! That would not have been pretty.* She opened her pack, retrieved the phone from her purse, plugged in the charging cable, and left it on the counter. *That should buy me some time. The dudes tracking my phone will think that I'm still at home.*

Rolling her eyes at herself, she closed up the pack again. *Finally ready.* She eyed her knapsack, which was bulging out the sides and stuffed to the brim. With a groan, she lifted the bulky bag and headed for her balcony. *This is going to be miserable. Never rode with a pack stuffed this full before. My shoulders are never gonna forgive me.*

45

Ariele opened the sliding door to her balcony, slipped out, closed it behind her, and turned around to proceed with her getaway. *Oohh!* She found herself in a quandary. *Forgot I was on the second floor.* How was she going to lower her bike to the ground? *Umm,* p*arachute cord.* She opened her pack, dug out her purse, and retrieved the hank she had been carrying for years just in case. Solution in hand, she jammed the purse back into the pack and recinched her straps. Hastily she unraveled the cord, tied a round-turn and two half hitches onto her seat post—a knot she had learned from a sixties-era Boy Scout Handbook she had found at a flea market— added a few extra hitches because she found it hard to trust such a simple knot, and looped the cord around the railing for a brake.

Holding the brake end in her left hand, she lifted her bike over the rail and lowered it until the cord was taut. Then, using both hands, she payed out line until her bike touched the ground and flopped on its side. With a silent whoop, she removed the loop from the railing, tied the loose end of the cord to her pack, and lowered it to the ground. Her hands felt like they were on fire—*yikes!* A quick inspection revealed several nasty rope burns. *No time to worry about that now.*

She tossed the cord down, scrambled over the railing, hung momentarily from the top rail, kicked her legs out, pushed away with her hands, and dropped. She landed hard on her right ankle, crumpled to the ground, stood up with a wince—*scratch the Hollywood stunt-woman idea*—and hastened to her stuff.

Feverishly she untied the knots on her bike and pack, wadded up the cord, and shoved it in her pocket. Then she slung the pack onto her shoulders, hopped on her bike, and peddled hard, heading almost straight across the courtyard, away from the black SUV and out of its line of sight. She hadn't had time to plan her route, so she had to improvise. *Let's see. Zigzag through the streets and alleys of the business district and industrial park and hit the trails in Elysian Park. Both would make it tough for anyone tailing me. Then make my way to Stadium Way somewhere north of Dodger Stadium. From there take Riverside under the interstate and make my way to Rosa's. That ought to do it. Game on.*

She worked her way north and east out of the complex, weaved her way through the industrial neighborhood, got on North Main, crossed the canal and the Metro tracks into Taylor Junction, worked her way back north and west to Broadway, crossed the canal and the Metro tracks again, and then accessed Elysian Park off Park Row Drive.

Once she hit the trail system, she slowed considerably.

Her legs felt like jello and she was gasping heavily. She tried to convince herself not to worry about her slowed pace. *Pretty sure I lost them by now if they were trying to follow me.* She weaved her way northwest on the streets and paths looking for Stadium Way, getting more and more nervous that she had lost her way because her ride was taking longer than expected. When she finally came across Angels Point Road, she shouted *Kowabunga!* Now she knew where she was and how to get to Stadium Way.

Upon reaching Stadium Way, she followed it northwards to Riverside Drive, which took her under the interstate, then she headed southeast along the canal to North Figuroa Street. She stopped at the intersection for several minutes to catch her wind. When she started again, her pace was slowed even more by wobbly legs that begged to be relieved of duty. But she steeled herself, remembering a statement, possibly from the Tanakh, that she had heard a rabbi once say with great vigor. "This too shall pass." Block by painful block, she pedaled her way to York Boulevard, then San Pascual Avenue, then South Arroyo Boulevard, and finally to West California, the street Rosa's was on. Now she was close.

A block and a half before Rosa's, she turned north up the alley for a couple blocks, then rode east for a block and a half, then turned south. Just north of Rosa's, she turned into a parking lot shared by two businesses. On the back side of the building on her left, she parked her bike out of sight of the street. Shaking from her exertion, she removed her pack from her weary shoulders and dropped it next to her bike. *Hope this is safe. Too tired to take it with me.* She struggled over the fence onto the next property, then hugged the building as she walked south, feeling a bit self-conscious for sneaking around like a spy in a movie.

When she reached the corner of the building, she spied Rosa's, angled across the lot, and hopped over the hedge into Rosa's lot. She didn't make it. Though it was only eighteen inches high and two feet across, her weary legs weren't up to the task. Her feet caught on the edge, and she sprawled out over the top, skinning her palms on the blacktop on the other side. *Hope nobody saw that.* She picked herself up, hobbled to the back entrance, leaned her head on the door, and stood there, her body trembling and dripping with sweat. The draining ride, some fifteen miles in length, had taken her an hour and a quarter. *Mission accomplished.*

46

When Woody drove away from the Cahill Center at 4:30 in the afternoon, he noticed a black Tahoe follow him out of the parking lot. *Looks like the same vehicle that was here earlier today. Sheesh! Don't they understand that black SUVs and men in suits and ties are a dead giveaway? How ridiculous is that? Nice to see our tax dollars subsidizing ineptitude. But what can you expect? Common sense and government never did mix very well.*

The Tahoe tailed him all the way to his house and parked a half block down the street. It was still sitting in the same spot when he checked fifteen minutes later from the second story hallway window. And when he left for Rosa's at 5:30 p.m., it turned around and followed him. *Maybe a little more subtlety might be in order?*

At 5:53 p.m. Woody pulled into Rosa's parking lot, parked in the third space on the left side, and futzed with his briefcase for a few minutes, intentionally delaying his exit from his Jeep. He wanted to see where the SUV parked. As he suspected, it pulled into the gas station kitty-corner from Rosa's and parked under the sign, giving the agents a clear view of Rosa's parking-lot entrance and the front door. From that vantage point they could, or so they assumed, observe everyone coming and going. *Bet they're tailing me to see if Ariele meets up with me. Hope they like the taste of humble pie, 'cause they're not gonna see their target coming or going.*

When he entered the building, he headed straight for the table he wanted, the only one on East California Boulevard that didn't have a full window. This table gave him two advantages. The sliver of window on his side of the table, the west side, allowed him to keep his eyes on the agents across the street. And the wall on the east side, which covered two-thirds of the table, would keep Ariele out of their line of sight. They wouldn't be able to see her.

A few minutes after he sat down, Ariele entered Rosa's through the back door, hastened through the kitchen to the dismay of the cooks, barged through the service door to the dining area as if she worked there, and spotted Woody sitting at a corner table. He saw her as she made her entrance, rose from his seat, pretended he was stretching, and discretely motioned for her to hug the side of the wall. She drifted to her left and sidled into the booth across from him.

Woody briefly glanced at her—reassuring eye contact—then set his briefcase on the table broadside to the window, opened it up, shoved it forward a bit, took out his leather portfolio, and opened it on the table in front of him, exposing his legal pad and the latest copy of *Fly Fisherman*. Ariele was a little puzzled. *Must have something he wants to show me. Hope it's not a fly fishing story.* Then he bent low over his pad and whispered, "Keep tight to the wall. Feds are parked across the street. I think they're looking for you." Ariele bit her lip. She didn't like the news. But at least his unusual antic made sense now. He didn't want to be seen talking because that would imply the presence of another person, so he had used his old-fashioned leather briefcase for a wall. It obscured his lower arms and hands, and it concealed his head when he bent down as if working on something. *Got to hand it to Woody, he's pretty clever. Can't do that with the new-fangled man purses the guys are carrying now.*

Ariele replied in a subdued voice, "I think federal agents are watching my apartment too. I slipped out the back and climbed down from my balcony. Glad I don't live on the third floor."

Woody gestured downward with his hand indicating that she should lower her voice even more.

She nodded her head and dropped to a hushed tone. "This is insane. Why is the FBI involved in this? Why should an astronomer be in legal trouble simply for questioning NASA's interpretation of an astronomical phenomenon?

"I can understand the gatekeepers requiring belief in the favored theories because that has long been the case in the academic world. What I don't understand is the government's strong-armed tactics in the matter. For crying out loud, why should they care whether the phenomenon is a comet or a manifestation of a black-hole jet? Why should they care that I believe that the occultations are caused by a huge comet? Why would the FBI be after me?" But she was just venting her frustration. She knew perfectly well why.

"The fact that the government regards you as a threat," he replied, "merely for knowledge of the comet implies that they regard it as a serious—potentially catastrophic—threat to Earth. They don't want the public to learn of its existence. Knowledge of this threat would result in chaos, which would hinder their efforts to prepare for it.

"So they have implemented Orwellian policies designed to keep all information on the comet out of the hands of the public. And they have invented the official narrative with its black-hole-jet nonsense as a cover for those like yourself who stumble upon occultations which suggest its existence. But you aren't playing by their rules. You challenged their explanation of the phenomenon, so they regard you as a threat. And they fear that you might leak news of the comet to the public."

"Well, they ought to fear. I intend to disseminate this information to the public. They have a right to know and to prepare."

Woody stared at her, impressed at her conviction but worried for her safety.

She continued, "I don't think that I'm the only one who knows about this. I heard on the radio last week that the feds arrested a dozen webcasters who broke the news about a possible Planet X candidate out beyond Neptune. I think they were referring to Irina's comet."

"You're definitely not the only one," he confirmed. "My cousin Jack at NASA knows about it too. Years ago, we agreed on a secret-message system to warn each other of an imminent extinction-level threat in the heavens. Whoever became aware first would warn the other with the message. He sent the message yesterday."

Ariele stared at him, eyebrows raised.

"Jack's a sober man, fact-driven and not susceptible to the myths and yarns that attract the gullible and make waves on the internet. The fact that he would risk his career and time in a FEMA camp to send me the message is a strong substantiation that you and Irina are correct about a massive comet out beyond Neptune that poses a threat to Earth."

The waitress showed up and asked Ariele if she wanted coffee. She answered, "Yes." But Woody countermanded the order, "No, she won't be staying long." Then he leaned over and whispered, "Listen, Marlene. If anyone asks, she wasn't here. Okay?"

Marlene laughed and said, "Sure, Woody. Whatever you say." Then she walked away, smiling and shaking her head.

Woody noticed that Ariele was eying his cup of coffee, so he shoved it across the table. The frazzled gal picked it up with trembling hands and sipped it gingerly. "So, what am I supposed to do?"

His answer was blunt. "Listen, Ariele. I don't think your life is in danger. But you do have to flee. If you stick around, you will face interrogation. After that, you will have a lot of free time on your hands for reading, though I suspect that the libraries in the FEMA camps leave a little to be desired."

She balked at the idea. "Maybe I can just go back to my apartment and carry on like nothing significant happened.

Maybe they talk to me a few times, I play the compliant game, and the problem eventually goes away."

"Not gonna happen," he said, shaking his head. Sterling talked to the FBI today and gave both you and Sally a very negative report. I overheard him while I was in the break room. Sally won't be able to cover for you any longer. She is in hot water herself now. I suspect that the FBI intends to aggressively question you—hook you up to Casper. They will ferret out every detail that you are trying to hide. After that, they will prosecute you as a security threat under the Security Act. Then they will hustle you away to a secretive FEMA camp, where you will disappear. Nobody will have the slightest clue where you are, not family, not friends."

Ariele sat in silence, her eyes moist and her lip quivering.

Woody sensed her fear. *I think she has gone from hoping this wasn't as bad as it looked to realizing it's worse than she thought.* "You have to flee. You can't go back to your apartment. The situation is too hot. Think about it. You left in an unorthodox manner and won't be able to tell them where you went and why. They will want answers, and they will introduce you to Casper. And when they find out that you came here and talked to me, it will get pretty hot for me too."

He patted her hand. "I know it's not in your DNA to flee and hide. You're a fighter. But this is not the time to stand and fight. It's the time to flee and fight. Think guerilla warfare." He paused again. "Ariele, this information needs to be in the hands of trustworthy folks who can and will disseminate it to the American public. The best way to do that is to flee, flee to people who have the means and ability to help. It's not in the best interest of the American public that you are sitting in a detainment camp somewhere whiling away your days away watching reality TV."

"I know," she agreed. "Deep down inside I know that you're right. But where can I go? Where should I go? I don't have a clue."

"I have a plan," he assured her.

She brightened a little. "I thought you might."

"Get yourself to Montana somehow and look up a friend of mine, Bob Reddington. Tell him that you are a friend of mine and that you have critical information on a potentially apocalyptic scenario that the government is covering up. He will see to it that you have a place to stay and that you are taken care of. He will also introduce you to several others that you need to meet, like pastor Jordy Backstrom, who is an expert on Bible prophecy and the apocalypse, and an amateur astronomer by the name of Blake Steele."

Woody stopped talking and started writing on a napkin. When he finished, he shoved it across the table to her. It was Bob's phone number and a crude map to the Compound.

She glanced at it and stuffed it into her pocket. *Gotta remember to put this in my purse, or I'll lose it.*

Woody flashed one of his heart-warming grins. "Don't be surprised if I show up in Montana too. I suspect that my time here in California is quickly coming to an end."

Out of the corner of his eye, he noticed the Tahoe pull out onto the street and stop at the light. He suspected that it would turn left onto California, then right into Rosa's parking lot. "Bend down low," he told her, "like you're tying your shoe, and stay down."

She obeyed—retying both of her shoes.

The Tahoe did as he had anticipated. *No creativity. No originality. No element of surprise. How do they expect to nail anybody? They go about their work like they're ten-year-olds doing a paint-by-number picture.* When the SUV passed out of view of the last window that offered a view of their booth, Woody gave Ariele his final instructions. "Get out of here fast. Use the front door. Go east on California one block. Then work your way back to wherever you parked your bike." As she stood up, he touched her arm. "Be careful Mox. I'll see you in Montana."

47

Ariele scurried out the front door, bolted across the street through the traffic, briskly walked one block east, turned north, started jogging, turned west at the corner, jogged one block, crossed the street, then turned south and began to run. Her heart pounding, she dashed into the driveway of the lot where she had parked her bike, rushed to the backside of the building on her left—*thank God my bike and pack are still here*—slung her knapsack over her shoulders, hopped on her bike, and pedaled back out to the street, where she headed north, riding as if she was being chased by the devil himself.

Her mind in a tizzy—*where am I going to go?*—she decided to turn west on East Del Mar and head for Central Park. When she arrived, she took the first path she saw. After meandering across the park on its paths, she exited out the west side onto Valley Street and turned up an alley. Halfway up the alley, she felt an impulse to make her way to Scholl Canyon Park. *I'll figure out my next step after I get there. Better*

315

take a back route though. Less chance of being spotted. Need to make my way to the Annandale Country Club. From there catch Glen Oaks Boulevard. Follow it all the way up the hill. Left on the dirt road that leads to the landfill. Ride along the edge of the landfill till I get to the park. Definitely not looking forward to this. My legs aren't recovered from the first ride.

Her plan made, she turned left on Dayton, made her way to the Green Street Bridge and crossed the interstate, turned north on Orange Grove Boulevard and crossed 134, then hung a left on West Holly Street. She relaxed her pace. She had been pushing herself hard. Her legs were cramping and she was exhausted. Besides, she didn't think she had been seen or followed.

The next stretch of her ride would have been enjoyable if she wasn't on the run. Winding streets sprawled their way through the hilly terrain, revealing many gorgeous homes worthy of *Better Homes and Gardens*. She recalled several rides she had taken in the neighborhood with her friends, but she hurt too much to enjoy the memories. Breathing hard, her throat as dry as Death Valley, she willed her legs to keep peddling. *Can't stop. Gotta keep moving. I'll rest when I get to the park.*

On and on she pressed, turning left on Linda Vista, then right on Fern Drive, then weaving her way northward on the residential streets on the east side of the country club until she caught Glen Oaks Boulevard. When it ended, high up the hill and past the last house, she turned west on a dirt track, into the lowering sun, and followed it to the south gate for the landfill. It was closed and locked. Her heart sank.

Nuts! The fence was also higher than she remembered. She cocked her ear and listened, but didn't hear any equipment running. A glance at her watch revealed that it was 7:32 p.m. *They must be done for the day.*

She hopped off her bicycle and walked it into the brush on the right side of the gate, where the fence was lower—about eight feet high—determined to get over the obstacle. With a grunt, she threw her backpack over the fence. *Hope nothing broke.* With another grunt, she hoisted her bike over her head as far as she could and realized that she was short of being able to flip it over the top—quite a bit short.

As she lowered the bike, she was consumed with angry determination. Balancing the bike awkwardly on her arms, she began to climb with the fury of an enraged bull. Inching her way up, stabilizing the unwieldy object against the fence with her upper body and head, wincing in pain from the battering her fingers and arms were taking, she gained the needed height. With her left hand clinging desperately to the fence, which allowed her to lean back for a better angle, she pushed the bike up with her right hand, felt it hang up on the top of the fence, and gave it a desperate shove upward and forward, which flipped it over the top. It landed on the other side with a clatter. *No one is gonna believe I did this.*

Gingerly she placed her hands on the top of the fence—*I hate chain-link fences with pokey tops*—pulled herself up, worked her upper body over the top, and tried to flip her legs over. She lost her balance, tumbled over, and landed next to her bike, banging her elbow, bruising her ribs, and scratching her face on the brush.

Grimacing, she stood back up, dusted herself off, and checked out her injuries. She noticed that her blouse displayed several grease marks and a six-inch tear on the right side. She groaned. *What was I thinking? Why did I have to wear my favorite peasant top? Why didn't I just wear a t-shirt and sweat pants?* There was no necessity to look her hippie-chick best, not under these circumstances. Stewing over the matter, she rummaged in her knapsack, dug out a fresh blouse, and made herself presentable.

After she had closed her pack and put it on, she picked up her bike and walked back to the road. With her stiff legs complaining, she mounted up and peddled, following the road until it merged with a track on the edge of the landfill. When the track turned toward the interior of the facility, she continued forward across a grassy field into the equipment yard, weaved her way through it, and caught another dusty track, which took her to the turn-around at the southwest corner of the landfill on the border of Scholl Canyon Park. *Almost there. Unfortunately, there's a stretch of off-roading between here and there.*

She nosed her bike over the edge, uttered *Geronimo* in mock enthusiasm, and careened her way down the ravine toward the park facilities, negotiating a gauntlet of rocks, brush, and trees.

After a bone-jarring ride and a nasty spill, she arrived at the parking lot, scratched, bruised, and whipped. She took a moment to orient herself, then pedaled to the playground equipment, leaned her bike against a tree, and flopped onto the grass. Her legs felt like she had just done a thousand squats with a gorilla on her shoulders. They were throbbing with pain and cramping up. *That is the hardest five miles I have ever ridden.* With a moan, she forced herself to sit up and open her pack. She needed sugar and electrolytes. After she drained a sports drink in one shot and wolfed down a Clif Bar, she lay back down and stared into the dappled canvas of green treetops and brilliant blue sky, trying to figure out what she should do next.

48

Rosa's Diner, Pasadena, California
Tuesday evening, June 4, 2019

After Ariele rushed out, Woody pushed his briefcase a little farther away, opened his copy of *Fly Fisherman* to a picture of a fisherman on the shore of a magical lake in the Sierras, put his head in his hands, and brooded. *Maybe I shouldn't have warned her today. Now there is no turning back. Maybe she would have been okay ... no ... I had to warn her. She had to flee. She would certainly have been questioned under Casper and sent to a FEMA camp.* His thoughts shifted to a slightly different track. *I'm probably a suspect now too. They know Ariele and I are friends. They know I have a reputation for being a maverick.*

While he was contemplating the difficulties that he and Ariele faced, the two agents entered through the side door, walked past numerous empty tables and booths, and chose a table that allowed both of them to keep an eye on him. Woody ignored them—never even glanced at them. Instead, he flagged the waitress, asked to have his coffee refilled, and ordered a slice of Rosa's famous Mexican apple pie with ginger shavings, minced green chiles, lemon juice, and pine nuts. He wasn't going to give them any satisfaction, but he was definitely going to give himself some.

After he finished his pie, he reached into his briefcase and retrieved a volume on redshift that he had recently purchased, a well-written challenge to the standard model. *Why can't men see the false assumptions on redshift?* He answered himself. *Same reason they can't see their false assumptions on anything else. Prejudice.* He grumped, *"Ideas rule the world,"* and *most of the ruling ideas are false.*

He pretended to be engrossed in the book, even taking notes. From time to time, on the edges of his peripheral vision, he noticed one or both of the agents staring at him, trying to evaluate him. *Not much to see boys. Just a man reading a good book, exercising his gray matter. Ever think of trying that?* This was a battle of the will. He wasn't going to budge. He would stay until closing if he had to. Whatever it took, he was going to make them leave first. Fifty-five minutes later, the agents grew tired of the game and got up and left. Woody shook his head to himself. *Amateurs.*

49

Ariele puzzled over her dilemma. How was she supposed to get from Glendale to Montana? She couldn't go home and get her car. Her apartment was probably still being staked out. She couldn't risk using public transportation. There were too many cameras. She would likely be spotted. She couldn't rent a car. Even if she dared to try and access her savings account, it was probably frozen. And there was no way she could ride her mountain bike that far. *You're going to have to come through here, GOD. This is way out of my league.* She smiled at herself. *Sure doing a lot of praying lately for a secular Jew.*

Her nervousness about her plight was on the verge of collapsing into panic. But a voice from the past, like a bolt out of the blue, held out an offer of hope. "If you ever have any needs, don't hesitate to call me." She cringed and hesitated. *Not sure I want to go there. Don't want to encourage him. Risk his unwanted attention. Risk hurting his feelings.* But she was in a jam. She had no one else to call. Her family and friends were likely being eavesdropped by the NSA. Besides, he had extended her an open invitation if she was ever in need. *I definitely got a need now.*

She revisited her connection with the young man. He was a dorky friend of her Caltech classmate Irina. The two had been introduced by a mutual friend who thought they were both Russian. While that wasn't true, they did discover that they shared much in common. Both were immigrants from former Soviet Bloc nations. He from Lithuania. She from Ukraine. Both were evangelicals, and both had an interest in prophecy. They ended up forging a friendship, but there was never any romantic attraction between them, at least not from her side.

Ariele had met him several years ago when she had gone to church with Irina on Easter Sunday. Irina had introduced them, told him that Ariele was Jewish, then wandered off and left her alone with him. It soon became obvious that he was attracted to her. He kept trying to stand in her personal space and she kept backing up, a few inches here, a half foot there. She grimaced, She still got a bad taste in her mouth when she thought about that awkward situation.

When he found out that she was an astronomer with an interest in asteroids, comets, and NEOs, his eyes lit up. He animatedly informed her that the book of Revelation in the New Testament mentioned numerous asteroids that would slam into Earth, bringing widespread devastation. This led to a fifteen-minute conversation, very much one-sided, on the relationship between astronomy and prophecy.

As they were parting, he had informed her that she could

contact him if she ever had any questions or needs. Then he wrote his name, cell-phone number, and email address on a slip of paper and handed it to her, reiterating his offer. At the time she suspected that it was one of those over-chivalrous gestures that young men sometimes make when they crush on a girl, and she had been inclined to throw it away when she got home. However, when she reached out her hand to drop it in the trash, a mysterious hunch that she might need it someday kept her from following through. Three times since then, she had cleaned her wallet, and each time the same strange premonition had moved her to keep it.

But what was his name? She tried to remember. Nada. She pulled her purse out of her pack, fetched her wallet out of her purse, and rummaged through her credit card pockets until she found the crumpled piece of paper. *Oh yeah. Now I remember. Andrius Markunas.* His phone number, though smudged, was still legible. But his email address had bled so badly that it was unreadable. *Must have come in contact with suntan lotion or something like that.*

Now she faced another problem. How was she going to call him? She didn't have a phone. She had intentionally left hers in her apartment. Pay phones were nearly extinct. And it probably wasn't wise to walk into a business and ask to borrow their phone. As she wrestled with the question, she heard the sound of children laughing and screeching behind her. She turned to see the source of the commotion. A young mother had brought her youngsters to the park to play on the playground equipment. Ariele walked over, chatted with her briefly, and asked if she could borrow her cellphone, explaining that she had left hers at home. The woman smiled, said "Absolutely," and handed over her phone. Ariele turned, walked away about twenty feet, and dialed Andrius' number.

He answered on the third ring. "Hello."

"Hi, Andrius, this is Ariele Serrafe. Do you remember me? Irina's friend. We met at church three years ago."

"Oh, I definitely remember you. How could I forget?" he blurted with more warmth than she bargained for. A short, awkward silence followed. "We talked about asteroids and Bible prophecy," he continued. Another moment of silence. "What's on your mind?"

She rolled her eyes to herself. *This is starting badly. He sounds like a giddy kid whose grandparents are taking him to the toy store.* But she brushed her uneasy emotions aside and spoke as sweetly as she could given the circumstances. "I need to talk. Can you come to Scholl Canyon Park and pick me up? I'll be hanging out under the trees near the playground equipment."

"Anything we can talk about over the phone?"

"No, it's complicated. I'll tell you what's going on after me and my bicycle are in your car and we're a few miles down the road."

"Okay. No problem. Good thing I drive a van. I'll be on my way in less than five minutes. The drive will take about twenty, so I'll see you in a half hour. I'll be in a blue van."

Ariele replied, "Thanks. See you when you get here," hung up, and groaned. *Nothing like a convenient solution that makes you feel uncomfortable.* She sighed, walked back to the young mother, and returned her phone. Then she returned to her stuff and sat down, leaning back against a eucalyptus tree. She took a few deep breaths, indulging the aromatic scent, and began to relax. She loved trees. When everything else in life was falling apart, they remained solid and supportive.

Twenty-seven minutes later, Andrius showed up in his seventies-era Toyota HiAce, its faded blue paint showing a little rust in several spots. Ariele jumped up, slung her pack over one shoulder, and jogged her bicycle over to the van. Their meeting was a bit awkward. He leaned in to give her a hug, realized she wasn't interested, then stepped back and offered his hand. Quick as a mongoose, she thrust out her hand, grabbed his, pumped it once, pulled her hand back, looked him in the eyes, and declared, "We have to go."

"Sure. Okay. Let's do it." He led her to the back of the van, opened the door, lifted her bike and rolled it in, and secured it with a bungee strap. Ariele was impressed with his ingenuity in maximizing the small space. The driver's side was taken up with floor-to-ceiling bins and shelves, mostly filled with electronics and computer stuff. The passenger side contained a narrow bed with storage underneath, a deep cubbyhole cabinet overhead, and a two-foot-long clothes bar over the foot of the bed. *Looks like he lives in here.*

Andrius observed her quizzical look. "I often stay here on the weekends when helping friends on projects." She nodded. When she didn't pursue the subject, he grinned and said, "Well, let's go."

As she climbed in the passenger door, she remarked, "Sweet ride by the way. I have a thing for retro stuff, especially the sixties and seventies."

"Thanks. I put a 1972 HiAce body on a 2002 chassis, added a recently rebuilt engine, and modified the dash to accept modern components. It gives me the best of both worlds. I get to enjoy the classic look and feel. And I get the benefit of new parts when things break down." He looked at her. "So, where do you want to go?"

"I don't know. Anywhere but here."

He was perplexed.

"Can we just drive and talk for a while?"

"Sure. We can do that. Where would you like me to drive?"

"I don't care. Just avoid the main roads and highways. And don't get stopped for speeding or rolling through a stop sign or anything else."

He looked at her with arched eyebrows, a little nervous. "Are you in trouble with the law?"

"No … yes … well, not really … well, yeah, kind of."

"You're making about as much sense as sauerkraut on ice cream."

She started to tear up. "Please. I need some time to think and sort things out. Take me up on the Verdugo. It's been a while since I watched the sunset from up there."

Andrius nodded and started the van. She sat quietly while he made his way to East Chevy Chase and then worked his way over to the Oakmont Country Club via Cherry Canyon Motorway and Pasa Glen Drive.

After they had left Beaudry Boulevard and headed up the first of several dirt roads that they needed to take to reach the Verdugo, he noticed that Ariele looked much more relaxed. She caught him looking at her, cracked a feeble smile, and asked him about the huge pile of electrical and computer parts in his van. They made small talk for the next half hour as they worked their way up the ridge roads, chatting about his hobby-work in computers and electronics, his income-work in welding, and his childhood in Lithuania. She offered a few hints about herself, like her interest in back-to-the-land living. He even made her laugh a few times telling her about several hilarious faux pas he had made after his family had immigrated to America. But she remained aloof and offered nothing about her situation. That frustrated him a little, but he consoled himself with the hope that she would talk once they got on top. She had, after all, implied that she would.

They had been traveling west on the Verdugo for about ten minutes when Andrius turned onto a pullout that offered a spectacular view of the Los Angeles area below and the sun that was setting on the horizon. He parked, shut the van off, turned to Ariele, and vented, mildly perturbed. "This has gone on long enough. You called me out of the blue after three years because you are in trouble and wanted my help. But you didn't want to talk until your emotional needs were met. Well, they are met now. You have plenty of distance between you and the park. You have had more than enough time to think. You are up on the Verdugo. You have your great view of the sunset. Now you need to talk, or I'm going to turn the van around and take you back to the park. So, tell me, what in the world is going on?"

Ariele sat silently for a few moments, biting her lip and fighting back the tears. She turned her head slightly away and down. How much could she share with him? Some? Much? Most? Everything? She wanted to trust him. But could she? Should she?

Snippets of his conversation in the church lobby came back to her. In the last days, Earth would be visited by the heavens. Asteroids would play a big part. America would have a Big Brother government. As she reflected on his sentiments, she realized that they resonated with what was going on now. His prophetic beliefs seemed to put him on her side.

She got sidetracked by the Bible prophecy issue and found herself questioning her long-held agnosticism. *Maybe the Bible is true after all? Stop! Focus! Don't have time to think about prophecy now. Focus on getting out of this predicament.*

Her thoughts came back to her awful bind. Her only way out was to trust someone, soon. And she had no options but him. After going back and forth several times, she decided not only to trust him but to share everything with him. There was little to lose if she did and much to lose if she didn't.

Ariele swung her head back to Andrius, ready to talk. He was watching her, waiting for her story. She started from the beginning, recounting every salient detail. The disturbing package she received from Irina revealing the existence of a massive comet that was headed for Mars ... the efforts of the government to conceal the comet from the public ... the ban on research in Taurus ... the official explanation that the stars were occulted by the shock horizon of a growing jet from a black hole ... her six months of observations ... broaching the subject with her boss, Sally ... Sally's efforts to cover for her ... being interrogated by FBI agents ... Sterling trashing her and Sally to the FBI ... Woody's message that she was in danger ... FBI agents tailing her and staking out her apartment ... sneaking out of her apartment ... her long bike ride ... meeting Woody at Rosa's ... the Sundown River message Woody received from his cousin Jack ... Woody's counsel to flee to Montana and look up Bob Reddington ... the agents staking out Rosa's ... her flight to the park ... her need for help to sneak out of California and get to Montana safely. As the sun dipped below the horizon, she closed with a plea, "You were the only person I could think of that I could call for help. Please help me." *Kind of fitting*, she thought to herself. *As the sun has set on the horizon, so the sun has set on my life as I know it.*

Andrius listened patiently for twenty minutes while she unfolded her story, nodding at timely points or interjecting the occasional *wow* or *whoa*, but never interrupting. She was impressed. *A guy that actually listens. How cool is that?* Once she stopped speaking, he sat in silence, considering his options. He was hesitant. Ariele was a handful. A red-headed spitfire with an engaging but feisty personality. She claimed she was fleeing the FBI for trying to expose a massive cover-up about a Nibiru-like comet. It all sounded over-the-top. He wasn't sure she was telling the truth. Not to mention, she obviously wasn't interested in him. She was only using him.

She looked at him expectantly, hoping his help would be substantial, like hauling her onboard ship, not meager, like tossing her a life preserver and telling her to hang on while he goes for help. Their eyes locked, her green eyes pleading for help. Any reservations he had melted away. With a little gallantry in his voice, he said, "I'll tell you what. I've been thinking of moving to the oil fields in the West for a while now, and this is as good a time as any. So, I'll take you to Montana. But I have to give my boss a two-week notice. We won't be able to leave until two weeks from tomorrow." He quickly checked his phone. "That will be Wednesday, June 19."

"Yes!" she shrieked. "Thank you!" She hugged him and impulsively gave him a peck on the cheek, immediately regretting it. "Treasure that," she said, a little embarrassed at her own forwardness. "It's probably the only one you'll ever get from me."

He continued, ignoring her unrestrained expression of gratitude. "In the meantime, you can have my bedroom. I'll sleep on the couch. And please remember, you are going to have to lie low—real low. No listening to music. No noise. No social media. No using my phone. No calling or contacting family or friends. If my mother or friends find out that I have a woman living with me in my apartment, it won't be pretty."

"Not a problem," she replied. "I can live with that." But inwardly she was rolling her eyes. *I'm running from the feds and you're worried about your mother and friends?*

He started his van and turned it around. "I know that you wanted to do the Verdugo, but it's already a long drive from here to my apartment, and I have to be at work at seven in the morning."

"That's fine. I got what I needed. I got a hilltop view of the sunset and a solution to my predicament."

He stole a glance at her. She was smiling. She shone like an angel when she smiled. When she noticed him looking at her, her smile quickly faded. She forced a weak smile, then turned and looked out the window at the crimson glow on the horizon and Mercury twinkling in the evening sky. A few minutes later, the redhead faced forwards again, revealing moist, red eyes. He motioned to the glovebox. "There's a box of tissue in there."

Andrius puzzled over her rapidly changing emotions. *Females. Amazing creatures. But it's difficult to read them. Much easier to read electrical engineering textbooks.* He suspected that her tears were mostly a release of pent-up emotion now that she had a ray of hope in her difficult situation, but who could know for sure? Just like men are not always certain what they are angry about, so women don't always know what they are crying about. At any rate, he thought it best to let her have some time alone in the heaving seas of her emotions. And she was glad to be left alone.

50

During the morning coffee break, Andrius pulled his supervisor aside and gave him his two-week notice. When the old timer enquired about his plans, he answered a little evasively, "Somewhere out West, in or near the Rockies. Not really sure where. I'll look around once I get there. Since I'm certified in MIG, TIG, aluminum, and stainless, I figure I won't have any problem finding work in the oil fields." His boss laughed. "Wish I could afford to pay you what you'll be making in the oil fields."

While Andrius was at work, Ariele explored his unkempt apartment and found herself feeling a little miffed with her new roomie. His fridge contained two twelve-packs of Coca-Cola, a half gallon of milk, two packages of hot dogs, a half bag of cheese curds, a small package of Kraft slices, catsup, and mustard. His freezer held a half-dozen frozen pizzas, a box of corn dogs, and ice cream. His cupboards held cold cereal, macaroni and cheese, sugar, salt, and pepper. On his countertop were a package of hot dog buns and two packages of cookies. For cooking, he had a George Foreman grill, a countertop broiler, and a microwave. *Taking bachelorhood to all-time highs.* There was no teapot or tea. No coffee pot or coffee. Not even instant coffee. *Gonna have to put my foot down. Gonna be a few changes around here.* In stark contrast to the sparsity in his kitchen, his living room was piled high with boxes of books and magazines on welding, computers, programming, networking, electronics, physics, mathematics, prophecy, apologetics, and science fiction. *The guy is a nerd on steroids.* She rolled her eyes and groaned. This was going to be a long two weeks.

When he returned from work at 4:45 that afternoon, tired and in need of a shower, she met him at the door, presented him with a shopping list, and declared that she would make supper for the next two weeks if he would go shopping and pick up some necessary items. He was caught off guard but agreed to the deal. *Seems more like a directive than a trade if you ask me. She's like a little bulldozer. Got a knack for getting her way without being offensive. Glad this deal only lasts two weeks. A guy could burn up his entire savings on a cute chick who has already decided that he is friends-only material. Not much upside for the investment.*

The overwhelmed male returned from his errand an hour and a half later with five bags of fresh supplies—three trips from his van—including a coffee pot, a bean grinder, two pounds of organic coffee beans, the ingredients for fajitas and guacamole, fresh fruit, shampoo and soap, new towels, new sheets, and some clothing that she desperately needed. He gave her a pained look as he handed her the last bag. "Do you have any idea how embarrassing it was to shop for women's clothes, especially dainties?" She laughed at him and chided him playfully, "No room for whining when you volunteer to be chivalrous."

51

That evening while Andrius relaxed in his threadbare recliner with a technical treatise on the physics of welding, Ariele removed a stack of old *Omni* magazines from the top of the coffee table, set up her laptop, and inserted the thumb drive that contained the emails she had pilfered from Sally's computer. Anticipation tingled in her nerves. She expected to find a trove of useful information. Every email was classified TOP SECRET and labeled with the SCI code (Sensitive Compartmented Information code) MINOA. Most also bore the secondary SCI code RESEARCH TEAM. She was curious about the use of secondary SCI codes. *Never read about that before in any spy thriller.*

She emerged from her research two hours later, after examining the entire batch, with a significantly expanded understanding of the Minoa Project. Three other secondary codes fell under the code MINOA: an EXECUTIVE TEAM which included the President, the Vice President, the National Security Advisor, and the Joint Security Council;

an ENFORCEMENT TEAM that included a handful of officials in the FBI, the CIA, the NSA, and the Department of Homeland Security; and a PREPARATION TEAM which was headed by a distinct leadership team drawn from the Department of Homeland Security.

The tens of thousands of federal, state, and contracted employees working under the Preparation Team appeared to be operating in the dark, unaware of the real reason behind the readiness programs they were instructed to carry out. According to their instructions and in their minds, they were engaged in preparing for the most probable disasters, like a nuclear detonation at the hand of terrorists or rogue nations, a nuclear strike from Russia or China, World War III, an 8.0 earthquake, a massive EMP, or a small asteroid less than one kilometer in diameter.

She also uncovered some illuminating information on the Rogue itself, referred to in the emails almost exclusively by its official designation RN13.

Its albedo was phenomenally low—apparently far below 0.02—which is why it was yet invisible to the most powerful optical telescopes on Earth.

Its diameter was verified at 5560 kilometers according to the latest data obtained from NEOCam, WISE, and Spitzer. This was significantly larger than the figure that had been leaked by Anonymous six months prior. A quick calculation revealed that it was eighty-two percent of the diameter of Mars.

Its composition caught NASA by surprise. According to data obtained by the revitalized Spitzer, it was composed primarily of iron and nickel, with significant amounts of platinum-group metals and heavy rare-earth minerals. This implied that the comet was so dense that its mass likely approached that of Mars despite its smaller diameter.

Its orbit, according to NASA's latest calculations, would take it inside the asteroid belt in March 2024 and bring it within 18,000 miles of Mars in August 2024. This closely coincided with the findings of Dr. Youngblood and the Anonymous leaks which had been purloined from NASA servers.

She found it unnerving that the correspondence referred to the Rogue's near pass with Mars as *Zero Hour*, a term that evoked images of war and cities reduced to rubble. It also implied that the Minoa leadership expected the Rogue to interfere with Mars and cause problems, sending one or both bodies careening on new orbits, and potentially placing Earth in the path of the angry heavens.

Another interesting tidbit she discovered was the real story behind the ESA's decision to delay the launch date of the ExoMars mission, moving it from the summer of 2018 to February 14, 2019. At the insistence of President Weston himself during a special summit meeting in Brussels in February 2018, the Mars mission had been secretly switched to a Rogue mission. The code name of the new project was Cupid. Only a tiny handful of individuals were privy to this change: the heads of state of the nations involved and select cabinet members, a handful of ESA and NASA executives, and a skeleton team of ESA technicians, bolstered by a few technicians and engineers from NASA and JPL.

The new launch date, not surprisingly, had been panned by aerospace scientists around the world as ridiculous timing for a Mars mission. Several periodicals had savagely ripped the ESA and its directors. But the greatest frustrations were felt by the ESA technicians and engineers, who went about their work oblivious to the mission change, wondering why in the world the directors had changed from an optimal date to a mediocre one. After a season of griping, they resigned themselves to their fate, believing that their intelligence and hard work were being used to further yet another government led snafu.

Ariele startled Andrius with a whoop, "Hey, Android!" She smiled to herself. That seemed like a fitting nickname for the braniac across from her. "Here's the summary of what I have discovered about the Rogue and the government cover-up."

He smiled, closed his book, and listened politely while she animatedly filled him in on the details. As she wrapped up her report, she eyed him, looking for his response. He sat silently, his mouth tweaked to one side and his head slightly cocked as if he wasn't sure what to say. She suspected that he was skeptical. "What's the matter? Is it hard to believe it because you didn't read it with your own eyes? Or maybe you don't trust my reading comprehension skills? Or maybe I forged all one hundred forty-two emails?"

The bookworm grinned like an imp, unwilling to defend himself. He knew that he was a hard sell, perhaps too hard. She pulled up five letters that contained the meat of the conspiracy and another letter summarizing what NASA knew about the Rogue, then handed him her laptop. He felt guilty already, knowing that he was probably wrong to doubt her. But the whole story seemed so far-fetched, more like a screenplay for a Hollywood film than the world he was used to living in.

The emails turned his perspective upside down. They left him numb, banging his head on the iron wall of cognitive dissonance, yet unable to deny the facts. Up to this point, he had believed that Ariele was a little delusional and had exaggerated the danger they were facing. In his mind he had pictured an average-size comet, less than five kilometers in diameter, which was going to come close to Earth. Now he had to swallow his pride. He had been dead wrong.

Staggered at the size, mass, and path of the comet, his brain almost over-heating with concern, he started to ramble. "This is insane. Apocalyptic catastrophe headed this way. A planet-sized behemoth. The situation is terrifying. The depth and breadth of the cover-up are astounding. This explains the flurry of construction that Homeland Security has been engaged in. A new generation of underground shelters and emergency government offices. Several will rival Cheyenne Mountain Complex and the Raven Rock Mountain Complex when they are done. It also explains the rapid expansion of the FBI and Homeland Security over the past eighteen months." He fell into silence, his mind struggling with the situation.

If I was wrong on the comet and the cover-up, maybe I'm wrong on the FBI stuff too. His chagrin was painful. He had been fairly certain that she wasn't really in trouble with the law, just paranoid about an interview with federal agents who had been at Caltech for the quarterly security instruction that is required for every business and institution involved in the military, aerospace, and astronomy sectors. *So what's my next step? I need to verify the rest of her story, find out if she really is on the lam from the feds. But how?*

The light came on. He jumped up—Ariele staring at him wide-eyed—raced to his closet, pulled out his police scanner, raced back to the kitchen, set it on the counter, plugged it in, and tuned it to the CHP recent-reports channel. Ariele sidled up to him and sat on the counter next to the scanner, swinging her legs. After listening to thirty-odd reports, mostly arrest-warrant bulletins for robbery suspects and drug dealers, he heard what he hoped to hear, a federal bulletin from the FBI on Ariele Serrafe, an employee at Caltech who was wanted for security violations under the Homeland Security Act and was believed to have fled her apartment on a bicycle. Ariele looked at him coyly, twirling her hair with her fingers. "Do you believe me now, Mr. Skeptic?" He nodded, trying to squash his embarrassed smile. They were both relieved. He was relieved to confirm that she was telling the truth. She was relieved that he finally and entirely believed her.

This changed his plans somewhat. Originally, his decision to take Ariele to Montana hadn't been so much a sacrifice as it had been a convenient occasion to pursue a dream. For months he had contemplated a change of pace, inclined to the lucrative opportunities in the oilfields. Now he was going to get more change of pace than he had anticipated. Now that he was privy to the comet and the conspiracy, which were classified secrets, and now that he was guilty of harboring a federal fugitive, a federal offense, he was in just as much danger as Ariele herself. *Hope they got room at this hideout in Montana for an electronics whiz. If they're looking for back-to-the-land types or macho guys like Bear Grylls with survival skills, I'm out of luck. I can barely start a fire with gas and matches. I'm scared to eat berries that weren't purchased in a store. And I have never enjoyed gardening or farm animals.*

Andrius turned to Ariele. "We have a lot of planning and preparing to do. Make a list tomorrow of the things we'll need for the trip: food, clothes, personal items. Make another list of the stuff we'll need for an extended stay. We'll buy what we need this week and load it in the van."

She smiled sweetly and saluted in a playful manner. "Yes, sir. Ready and raring to go."

"Tomorrow after work, I'll sort through the bins in the van and make room for our gear. Wow. I got a ton of stuff to think about. But I'm drained. It's been a long day. I'm going to take a hot shower and go to bed."

He walked into his bedroom, fetched his pajamas and clothes for the next day, and headed for the bathroom.

Ariele grabbed his arm and stopped him. "By the way, thank you for hearing me out and believing me."

His face lit up, and he nodded, but he said nothing. Once in the shower, he hung his head, feeling guilty that he had regarded her as crazy and her story as inflated if not pure fiction. But there was no way he could make a full disclosure to her. No way he could confess how deeply his doubts had run. *Probably not a good idea. Not with that feisty chick.*

Ariele retreated to the bedroom, still feeling a little hurt at Andrius' reticence to trust her story. *Pretty slow to get on board. At least he's all business once he did.* But her chief emotion was relief. She felt relaxed for the first time in days. She sat on the edge of the bed and perkily kicked her shoes off. Things were going to be okay. She trusted Andrius entirely now. He really was going to get her to Montana. And she was starting to appreciate the nerdy-smart guy as a friend. His sweetness and considerateness were world-class. *If he could just lose some of his bachelor ways and tone down the tech-wonk stuff.*

52

Glendale, California
early June 2019

Andrius kept himself busy almost every waking moment outside of work getting ready for their adventure, but Ariele managed to engage him in snippets of conversation. He was interesting—unique. His approach to science and religion intrigued her. It was refreshingly different from the dichotomy she had learned in college. According to him, she didn't have to choose between science and religion. There was no controversy between unbiased science and the Bible. The God who wrote the Bible also wrote the book of nature. That made sense to her. She wanted to believe it.

He was also a strong believer in taking the Bible literally, including the early chapters of Genesis: the creation, the fall, the curse, the flood, the tower of Babel, and the table of nations. And based on his belief in the worldwide flood, he opined, to her skeptical amusement, that every impact crater evident on the face of Earth was less than 4500 years old because the flood in Noah's day had swept the entire surface of the planet clean. This view required one to believe that even the largest craters on Earth, like Chicxulub and Popigai, were formed in recent history. This was tough for her to swallow. She had been taught that craters that size were caused by extinction events millions of years ago and that it would have been impossible for humans or large animals to have survived those devastating blows. No place on Earth would have been safe.

The most interesting thing she learned about him, though, was his love for prophecy. He talked at length about the last days and God's promises which he had made to the people and nation of Israel—the Jews. His belief in these promises touched her heart in a way that religious things had never done before. She was used to thinking of the Bible as ancient mythology, dusty traditions, and passé platitudes. He made it sound like the Bible was real history and God was a real person making and keeping real promises. She mused to herself. *I could get used to that. I hope it's true.*

Despite the fact that she enjoyed their conversations, the two weeks of waiting before their departure for Montana seemed like eternity to her. She was antsy the entire time. The conditions imposed on her would have been difficult for anybody, but they were unbearable for the boisterous young lady. She wasn't allowed to look out the windows, much less go outside. When home alone, she couldn't listen to music, run the microwave, or make noise of any kind. Even when he was home, she was forbidden to talk loudly or listen to music except for his Christian music. Dancing and jazzercize were out of the question. There wasn't much for her to do except read. She quickly tackled the lone Ayn

Rand title on her Kindle that she hadn't read yet. Then she ransacked Andrius' disorganized library, a painfully boring task. Thankfully, she found several titles on Israel and Judaism that seemed fascinating enough to warrant reading, including one which claimed that Jesus was a Jewish rabbi.

53

Woody lay awake contemplating the situation, worrying about Ariele. He hoped and prayed that she was safe. While exceptionally bright, she had no experience in evasion and escape. Dull pangs of guilt reproved him for sending her off on her escapade alone, but there was nothing else he could do on such short notice.

His thoughts turned to his own circumstances. He knew that his days were numbered—did he have days or weeks?—and he felt irked at himself. He had sensed trouble brewing for over a year and hadn't devised a plan. This was definitely not the right way to operate when you are in a situation that might demand an escape and evade operation with little or no notice. Jack's advice mocked him. "Have a plan ready at all times, Woody. Otherwise, when the time comes to flee, you'll be flying by the seat of your pants." Well, now he was flying by the seat of his pants.

One thing was certain. Whatever he came up with for a plan had to meet three conditions. First of all, it had to fall within his normal patterns of summer activity so he wouldn't tip anyone off that he was up to something. Secondly, it had to give him an edge. He needed to create a situation where the advantage was on his side, not his pursuers. Thirdly, it had to give him a head start. He figured he would need at least a twelve-hour jump if he was going to evade those who would be pursuing him.

After weighing various ideas, he decided that a hike in the wilderness was the only one that met all three conditions. It met the normal-pattern condition. Everyone knew that he loved the Sierras and made two week-long trips into the high country every summer, pursuing trout bliss with his fly rod. Nobody would suspect him of unusual activity were he to plan and execute a June trip, something he had done for many years. This idea also offered him an edge. He had been hiking in the region for twenty years, so he would know the terrain better than his pursuers. And it gave him a head start. If he got up in the middle of the night and left camp, those tracking him would think that he had gotten up early in the morning to wet a line in another lake or stream. If this played out the way he hoped, he might actually get the twelve-hour head start that he desired.

But where should he go in the mountains? Obviously, it had to be somewhere that was only a one-day hike from the transportation he was going to use to get to Montana. But what kind of conveyance would be best? Public options like buses, passenger trains, and flying were out of the question. They were far too dangerous. He would certainly get caught. Ditto for renting a car. Taking a cab or using Uber was a little safer, but still dodgy. Hitchhiking was also problematic. That left him one option, hopping a freight train. As he considered the idea, an inspiration flashed into his mind. *I could hop the train at the hairpin curve near Donner Pass, then ride the rails east and north. Actually, sounds kind of fun. Used to dream about being a hobo when I was a kid.*

He needed a few things, however, to transform his rough idea into a plan: an entrance point, a route, and logistics. Galvanized, he sprang out of bed, slipped into his Woolrich robe and moosehide slippers, and hastened to his study. He yanked his backpacking file drawer open and pawed through his maps till he found one that covered Donner Pass and the wilderness areas south of it. He spread the map out on his table and surveyed it carefully. After a few minutes weighing his options, he determined that he would be better off hiking into the Desolation Wilderness than the Granite Chief Wilderness. It was so far away from the railroad tracks that nobody would suspect when he went missing that he might have been headed in their direction.

This brought up a logistics issue. No matter where he made his trailhead in the Desolation, it would take at least a week to hike all the way to the tracks on foot—far too long. If law enforcement was keeping close tabs on him, and he figured there was a strong probability that they would tail him into the woods, then his escape margin was going to be slim. He figured, assuming a stealthy departure in the middle of the night, that he might have twenty hours before they figured out that he wasn't coming back to camp, maybe thirty hours before the entire area would be crawling with law enforcement. He had one day. That's all. So he needed a plan that would get him to the tracks in one day whether on the train or holed up waiting for it, a plan that had him far outside the search area when the sun went down.

Roads. That was his only option. He was going to have to use the forest roads. He scrutinized the map. A plan came together. His jump-off point would be the trailhead at Echo Lake. From there he would hike to Susie Lake and set up his base camp. In the middle of the night, he would set out on a grueling hike across the wilderness to the point where the Barrett Lake Jeep Trail crosses the stream below Barrett Lake. There he would rendezvous with pre-arranged transportation that would take him, via forest roads, to a jump-off point south of Donner near the hairpin curve. Then he would hike cross-country to the curve and hop the train.

He wanted to go farther with his planning, but the next step involved computer research on his route and logistics, and he didn't dare do that on his home computer. If he was under suspicion, and he suspected that he was, then his home network was probably bugged. He would have to pursue this tomorrow, maybe at the Sierra Coffee Company after work. That was just as well. His eyes were heavy and a few hours of sleep sounded good. *Might even be able to fall asleep now that I have a workable plan.*

As he walked back to his bedroom, one thought did give him a little discomfort, though not enough to rob him of his sleep. His wilderness trip plan was doable, but it was going to kick his butt. He started to wish that he had kept himself in shape as Jack had, but stopped himself. The truth was, he was glad he hadn't. Jack's path was ... well ... too much exercise and not enough ice cream. He didn't try to flatter himself that he had struck a healthy balance because he knew that wasn't true. He just wasn't a fitness buff, and he never had been, not even in the Special Forces. He was, as he liked to conceive it, an above average man in an average body. And he was content to be just that. His body always complained when he abused it in the mountains, but it performed well enough to get the job done. And that was all that mattered.

54

On his way home from work, Woody swung by Best Buy and purchased a new android phone. He knew that his phone and laptop were under surveillance. Then he doubled back to the Sierra Coffee Company. After picking up his Cinnamon Griz', he took a table in the back with his face toward the room, retrieved his laptop from his briefcase, and booted it up. He opened up several tabs with web pages advertising fly-fishing tours for peacock bass in the Amazon. *Too bad this is just cover. I would love to go down there for real.* From time to time he scrolled, changed pages, clicked on pictures, and wrote notes on his legal pad.

Next, he turned on his new phone and activated a prepaid program under a pseudonym. Then he downloaded Orfox and Orbot. Now he was ready. He logged into the Wi-Fi for the business across the street and searched for things he had never searched for before—macramé, mate, and mascara—leaving tabs open to several of the websites. He wanted to leave obscure footprints that made it difficult to trace this research to himself if they were somehow able to get around Orbot. Only after he had erected his smokescreen, did he begin his route investigation.

He tackled the railroad part first. He discovered that the stretch of track he was interested in belonged to the Union Pacific Railroad and that an eastbound freight train traversed the hairpin curve daily between 6:30 and 7:30 a.m. *Perfect.* Moreover, he could ride the train all the way to Gillette, Wyoming, via Reno and Ogden. At Gillette, he would have to switch to the Burlington Northern, which would take him to Billings, Montana. Once there, he would call Red for transportation to the Compound.

Next, he sought a solution for the road stretch. It was too far to walk, a good eighty miles. Besides, he couldn't risk being seen along the road. What he needed was somebody to pick him up where the Barrett Lake Jeep Trail crosses the stream below Barrett Lake and then drop him off at his jump-off point. Cabs were not an option. His request would make the company suspicious. They don't normally pick people up or drop them off at obscure locations in the woods. Arrangements with family or friends were way too risky. They would almost certainly get interrogated, and everyone involved would be busted. *I need a neutral stranger. Somebody willing to pick me up in the mountains under unusual circumstances and transport me over mountain roads. Wait a minute! A transporter. That's it! I need to locate someone who hauls goods and people for a fee, no questions asked, like in the movies.*

Craig's List came to mind. He scrolled through the

transport listings for the greater Los Angeles area. There were several dozen. Most were generic shippers or couriers, but he did find several that looked promising. They all said more or less the same thing, "We haul anything that fits in a van (or a truck), half up front, half upon completion. He decided to try Conveyance Unlimited out of East Los Angeles and memorized the phone number.

***

That evening after dinner at home—take out chicken and coleslaw—he dug a burner phone out of a box of survival supplies that Jack had given him and called Conveyance Unlimited. He got no answer, so he left his burner number and a brief message: "I have a transport job approximately two weeks in the future. It is confidential. No illegal activities or controlled substances are involved. I work indirectly for the federal government under a federally funded program. Call this number tomorrow evening between 7 and 9 p.m. if you are interested. My handle is Tenkara."

His project at a hurry-up-and-wait point, he sat down in his recliner with his laptop, hoping to catch up with the world news from his favorite conservative websites. But he was unable to concentrate. He ended up drifting, thinking about his cousin. *Good thing Jack gave me a half-dozen burners for an emergency. Gotta hand it to him. I honestly thought I would never use them. He was right about a lot of things. No, he was right about everything.*

Jack was dead serious about preparation and security. He

was thorough. He didn't just think three or four steps ahead. He thought miles ahead. When he and Woody started taking their annual trip to Montana in August 1998 to fly fish and scout options for their Sundown hideout, he had insisted that they use cash and prepaid cards for the entire trip—gas, groceries, and supplies—so that they left no tracks. He also insisted that the Montana portion of their trips remained a secret. When folks asked about their trip, they were regaled with pictures and tales of their adventures in Idaho, Utah, Wyoming, and Colorado—wherever they had fished outside of Montana. But not a whisper of the Big Sky State.

While Woody had pooh-poohed these steps as excessive precautions, his cousin had defended them tenaciously. If a Sundown event ever forced them to retreat to Montana, he didn't want the feds to be able to figure out from their past trips that they had probably fled to familiar territory in Montana. Woody, though unconvinced, went along with the inconveniences. There simply was no arguing with Jack if he was convinced that something was important for the security of their Sundown plans. He wouldn't holler or get mad when Woody disagreed. But neither would he let the point go. He just played a calm but unyielding game of tug-of-war until Woody eventually gave up and let him have his way.

While he hadn't appreciated Jack's plans and adamance in the past, he sure was thankful now that his cousin had had the foresight and the bulldogged determination to secure the best possible odds for them if they ever had to face a Sundown situation. Eating crow had never tasted so good.

55

The next evening, a few minutes past eight, the contacted transporter called back. "Hi, this is Randy with Conveyance Unlimited returning your call. Sorry. I can't, I don't, and I won't do the kind of work you are inquiring about. You might be telling the truth, you might really be on the up-and-up and not doing anything illegal, but I don't do any kind of confidential or secretive transports. All my transports are above board with manifests and records. I require photo ID, current verifiable address, and phone number. But I do have an acquaintance that does do confidential transports. I'll give him your number. If he's interested, he'll call you. If you don't hear from him by the end of the weekend, it's because he's not interested.

"By the way, no transport business that posts on Craig's List does confidential transport. That's way too risky. One other thing, the fact that you would call a transport business that posts on Craig's List indicates that you're a rookie who has never used confidential transport services before. Take a few words of advice. Don't balk or haggle at their prices. You will offend them and they will walk away. If they ask for cash up front, it's okay to counter with half up front and half upon completion. Act distant and indifferent. Friendly makes them nervous. And do not show desperation or panic. That sets off warning bells. Good luck, rookie."

Woody hung up, set his burner down on the end table, and settled back in his recliner. *So much for that. Back to the waiting game, round two. Either Mr. Real McCoy transporter calls me back or he doesn't. If he doesn't, it's back to the drawing board. Hope that doesn't happen. But not gonna worry about it now. Just gonna let it play out.* He reached for the latest edition of Fly Fisherman, turned to the article on trout fishing in Mongolia, and daydreamed about fly fishing for lenok and monster taimen until he couldn't keep his eyes open any longer.

56

After Ariele had missed two days of work and failed to show up again Friday morning, Woody enquired about her. "Hey, Sally. I haven't seen Ariele for a couple days. Is she sick?"

"I have no idea," she replied. "We haven't heard from her. At this point, her absence is being regarded as unexcused."

Woody raised his eyebrows and donned a shocked expression. "Unexcused? That's so unlike her."

"I know, I know. It sure isn't like her. But it is what it is. If you hear anything from her, let us know."

"Will do. Did anyone check her apartment?"

"Her apartment has been checked. Her car is there. Her phone is there. But her bicycle is missing."

"I hope she isn't in trouble. She does live in a rough neighborhood. Did anyone call the police department and report her missing?"

Sally hesitated for a moment—she looked pained—then recovered herself. "Yes, law enforcement is involved."

Woody didn't miss her emotional misstep. *Bet she knew*

Ariele was on the lam the first evening. Nonetheless, he said nothing. Showing too much interest might be detrimental to his own situation. Instead, he shook his head as if he were baffled and brought the conversation to a close. "You seem to have the bases covered." Then he retreated to get himself a cup of coffee.

Sitting at his desk, nursing his morning java, Woody brooded over the situation. He was nearly as worried for himself as he was for Ariele. Sterling had never liked him. But ever since she had gone missing, the suck-up seemed to hold him in unusual suspicion. *Watching me like a hawk.* If he was going to extricate himself from this dicey situation, he was going to need all his savvy, lots of pluck, and a bit of luck.

***

Shortly after lunch, Sally summoned him into her office, where he was questioned by two agents. First, they plied him with questions about Ariele's indiscretion. He replied that she hadn't shared much with him about it. He did know that she had been doing some general research on NEOs, that she had stumbled upon an interesting lead and followed up on it, that she had taken it hard when she had been rebuffed, and that she had taken it even harder when the FBI had gotten involved. When she had come to him, he had advised her to look at the situation from its bright side and take something positive from it.

Next, they asked him about her disappearance. He told them that the last time he had seen her was at work and that he had no idea where she was.

"You have no idea where she went?"

"No, I don't. To be honest, I'm more worried about what might have happened to her than where she went. She does live in a pretty bad neighborhood."

"We appreciate your concern, Mr. Lundstrom, but we are worried about *where* she went. We have reason to believe that she has fled to avoid prosecution for security breaches that are punishable pursuant to the Homeland Security Act."

Woody just shrugged his shoulders. "I've got no idea."

"Of all of her friends and acquaintances that you know, who would be the most likely to help her out if she was fleeing from law enforcement?"

"Well, come to think of it, she did have a chat-room friend by the name of Boondocker who lives somewhere in central Oregon. The guy is a bit of a fruitcake—a Green Peace, anti-Big-Brother prepper. Built himself an off-the-grid underground home with an attached grow hole. Ariele showed me pictures of the place once. It actually looked like a pretty cool place to visit if you wanted to eat organic vegetables, drink herb tea, and hang out with tree huggers."

After the questioning was over, and he was back at his desk, he struggled a bit with the answers he had given the agents—fabrications and whitewash apart from the account of Boondocker. But he wasn't struggling with the propriety of what he had said. He believed that tactical deception was justified on the battlefield. He simply wondered whether his diversionary efforts were good enough. And he wondered how well he would do if they questioned him again while connected to a polygraph.

Could he internalize his ploys well enough to pass a polygraph? He doubted it. He tried to rehearse them. *I last saw Ariele when I was at work, hard at work trying to help her escape. I have no idea where Ariele went, immediately went. Don't ask me where she is ultimately going.* But the time invested was probably wasted. While he would likely remember to keep his subtleties in mind while hooked up to the polygraph, he probably would not be able to internalize them enough to affect his emotional response. *Pretty much toast if they polygraph me.*

57

Deukmejian Wilderness Park, Glendale, CA
Sunday evening, June 9, 2019

Woody started getting anxious after dinner knowing that the window for a call from the transporter was drawing near, so he drove to Deukmejian Wilderness Park and went for a hike. Walking in the hills always relaxed him. He loved the Southern California chaparral, especially when flowers were blooming, like bush mallow, chamise, and sage. About a mile up the trail, his burner vibrated in his pocket. "This is Tenkara."

"This is Ghost. What are you looking for?"

"I need to be picked up in the mountains in northern California near the Desolation Wilderness and driven to a drop-off site near Truckee. Drop-off needs to occur after dark. A four-wheel drive will be needed to access and depart the pick-up point."

"The job won't be a problem," Ghost replied. "I have a 4WD pickup with spare parts, spare gas, and a winch. What are the expected pick-up and drop-off times?"

"10 a.m. pick-up and 10 p.m. drop-off. The drive will

only take about half that time, so we will need to hole up somewhere and burn up a few hours."

"I charge one hundred dollars per hour, plus vehicle expenses, plus whatever extra charges I feel like adding due to the difficulty or danger of the job. You will be taking up, I'm guessing, probably fourteen hours of my time, which comes to fourteen hundred dollars, plus six hundred miles of wear and tear and gas, which comes to another six hundred dollars, plus I don't know you, which is a risk, so that's another two thousand dollars. That's a total of four thousand dollars, which I want up front."

Woody countered, "How about two thousand up front, a thousand at pickup, and a thousand at drop-off?"

"That's cool. When does this job need to get done?"

"Approximately two weeks in the future."

"I will need a week advance when you finalize the date and the times."

"No problem. I have one more request."

"Yeah?"

"Can you pick up a duffel bag for me from a locker at the Greyhound Bus Station and bring it with you?"

"That will be another thousand dollars since picking up and hauling bags is dangerous. You never know what might be in the bag you're hauling."

"Fine. How about five hundred up front and five hundred when I get my bag, unopened and not tampered with?"

"Done. Anything else?"

"Nope."

Ghost gave Woody his instructions. "Meet me at 5:30 Tuesday morning at the Redondo Municipal Pier. I will be wearing black pants, a gray sweater, and a gray newsboy cap. I will be alone. You must be alone too. Stand at the inside rail in the middle of the wide section just past Kincaid's. I will approach you and ask to borrow your phone. You got that?"

"Yep. Got it."

"What will you be wearing?"

"Jeans, sagebrush-green shirt, olive-drab patrol cap with Special Forces insignia, brown leather bomber's jacket."

"Nice. Definitely a rookie."

Woody cringed at the sarcasm.

"Bring the cash," Ghost directed. "Bring your locker key. And don't forget a note with the locations and times for your pick-up and your drop-off. GPS coordinates are preferred, but landmarks are acceptable. Have the cash, note, and key inside your phone case. I will ask to borrow your phone. You will toss it to me. I will walk away, turn my back to anyone near enough to watch, remove the items, count the money, then pretend that I am on a call. Got all that?"

"Yep."

"Good. Another thing. I can call the deal off when we meet if I feel uncomfortable or don't like you. But you can't call the deal off."

"Fair enough. See you Tuesday."

Ghost responded with a little bristliness in his voice. "Maybe. Maybe not. If I don't walk up to you at 5:30 sharp, it won't be because I didn't show. I will show. I always show.

It will be because I saw something that made me feel uneasy. If I see anything that makes me nervous, I will turn around and leave. You will not see me, and the deal will be off. If that happens, you will not attempt to contact me."

"I understand."

Ghost fired off one last salvo. "Be standing at the rail at 5:25 Tuesday morning. Don't be early. Don't be late. No dogs. No friends. No nonsense. Got it?"

"Got it."

The transporter didn't say goodbye. He just hung up.

Woody was glad the phone call was over. Talking with Ghost made him feel uneasy in a way he hadn't felt since he had been forced to deal with the underworld in the Balkans. The Special Forces had helped local authorities handle the Russian mafia, who were selling drugs and illegal arms and murdering any locals that stood up to them. He still got the chills whenever he thought of arresting and interrogating those Mafiosi. They hardly seemed human. They were cold, ruthless devils without heart, conscience, or moral compass. Dealing with Ghost gave him the same chills. He wished he had other options, but there were none. So he steeled his soul to do what he had to do—"necessity knows no law"— and looked forward to putting this behind him.

When he returned home that evening, he dug out his digicam parachute bag, rummaged through his preparation cache, and packed the bag with everything he would need for a week-long trip by rail to Montana: food, water, water purification tabs, cookware, clothing, shelter, personal items, his burner phones, and coffee. *Can't forget the coffee.*

Then he added some supplies he wanted with him at the Compound: two knives, an extra tenkara rod, six tenkara lines, four boxes of flies, a hacky sack that Joby had given him, and a set of mini-screwdrivers. Lastly, he packed several mementos that he couldn't bear to leave behind. After a little rearranging, he zipped the well-stuffed bag shut and zip-tied the zipper to the end loop. *Ready to hop a train and roll.*

58

Los Angeles
Monday, June 10, 2019

Woody worked through his lunch break and left work early, shortly after 1 p.m. He would have to make up the lost hours later in the week. Right now, a critical mission demanded his attention. Forty-five minutes later, in a part of Los Angeles he preferred to avoid, he turned off South Main Street onto East Seventh Street and headed into Skid Row, keeping his eyes peeled for a suitable runner. At the corner of East Seventh and Crocker, he saw a lone Hispanic fellow, who looked to be around twenty, leaning against a building. Woody pulled into a no-parking zone, stopped, rolled down his passenger window, and beckoned. The young man walked up to the car warily, sized up Woody, and asked, "What's up?"

"How would you like to make two hundred and fifty dollars?"

"I'm not queer."

"Not looking for a date. I'm looking for a runner to do an errand. I need someone to take my duffel bag to the bus depot, put it in a locker, and bring me the key. It will only take fifteen or twenty minutes."

"Okay. I'm game. I want the money up front though."

"I'll give you fifty up front, the other two hundred after the job is completed. Hop in. I'll drive you to within a couple blocks."

The young man hopped in the car, reached out his hand, and said, "Roberto." Woody grabbed it, and said, "Ace." He didn't know why. It just popped into his head. Then he put the Jeep in gear and took off. A dozen or so blocks later, he crossed Alameda, turned right on Channing, and parked on the side of the street.

He turned to Roberto, handed him the duffel bag and a crisp fifty-dollar bill, and warned him. "Make sure this bag gets in a locker and bring me the key. See this fisheye-looking thing on the zipper? That's a camera. I'll be watching the whole operation right here on my phone. I will know whether this bag gets stashed in a locker or not. I will know if someone tries to open my bag or walk away from the bus depot with it. And if someone does try to cheat me, I can track them, find them, and make them wish that they hadn't crossed me. Comprende?"

He nodded. "I know the drill. This isn't the first time that I've run errands for dealers." He opened the door, jumped out of the Jeep, and briskly walked back toward East Seventh Street. As Woody watched in his rearview mirror, the young man turned the corner and disappeared.

Fifteen minutes later, the runner returned, opened the Jeep door, and handed Woody the key. Woody handed him the remaining two hundred dollars along with a twenty-dollar McDonald's gift certificate as a tip. Roberto snatched them from his hand, mumbled "Thanks," and hurried away. Woody sighed and relaxed. A burden was lifted. He whipped a U-turn and headed for home, emotionally spent. *Glad this little foray is out of the way. Next step, meet with the tough-talking transporter. Not looking forward to that. The mountain-trek part looks easy compared to this seedy, underworld stuff.*

59

Woody pulled into Kincaid's parking lot at the Redondo Municipal Pier at 5:16 a.m. *A little early, just enough time for some coffee.* He poured himself a cup from his battered thermos, a wedding present from Anne twenty-eight years earlier, and found himself teased by her memories. He had proposed to her on this very pier in June 1990 while home on leave from the Special Forces. He sighed. The passing of time hadn't healed the pain or filled the void. The ache, the emptiness, was still there.

Five or six dozen fishermen were on the pier already, mostly midsection. Dawn was starting to break, a glorious red glow brightened the east over the mountains. A few bright stars still twinkled on the western horizon. The chug of fishing boats reverberated across the water as they made their way toward open water. Gulls were swarming the beach like raucous marauders. A gentle breeze wafted the salty smell of the ocean inland. He never tired of the fragrance. *If I was given the chance to do my life over, I could picture myself on a carrier, the queen of the seas.*

He glanced at the clock on the dash. It was 5:20 a.m. He set his coffee cup down, slipped on his jacket, walked out onto the pier, and slowly made his way toward the meeting place. He lollygagged a little bit so he wouldn't get to his destination early. At 5:25 a.m. he leaned against the rail as directed. Resisting the urge to look around for Ghost, he turned his attention to a fisherman around seventy-five feet away, his rod bent and straining as he shouted to his buddy on the other side of the pier, "Fish on!" After several minutes, the fish rolled near the surface and the angler hollered, "Halibut!"

"Can I borrow your phone?" Woody turned and faced the transporter, a big, burly man with wavy blonde hair, probably in his late twenties, who looked like he could handle any trouble that came his way. Woody reached in his jacket pocket, retrieved his phone, and tossed it to him. Ghost caught it, turned, and walked away from Woody and the nearby fishermen. Thirty feet away, he started pacing back and forth, phone to his ear, pretending he was enquiring about a charter boat for bonito. Abruptly he flipped the phone shut—Jack's burners were all flip phones—walked towards Woody, tossed him his phone, whirled about, and hastened shoreward. Woody shook his head. *Bad business manners must be standard protocol in his line of work.*

Woody returned to watching the fisherman, whose friend was attempting to gaff the halibut. After the fish had been hoisted aloft, he started walking toward the end of the pier to find a seat and watch the sunrise. *Might as well enjoy creation for a little while. It's the only pay I'm going to collect for the day. Feels a little strange to be putting in hours this week and next for which I will never get paid.*

60

Woody woke in the wee hours of the morning and began worrying about the vacation request that he was going to put in that morning. He hoped that requesting time off wouldn't set off any alarms, that it would be viewed as just a routine request for a week off in June as had been his practice for over a decade. But he knew that he was being watched with suspicion by Sterling and the FBI.

He was so anxious when he arrived at the Cahill Center that he barged into Sally's office, before he had even poured himself a cup of coffee, and made his request. "Mornin' Sally. I'd like to take a week off, the week of the 24th through the 28th."

She checked her planner. "That will be fine. There's nothing going on that week that concerns you."

Woody grinned. "Thanks."

She returned his smile and enquired, "Going on another one of your Sierra adventures?"

"I sure am. This just might be my biggest adventure yet."

"So what do you have planned?"

"I'm heading north to the Desolation Wilderness. I hope to catch the damsel-fly hatch, which typically happens in late June at the lower elevations. That usually means really good trout fishing. And I would love to get into some good golden trout fishing too." He reached in his portfolio, ripped the top page off his legal pad, and handed it to her. "Here's my itinerary, just in case something happens."

She smiled at him and read the outline. "Desolation Wilderness trip on Pacific Crest Trail, June 2019. Starting point is Echo Lake on Saturday, June 22. Day one: stops at Aloha Lake and Heather Lake, camp at Susie Lake. Day two: up early, day hike down to Grass Lake and Glen Alpine Creek for brook trout, back in camp around dark. Day three: hike around Susie Lake, try stream above. Day four: hike to Gilmore Lake, make camp, hopefully catch a big laker. Day five: stay in the area, fish Gilmore Lake and Half Moon Lake. Day six: hike to Dicks Lake, make camp, fish Fontanalis Lake and Dicks Lake. Day seven: stay in the area. Day eight: hike to Velma Lakes and camp. Day nine: hike back out to the highway via the Eagle Lake Trail, hitch a ride back to my Jeep."

Sally looked up at the rugged gentleman, marveling, and said, "Wish I was going with you. I would love to learn to fly fish." She sighed wistfully. "It's been a long time since I went camping. The last time was when I spent the summer with my grandpa at his cabin in Oregon when I was twelve."

Woody was nonplussed. The tone of her voice, her eye contact, and her twosome comment made his heart skip a beat. But now was not the time to pursue romance. He was hitting the road soon and would never be coming back. In his anxious haste to avoid the awkwardness of dead-air time, he responded with the lame reply, "The local fly shop offers lessons."

Her countenance fell, and she reverted to her usual reserved demeanor. "Thanks. Well, I should get back to work."

Woody turned and walked out, relieved that his vacation had been granted but annoyed with himself for his bumblings and bunglings when it came to Sally. In the past when she had seemed to show interest in him, he had ignored her clues, afraid of reading romantic interest into attention that may have been nothing more than friendliness. He recalled his old feelings of helplessness. *I can read the woods. I can read a trout stream. But I can't read Sally. She's as mysterious as she is enchanting. I feel like a compass in an iron mine. No idea where I stand in relation to her.*

This time was different. He was certain that she was interested. And he had hurt her when he brushed her off with a line that suggested that he wasn't interested. He felt stupid. *Talk about poor timing and bad luck. Oh well. Nothing I can do about it. I am going. She is staying. Our paths will probably never cross again. Best to put it out of mind.*

61

On Monday Woody wore his favorite fishing hat to work, its ragged fleece band sporting a few of his favorite patterns: an elk hair caddis, a stimulator, and a golden stonefly nymph. While his fishing spirit was dampened by the danger hanging over his head, he needed to put up a good front as if nothing was out of the ordinary. His associates had come to expect that he would get into the fishing spirit in June with his first Sierra trip and that his enthusiasm would last until the last hatches in October.

He kept this show up for the entire week. Tuesday, he brought his new tenkara rod and showed it off, a shortie-stick from Patagonia for small, brushy streams. Wednesday, he brought a collection of Japanese patterns, dry and wet. Thursday, he brought a dozen Russian patterns, including a massive mouse for Siberian taimen. And Friday, he brought smoked trout, his own apple wood and juniper berry mix, a treat which everyone appreciated.

As he and his colleagues nibbled on trout, cheese, and

crackers in the break room, he experienced a few waves of nostalgia. He was going to miss these folks, most of them at any rate. Sadly, he couldn't say goodbye. That was hard. For a moment he had to fight back tears and a lump in his throat. Though he hated to admit it, sometimes he was just a little too sentimental for his own good.

62

South Lake Tahoe and Desolation Wilderness
Friday, June 21 and Saturday, June 22, 2019

Woody jumped into his Jeep after work and headed for Interstate 5 North. While he had gone straight from work to a camping trip before, this time was different. He wouldn't be coming back. The blues visited him with a vengeance. It was sad, painful, to be leaving permanently, never to see his home again. Memories overwhelmed him like a flood. His only Christmas with Anne. Her excitement over the antique crystal dove her grandmother had given her. Watching her gingerly hang the dove in the tree. His daughter Katrina and her friends in junior and senior high school and in college. The informal Cahill Center get-togethers twice a year at his house when Sally loosened up and laughed infectiously after a couple of glasses of wine. He was going to sorely miss the house and those who were part of it.

Life had taken him on a vastly different course than the one he had anticipated, one filled with broken dreams. He had lost Anne in childbirth. And with her passing, he lost his dream of having boys. He had suffered a brutal compound fracture of his left femur, which ended his special-ops career. He had been blacklisted by the intellectual elite of the astronomy world over his "heretical" rejection of relativity. And now he was forced to go on the run and lose all his worldly goods. Was there any meaning in all of this? Jack had often told him that everything happens for a reason. God allows and ordains with man's good in mind. He wanted to believe that.

The melancholy drive took eight and a half hours. At 12:35 a.m. Woody checked into Marriott's Grand Residences in South Lake Tahoe, carrying everything he needed for the night in a duffel bag, and asked the clerk for a 6 a.m. wake-up call. When he got to his room, he went straight to bed. He hadn't slept well the past few nights, today had been a long day, and tomorrow would be longer yet.

In the morning he shaved and showered, then headed downstairs to the Driftwood Cafe, where he gorged himself on a hearty breakfast: pancakes, eggs, two hash browns, and three orders of bacon. *It'll be a while before I get a good breakfast again.*

At five minutes past eight, he parked his Jeep at the Echo Lake trailhead, unloaded his pack, started to lock the Jeep, then hesitated. Should he lock it or leave it unlocked? After all, he wasn't coming back. Should he leave it conveniently unlocked for whoever had to tow it? *Nope. Have to lock it. Everything needs to appear normal.*

Woody lifted his pack to his shoulders, cinched up the straps, then turned to bid farewell to his Jeep. They had been partners on well over a hundred fishing, hiking, and hunting trips over the past twelve years. Respects paid, he wheeled around and headed for the trail. *No turning back now. The bridges are burned. Today I start my new career as a "criminal" on the lam.*

On the trail he set a leisurely pace, drinking in the scenery and frequently stopping for breaks, knowing that this was his last trip in the Sierras. At Heather Lake he broke out his spinning rod, which he rarely used, tossed a small spoon for an hour, and caught two fourteen-inch browns. Around 4 p.m. he arrived at his destination, Susie Lake, one of the crown jewels in the Sierras—nestled in a rugged, tree-lined basin. He found himself a decent campsite, pitched his tent, inflated his air mattress, and rolled out his sleeping bag.

As he was retrieving a mini flashlight from his pack that he hung in his tent for a lantern, he noticed movement out of the corner of his eye. Two men were walking past his site, the same two that had been sitting in the parking lot when he arrived at the trailhead and that he had seen several times on the trail behind him. They continued on past his campsite, stopped about 150 yards up the trail, dropped their packs, and wandered around for several minutes, gesturing and talking, probably trying to decide where to pitch their tent.

He pulled out his binoculars and scoped out the situation. The two men grabbed their packs, moved them about fifty feet, pulled out their tent, and started setting up camp. He took a close look at their gear. *Interesting.* Their tent was a Eureka Combat Tent in Scorpion OCP, their packs were Molle Assault Packs in the same pattern, their bags looked to be Modular Sleep System inner bags with Coyote Brown bivy covers, and their boots were Coyote Brown ACUs. Everything appeared to be brand new.

But something seemed out of place. It wasn't that they were wearing civilian clothes while carrying military gear, for that wasn't uncommon when soldiers went camping on a weekend off. What was it? It was their haircuts. The style wasn't military. Nor was it a style that was common in the civilian world. It was the style sported by the FBI agents he had seen at Caltech over the past two years. This seemed to confirm his suspicions. He was being trailed. The feds had assigned agents to keep tabs on him.

Woody chuckled. The FBI was after him, and he was more indignant than nervous. *Is this really the best they can do? The stupidity of government bureaucrats knows no bounds. Judging by the tactics and the agents they're using to trail me, they must think that I'm dumber than a box of rocks. Do they really think that a couple of rookies, who are little more than boy scouts, are gonna do the job justice?*

He shrugged his shoulders and decided to ignore them. As he started to turn away, he observed one of them pulling a pair of binoculars out of his pack. He stowed his binoculars in their proper pocket, lifted his water bottle to his lips, and took a drink. Then he went about setting up camp as if he were preparing for a comfortable stay. He set up his folding camp chair, a favorite camping luxury. He put up a clothesline. He filled his solar shower and hung it on the south face of a large pine. And he filled his bag-style water filter and hung it on the opposite side of the tree. Then he sat on a rock and changed his socks. When he was done, he rinsed his old socks in the lake, wrung them out, and hung them, dripping, on the clothesline.

Dinner was next on the agenda. He hauled out his stove, attached a canister of IsoPro (isobutane and propane blend), and put on a quart of water. Five minutes later, when it was in a rolling boil, he whipped up a batch of macaroni and cheese with diced jalapenos and onions, his favorite meal in the mountains. When it was done, he set the kettle aside to cool, and put on a pot of coffee. Then he settled into his chair for his dinner, savoring every bite. *Food always tastes better when you're camping.*

As he finished washing his dishes, he noticed that the sun was low enough over the mountains that the trout would probably be rising within tenkara range. He picked up his rod, tackle bag, and waders, and made his way to the lake.

Sure enough, a damsel-fly hatch was on and the fish were rising within easy casting distance. He perched on a rock, connected his level line to the lillian with a stopper knot, attached his tippet to the level line with a nail knot, and tied on a #14 damsel fly pattern with a classic fisherman's knot. Though he loved the tenkara style, he mostly used American fly patterns. Then he climbed into his waders, extended his rod, waded out to a flat rock near shore, and began to cast to the cruising and rising trout. This was his happy place. *Nothing like a wilderness setting and crystal clear trout water.* He was enjoying the moment so much that he almost forgot that he was being followed. Over the next hour, he caught and released twenty-three small brookies.

When darkness began to settle on the basin, he returned to camp and set the coffee pot on the stove to boil water for hot cocoa. As he sipped his piping hot mug and gazed at the stars which were beginning to appear, his mind turned to the next step of his adventure. Would his plan work? It had to work. There was no backup plan. He walked himself through the steps once more, from wakeup at zero-dark-thirty to meet-up with the transporter. While not fool-proof, it was a workable plan, worth a Bravo Zulu. A smile crept across his face as he thought about how sheepish the rookies were going to feel when they found out how badly they had been duped. "You're out of your league, boys," he whispered. Then he tipped his cup of cocoa, drained it, and went to bed.

63

At 1:30 a.m. the vibrator alarm on his watch went off. Dazed, he struggled to figure out what was going on. *Whaaat? Huhh? Oohhh! That's right. I set my alarm.* He touched the *light* button on the watch. It was now 1:31 a.m. *Holy smokes, I'm tired.* He wished he could catch a few more hours of sleep. *You can sleep tomorrow night soldier.* Still groggy, he dragged himself out of his sleeping bag, quickly dressed in the dark, and wolfed down two chia bars, leaving the wrappers on the floor. Then he grabbed his assault pack, ready to go with everything he would normally take for a day fishing trip, plus extra food and emergency gear, set it outside the door, and crawled out of his tent.

Sitting on a rock about a hundred feet from his tent, he opened his pack and removed a package of Kevlar-reinforced boot covers with Kevlar-webbed felt soles. He soaked the felt and the sides liberally with a deer-urine and animal-musk mix. Then he pulled the boot covers over his boots and laced them up. Finally, he smeared the oily mix on his pants, shirt,

384

hat, hands, and face. *This should cover my scent. Throw the dogs off. Wish I could see the frustration on their faces when the dogs can't pick up my trail.* He stood up, shoved the empty packaging and the scent bottle deep in his pack, threw his pack over his shoulders, and struck out on his journey.

He left almost all of his gear behind: tent, sleeping bag, sleeping pad, bear container, clothesline, shower bag, chair, spinning rod, water purifier, stove, and battered coffee pot. If everything went as planned, the rookies and their superiors would figure that he got up early to go fishing and would be back in camp around dusk. No one would suspect that there was a problem until it was dark and he wasn't back. By then he would be long gone.

Once on the trail, he checked his watch. It was 1:44 a.m. *Sweet.* From the time his alarm had gone off until he was on the trail had only been fourteen minutes. He took a quick glance at the stars and marveled at Orion as he so often did, then headed back down the trail toward Heather Lake at a fast pace. He had a lot of ground to cover before morning. He wanted to be over Mosquito Pass and in the Rubicon drainage by dawn. That was doable if he pushed hard.

He hadn't even gotten his trail legs when Heather Lake appeared on his left. *That went fast.* The trail skirted the lake, then started climbing. He geared down a little but still maintained a brisk pace. When Lake Aloha came into view shortly afterward, he knew that he was close to the Rubicon Trail. A few minutes later, he stumbled upon the cairn that marked its lonely track. By 3 a.m. he was winding his way up Mosquito Pass. *Making good time.* At the top, he stopped for a brief break and marveled at the shimmering moonlight dancing on Lake Aloha, the orb itself low over the eastern mountains. He allowed himself a small drink of water, his first since he woke up. This wasn't a matter of water conservation, but a matter of savvy. He didn't want to pee, which would leave his scent, until he was outside the probable search parameters that would be imposed once they realized that he was missing.

He headed down the other side, passed the Clyde Lake trail, and then crossed the Rubicon River. He smiled. *How fitting. Crossing the Rubicon. May I prevail in my crime as gloriously as Julius Caesar did in his.* The crossing was a key landmark in his memorized trail notes. *I cross the Rubicon twice more, then leave the trail and turn left, up the small stream that flows out of Lake Doris, then follow the right fork to the unnamed pothole.*

The darkness was starting to recede when he arrived at the unnamed stream where his route left the trail. He checked his watch. It was 5:32 a.m. Sunrise wasn't too far away, though it could be an hour yet before the sun actually peeked over the mountains. He stopped for a short break, pissed in the creek so his odor would dissipate, chugged a Gatorade, devoured a Clif Bar, and ate a Pink Lady apple, core and all. *No trace. No scent. No DNA.* Then he stowed the wrapper and bottle deep in his pack.

Though he was fatigued, he forced himself to stand up, climb back into his pack, and head up the creek. *Can't afford to extend this break.* His plan from here on out was to stay off trail as much as possible, which would minimize the odds that he might run into other hikers. He hadn't run into anyone yet. He hoped it stayed that way. It could be costly if folks saw him hiking and later recognized his picture in a police bulletin. The less the government knew about his direction, the better.

When he reached the fork, he followed the rivulet on the right to the unnamed pothole. From there he headed west, angling up the slope until he rounded the shoulder of the mountain and found himself overlooking the south shore of Lake Lois. On the shore below, he observed several tents and campers milling around. *Glad I didn't hike down to the lake.* He continued west until he came to a streamlet babbling with fresh snowmelt from the white banks above, then followed the noisy waters upwards.

After a few awkward moments, when he nearly fell while boulder hopping up the slope, he sat down for a breather. He was exhausted, wobbly on his legs. That worried him. The next stretch was the hardest. He downed another Clif Bar and a bottle of water, stretched his legs, took a salt tablet and a vitamin C to fight the cramps, grabbed a piece of jerky for the trail, and struggled back to his feet. It was now 7 a.m.

On his wasted legs, it took him an hour and a half to work his way up the streamlet, cross the saddle, and follow the stream on the other side down to Top Lake. When he finally glimpsed its waters, he collapsed at the base of a tree for a five-minute break. The five minutes stretched to seven. He had to get going again. With a facetious "hooah," he willed himself to stand. Limping slightly, he worked his way over the small ridge on the south side of the lake, found the stream that flowed into Barrett Lake, and followed it until he figured he was about three hundred yards from the lake.

He glanced at his watch. It was now 9:03 a.m. Since he still had fifty-seven minutes until rendezvous, he decided to hole up for fifteen minutes and give his weary body and spent legs a rest. He shucked his pack and sat down with his back against a convenient rock. Every muscle ached. Cramps were tightening up his legs. Spasms were shooting up and down his back. He felt weak, like he might faint, and didn't want to move. But he forced himself to open his pack, retrieve his last sports drink, and grab his food bag. Though his arms were shaking, he managed to down the beverage fairly quickly, followed by a dark chocolate bar, a box of raisins, and two pieces of jerky. Then he just sat, numb and quivering, hoping that a little energy would return.

At 9:18 a.m. he picked up his pack, slung it on his weary shoulders, and stumbled his way cross-country, westerly, aiming for the stream that flowed out of Barrett Lake. He figured it was about four hundred yards away. When he reached it, he followed it downstream for a few hundred yards until he could see the road. Then he stopped in a spot partially hidden from the road by brush and trees, dropped his pack, and waited for his ride. He checked his watch. It was 9:47 a.m. There were still thirteen minutes to go, which seemed like a century to him, for he was more tired than he had been since his Delta days. His eyes were heavy like rocks. *Not good. Hopefully, I won't fall asleep. Have to focus somehow.* He began to recite Robert Service's poem *The Ballad of Hard Luck Henry* in a quiet voice and managed to stumble through all seven verses. But the effort only ate up six minutes.

64

The next seven minutes passed in nods and fears. Would he fall asleep and miss his ride? That would be ugly. Would his ride show? Would Ghost find the rendezvous point? He hoped so. The location he had given him seemed pretty straightforward—where the stream crosses the Barrett Lake Jeep Trail about halfway between the University of California Cow Camp and Barrett Lake. It would be a long walk if the transporter didn't show. He would be forced to spend the next two weeks in a miserable situation, walking at night, concealing himself from traffic, and hiding out during the day, with little food. *Don't even want to think about it.*

He was starting to fear the worst when he heard a truck. A dark-green Ford crew cab rolled around the corner and stopped at the stream. His watch showed 9:59. *Thank God!* He stepped out from his hiding place, hobbled to the truck with his pack in hand, grabbed his parachute bag from the back seat, set his pack on the front floorboard, and climbed into the front seat with his bag on his lap. Ghost sat staring emotionless.

Woody examined his bag. The two zip ties that tied his zipper to the end ring—one black and one olive drab—were still intact, so he knew that no one had opened it. Woody pulled a wad of Franklins out of his pants pocket—he had counted out one thousand dollars for his pick-up and five hundred dollars for the duffel delivery while he was waiting—and handed it to Ghost. The transporter quickly counted the money, shoved it in his pocket, turned the truck around, and headed back down the jeep trail.

As the truck bounced down the road, Woody opened his parachute bag and examined the contents: a small MSR stove and two IsoPro canisters, freeze-dried meals, MREs, chia bars, Clif Bars, oatmeal, toilet paper, baby wipes, clothes, Kelty tarp, ultra-light sleeping bag, air mattress, titanium cookpot, small coffee pot, pound of coffee, survival knife, hank of parachute cord, six bottles of water, a stuff sack of personal items, his Montana stuff, his mementos, and four stuff sacks with loose items. It was all there. He stowed his clothes, sleeping bag, pad, and tarp in his pack, left the rest of his gear in the bag, and strapped the bag to the bottom of his pack. Then he shoved the pack into the back seat.

***

The route to Soda Springs was tiresome, six hours on backcountry tracks and rural roads. They worked their way back down the Barrett Lake Jeep Trail to Wright's Lake Road, then made their way to Ice House Road. From there they worked their way over to French Meadows Road, which they followed to Soda Springs Road, which took them into Soda Springs. Woody was uneasy the entire time. He found it hard to trust a shady character whose gods were money and street cred.

They made a brief stop at the Soda Springs General Store so Ghost could buy a couple six-packs of Samuel Adams. Before they pulled into the parking lot, Ghost told Woody to lean back in his seat and pull his hat over his face as if he were napping so the camera couldn't catch his face.

Once Ghost was back in the truck, they headed east on Donner Pass Road. When Woody noticed that they were entering Donner Lake and getting close to the drop-off point, he looked over to Ghost, questioningly. He stared back with a look that was half glare and half wry smile. "We'll burn up a few hours here. No worries. You'll be dropped off after dark as planned. I always keep my word. Those that keep their word in this business make money. Those that don't, disappear."

A few minutes later, Ghost turned south on South Shore Drive, and they wound along the lake. Near the middle of the south shore, he turned into the driveway of a lavish home. Barely off the street, he stopped and sent a text message. The garage door opened, he drove in, and the door closed behind him. Ghost stepped out of the truck, turned to Woody, and said, "Just paying a visit to old friends. You stay here. You can use the bathroom on the NW corner of the garage if you need to. Other than that, don't get out of the truck. And don't touch anything." Then he grabbed the six-packs, stepped up onto the landing, walked into a hallway, and turned right.

***

When the transporter emerged from the house five and a half hours later—10:05 p.m. by Woody's watch—he was staggering and looked burned-out. *Great! Just what I need. Obviously been drinking and smoking pot. If we get stopped for a traffic violation, I'm toast.* But there was nothing he could do about it. He forced himself to look at the bright side. In just a few minutes, he would be on his own. No more sleaze-ball partner.

Ghost looked at Woody and nodded toward the front seat. Woody shook his head *no.* He had climbed into the back seat while Ghost was in the house, partly to catch a nap and partly to make sure that he and his pack were together when the truck stopped to let him out. He had no interest in moving back to the front seat. There wasn't enough room to set his pack on the seat next to him so he could slip out the door with it fast and easy. And there was no way he was going to sit in the front seat while his pack remained in the back. Ghost watched his response, shrugged, and climbed into the cab.

Once they hit the street, Woody kept one hand on the door handle and one hand on his pack, ready to be out the door in the blink of an eye. Ghost continued east on South Shore Drive, got back on Donner Pass road, and turned south on Coldstream Road just outside Truckee. A little over a mile down the road, he stopped, executed a two-point turn, pulled onto the right shoulder, and nodded to Woody. Woody handed him the last thousand dollars, then hopped out with his pack, the parachute bag strapped securely to the bottom. When he shut the door, the truck roared off. No goodbye, no wave. Woody shook his head. *A cold-blooded man in a cold-blooded business.*

There was no time to waste. He didn't want to take a chance of being seen on the road. Holding his pack in hand, he quickly walked down the hill. Once deep in the shadows, he stopped to put his pack on, then continued on his way. At the bottom, he forded the stream and climbed the hill on the other side toward the railroad tracks. When he reached the tracks, he crossed them and sat down on the other side. He needed a short break, more for emotional release than exhaustion. He ate his last Pink Lady apple, taking the time to savor its tang, sipped a lemon sparkling water he had been saving, then checked the straps that held his bag to his pack. They were tight and secure.

He was finally starting to relax after a tension-filled day. Nothing big to worry about until tomorrow morning when he would attempt to hop a moving freight train. He stood up and began walking down the tracks, taking his time and—oddly—relishing the moment. The experience took him back to his childhood when he had often hiked on the tracks and picked berries in the thickets along the edges. The sky was moonless. For that he was thankful. It made him feel more secure because he was less likely to be seen. Somewhere in the distance, he heard a coyote yip, a sound that he found comforting. About two miles up the rails, he came to where the stream passed under the line. He cautiously made his way down the steep bank near the trestle, then pushed his way upstream looking for a place to make camp. About a hundred and fifty yards upstream, he found a dense thicket of pines well away from both the tracks and the nearby road. *Perfect.*

He quickly strung his tarp, laid out his bedding, and started a small fire. Then he grabbed a few flat rocks that were suitable for balancing his pot. Before long, a kettle of water for chili-mac and a coffee pot of water for hot cocoa were perched over the cheering flames. While he waited for the water to boil, he waded out into the stream and took a brisk splash bath. *Might be a while on the train before I have access to a bath or a shower.*

With a hot meal in his belly, Woody decided to stay up a little longer. He had managed to get some sleep in the truck and wasn't as exhausted as he had been earlier. He stirred the coals, added a few sticks to the fire, and watched the flames burst into life. As he sipped his hot chocolate and watched the flames dance, he grew philosophical. *Life sure knows how to throw a guy a curveball. A month ago I was just a few years from retirement. Now my retirement funds are gone. Likewise my possessions and savings. At least I have hot cocoa and a warm sweater and somewhere to go. Many a man has far less than that.*

There was one painful thought, however, which he could not assuage—Sally. Ever since she had arrived at Caltech five years ago, he had secretly admired her. During her first two years, they had suffered a few tiffs. Since then, they had developed a strong relationship that was easy and friendly but had never gone further. He found himself wishing that something had worked out between them. She was talented, intelligent, and attractive, and had a magical way about her. Being around her was like sunshine, intoxication, and dessert in one package. He sighed.

His thoughts turned to worrying about her. She probably shouldn't have given him permission to go on his camping trip. Her higher-ups in Minoa would likely have forbidden it at the bidding of the FBI if she had asked. But he had an inkling that she would say *yes* if he asked, completely on her own initiative, and she did. Now he felt guilty, like he had exploited her. Regardless of whether she had suspected that he might run or was just allowing him to go fishing, she was probably in hot water. He wasn't much of a praying man, but he turned to the Father in heaven. *Look out for her and keep her safe, and …* He hesitated. He couldn't pray for it though he wanted it. He had to let it go. He spread his coals, poured a kettle of water on them, and went to bed. Tomorrow was a big day.

65

Woody's watch alarm went off at 5 a.m., and he rolled out of his bag groggy. *Too little sleep and too much sugary hot chocolate.* He fired up his stove to boil water, then got dressed and broke camp. He wanted to be waiting beside the tracks at the curve by 6 a.m. in case the train was early. Within twenty minutes, he had broken camp and was sitting on a log eating breakfast—cinnamon oatmeal with raisins. His pot was on the stove, the hearty scent of fresh coffee wafting in the gentle morning breeze.

At 6:05 a.m. he was hunkered down in the trees below the tracks, waiting. It proved to be a long wait. Not longer than he had anticipated, but harder. His legs started to cramp up, forcing him to stand. His guts were churning. Was it a bug or something he ate? Or perhaps he was just nervous about hopping a moving train. It had seemed like a brilliant idea when he first thought of it. Now it seemed dangerous. There were too many unknowns. Too many things that could go wrong. But he had no choice. It was hop it or hoof it, and he definitely wasn't going to hoof it.

At 6:57 a.m. the train whistle blew in the distance, faint and haunting. The moment of truth was near. His heart jumped and his pulse picked up. He started mentally preparing for his risky endeavor. Eight minutes later, the train entered the hairpin curve, going faster than he anticipated, maybe seven miles per hour. *A fast jog, on gravel no less.* He picked up his pack and stood, ready. After the engines had passed, he scrambled up the bank to the tracks and started looking for a car that offered both ladder and shelter.

A string of flats carrying shipping containers and trailers passed, then several empty gondola cars, then eight closed boxcars. Nothing suitable for a wannabe hobo to find shelter from the elements and concealment from railroad bulls. Then a grain car passed by, and he noticed that there was a small porch on the back along with a porthole opening that led to a cubby hole. The next car was the same kind. He determined to make it his target and started jogging down the tracks, his pack heavy in his right hand, trying to keep his speed close to that of the train. His legs throbbed with pain, a combination of old age, his old femur injury, and aches and bruises and scrapes from his rugged jaunt across the Sierran wilderness.

The rear ladder crept into his peripheral vision. He turned slightly, tossed his pack onto the porch, grabbed the front rail with both hands, swung his hind leg up onto the first rung, and started to pull himself up. *That wasn't so bad.* But the train jolted as he was attempting to move his right hand higher up the rail, causing it to slip. He swung wildly backward, his feet slipped off the rung, and he started to spin. Holding on for dear life with his left hand, his body came completely around, slamming his butt hard into the third rung and his calves into the first. In desperation he threw his right arm upwards and backward, frantically reaching for the rear rail. Thankfully, he found it. Gingerly he tucked his feet back up on the first rung, calves throbbing.

He perched in this awkward position, stunned. *Think I'm gonna have to do this a little differently next time.* His arms and shoulders ached from strained muscles and his backside was bruised. *Gonna feel this for a while. Haven't hurt like this since my rugby days in the city league.* He was in a predicament. He couldn't stay where he was, and he couldn't easily turn around. *This is ugly in every color it comes.*

After a moment of reflection on his quandary, he crossed his arms behind his head, placing his right hand on the front rail and his left hand on the back rail. Then he slipped his left foot behind his right leg and moved his right foot as far forward as he could, turned as far inward as he could. He shook his head, frustrated. *This is as awkward as a cat in a blender.* He steadied himself, then tried to stand up slowly. He didn't get very far. *Rats! Not a lot of room to work here. But I need to get turned around before my arms and legs give out.* With a guttural "Aaargh!" he executed a hazardous twist. *Hallelujah!* It worked. He was still perched on the train rails, and he was facing inward. He cautiously moved his hands up the rails, adjusted his feet on the bottom rung for better footing, and leaned his head on the rung in front of his face to rest for a moment.

Adrenalin still rushing in his veins, he climbed around the right side of the ladder and sprawled himself onto the deck, landing on his pack and banging his head on the bulkhead. *Talk about adding insult to injury.* He lay there for a minute contemplating the situation. *That would have been a miserable way to die. Laying on the tracks, missing both legs, and bleeding to death.*

With a groan, he grabbed his pack, shoved it inside the porthole, and crawled in after it. Then he dug out his coat for a cushion, put on his stocking hat and pulled it down over his ears, more to mask the noise than anything, and cozied up next to his pack, hoping to sleep for a little while. The past few days had been grueling, physically and emotionally, and he was sleep-deprived. In drone mode as they used to say in Special Forces. After a few minutes, his eyes grew heavy. The rhythmic clickety-clack was almost soothing. His last conscious thoughts were whimsical. *On an adventure fit for a boyhood novel. On my way to Montana. Sweet Montana.*